"Kiss me, Maggie.
Kiss me and tell me we're wrong."

He pulled her tight against him. He enveloped her, his arms, his heat, the ardent pull of his hard body. Her hands fluttered at her sides, straining to touch something that was not him, but there was nothing except moonlight and shadows and man. He grabbed her wrists, pulling them up to her shoulders.

"Hold on," he murmured.

A strange ache flooded her body. She moaned softly and leaned into him. His arms came around her, holding her tightly, and she clutched at his shoulders, but it wasn't enough.

She was lost, helpless. Drifting somewhere beyond place and time, where even the angels trembled.

He pulled back and gazed down at her—eyes of midnight, lit with stars . . .

KATHLEEN ESCHENBURG

The Nightingale's Song

HarperTorch
An Imprint of HarperCollinsPublishers

❦

HARPERTORCH
An Imprint of HarperCollins*Publishers*
10 East 53rd Street
New York, New York 10022-5299

Copyright © 2001 by Kathleen Eschenburg
ISBN: 0-380-81569-9

First HarperTorch paperback printing: November 2001

HarperCollins ®, HarperTorch™, and ❦ ™ are trademarks of Harper-Collins Publishers Inc.

Printed in the United States of America

Visit HarperTorch on the World Wide Web at www.harpercollins.com

10 9 8 7 6 5 4 3 2 1

For my mother, Mary Lou Stevens,
a woman of uncommon courage, boundless love
and the heart of this book

Prologue

She no longer had a home. No family. No country.

Beside an official-looking man stood a priest with hair as black as her own. His gaze swept over the line of immigrants and then came back to rest where she waited with the red-haired O'Connor family.

The soldiers would be coming for her now. Mum had escaped, dying from the wasting sickness only two weeks out from Limerick. Maggie was caught, a twelve-year-old orphan in an immigration shed.

She felt Padraig O'Connor's big hand on her shoulder. " 'Tis only a priest, Mary Margaret," he said. "Though a fancy sort, never meant to be in an immigrant shed."

Maggie looked up at Mr. O'Connor, then back to the priest. A frown creased his brow as he started toward her and she feared to so much as breathe. Sick, so sick in her empty belly. She hugged her cloth sack tighter to her chest, but the pain didn't ease inside her heart or her flipping stomach.

Oh, Mum.

She stiffened her back and locked her quaking knees as the priest knelt in front of her. For the longest time, he studied her face. She wanted him to smile, but he didn't.

He *was* of a fancy sort: a mirror image of the earl. For a moment, she saw Geoffrey Fitzhugh, the twelfth Earl of Lachlan, in this man kneeling in front of her, saw the lurid orange glow of dancing flames across his face as he held her back from the fire while the terrified screams of his horses filled the night. Maggie shuddered.

The priest seemed to sigh. His eyes were green and filled with a tenderness, unlike the earl, and something more, something sad. A nobleman's face over a priest's collar, with an Irishman's eyes.

"And sure as I'm standing here, you are Mary Margaret Quinn," he said.

"Aye." Her voice sounded like a frog's croak.

"Well, I'm Father Hugh Fitzhugh, and I've been waiting for you." He pried the sack from her grasp. As he fingered the sack, an odd expression came over his face. "A fiddle, *mó cailín?*" he asked softly.

"Aye."

She heard sudden music in her soul as a slow smile took shape at his lips and the warmth in that smile chased the chill from her bones. Raising up to his full height—and it was a grand height, so that she had to tilt her head back to see his eyes—he held out his hand, palm up.

"I play the harp, myself, Mary Margaret Quinn. If I teach you the harp, will you teach me the fiddle?"

Without a moment's hesitation, she placed her hand into his keeping. She didn't ask herself why. God, with the aid of the Earl of Lachlan, had sent her a good shepherd of her very own.

Chapter 1

Maggie's hand tightened on Clare's as they picked their way through the crowds and horse-drawn streetcars. Though few decent women traveled unescorted down these streets, Maggie was a frequent visitor. She didn't fear being mistaken for a woman of questionable character, so she kept her chin high and a firm clasp on Clare's hand, and tried to ignore the shadowy figures lounging in the doorways of leaning buildings.

As they started down the hill, she caught the first odors of the harbor—exotic spices, coffee, oakum—an amalgam of the perfumes of the world quickening inside Baltimore's warehouses.

A beggared old man sat huddled beneath a lamppost, his face expressionless, his eyes blank. His fingers curled clawlike around a tin cup, gripping it loosely atop his thigh. Beside him sprawled a dog whose ribs showed stark beneath nondescript brown fur. The dog watched the passing shoes and trousers as if lifting his drooping head to see a human face were not worth the effort.

She let go of Clare's hand, rummaged in her market basket and pulled out a half-loaf of bread. She thrust the bread onto the old man's lap and dropped a quarter into his cup. He blinked as the coin hit the bottom of the cup with a tiny metallic plink.

She couldn't linger today, not with Clare in her company on these rough streets, so Maggie grasped Clare's hand and started onward, almost dragging the reluctant child. Behind them, she heard the dog whining.

"I have bread too, my Maggie."

"Aye, the sweet roll I bought you." She stopped and looked down into Clare's blue eyes, feeling a measure of pride in this child she loved as her own. "Do with it as you will."

Clare reached for the basket slung over Maggie's forearm. Lifting the lid, she studied the contents and then pulled out her treat. Clare ran back to the dog. She knelt and placed the bun on the cobbled street. The dog wolfed down the sweet roll and settled his head between his paws.

"Neddie thanks you."

"Is his name Neddie?" asked Clare, her small fingers stroking the ruff at the dog's neck.

"He's a lucky dog, with old Neddie to keep him company and Saint Maggie to look out for the both of us." He looked up, his pallid eyes unseeing. "She's a young one, Mary Margaret."

"Aye, we'll not be tarrying today," said Maggie, hearing the gentle chiding beneath the words. She took Clare's hand into her own. "I won't be back before Saturday . . . the concert."

The old man's fingers trembled against the hard-crusted bread as he nodded. "And then your Father Fitzhugh leaves for Richmond."

"It's a grand honor for our Father Fitzhugh to be made a bishop."

"An honor that's breaking your heart, girl."

She glanced at Clare, who had shifted her attention from

the dog to Maggie's face. Maggie forced a reassuring smile for the child. "An honor that makes me proud of him, Neddie."

The old man huffed a breath. Maggie tugged on Clare's hand. "Come along, Clare," she said softly.

After one more lingering glance at the dog, the child fell in beside her. An oyster lugger rolled past, its wooden wheels clacking over the cobblestones. She hadn't yet placed Mrs. Gottlieb's order for fresh oysters; but the day was overcast, threatening more rain, and Maggie quickened her pace, suddenly anxious to get Clare away from the stink of fish wharves and seedy bars. She turned down a narrow street lined with brick row houses.

"Why does he call you Saint Maggie?" asked Clare.

" 'Tis meant in jest."

"Because you sent away Jamie O'Connor when he came courting?"

"Because I've yet to take my vows." Maggie stopped and set her market basket on the ground, then turned to Clare. "And what will the sisters be saying if you come down with a fever?" she said as she pulled the coarse woolen hood over Clare's shiny curls one more time.

" 'Tis a grand, soft day," said Clare, wrinkling her nose and shoving the hood back so it fell on her narrow shoulders like a cowl.

Maggie deftly turned her laughter into a small cough and pulled the hood back in place. "You've quite the gift for mimicry, *mó cailín*, but don't be copying my sorry accents."

"I like the way you talk. It's pretty, just like when you sing," said Clare with a toss of her head that caused the hood to tumble back down. "Father Fitz talks just like you when he's nipped the brandy decanter."

"Clara!"

A peal of childish laughter was her only answer. With a thoughtful frown on her face, Maggie followed Clare as the child skipped ahead up Aliceanna Street.

Christened Clara by the nuns, the child had always been a

mystery. She'd been brought to the orphanage as a tiny infant, dressed in expensive linen and lace, delivered by a maid traveling in a hired coach who claimed to know nothing of the child's background. To the danger of her immortal soul, Maggie both wanted a good family for the child and dreaded the day when Clara would be chosen.

Now the possibility of adoption for the five-year-old seemed very real. Two days ago, a Mr. Cromwell had come to call at the orphanage. Mr. and Mrs. Cromwell were seeking a girl child to take the place of their own daughter, who had died from a childhood fever. When brought in to survey the children gathered in the playroom, Mr. Cromwell had pointed to Clara and asked to speak with her.

Maggie hadn't yet found the courage to question Clare about the interview. To her knowledge, Mr. Cromwell hadn't returned to the orphanage since that afternoon.

They passed Mrs. White's boardinghouse and her steps slowed as she saw the hand-lettered sign in the front window. ROOM TO LET. NO IRISH NEED APPLY.

Maggie shifted the heavy basket to her other arm. Had Clare frightened Mr. Cromwell away by using her gift, mimicking an Irish brogue? But a five-year-old could not be that devious, that wise to the ways of the world. Or could she? And why?

"You didn't answer my question, Maggie. Is it because I ask too many questions? Sister Josephine says I ask too many questions."

"A grown-up tells a child she asks too many questions for one reason only."

"What?"

Maggie bent over so her face was close to the child's. "They don't know the answer." The sun peeked through the clouds and shimmered in Clare's eyes. Maggie straightened. "I didn't hear your question, *mó cailín*."

"Whose carriage is that?"

Maggie looked around, suddenly realizing they had walked the entire distance back to the rectory. A strange carriage was parked in the alley between the rectory and orphanage. A tall man stood with his back toward her, conversing quietly with the Negro driver. A gentleman, everything about the man bespoke wealth, from the shiny black carriage and well-bred horses to the understated elegance of the fitted frock coat covering his broad shoulders.

"Here, Clare," said Maggie, holding out the market basket. "Take this in to Mrs. Gottlieb. I'm thinking the gentleman is here to see Father Fitzhugh, so maybe you'd best be warning her to put the teakettle on."

As Clare skipped through the gate, the gentleman turned. A single ray of sunlight sought him through the parting clouds, kindling the burnished gold of his hair and lighting the depths of his eyes. Maggie's breath caught. Surely she must be imagining such a vision, such a flawless, golden man. He was Gabriel set down among mere mortals, with a most devilish smile taking shape at his lips.

"I seem to be at a loss, Mrs. . . . ."

She couldn't find her voice. She watched the tiny lines at his mouth deepen as his rogue's smile broadened. Embarrassment alone forced her to speak. "Miss Quinn. Perhaps, I may be of help?"

He took several steps forward, stopping a mere arm's length away. His eyes were as deep and dark a blue as Clare's. She felt a shiver of apprehension; her stomach took a tiny flip and she wondered if she was going to be sick.

His eyes, with thick, long lashes shades darker than his hair. So like Clare's arresting blue eyes, even to the tiny slant at the corners.

"Perhaps you may, Miss Quinn. I have an appointment with Father Fitzhugh on the half-hour, but I've been told there's a Sister Bernadette here. On the chance it's the same nun I had the good fortune to meet many years ago . . . Well, it seems I don't know the proper etiquette to make myself known at a convent."

"It's Mother Bernadette now and she'll be in her office at the orphanage. If you have a card Mr. . . . ."

"Kincaid," he said, reaching into his pocket and withdrawing a silver card case.

Another thought struck and she felt instantly foolish. His manner of speaking was the soft drawl of the upper South. St. Columba's unseen benefactor these past five years was a Mr. Peyton Kincaid from Virginia.

"Mr. Kincaid, as much as I'm certain Mother Bernadette will see you, perhaps I should show you in to Father Fitzhugh's study first."

Something flickered in his expression, quelling his visible amusement. "The name Kincaid is familiar to you."

It wasn't a question, but she nodded as if it were and gestured toward the orphanage, where a new wing jutted from the back of the building. "Kincaid Hall," she said, allowing a tiny smile to show. "In honor of Mr. Peyton Kincaid."

She accepted the card he held out, feeling painfully shy and awkward when their fingers made brief contact.

"Peyton Kincaid is dead, Miss Quinn. I'm his second son."

"Oh. I'm so sorry. We will remember him in our prayers."

His mouth turned up at the corner, as if he found that thought amusing. "Just lead the way to Sister Bernadette. If it's one and the same woman I remember, she'll have you saying prayers for me before nightfall."

He crooked his arm, a gentlemanly action, and yet she couldn't bring herself to take it. She ducked her head away from the knowing laughter in his eyes and started walking toward the orphanage. She heard a sound that might have been a chuckle and then he was beside her, his body so tall, his presence so . . . so imposing. Maggie quickened her pace, anxious to be done with him. This was her peaceful world, and it didn't feel quite as safe just now. Not with him in it.

She was tall for a female, thought Gordon, primly buttoned up in a stiff white shirtwaist and slim black skirt that hinted of long, slender legs beneath. She was careful not to look at him and he didn't know whether to feel amused or chagrined.

Since he couldn't think of anything he'd done or said that could be considered forward, other than inadvertently touching her fingers as she took his calling card, he settled on amusement.

She opened a door to the left, across from the narrow stairway, and gestured. "If you'll be so kind as to wait here, I'll inform the mother superior."

Her light brogue had thickened somehow in the short walk through the alley. He controlled his urge to smile as she took one unnecessary step back to avoid any chance contact with his coat sleeve. Apparently males were infrequent visitors at St. Columba's stone-walled fortress of a convent-orphanage.

He suddenly regretted his own presence here. But it was a stipulation of Peyton's will that he seek out Sister Bernadette, and one top racehorse hung in the balance. He would endure fifteen minutes of verbal sparring and leave as the owner of Firenza, a two-year-old colt of tremendous promise. In the next Preakness, Firenza would run under his colors, not Riverbend's.

The parlor was small and fashionably dark, with the heavy green drapes pulled tightly closed. He doubted there was much of a view from the window anyway; working-class Baltimore had little to commend it in the way of either architectural or natural beauty. When he turned back to the door, his quiet, oddly intriguing guide had already disappeared.

He considered seating himself on one of the horsehair chairs—no supple leathers or rich brocades here—but felt the need to pace. He did neither. He fingered his hat, listened to the distant sound of children's voices and studied the picture hanging above the unlit grate.

The wood-framed watercolor depicted a gentle-faced Jesus surrounded by children. A growing unease settled over him, as if even the painted walls and threadbare carpet considered him an infidel in this house of obvious piety.

"Sister Agatha painted that scene," came a lilting voice from the vicinity of the doorway. "I fear it's not the least subtle for Mother Bernadette to display it thus in the visitors' parlor."

Gordon turned slowly. The spinsterish not-nun stood in the doorway with a smile threatening to bloom at her lips. "Mother Bernadette will see you now, Mr. Kincaid. The first door on your right at the head of the stairs."

"You're not going to show me up?"

"I have other duties, sir. I trust you won't be finding yourself lost in such a distance."

He heard the swish of her skirts, followed by the closing of the front door. Gordon drew a deep breath and made his way to the stairs.

"You look well, Gordon. How is the leg?"

"Good enough."

Ten years had left little mark on the oval face taking stock of him from beneath a black wimple. Mother Bernadette, the upper-class Philadelphia nun who had nursed him back to precarious health after his wounding at Gettysburg, had brought him the news of his wife's death and then, by sheer force of will, forbade him to give up and die from a prison fever.

"The doctors said you'd never walk again," she said in an even tone, as if they were discussing the weather.

"Doctors can be wrong."

She didn't rise, merely peering at him with her steely-eyed gaze. He'd forgotten the piercing quality of those ice-blue eyes. Gordon was suddenly overcome by long-buried memories—back in the war and fighting for his life, threatening to kill the Yankee doctor standing over him wielding the knife.

Sister Bernadette in those days, she hadn't recognized colors of uniforms. Yank or Reb, she'd treated them all the same. He owed this woman not just for the timely intervention that saved his leg but for his very life. At times, he still hated her for that kindness.

"I've been waiting years for you to find me. Please, be seated," she said, gesturing toward a spindle-backed chair.

"I didn't find you, but then, I haven't been looking for you either." He seated himself, pleased that his voice sounded normal, and settled his hat in his lap. "I suspect you know it's Peyton's work bringing me here now."

"How is your father?"

"He's dead."

Mother Bernadette drew a slow breath. "I'm sorry, Gordon," she said. "Truly sorry. He was a fine man."

A fine man. Trust Mother Bernadette to come up with the most fitting epitaph for Peyton Kincaid he'd heard in these last, difficult weeks. The man he called Father was dead and Gordon wasn't quite ready to accept that fact. He felt a weightless sensation, as if he himself hovered over the black void. He hid it behind his best sham smile.

"There's one last, good-sized bequest to the orphanage. I'm supposed to hand-deliver the check to a Father Fitzhugh."

"Why did you ask for an audience with me, then?" she asked.

"Old times' sake. Remembering better days. Foolishness. Take your pick."

"Still so bitter, my friend?"

"No," he said on a low breath.

She set her pen aside on a sheaf of paper and then capped the inkwell. For a minute the only sound was the ticking of a mantel clock. She leaned back in her seat, folding her hands together at the edge of the maple desk. He tried to read the expression in her eyes and couldn't manage it, yet he knew the sparring round was about to commence. What he didn't understand was the whys. Why was he here? Why had Peyton sent him on this journey into a past he wanted only to forget?

"You haven't remarried?" she asked.

"You know the answer."

"And your son? Doesn't he deserve a mother?"

"My sister-in-law had already assumed that role by the time I was released from Fort Delaware—and you already know the answers if you've been corresponding with my father."

Suddenly impatient with being a pawn in Peyton's last impenetrable game and loath to subject himself to Mother Bernadette's uncanny mind-reading skills, he made a motion as if to rise. "I've come. If you'll be so kind as to send word of our visit to Peyton's lawyers, I'll leave you to your work."

"Not yet," she said, gesturing for him to remain. "You remember I first began corresponding with your father while you were sick in the prison camp," she said. "After the war, we exchanged a few letters. He was a learned man, well spoken, and I enjoyed our correspondence. Our letters eventually ceased as he grew older and my duties increased."

She shrugged and then pushed back her chair. "I would ask after you and he would respond, but the majority of our discourse was a heated debate on Saint Thomas Aquinas."

He remained silent as she rose and crossed over to a massive cupboard. She opened the cupboard door and reached inside.

"When this came, I felt compelled to resume our correspondence," she said, pulling out a small lacquered box and turning to face him. "Have you seen this before?"

Gordon chose to leave all his options open. "It seems a very ordinary box."

"Quite, until you look at the detail work."

She rubbed her fingers over the gilt-painted flowers on the lid and then held out the box. He took it, his larger hand spanning its shape as he turned it over and stared at the mark on the bottom. He froze inside.

"Where did you get this?" Already, his mind was spinning, in denial, in self-directed anger—in pure panic.

"It arrived quite unexpectedly five years ago. Open it, please."

Gordon lifted the lid. Inside, nestled against the crimson velvet lining, was a lace-embellished baby's bonnet. Slowly, he lifted the bonnet, the lace catching on the roughness of his hands. Beneath the bonnet was a gold-framed miniature, face up so that he couldn't even delay the final proof of what he suddenly knew and didn't want to believe.

Aurora, Mrs. Leland Hammond. He hadn't seen her in over five years, but he remembered now as if it had been just yesterday. An illegal duel on the fog-shrouded Richmond dueling grounds, a near hit because he deloped. Guilty as hell, he couldn't add insult to injury by killing the wronged husband. Peyton's anger, Royce's disgust, a hasty trip to the family's ranch in Texas . . . the devil take it, he remembered it all.

Dammit, Rory, why didn't you tell me?

"Your face is not one easily forgotten, even by a nun," said Mother Bernadette, her normally soft voice becoming even softer. "The miniature was a gift from you?"

"I was arrogant enough to oblige her when she asked." He shrugged, as if it didn't matter. "How did these come into your possession?"

Gordon felt, rather than saw, the shift in Mother Bernadette. Still, he sat motionless as the tension surged in him, unable to rise, knowing the charge had been set and waiting stupidly for the explosion.

"The box was brought by the same maid who brought us the baby. We got nothing out of the silly girl. She claimed she'd been hired that morning by a 'well-dressed spiff of a gentleman.' Her instructions were to deliver the infant and the box to this orphanage." A hand landed gently on his shoulder. "Please tell me you weren't the gentleman."

He wanted to deny it all. The baby wasn't his, would be Leland's child. But Leland had been traveling on business, gone for months.

So it was Aurora's doing. She didn't want another child, was about as decent a mother for the two she already had as he was a father for his own single son.

The baby was probably his own issue. And Peyton had at least suspected, strongly suspected.

The cash gifts his father had made to a distant Catholic orphanage suddenly made sense. The final game was no longer impenetrable. The pawn was to do the decent thing, search out the child, seek out the truth, and give his bastard child a name.

No, Father. I can't. I'm not you.

"I never knew," he said in a voice devoid of emotion. "I never even knew she was pregnant."

"You couldn't marry her?"

He didn't answer, knowing his silence would speak volumes.

"I could send for the child if you'd like."

He opened his mouth, but no sound came out, so he covered his difficulty by slowly closing the lid. "I'll come back. Another day, maybe tomorrow."

After a long moment in which the blood pounded in his ears and guilt fired his gut, she said, "I named her Clara, in honor of Miss Barton."

A girl child.

"You believe this child is mine," he said, one last grab for a lifeline. "With Auro—given the child's mother, this . . ." He gestured with the box. "A trick."

"I make no judgments on Clara's mother, Gordon. Whether she was married or unwed, and I won't ask which, she suffered in giving up her child. When you see Clara, you'll understand why I have no doubts as to the identity of the father."

No way out.

Sitting paralyzed, staring insensibly at the baby cap in his hand, he knew he was yet in flight from himself. Running panicked from his failures, his guilt, his damned loneliness. And he knew more. He knew that until he stopped and faced his fears and his failures, his existence would never be anything more than a living nightmare.

The deuce of it all, Mother Bernadette knew it too.

It was the sound of Clare's voice that stopped her just inside the door, still hidden in the shadows cast by the gambrel roof over the back porch. The child was playing in the backyard of the rectory, her cloth doll perched in a child-sized chair and drawn up to a child's table, ready for afternoon tea in the garden.

Maggie's heart swelled at Father Fitzhugh's kindness, his habit of giving each child in the orphanage special time with him at the rectory. For each, it was an opportunity to sleep alone in a bed, dine at a table with him and his housekeeper, Mrs. Gottlieb. This was Clara's time. Maggie wondered if the new priest would be such a father to them, because the children would miss this so much.

"If you'll be looking for my Maggie, now, you'd best go to the front of the rectory, the back door 'tis for service."

Clare's singsong voice had shifted into a thick brogue. Maggie eased from the doorway so she could see more of the yard. She saw Mr. Kincaid then, standing on the far side of the gate, gripping the iron points of the railing so tight she thought it must cause pain.

"No." He paused, as if lost in thought. "Who is Maggie?"

Clare turned her attention back to tying a baby bonnet on the head of Clancy, Father Fitz's obliging tomcat. "You were speaking with my Maggie before. She took you to the orphanage."

Mr. Kincaid nodded with this information, yet nothing else moved in him. He was rigid in every sinew, taut as a fiddle string wound too tight and ready to snap with a touch. Clare looked up from her task.

"And sure it is you've come for a child, then. Perhaps your own wee *cailín* has died from the fever and you'll be needing another to take her place?"

"I came to see Father Fitzhugh."

Clare set Clancy on another small chair, where he curled into a yellow ball, his bonneted head tucked over his paws. Mr. Kincaid stood immobile by the gate, staring at Clare. Neither seemed aware of Maggie's own shadowed presence.

Clare brushed her small hands together. "Father Fitz says Americans aren't civilized enough to take tea. He's from Ireland," she said. "Don't eat all the scones either. Father Fitz likes scones, Mrs. Gottlieb makes them just for him."

The brogue was gone from her voice. Maggie's suspicions were suddenly confirmed. The bright little girl used language to frighten away prospective parents.

"What's your name?" asked Clare.

"Mr. Kincaid."

"Mother Bernadette said we had to name the new wing of the orphanage Kincaid Hall even though he's Prot—" She waved her hand as she stumbled over the big word. "Prosatint. Is that you?"

After a small hesitation, Mr. Kincaid shook his head, apparently oblivious to Clare's mispronunciation, while Maggie herself was softly smiling. He seemed to be having great difficulty finding his own words to speak to the child.

Anger, wariness and some deeper suffering were apparent in his face, his stance, the way his fists opened and closed on the iron stakes—once, twice, three times. His throat convulsed above the silk cravat as he swallowed hard. Maggie made a motion to intervene—whether to rescue the child or the man, she was uncertain—but he spoke again and she stopped.

"A pretty little girl like you must have an equally lovely name," he said in an even voice that showed none of his bodily tension that was so obvious to herself.

"Sister Josephine says it's not polite to ask questions. She says I'm always asking too many questions." Clare turned back to the table, where she poured hot chocolate into a chipped teacup. She tested the temperature first with her index finger, then with her tongue. Apparently satisfied, she set the cup beside Clancy.

Clancy raised his head and sniffed at the cup of chocolate, then dipped in a pink tongue. Clare brushed the cat along the length of his back, ignoring the man at the gate, who stood with his legs spread slightly, still gripping the stakes.

Maggie thought it a strange, unsmiling conversation; all

fits and starts, as if the child and the man were each probing for weaknesses.

"Let me tell you a secret, little girl."

Clare looked up, apparently unable to resist the sudden playfulness in his voice.

"When a grown-up tells a child she asks too many questions, it means the grown-up doesn't know the answer."

"My Maggie already told me that secret."

Maggie stepped forward, out of the shadows and into the sun, as she traversed the four back steps. "You'll be answering Mr. Kincaid, *mó cailín*. He asked you your name and most gentlemanly he was to do so."

Clare lifted the chocolate pot. "Orphans don't have names, not until they're either adopted or grow up," she said, avoiding Maggie's disapproval by watching the rich liquid pour into another chipped cup.

"Clara!"

Maggie looked to Mr. Kincaid with an apologetic smile on her face. He had stiffened ramrod straight. A small muscle worked along his jaw as he stared at the child.

His lips moved, as if he might speak; then, after another hesitation, he whispered vehemently, "Dammit, Rory."

She stepped forward another step and placed her hand on Clare's shoulder. "I'm afraid our Clara has been most rude, Mr. Kincaid. I assure you, she's usually a sweet child."

He pulled his gaze away from Clare and settled on Maggie's face. She saw a moment's confusion in his eyes, followed by a rapid transformation. His body relaxed and his lips turned up in that roguish smile.

"Miss Quinn," he said.

"If you're finished with Mother Bernadette, I'll show you to Father Fitzhugh. Mrs. Gottlieb is steeping the tea and Father Fitz is most anxious to meet you."

"I'm sorry, but a matter of grave concern has suddenly come up. Tell Father Fitzhugh I'll make arrangements for another visit."

Maggie took one step forward. "But—"

"Good day, Miss Quinn." A small nod. "Clara."

The driver opened the door of the carriage as Mr. Kincaid approached.

"Mr. Kincaid?" It was Clare's voice from behind Maggie. "I'm sorry, Mr. Kincaid."

He turned. A passing cloud cast a shadow across his face and her breath caught. The classic, sculpted lines of the bones beneath his skin. His hair, darker gold, more loosely curled, but coupled with those distinctive blue eyes . . .

The very air grew still as he studied the child another long moment. Maggie didn't need to look at Clare to know the answer he was seeking.

"No, little girl," he said finally. "There's no reason for you to apologize. The fault is all mine."

He took a step toward the carriage and his leg seemed to give out from under him. Maggie reflexively jerked forward, although there was no way she could prevent a fall. His driver was closer and caught Mr. Kincaid's arm. For the briefest moment, Mr. Kincaid leaned against the burly driver, then straightened.

"It's nothing, Franklin," he said, impatiently brushing away the driver's assistance.

Not put off so easily, the driver hovered close by as Mr. Kincaid made the rest of the distance to the carriage, his limping gait hampered by the mud in the alley. Odd, but she hadn't noticed him limping before.

Clare slipped her hand into Maggie's. They watched in silence as the carriage pulled away.

"I'm sorry, my Maggie. He really was a nice man."

"Remember that, *mó cailín*," Maggie said around the knot in her throat.

She hoped the child was right, for as sure as there was a pot of gold at the end of the rainbow, Clare had just met her father.

*　*　*

Gordon idly drummed his fingers on the window frame as the carriage slowed to make the turn onto Light Street.

Gordon Kincaid had unknowingly fathered a daughter.

On the seat next to him was a bushel basket filled with potatoes. The blue leather seat across from him held more baskets filled to overflowing with cabbages, turnips, fresh peaches, tomatoes and leaf-wrapped ears of corn. The boot was stuffed with bags of flour, rice and beans. And wedged next to his feet was a wrapped slab of beef, its pungent aroma becoming more and more unpleasant with every click of the carriage wheels over the cobbled stones.

Indeed, the coach was so crowded he had no room to straighten his bad leg, which was becoming so cramped he wouldn't be able to walk if he didn't stretch soon. He yanked the bell cord to signal his driver, and thought again of what a poor excuse of a father he was. The food surrounding him now, and the orders he'd placed for delivery later, would go a short way in improving the diet of orphaned children. It did nothing to assuage his sense of guilt.

The carriage slowed and rolled to a halt. Gordon pushed the door open and climbed out, carefully taking his weight on his good leg. Not many people were about this time just before dusk. But the two who were—a waterman sitting on a stoop mending a crab trap and a rag picker pushing his cart home from a rubbish pile—had stopped to gape and stare at the black-lacquered carriage and matched horses in leather harness.

He looked up to see Franklin's round, dark face studying him. "Deliver this food to the orphanage kitchen at Saint Columba's," he said. "I'm going to walk back to the hotel."

Franklin took a slow look around. "Not the best part of town, Doc."

"Not the worst either." Gordon gestured with his hat. "Go on. I won't need you again until tomorrow."

Franklin scowled at the rag picker until he moved on, then they spent a few minutes making plans for the next day and finally Franklin took the traces in hand and pulled away from the curb.

At the far side of the road, the buildings opened up and the river winked a tarnished gray between them. The steamship wharves were deserted. Gordon crossed the street and walked along a stone jetty.

He stopped to watch a flock of gulls circle above a listing wooden dock. His fingers kneaded the ache in his thigh while he wondered in some idle way over the vagaries of life. What fate had placed him, his faithless mother's bastard son, in the household of a man so honorable Gordon learned the truth of his parentage only from overhearing slave gossip? And what crueler fate had condemned his own bastard daughter to an orphanage? It didn't help that it was Aurora who made the decision to discard the child.

The child had been discarded.

He felt a wave of sorrow that Peyton had died, to be forever silent on the subject of this girl child with the flaxen curls and his own oddly shaped eyes. Alone of all the men he knew, Peyton could offer guidance.

Well, he would have to find the proper path on his own.

A gust of damp wind plucked at his hair. Two men jumped from one of the skipjacks onto the dock, startling the gulls into flight. The wind carried their voices across the water. The language was Irish, but they were among that hard breed of Baltimorean who earned a living from the sea. Gordon turned his steps to the small dock. He would order some shellfish from tomorrow's catch. Crabs, oysters—surely those items were rare delicacies on the dining table of a home for discarded children.

The traffic lessened as Maggie made her way to the wharves, the smells subtly shifting to the tang of salt air and guano. A swarm of gulls wheeled in shifting light and shadow as a thin fog settled over the water.

She saw the O'Connors, father and son, standing in front of their skipjack, The *Molly-O*. Dressed in dark pea jackets and rolled stocking caps pulled low on their heads, they looked like what they were, Irishmen who labored hard to scratch a living from the waters of the Chesapeake. Padraig O'Connor was conversing with a third man, a man with golden hair and broad shoulders covered by an elegantly tailored black frock coat.

Mr. Kincaid must have seen her before she saw him, for he stood facing her, his back to the wind and the water. In the failing light, she couldn't see his features well, but she recognized him by his tousled golden hair, and his very presence stopped her midstride.

The slow-moving river slapped against the pilings, rocking the line of weathered skipjacks drawn up alongside the wharf. Jamie O'Connor lifted his hand and waved to her, and she smiled as she waved back. When she drew closer, she could hear bits of the conversation between Mr. Kincaid and Jamie's father.

Mr. Kincaid was buying jimmies, the blue crabs of the Chesapeake, and her footsteps faltered when she heard him request a delivery of shelled crabs to St. Columba's kitchen.

Maggie gathered her trailing skirts and stepped between the piles of coiled rope and bushel baskets. As she neared the men, her toe caught in a warped board and she tripped. Mr. Kincaid reached out and grabbed her elbow to keep her from falling.

His fingers pressed hard through the fabric of her sleeve. Something strange, breath-catching and near to panic swamped her. She stiffened, making a sound that was almost a gasp.

"Watch your step," he said. His voice was cadenced with a graciousness that shouldn't feel menacing yet was, somehow.

I'm sorry, she almost said, then realized how foolish that would have sounded, since she had nothing to be sorry for. She didn't know why she should be so flustered, but his mere presence seemed to shake the common sense right out of her head.

"Aye, thank you, Mr. Kincaid," she said. He had already

let go of her, both of his gloved hands curled around the brim of a black silk hat. They were large hands, graceful, with the long, narrow fingers of a gentleman.

"You two have met?" asked Padraig, his voice sounding surprised.

"Miss Quinn was kind enough to show me around the orphanage," said Mr. Kincaid. "Or to the lair of the mother superior, anyway."

She ignored his tone of sardonic amusement and stared at his black hat, at the way his fingers curled around the brim. Slowly, she lifted her gaze, and then she was looking into a pair of midnight-blue eyes.

His face matched his hands. An aristocratic face with strong, angular bones and lips that were curled as if in enjoyment of a joke only he understood. His nose was straight, his skin slightly bronzed and unlined except for tiny wrinkles at the edges of his eyes. She would like to think those were the marks of laughter on his face, but his eyes would give him away. This was a man whose laughter was not of pleasure, but of something else, something ironic, maybe, or maybe bitter.

The wind whipped her skirts around her legs. She tore her gaze away from Mr. Kincaid's. "Father Fitzhugh is wanting some oysters for his dinner come Thursday, after the concert," she said to Padraig O'Connor.

"He'll be leaving soon after?"

"You'll not be frowning, now, Mr. O'Connor. It's a grand honor for our Father Fitzhugh to be made bishop."

"Richmond," said Jamie with a snort of disgust. "And sure there's not an Irishman to be found in that den of Rebels."

She suspected Jamie was exaggerating his brogue, flaunting his Irishness in front of Mr. Kincaid, the Richmond Rebel. Jamie stood bulky and tall against the gray sky, his muscled shoulders squared and his stance aggressive.

" 'Tis not the Irish who called our Father Fitz to Richmond, but the Church," she said. "I'll be thinking our Lord is just as interested in the souls of former Rebels as He is in the souls of the benighted Fenians."

Jamie threw back his head dramatically, his eyes beseeching the slate heavens above. "God save us all, and the next thing she'll be accusing me of sending my scarce dollars to the United Brotherhood, and me an American citizen and my da himself a veteran of Grant's army."

"Aye, and reminding you too that every dollar you send is a dollar used to buy guns, and who dies from those guns, Jamie O'Connor? Not the earls and the landlords. Not even the British soldiers. It's our own who die, swinging by their stupid necks from the gibbet."

He startled her by moving forward suddenly, and then Mr. Kincaid moved, insinuating his shoulder between them. But her temper was up, and she stepped around Mr. Kincaid's bulk and went toe to toe with Jamie O'Connor, waterman, Irishman.

Jamie glared down at her, his jaw thrust forward with his own rising temper. "Aye, freedom is a rare and wonderful thing." His voice was a rasp, like the pull of a clam rake through wet sand. "But perhaps if you think on it a bit you'll agree there was another fever that drove poor Seamus Quinn into the arms of the Brotherhood."

She gasped in a breath that tasted of brine and caught in her throat with a physical pain. She turned her back to him and folded her arms across her waist.

"Ah, Jamie, lad, if those be your courtin' ways, you'll be finding yourself an old man in a cold bed," said Padraig O'Connor.

Maggie looked over her shoulder at him. For an instant, their gazes caught and she saw in his eyes a reflection of her own sad memories.

"The fine, fat oysters for our Father Fitzhugh," he said, smiling a little. "I'll bring them myself come Thursday."

"Aye, thank you." She took a step and Mr. Kincaid stepped beside her, startling her again so that she stopped.

"I'll see you back to the orphanage," he said. "It's getting late and this part of town is no place for a lady traveling alone."

"I'll walk her home," said Jamie from just behind her, and she heard the fight in his words.

She was no longer cold, caught between two large men as she was, enveloped with the heat of their bodies and the anger swirling just beneath the surface.

Her head fell back as she looked up at Mr. Kincaid. Where it should be Jamie O'Connor making her think of pirate barques sailing moonless waters, of muffled oars and the dark, shadowy figures of dangerous men, it was the silent, assessing Mr. Kincaid of the golden hair and haunted eyes who brought the fanciful vision to her mind.

He stared down into her upturned face, and it was as if Jamie and his father faded from sight so it was only Maggie Quinn, with her heart pounding so loud in her ears, waiting for Mr. Kincaid to do . . . something. After a moment, he simply nodded and stepped past her, passing so close she felt the sleeve of his coat brush her arm.

She turned and walked a few paces in the opposite direction, stopping at the edge of the dock. A seagull wheeled and cried over the river. She pretended a fascination with the strings of seaweed that wrapped around the pilings while she listened for the thud of Mr. Kincaid's boots fading away against the boards. When all she could hear was the melody of the river and wind, she turned around to see Jamie come up beside her. She looked away and watched a distant skiff rock in the river's dark current.

"I'm sorry, Maggie," he said after a long silence between them. "I know it pains you, losing your da as you did. But you don't see it and I needed to make you see it. Since we were children I've cared about you, and God save me, I fear I always will."

"Jamie, you're a good man, and I love you, but not in the way you'll be wanting. Somewhere, there's a woman who will love you for your good ways, your hard work, and she'll want to be your wife and the mother of your children." She looked up at him then, and spoke the words she no longer fully believed. "I'm meant to be a nun."

"Aye, then, be a nun if that's what will make you happy. But don't be making your poor mother's mistake, my Maggie. He's not our kind."

"And what kind will he be, Jamie? This is America, not Ireland."

"And isn't it the same everywhere? There'll be those that own the land, and own the people who work the land. He's the landlord we left behind us in Ireland and the slaveholder who shot my father in the Americans' war."

She turned around then, but Mr. Kincaid was gone. It was growing darker with the fog settling in, and quite cold. Jamie removed his pea coat and placed it around her shoulders. The damp wool smelled of salt water and a man's honest sweat. She reached up and drew it close to her throat, but still her body shivered.

"No, he's not our kind, Jamie," she said softly, and wondered if Mum had felt so strangely cold, and excited and fearful. Wondered if Mum, who had loved her only child, had yet regretted the birth of that child. For it was no secret Mum had loved the man who wouldn't marry her, and had married the man she couldn't love.

Chapter 2

*M*aggie intended to speak with Mother Bernadette about Clare, the way she'd overheard the child speaking in brogue and her own conclusions on the matter. She wanted to ask the mother superior a hundred questions about Mr. Kincaid.

She did neither. She hadn't the time, not with the fund-raising concert so near and the children's choir being placed on the program by the famous Mr. Tilghman himself.

Maggie taught at the school run by the nuns, reading and penmanship to the daughters of rich men who could afford the tuition at the convent boarding school. Through teaching, she earned a tiny room on the third floor of the orphanage, meals with the children and enough coin to keep herself clothed.

Her real passion was the children's choir of St. Columba's parish. And tonight, the poor children of first- and second-generation immigrants were going to perform on the stage of the new Halliday Street Theater along with the famous Mr. Tilghman from Boston and his musicians, before a sellout crowd of eighteen hundred.

She hastened her steps as she passed the gray-stone edifice of St. Columba's Church, its stained-glass windows reflecting the orange glow of the setting sun. The late traffic was noisy. A streetcar, drawn by two horses, lumbered by on a circuitous route to Camden Station. After it rattled past, she saw Father Fitzhugh standing in front of the rectory.

A handsome black carriage was pulling away into the steady line of traffic. Maggie recognized the driver, the man who had driven Mr. Kincaid last Monday. Father Fitzhugh turned his head, catching sight of her. He lifted his hand and waved.

She paused at the curb, waiting for a gig to go by. Father Fitz was smiling, but for Father Fitz, smiles came easily. Her own face was set in a thoughtful frown. *Mr. Kincaid.* Had he come to visit Clare today? When the trap had rumbled on, she lifted her skirts and crossed the street.

"Are the children ready?" asked Father Fitzhugh as she stopped beside him.

"Aye, excited . . . silly." She paused, trying to formulate a question so she wouldn't sound too curious. She failed and settled on another. "The oysters? Did Padraig O'Connor bring the oysters?"

Father Fitz slanted her an amused glance. "*Jamie* O'Connor." She nudged her chin higher and ignored his amusement. He shook his head. "Maggie, I fear you're much too hard on mortal men. Few are meant to be saints."

"No more than I am meant to be Jamie O'Connor's wife."

"Maybe not Jamie O'Connor's—"

"Father Fitz, please, not today."

She was already nothing but nerves, with the concert only hours away. The last thing she needed was another discussion of her suitability for the religious order, especially with her own growing uncertainties. Father Fitzhugh leaned against the wrought-iron railing and crossed his arms on his chest while he studied her.

He expelled a breath and then gave her the slow half-smile that always worked. She tried to harden her heart, not even knowing what horrible task his soft heart wanted to gift her with this time.

"I'd like you to join us tonight after the concert. Mother Bernadette is a fine lady, but I'd prefer you to serve as my hostess, given the company."

She gave him a startled look. "Me? I'm not suitable—"

"You're more than suitable, you're perfect for the occasion. Mr. Tilghman finds you charming, to use his own words, and you've already made the acquaintance of Mr. Kincaid."

"Mr. Kincaid?" His name came out on a breath.

"Yes. He's bringing a friend as well."

She started to shake her head, but Father Fitz interrupted.

"His family has been more than generous to our parish, my Maggie. Just now he presented me with a check for five thousand dollars. Would you have me treat him so poorly as to give him just a tour of the orphanage and then send him packing?"

"No, Father," she said. "It's just that I don't . . ."

Don't what? Like him? Trust him? Or was it those strange, breath-catching sensations that rushed through her, was it herself she didn't trust?

"Maggie?" There was a small frown on Father Fitzhugh's face. "Are you afraid of Mr. Kincaid?"

"Blessed Saint Brigid. Why should I fear him?"

Father Fitzhugh surprised her by laughing. And then it was the strangest thing—she suddenly felt as if she could tell him everything about the meeting down on the wharf, about Jamie and Mr. Kincaid squaring off like gamecocks, and about that odd rushing in her ears when Mr. Kincaid only looked at her, and they could laugh together over her foolishness. Yet no sooner did that thought enter her head than she remembered her mother, and she knew she would never laugh over such a thing.

A pensive look came into his eyes. "I'll be leaving for Richmond next week."

"Oh, Father Fitz." She folded her arms across her waist and stared, unseeing, at the traffic.

"I'd like to carry the memory of you on this big night with me."

She nodded in acquiescence and turned toward the orphanage.

"Maggie?"

She stopped.

"There's a package in your room. A birthday gift from me and the children. Wear it tonight."

She turned and looked at him. He was standing straight now, so tall. Sometime in the past years, silver threads had come into the black hair along his temples, but this minute she didn't see them. She saw Father Fitz as he was that long-ago day in the immigrant shed, so tall and broad-shouldered and kind. A frightened child's dream of a protector.

"Wear it for me."

"Aye, Father."

She couldn't wear such a dress. Maggie stepped back several paces, trying to see more of herself in the small, cracked mirror hanging over the dry sink in her room. What she saw was not immodest, with the high collar of ivory lace and long sleeves cuffed at the wrist. She twisted, trying to see the back. No bustle, she didn't own a bustle, but the dressmaker had improvised, creating a wide, stiff bow gathering the material at the small of her back with yards and yards of ivory lace flounces tumbling beneath.

The dress was beautiful. And too rich, much too rich. She pulled open the door to her clothes cupboard. The skirt and shirtwaist she wore for teaching wouldn't do for tonight, nor would the old black serge she wore for marketing. She fin-

gered the gray silk, her Sunday dress, the one she'd planned
to wear. Behind her, a light tapping sounded, followed by the
swish of the door being pushed open.

"Mary Margaret Quinn, you will not change."

Maggie pulled the gray silk from the cupboard. " 'Tis not
a suitable dress for the likes of me, Sister Agatha."

"You'll disappoint the children. They've been keeping this
secret for weeks."

"How?" asked Maggie, turning around. "Why?"

"As to how, a few pennies from each of the children, Mrs.
Brennan's time and sewing machine and the rest from Father
Fitz. As to why?" Sister Agatha shrugged. "They love you,
maybe?"

"They shouldn't have."

"They did. So will you disappoint them?"

"No," said Maggie softly. She brushed one hand down the
silken skirt. "I don't deserve this."

"Pshaw." Sister Agatha came forward into the tiny room.
"I'll be backstage with you tonight to help keep the little hea-
thens under control. Right now I'm going to do your hair."

Maggie turned back to the mirror. Her hair was her singu-
lar vanity, thick and black and arrow-straight. Just combing it
out was a major task since it had never been cut, falling past
her hips when left unbound. At eighteen, when she was certain she was meant to join the sisterhood, she had delayed because it meant cutting her hair. No doubt she'd already
consigned her soul to years in purgatory with this one sinful
vanity. She sighed.

"I suppose it needs to be rebraided," she said.

"Leave it to me, dear."

Maggie sat at the foot of her narrow cot while Sister
Agatha combed out her hair and chattered. Of all the sisters,
she felt closest to Sister Agatha. One couldn't help loving her
because, unlike Mother Bernadette, there was no steel in Sister Agatha, only sweetness and light.

"There," said Sister Agatha, sounding pleased. "You look
as lovely as a debutante."

"Then I'll be looking very silly, me being twenty-six years tomorrow."

"Not silly, lovely." Sister Agatha gave her a gentle shove. "Look for yourself. If only we had some earbobs."

Maggie's hand reflexively reached for her earlobe as she shook her head, and then she caught sight of herself in the mirror. Her hand dropped to her side while she stared at the stranger's reflection. Sister Agatha had woven two ribbons into her hair, one of emerald, one of gold. With the braid coiled on top of her head, the effect was of a jeweled crown.

"What do you think?" Sister Agatha sounded so pleased.

Decadent, thought Maggie, feeling a strange combination of pleasure and guilt. For a fleeting instant, she wondered what Mr. Kincaid would think of this Maggie Quinn. Would his rogue's eyes glimmer in appreciation or in amusement at the airs of this foolish Irish immigrant spinster, dressed in the style of a lady?

"Come along, Maggie. Sister Josephine and I'll ride with the children. Father Fitz asked Mr. Kincaid to pick you up and his carriage should be arriving any minute."

Maggie swung around so fast her skirts swirled. "He did *what?*"

The laugh lines at Sister Agatha's eyes deepened. "We don't want that beautiful dress getting all crushed and wrinkled riding in a wagon with a dozen bouncing children, do we?"

Before she could move or even speak, the children were twittering outside her door and Sister Agatha was shoving her into the hallway. When they reached the main hall, she had time only to bend and straighten two collars on two fidgeting boys before a knock sounded at the door. Sister Agatha answered the knock while Maggie tried to soothe little Alice's stage fright.

Then, between ushering twelve jabbering children down the stairs and rushing back inside for Sister Agatha's shawl and seeing that the children were all situated inside the wagon with the two troublemakers, Billy Kohn and Timmy

O'Reilly, safely separated, she found herself suddenly presented with Mr. Kincaid's bow and offered arm. She had nothing to do but take it.

She was breathless, flushed and already rumpled. She felt sudden amusement with herself. What a picture she must make to this aristocratic gentleman, with her brow showing a sheen of sweat and her fine silk dress already crushed where dozens of little hands had gripped and pulled. With a faint smile tugging at her lips, Maggie allowed him to assist her into the carriage.

Maggie took the backward seat, wriggling a little in a vain attempt to keep from crushing the stiff bow at her back. Mr. Kincaid climbed in behind her and took a position beside a young woman who was already seated.

"Miss Hays," he said with a slight nod, "Miss Quinn."

And so much for gentlemanly introductions, thought Maggie as Miss Hays openly studied her. Maggie lowered her lashes and contemplated her gloved hands folded in her lap.

"Mr. Kincaid tells me you're directing the children's choir tonight."

Maggie could hear the ring of censure in Miss Hays's voice. A lady would never make such a public display of herself, even in the name of charity. She looked up, meeting Miss Hays's scrutinizing gaze. "Aye," she said simply.

Miss Hays's pert little nose wrinkled. "You're Irish?"

"Aye," said Maggie. One corner of her mouth lifted. "I trust it won't rub off on you if you don't come too close."

Mr. Kincaid cleared his throat. When she looked at him, he was smiling his rogue's smile. "When Rebecca heard I had tickets for tonight's performance, she begged to come along. Mr. Tilghman's fame, I suppose. I forgot to mention this was a special performance to raise money for a Catholic parish."

Miss Hays gave another dainty sniff, causing the bird of paradise perched amid the feathers in her hat to bobble like a living thing.

"Just keep telling yourself Handel and Haydn and maybe

a little Mozart, dear heart," said Mr. Kincaid as he gave Miss Hays's knee a pat, apparently unconcerned that Maggie sat across from them watching the untoward display. Maggie wanted to look away, but something in Mr. Kincaid's expression seemed to taunt her, so she didn't. "And you'll be Mr. Tilghman's dinner partner after the concert," he added.

Miss Hays stretched like a lithe cat. "Gordon," she murmured, peering at him from beneath her lashes, her hand stroking his arm while her lips turned into a seductive pout. "I declare, you do go on so."

Maggie watched, fascinated. If this was the way of the world, she wanted no part of it, because never, *never* could she imagine herself behaving in such a fashion. Miss Hays fluttered her lashes. Maggie sucked in her cheeks and turned to gaze out the opposite window.

For a long while, she listened to the clink of the harness traces and the bustle of traffic as they traveled with silence inside the carriage. Her mind raced between the children, their nervous excitement over performing, and speculation on Mr. Kincaid and Miss Hays, whom he seemed to tolerate with a condescending amusement. She felt a sudden and surprising wave of compassion for Miss Hays.

"Father Fitzhugh was telling me Mr. Tilghman donated his time for this performance."

Maggie turned her attention back to Mr. Kincaid, appreciating his effort to lighten the burden of silence, willing to aid him as much as she was capable.

"Aye," she said, and it was a stupid thing to say in front of Miss Hays and her wrinkled nose. Maggie nudged her chin up. "It was good of him, since the church must only pay the rent for the hall and that much more will go into the school fund."

"Father Fitzhugh is a very persuasive man." His smile faded. "It's a pity my father never made a visit to Baltimore. He would have appreciated your Father Fitzhugh."

His face was chiseled with light and shadow as they passed by a street lamp, beautiful and expressionless. But she thought she heard something in his voice, that same bewildered sadness she'd seen the other day as he spoke with Clare.

"There's much to appreciate in our Father Fitzhugh, as I'm certain there was in Mr. Peyton Kincaid," she said softly. She waited until he met her gaze. "We'll be missing Father Fitz when he goes to Richmond, but our loss will surely be your gain."

"Perhaps you're right, Miss Quinn," he said after a moment.

They lapsed back into silence as the carriage turned onto Halliday Street. The pavement in front of the theater was crowded with well-dressed gentlemen and ladies milling about while waiting their turn to enter. Maggie felt a terrible moment of panic; all these finely dressed society patrons come to hear Mr. Tilghman without a thought for the purpose of the concert. Her poor children were going to be made a laughingstock, singing their simple Irish airs.

Mr. Kincaid exited the carriage first, then assisted Miss Hays. Maggie was gathering her skirts to stand when he turned back for her. He was so tall and his shoulders filled the doorway. The gaslights cast a golden slash of color on one side of his face.

He reached into the carriage, and she thought for just the space of a heartbeat that if she touched him, she would lose something of her self. But she took his hand and allowed him to assist her from the carriage.

"Miss Quinn!"

She turned and saw Mr. Felan, president of the fund-raising board. Third generation Irish, owner of a grand emporium on Commerce Street, his rotund, richly clothed body fit in very properly among the society swells. He bowed to Miss Hays and favored Mr. Kincaid with a nod.

"If you'll follow me," he said. "Mr. Tilghman and Father Fitzhugh are already waiting in the Green Room."

"I must go to the children," said Maggie.

"No, no. Father Fitz was very specific," said Mr. Felan. "He wants you in the Green Room."

Maggie followed as Mr. Felan took Miss Hays's arm, and Mr. Kincaid fell in beside her. The crowd on the pavement parted, allowing them passage.

"All these people," she murmured.

"All this money," said Mr. Kincaid.

She looked up. Mr. Kincaid winked at her, as if they were conspirators in some grand scheme. But she couldn't come up with the first word to say to him.

By the time they reached the Green Room, Mr. Felan was already introducing Miss Hays, who seemed overcome by the proximity of the famous Mr. Tilghman. Father Fitzhugh separated himself and came forward to greet them.

He took both her hands in his, holding them out to the side while he studied her. "Beautiful, my Maggie. You'll do us proud tonight." He looked over to Mr. Kincaid and she saw a roguish smile greet a similar one. "What say you?"

"Far be it from me to contradict the word of a man of God."

Father Fitzhugh laughed at the sally. Maggie pulled her gaze away from Mr. Kincaid, wondering why she felt a twinge of disappointment. But she had no time for this silliness. The children were waiting on her.

"I must go, Father Fitz," she said. "The children—"

Mr. Tilghman interrupted. "No, Maggie."

"You'll be onstage with us," said Father Fitzhugh. "There wouldn't be a concert without the time you've put into this."

"But—"

"The sisters will keep the children in line," he said. "Mr. Felan, would you escort Miss Hays to the box to sit with you and your wife? We can meet here again after the program."

Mr. Felan is Irish, thought Maggie, barely suppressing a nervous giggle. Miss Hays shot a questioning glance to Mr. Kincaid, her blond ringlets jiggling around her diamond earbobs as she turned her head.

"Miss Hays," he said. "I trust you'll forgive me for not mentioning I'm to make the introductory speech tonight." He caught her hand and lifted it briefly, while bending forward and lowering his lashes. "It was most gauche of me, but it seems I'm cursed with a horrible memory. Am I forgiven, fair lady?"

Maggie wondered what fool would fall for that display, but her unspoken question was soon answered.

"We must work on your memory," said Miss Hays, apparently forgetting her distaste of the *Irish*. But then, Mr. Felan was third-generation and rich, so maybe he didn't smell quite so bad to that dainty, wrinkled nose.

Father Fitzhugh smiled. "Miss Hays might enjoy riding back to the rectory with Mr. Tilghman."

Miss Hays was going to gush all over Mr. Tilghman's fancy suit. At that moment, Mr. Tilghman saved himself by spreading his arms and fluttering his hands. "It's time, it's time," he said. "Let us all take our places so the performance can begin."

"Miss Quinn," said Mr. Kincaid, catching her arm as she headed toward Father Fitz. "Allow me."

He looked into her eyes and she wondered, was that the kind of look he'd used on Clare's poor mother? Even she, who had only been courted by the likes of Jamie O'Connor, and who had long ago decided on the chaste life of a nun—even Maggie could recognize the seductive power in that intense, cobalt gaze.

"The introductory speech?" she said by way of making conversation as Mr. Kincaid guided her from the room.

"Your Father Fitz is a very persuasive man."

She looked up. He smiled.

A smile that sad could make the angels weep, and in the next instant she thought *she* might weep. For him, for Clare. And maybe, for Maggie Quinn.

Their footsteps echoed as they stepped onto the bare wooden floor of the stage from the wings. Gordon glanced down at

the top of her head, where ribbons twined through the black
braid. The lace jabot at her throat fluttered as she swallowed
hard.

She was so quiet tonight, painfully shy in the wake of Rebecca's rudeness. The truth was Rebecca Hays, in all her jeweled and organdy splendor, faded into obscurity when
measured against the stately Miss Quinn. Maggie looked
stunning tonight, dressed in Irish lace and green silk that
deepened the hue of her eyes and rustled seductively with
every step she took.

He had thought her prim and unapproachable the first time
he'd seen her, that clouded morning outside the orphanage.
Later, when he inadvertently bumped into her at Light Street
Wharf, he had thought of her as brave to go nose to nose with
Jamie's belligerence.

He held Maggie's chair, adjusting it slightly as she took
her place beside Father Fitzhugh. He came around then,
flicking the tails of his evening coat as he took the seat on her
other side.

He was instantly conscious of every part of his body in
proximity to every part of hers. Her dress draped her body so
he could clearly see the outline of her legs, the curve of her
hip beside him, the mounds of her breasts. She had seemed
chaste when first they met; now she was nothing short of
sensual.

She was also nervous, maybe even frightened, if those
gloved hands squeezing in front of her waist were any clue.
Without conscious thought, he reached over and covered her
hands with his own.

His hand was so much larger and he fought the urge to
draw hers into his lap and take her fear as his own. There was
something about her that made him want to delve deeper into
her heart. And he knew himself a fool, for he understood how
glimpses into another's heart came at such tremendous cost
to one's own.

He withdrew his hand and heard her soft exhalation of
breath. She felt it too, whatever the mysterious pull was, but

unlike the widows and war spinsters who filled his social life, this woman would never give him an overt sign. Only her innocence left her open to his perceptions.

Mr. Tilghman lowered his baton to the sound of applause. So, it was time for his own performance. God, how he hated this quasi-political, quasi-charitable nonsense. He'd given up causes long ago, and wouldn't his brother laugh if he could see him now: dressed like a penguin, performing like a trick dog. But then, Royce had convictions and the courage to act on them. A monumental waste of effort, as far as Gordon could determine.

He stood and took a moment to center his weight, hoping his deuced leg didn't give out on him now. He stopped at the edge of the stage behind the wooden lectern and looked out over the floodlights, but could see little beyond the first rows of seats, each filled with a white face seeming to float in the dark theater.

He elicited a bit of laughter from them by opening with the dead frog he'd put in the church collection plate one Sunday morning as a boy, restive rustling of silk gowns when he shifted to the purpose of the concert, and desultory applause when he took his bow. All about par for this type of audience, who came to be seen in their gowns from Worth and jewels from Tiffany's while congratulating themselves for their benevolence in purchasing a benefit concert ticket. He felt a tug at his heart for those children who had rushed down the orphanage steps in a lather of excitement. They would get a poor reception from this crowd.

Mr. Tilghman lifted his baton, and the orchestra opened with Handel's *Magnificat*. Gordon was swamped in his own thoughts and didn't even know how far into the program they were when he cut the woman beside him an indirect glance, wondering why he had sensed no movement from her.

She had gone utterly still with the kind of intensity that wells up from deep inside. He heard the music; Maggie *felt* it. He could have sat for hours watching that kind of enchantment, but the music stopped.

Father Fitzhugh rose, and Maggie visibly started when the priest took her hand. They walked to the center of the stage, where Father Fitzhugh stopped to make his introduction while Maggie continued on to the far stage curtains. She gestured and the children marched out in a line and filed onto the risers.

They were halfway through the second song before one of the children standing in the front row shifted and Gordon saw the shimmering, shoulder-length curls of his daughter. He tipped his head back and closed his eyes.

His daughter, and he hadn't even noticed her in the confusion of children pouring out of the orphanage and climbing into the wagon. A Kincaid, riding in a farm wagon, while her father traveled to the same hall in the comfort of an enclosed carriage with two lovely women. Why hadn't Maggie said something to him?

Why would she say anything? Maggie didn't know young Clara was the bastard daughter of Gordon Kincaid. He hadn't known himself, before Mother Bernadette's staggering revelation. He still wasn't ready to accept it; believe it, yes—he could believe it simply by looking at the child.

The children's voices faded. He heard a few pockets of genuine applause, no doubt the children's families, but the rest of the society patrons clapped politely and without enthusiasm.

Anger tightened his chest. Get the children off the stage, he thought, but before Maggie could move, Mr. Tilghman was standing beside her. The conductor gestured and two musicians rose from the back of the orchestra pit. They carried a harp to center stage. Maggie jerked backward and sent a beseeching look up at Mr. Tilghman.

Father Fitzhugh leaned closer to Gordon. "I told him she'd refuse."

"She plays the harp?" asked Gordon, almost laughing at the absurdity of the image in his head. An angel and a harp, even the cherubs, if freckle-faced urchins even remotely qualified as cherubs.

"The harp and the violin," said Father Fitzhugh in a low murmur. "Of all the things I'll miss when I leave Baltimore, I think I'll miss Maggie's music the most."

Gordon realized that the priest was in earnest, that he honestly believed Maggie had the right combination of talent and skill to perform onstage in front of a discriminating audience.

Mr. Tilghman said something to her that caused her to look in their direction. She ignored Gordon, her gaze settling on the priest. Father Fitzhugh let out a breath and Gordon thought for an instant that Maggie was going to smile, or cry, but she did neither. She nodded, and seated herself on the stool.

Father Fitzhugh leaned his head again. "Have you ever heard 'Danny Boy'?" Gordon nodded. He hated that song, and if he never heard it again as long as he lived, then he'd die happy.

"I promise you," said Father Fitzhugh, "you've never heard it sung the way our Maggie sings it."

Wonderful. And he'd do his confounded best not to hear it tonight either. But he was sucked in, first by the play of the reflected lighting in her hair and across her face, then deeper still as he became aware of the fluid, graceful motion of her hands caressing a melody out of the harp strings. And then she added her voice to the notes from the harp and he was lost.

Her voice started soft, uncertain, then gained strength, and Gordon caught more than a glimpse into her heart. It wouldn't surprise him to see crimson at the tips of her fingers, because she bled with the music she created; her voice was glory and tears for the soldier gone to war.

He rubbed his sweating palms down his thighs, then crossed his arms on his chest, hoping he gave the appearance of ennui, knowing the motion was a vain effort to trap the pain inside. To encircle and contain it. And still, she thrummed the harp and sang of the soldier returning to kneel at his wife's grave.

He should have died. Soldiers were supposed to die, not the wives they left behind.

She finished and rested her head against the still-vibrating strings. For a long, endless minute, the hall was silent. His throat closed, choking off his breath.

Finally, a single clap broke the silence, joined by another and then the spell was broken with a thunderous roar of hand-clapping. There was a rustling in the audience. The rustle became a rumble and then a reverberation as wave after wave of people came to their feet.

Gordon stood, clapping with the rest. He concentrated on the children as they rushed down from the risers and circled around her, grabbing at her skirts as they clamored for her attention. She hugged each one, then gathered the last child in her arms. His child.

Maggie rested her cheek against the top of Clara's head and looked to the side where he stood with Father Fitzhugh. She gifted the priest with an ethereal smile that transformed her into the most beautiful woman he'd ever seen and then her gaze shifted to him. Their gazes locked and her smile faded.

She seemed to grip Clara tighter in her hold. He tried to swallow and thought a knife must have become stuck in his throat.

The pain, God, the pain. He wanted to believe he was all his daughter needed, all she would ever need. But a child's needs had to be answered, fulfilled, and he had recognized long ago that the man sent home from a Northern prison camp was a man destined for failure.

Gordon Kincaid, once the dreamer of dreams; Gordon Kincaid, now the broken man. So he gave his son to his brother to raise, willingly. Not from lack of a father's love but because he loved the boy too much to fail him. And Peyton had known this, yet still reached from the grave handing him one more chance at redemption.

I can't do it, Father. I can't raise a child alone.

Chapter 3

"You were wonderful," gushed Miss Hays yet again to Mr. Tilghman. "So wonderful."

"I think Miss Quinn turned out to be tonight's star," said Mr. Tilghman gallantly, for the sixth time, and was ignored by Miss Hays for the sixth time. Maggie had passed beyond blushing in embarrassment to flushing in irritation.

There were six of them seated at Father Fitzhugh's table. Father Fitz at the head, with Miss Hays and Mother Bernadette on either side; herself at the other end, with Mr. Tilghman and Mr. Kincaid at her left and right, respectively.

Father Fitz had not been thinking when he asked her to serve as hostess tonight. She was in over her head and knew it. Maggie sat primly on the edge of her seat and took several indirect glances around the table to see if anyone else recognized that simple fact.

With the meal over, Mr. Kincaid appeared very comfortable, pushed back from the table with his long legs angled off to the side while he idly toyed with his wineglass. Mother Bernadette had evidently had her fill of Miss Hays—Mother Bernadette could never abide foolishness—and was making an effort to direct the conversation to a more interesting path.

"Do you still practice, Gordon?" she asked.

Maggie was wondering what instrument he played when Miss Hays's silly giggle interrupted her thoughts.

"I keep telling Gordon if he'd set up a practice in Mount Royal he'd make bushels of money, but he just wants to see those sad old veterans, most of whom don't even pay him after he travels all that distance."

"Most of those sad old veterans don't have enough money to buy food, Becca," said Mr. Kincaid in a quiet voice.

Maggie looked up from studying the painted flowers on her plate, wondering if the surprise showed on her face. "You're a doctor?"

He sat very relaxed, with his elbow on the arm of his chair, his jaw propped against his curled hand, studying her from beneath lowered lashes. A strange shadow came into his eyes.

"Only for sad old veterans," he said.

She tucked her chin, hiding her urge to smile and thinking of his limp the other day. A war wound of his own, she supposed. Kincaid—she'd heard that name before in conjunction with the war, but she'd been new to this country then and couldn't place the name with either the North or the South.

"That's how you met Mother Bernadette, isn't it?" She looked over, catching the warmth in the mother superior's usually cool blue eyes.

"Gettysburg," they said in unison, and then he chuckled. "I lived to rue the day."

"Stay in Baltimore awhile longer, Gordon. I'll make a man of you yet," said Mother Bernadette, and Maggie had never heard that soft, affectionate tone in her voice.

"That's one of my greatest fears," answered Dr. Kincaid in a slow drawl, bringing a round of laughter from the other gentlemen.

As she watched him, he ducked his chin a little, his eyes

looking down, a half-smile at his lips. It was a look she'd seen before on young boys; a look that conveyed a bashful pleasure. But he spoiled the effect by lifting his wineglass to his lips and staring at her over the rim.

She had little experience with men, but she knew that sultry gaze through those thick golden lashes was that of a worldly, experienced man. Flustered, she broke eye contact, toying with her fork, and then, curiously sneaked a glance at Miss Hays, wondering if she'd witnessed the display.

Miss Hays looked like an unhappy china doll; even her sausage curls seemed to droop as she gazed at Dr. Kincaid. She loves him, thought Maggie, and didn't know why this should startle her so.

Father Fitzhugh folded his napkin on the table. "I can see Mr. Tilghman would like a cigar," he said. "If our guests would allow me the presumption, I'd like to suggest we all retire to the parlor for our coffee." He smiled at Miss Hays. "As a young man, I never could understand why the ladies were allowed to escape to the withdrawing room while we gentleman inhaled smoke, imbibed spirits and argued politics. I might be a priest now, but I can still appreciate finer company. Shall we flout that convention tonight?"

Miss Hays's eyebrow arched, then she looked at Dr. Kincaid, who nodded, a strange smile playing at the corner of his mouth. "Of course," she said.

Maggie thought that an excellent idea and couldn't understand why no one moved. Mother Bernadette stared at her fixedly, trying to convey some message. Maggie sat paralyzed, wondering what Mother Bernadette's eyes and stiff smile meant, fearing she was making some gross social blunder and totally at a loss as to how to fix it. From the corner of her vision, she saw Dr. Kincaid's napkin flutter to the floor. Their heads almost bumped as they both leaned over, reaching for the linen napkin.

"No one can rise until you do, Miss Quinn," he whispered.

"Oh," she mouthed as she handed him the napkin. He

winked again before straightening and instead of feeling chagrined, she wanted to laugh.

She managed to keep her face straight while she folded
her napkin and set it beside her plate. "Shall we adjourn,
ladies?" she said, pushing her chair back and rising. She
tilted her head slightly. "Gentlemen?"

Father Fitzhugh's eyes danced with amusement, as if he
knew exactly the sequence of events that had taken place at
the lower reaches of the tablecloth.

As the others settled into the parlor, Mr. Tilghman excused himself for a smoke, leaving the door ajar and allowing
the entrance of Father Fitzhugh's cat. Clancy, ever regal,
stalked directly to Dr. Kincaid.

"Clancy," said Father Fitz in a stern voice, which the cat
ignored, turning in slow circles and then settling into a yellow lump on Dr. Kincaid's lap.

Dr. Kincaid brushed the cat's back, seemingly oblivious to
the yellow hairs settling on his black dress trousers. "Have
you had your chocolate today, old boy?" he murmured in a
low tone, as if it were a secret between them.

"Down, Clancy," repeated Father Fitz, giving the cat a sus-
tained glare. Clancy didn't see the glare; his eyes were closed
and his motor running. Father Fitzhugh, heartless, got up and
physically removed the lazy tomcat, shutting him from the
room. Father Fitz returned, apologizing for his cat's bad
manners. Dr. Kincaid brushed off the apology as he brushed
off the first layer of cat hairs, and the conversation flagged.

Maggie would have liked to fill the silence, but her tongue
was tied in front of Miss Hays. She would have loved to ask
Dr. Kincaid about his medical practice, but decided such
questions would be forward unless he raised the subject.

She was studying the picture hanging above Father Fitz's
mantel, a beautiful oil painting depicting Castle Lachlan in
County Clare, when Dr. Kincaid spoke.

"Well, Becca," he said in a teasing drawl, "has it been as
awful as you expected—dining with priests and nuns?"

Maggie herself would have been hard-pressed to control her temper, but Miss Hays merely fluttered her lashes and said in a little-girl's voice, "Gordon, surely you jest. Miss Quinn is not a nun."

Father Fitz laughed. "Mother Bernadette looks at Miss Quinn and sees a nun, Mr. Tilghman looks at her and sees a musician. When I look at her, I see the little girl in a dirndl and brogans." He tilted his head, studying her. "What do you see when you look at her, Doctor?"

Maggie stiffened. "Father Fitz, please—"

"I'm curious, my Maggie. Let him tell us. Perhaps his insight will give you guidance the rest of us have been unable to offer."

She couldn't keep herself from turning her head to look at Dr. Kincaid, and once she did, she sat still as stone, her chest emptied of air. He unnerved her, he did, the way he was looking at her from beneath his lashes, the dark intensity of his eyes. He caught her looking, and after another moment his mouth softened.

Maggie yanked her gaze away, watching Mr. Tilghman return and take a seat on the maroon tufted wing chair near Father Fitz, while her mind spun objections and no words came from her paralyzed throat.

"Not yet a nun, not with that crown of black hair on top of her head," said Dr. Kincaid slowly. "Beautiful hair. I hate to think of it chopped and hidden beneath a wimple."

It was an unconscious response to his words—Maggie raised her arm and touched her hair, cocking her head just a little, and the movement brought him back into her view. Dr. Kincaid's face changed. Only a little, a deepening tension around her eyes and mouth, a hardness that should have made her feel cold inside, but felt like heat instead.

"She has Mother Bernadette's steel in that spine of hers," he said. "But I think I'm more taken with the warmth I saw in her with the children. I suspect she learned that from you, Father."

"Go on," said Father Fitzhugh.

"Gladly. Her face . . . well, her face wants to be stern, but she can't quite pull it off, although she has a way of lifting her chin that I'm certain puts the fear of God into her students. She's too tall to be considered fashionable, but dressed as she is tonight, she has a . . . shall we call it a presence?" He shook his head slowly. "Not at all spinsterish, fair lady, and hardly a black-robed nun."

Her face burned, with anger or embarrassment, she wasn't certain. "Enough, Dr. Kincaid."

"What do you say, Father? She's too much a pagan to be Saint Maggie. I'd call her Athena, of the spear and the thunderbolts."

"The owl and the olive branch," murmured Father Fitz.

A soft breeze stirred the draperies. Father Fitzhugh stood and walked to the sideboard, where he lifted the brandy decanter and removed the stopper. "My Maggie sings like her mother," he said. "Deirdre was a nightingale."

Heat pricked the back of her eyes. Father Fitzhugh caught her gaze, his green eyes soft and beguiling. And that sharp sensation of tears faded into a kind of diffused sadness, like a bruised place in the heart.

His mouth curved in a gentle smile, as if he knew, then he looked to his guest. "You like the horses, Doctor. Maggie's stepfather was head trainer for the Earl of Lachlan."

Until he was so foolish as to smuggle guns for the Fenians, she thought. Dr. Kincaid appeared intrigued by this new information.

"The Earl of Lachlan, Geoffrey Fitzhugh?" He grinned suddenly. "He's your brother, isn't he?"

"My twin," said Father Fitz.

Maggie's hand shook so hard the coffee cup rattled in its saucer and black liquid sloshed over the rim. Father Fitzhugh tilted the decanter toward Dr. Kincaid in a silent inquiry. Dr. Kincaid waved his hand to decline the offer.

"We bought a two-year-old from the Lachlan stables just before the war." Dr. Kincaid looked at her. "You might remember the horse. A big blue out of Diomed. I believe you called him Byerly, although we reregistered him with a different name."

"Aye, I remember. Has he performed well for you?"

"The horse was shot out from under my brother at the Battle of New Market," he said, his gaze fixed on the brandy snifter he held in his hand.

Silence settled over the parlor. The mantel clock chimed and Miss Hays stirred, causing her skirts to rustle, which seemed to recall Dr. Kincaid from whatever demons possessed him.

"If you like horses, Miss Quinn, perhaps you and Father Fitz would join me at Pimlico for the Dixie Handicap. I've a good horse running this year."

"I'll be in Richmond by then, Gordon—if I may call you Gordon," said Father Fitz. "I'd be happy to join you sometime at the Richmond races."

"Are you a betting man, Father?"

"I go for the pleasure of watching."

"Once my father's will is probated, I'll have sole ownership of a two-year-old colt who could fill your coffers. Firenza." He looked at Maggie. "Miss Quinn, you're still welcome to join us at Pimlico."

"I'm afraid I couldn't possibly . . ."

One corner of his mouth lifted. She thought he must understand all her reasons, which had everything to do with spending time in his company. Something about him unsettled her, all her tidy assumptions and certainties as vaporous as mist when she looked at him.

"Perhaps you'll change your mind. The invitation remains open." He directed his attention to the young woman he'd ignored for most of the evening. "Are you ready, Becca? Our hosts have obligations for the morrow." Miss Hays stood, looking relieved. "Can we drop you at home, Miss Quinn?" he asked politely.

"I have only to walk across the alley," she said. "Father Fitz will see me safely there."

He rose with a fluid, easy grace, and only because she was watching him did she catch the hesitation in his movement as his weight shifted. His leg, whatever the injury, must be a constant irritation, and one he hid well. He gestured to Miss Hays. "Becca, you can wait here while I walk Miss Quinn home."

Miss Hays spluttered and then resignedly settled back into the brocaded chair when Dr. Kincaid ignored her. Maggie shook her head, unwilling to be alone with him even for the short time it would take to cross the alley.

He took her hand and pulled her up. "I insist. It's the least I can do after the good father's hospitality."

She looked to Father Fitzhugh for rescue, but he was ignoring all her silent signals tonight, so she allowed herself to be led from the room by Dr. Kincaid.

"This is really unnecessary," she said as the front door closed behind them.

"No. I'm afraid I maneuvered you into this. I wanted to speak to you alone."

Clare, she thought in a slight panic. She was aware of his limp, more by the slight dragging sound of one patent leather shoe on the stones than by his gait. He was so tall, so finely formed. She knew instinctively he wouldn't appreciate her sympathy, but it seemed a sin for God to allow the marring of such perfection by men's violence. She waited for him to speak, and after a few more steps he drew in a deep breath and expelled it slowly.

"I saw Clara today," he said. She said nothing, unable to form any coherent thought. After another moment, he said, "I believe young Clara is my daughter."

"Aye, I guessed as much," she admitted.

He stopped at the end of the walkway and leaned his hip against the wrought-iron fence. A spill from the gas lamp on the corner cast his face into stark relief. A muscle twitched along his jaw.

"I was going to take her on an outing tomorrow, maybe

the park, but Mother Bernadette informs me that Clara will be leaving to spend two nights with another couple, someone by the name of Cromwell."

Maggie drew in a swift breath. "Clare does *not* want them for parents."

He studied her intently. "She told you?"

"It's the way she turns on the immigrant brogue, like she did with you the other day in the garden. Remember, she asked you if you were looking for a child to replace another?" He nodded, smiling slightly at the memory, and her heart softened toward him for that. "Clare wants to be wanted for herself. All orphans feel that way. The Cromwells make her feel as if she's second best, taking her only because their own daughter died."

"You are an orphan," he said, and it was more a statement than a question, so she only nodded. He gazed somewhere over her shoulder for a long minute, as if gathering his thoughts.

"Mother Bernadette tells me she'll allow the Cromwells to adopt Clara if they find her suitable for them." He huffed a bitter laugh. "She feels a married couple takes precedence over a bachelor, even if that man is blood kin."

Maggie struggled to keep her face blank as she absorbed that shock. She must think of Clare. What was best for Clare? The answer was so simple, so apparent. And it hurt like the devil's own fire.

Because she loved the wee *cailín,* she must let her go. Whether it was the Cromwells or this man, Clare deserved a home, a family of her own.

"I'm sorry, Dr. Kincaid. I can speak to her, but when the mother superior makes up her mind . . ."

He met her gaze. "I know Mother Bernadette, you don't need to explain."

She wanted to reach out and touch him, make him foolish promises she couldn't keep, anything to ease the suffering in his eyes.

"I elicited a promise from the mother superior that she

won't act in haste on this issue," he said. "After all, five years have already passed in the child's life, a few more weeks won't make a major difference." He tilted his head back and seemed almost to sigh. "I'll find myself a wife and take Clara home with me where she belongs."

"Miss Hays is auditioning for the position?"

"Miss Hays doesn't know that." .

"Why not Clare's mother?"

He stiffened. She probably had no right to ask that question, but he seemed poised to ask for her help somehow and she needed to know before she could make her own decision.

"Clara's mother is not an option," he said in a low voice.

She nodded without speaking because she didn't know what to say. All this time, he'd kept his gaze fixed on her, almost as if he were waiting for her condemnation. When it didn't come, his expression softened and she thought he might smile, but he didn't.

"My options are limited in this territory, Miss Quinn, as limited as my time. Miss Hays is available and interested."

"But Miss Hays . . . you . . ."

He did smile then, although she didn't know if he smiled because she herself was so inept or because Miss Hays was so flighty and foolish.

"It seems she's rather enamored of the name *Kincaid*; there must be some kind of cachet in marrying into an old Virginia family even now, after the war. My father was known in his own right, my brother is rather famous, but since I'm the only available Kincaid, she seems ready enough to settle on me." He shrugged. "I need a wife so I can take my daughter home. She wants a husband. Many marriages are based on less."

He looked at her intensely, his head tilted to one side. "I can handle that part; it's Clara and Mother Bernadette who give me pause. Will you help me, Miss Quinn? I know you love Clara."

She stared into his dark eyes while she grappled with her own tumultuous sense of loss. "Aye, as long as I can feel you'll be giving her the better home," she said finally, wondering why even as she spoke. But he *was* Clare's father and she suddenly wanted to believe he would love Clare for herself alone. "If I do, and Mother Bernadette gives her to you, will you promise you'll allow me to write and maybe even visit if I ever save up enough money to travel that far?"

"It's a promise." He pushed away from the railing and crooked her hand in his arm. "I'll be back in the morning for a short visit before Clara leaves with the Cromwells. Perhaps you'll walk with me and Clara if your time allows? Give me a little aid in courting my daughter?"

"Aye."

They had reached the marble steps in front of the orphanage and she disengaged her hand. "May I call you something friendlier than Miss Quinn?"

"Maggie will do."

"All right, Maggie."

She knew she should turn and go inside, but she didn't. For a long minute they gazed at one another. She suddenly realized how foolish she must appear.

"Dr. Kincaid." She inclined her head in farewell. He reached out and grabbed her shoulders and she looked up, startled, into his face. He lowered his head and kissed her, a quick kiss on the cheek, so quick she had no time to react.

"My name is Gordon, and I absolutely hate being called Doctor," he said, smiling, not at all abashed by his own behavior.

Her hand had reached up of its own volition, covering her lips, which was just as well, otherwise she would surely be looking like a fish out of water with her mouth opening and closing reflexively. His smile turned into that conscienceless grin.

"Good night, Maggie."

She said nothing and after a moment turned and climbed the stairs. She didn't intend to look back, but once she had unlocked the door and pushed it open, she peered over her shoulder.

He was already gone.

* * *

Father Fitzhugh escorted his guests to the door, watching until the last carriage pulled away. When he returned to the parlor, Mother Bernadette was busy collecting used cups and snifters, placing them on the serving tray.

Hugh Fitzhugh leaned against the doorjamb. "I'll help Mrs. Gottlieb in the morning, Bernadette," he said. "You've had a long day already."

She looked up and met his smile. "Once a mother . . ."

"How is your daughter?"

Father Fitzhugh knew better than most people that priests and nuns were not born, they were made. As a young woman, Mother Bernadette had been a wife and then a young widow—like himself, a convert to Catholicism. Her calling had come relatively late in life, which was one of the reasons he held her opinions in such high regard. She had lived joy and sorrow both inside the convent walls and outside. It made her a treasure to the Church.

"She's about to make me a grandmother," she said with a wistful little laugh.

"You'll let me know?"

"Of course."

They were silent a minute, comfortable with the silence. He was going to miss this woman, as friend and adviser and confidante. Right now she was shooting him little speculative glances and he tried to gird himself for the question. He decided another finger of brandy might be appropriate. As he passed by her on the way to the decanter, she pounced with the same stealth as Clancy.

"Have you given serious thought to what you're doing?" she asked.

He pretended bewilderment. She gestured with her hand in irritation. "Maggie, Hugh. You're throwing her to the wolves and you're not going to be here to rescue her this time."

"I rather liked Dr. Kincaid," he said, his lips turning up in half a smile.

"Hah, just as I thought."

He poured his brandy and then turned around, leaning against the sideboard while dangling the glass negligently with his fingers. "You've been fond of the young man since you nursed him at Gettysburg."

"That doesn't make him right for Maggie. And he's no longer a young man, in spite of what our years tell us. He's got to be thirty-two, thirty-three by now."

She gave a hunch of her shoulders and then settled into his own favorite chair, her elbows resting on the worn sidearms. "Maggie's spent her formative years in an orphanage run by nuns, her adult years inside the cocoon of Church-related activities. She thinks she wants to be a nun, for pity's sake!"

"And if you thought she was firm in that conviction you would have encouraged her to join the last class of postulants." He lifted his glass and took a drink. "Bernadette, believe me, I want what's best for her, whatever is going to bring her happiness. I just want her to be certain, and as you so kindly pointed out, she's basing her decision on limited experience. Maggie needs to be a part of the world before she makes the decision to leave it."

Mother Bernadette leaned her head back and sighed. "I can watch, but I won't intervene. I'm afraid you've started something you're going to regret."

"She has your strength."

"She has the makings of an abbess."

"Then why didn't you take her in the last class?"

Mother Bernadette opened her eyes and smiled. "Because I happen to agree with you."

"Hah."

"Hah, yourself."

Their gazes met and held for a moment and then he looked away, staring at the picture of Castle Lachlan, thinking of other leave-takings in his life as a priest. He guessed by her next question she was following his thoughts.

"Your brother was the heir?" she asked.

"The spare. I preceded him by five minutes." He heard her sharp intake of breath.

"You gave up all that for the Church?"

"It wasn't as difficult as you might believe." He almost chuckled at the lilt that had come into his voice. Her habit rustled as she pushed up from the chair.

"It couldn't have been as easy as you'd have me believe either."

He did chuckle then. "Shall I walk you back?"

She waved her hand in dismissal. "Half a block, I'm safe."

He set his glass down, determined to watch until the orphanage door closed behind her. They were in the kitchen before either spoke again. She looked up as he pushed open the back door.

"You knew Maggie's mother; did you know her father, too?"

He nodded.

"Your brother, the earl?"

He smiled faintly. "Good night, Bernadette."

She reached up, placing her work-roughened hand against his cheek. Reflexively, he leaned into her gentle touch for a moment and then took her hand down.

"Good night, Hugh."

Ah, Bernadette, you see too much, he thought.

He watched her climb the white marble steps fronting the orphanage and watched while she unlocked the door and watched until the door closed safely behind her. Then he watched the moon rise and wash its luminous light over the alley. A soft breeze ruffled his hair as he stood on the back stoop, listening to the night sounds.

A single carriage rattled down the street. When it had passed, he heard a different sound. Father Fitzhugh leaned against the porch railing, listening, caught in the remembrance of days long gone, while in the shadows beyond the moon glow, a nightingale lifted a song.

Chapter 4

"*I*'m allowing this against my better judgment."

"We've agreed that I'm her father. I shouldn't have to seek your permission to spend time with my daughter."

For the third time in a week, Gordon found himself seated on the hard chair in the mother superior's bare office. If he'd been a charitable man, he'd say the hard, uncomfortable chair could be blamed on low funds for such extraneous purchases as visitors' chairs. He wasn't overly charitable and knew the mother superior; the chair was intended to make the visitor feel like a naughty schoolboy sent to the headmaster's office for punishment. It was effective.

"Your daughter should never have been here in the first place."

There was little he could say to that. He leaned forward, his elbows on his thighs, and raked his fingers through his hair. "I'm trying to do the decent thing," he said, sounding almost as weary as he felt. "You're making it extremely difficult."

"I'm trying to do what's best for the child, who, I might add, has been my responsibility for the entire five years of her life." Mother Bernadette leaned back in her seat, her fingers idly turning the pen she held. "While we may both believe Clara is your daughter, there is no way to prove the point. The child is an orphan, legally a ward of this parish, and you have no rights as a father."

She tossed the pen onto the desk, where it landed with a small plunk. Gordon watched the pen roll and come to a stop at the edge of a sheaf of papers.

"You will not mention anything to Clara about adoption, your belief that she is your daughter, or any discussion that might turn the child against the Cromwells. Do I make myself clear?"

"Absolutely." Gordon stood up, wanting to use his height and size to full advantage. Two could play this game. "And you will speak to Miss Quinn about Clara's desires where the Cromwells are concerned."

He expected a look of startlement at best, impassivity in all likelihood, but was met with a soft smile on the mother superior's face.

"Clara is a bright child," she said. "I didn't know she'd picked up Gaelic words to add to her Irish stew. Perhaps she asked Maggie or Father Fitzhugh to teach her. Father Fitzhugh would encourage the child's gift for languages. Maggie?" Mother Bernadette shrugged. "I believe Maggie, given her different perspective, would turn those kinds of questions aside. What truly surprised me was the perception behind that little act Clara put on for Mr. Cromwell. For such a young child to understand so much." She paused, frowning, then said, "Yes, I too am convinced Clara was testing Mr. Cromwell."

"Did Mr. Cromwell pass Clara's test?"

Mother Bernadette gave him a shrewd look that told him she wasn't taken in by his verbal ploys. "The arbiter in these kinds of decisions cannot be a five-year-old child, Gordon. Mr. Cromwell meets every requirement we could hope for in a prospective father. He was quite taken with Clara. That carries great weight in my judgment."

Gordon decided to shoot Maggie's darts. "She doesn't want to be a replacement for a dead daughter. She should be wanted solely for herself."

He moved to the window and gazed out into a play yard. Several boys were rolling a hoop, which wobbled and fell repeatedly in the rough turf. More children gathered around a long jump rope. Clara was not among the group. He listened to the children chanting in rhythm with the swinging rope.

What was he doing here? He hadn't been any kind of father to Gordy; at this late date, didn't even know how to be a father. While he might have accepted that the child Clara was his own issue, the evidence was abundantly clear and the physical resemblance overwhelming, he didn't need to push the point now. Clara had someone, a couple ready and willing to adopt her. He could turn and walk out the door, telling himself it was all for the best. So why didn't he?

"Is the child ready?" he asked without turning. Wooden legs scraped against the bare floor as Mother Bernadette pushed her chair back. She came and stood beside him at the window. He wondered what she was thinking.

"You can wait in the visitors' parlor," she said finally. "Sister Agatha will bring Clara to you."

"Miss Quinn was going to accompany us."

She lifted one brow. "Miss Quinn, not Miss Hays?"

"I thought Clara might be more comfortable if she had someone along she knew and trusted."

Mother Bernadette studied him, her expression intense and serious. He was surprised to see a smile come over her face.

"A fine idea, Gordon. I'll send for Maggie too."

The visitors' parlor had little more appeal than Mother Bernadette's office. Gordon's gaze swept the shabby interior. He walked over and pulled the drapes open, allowing the morning sun to chase some of the gloom into the corners of the room. He heard the tap of footsteps and then a low laugh.

"A boy after my own heart," said a pleasant female voice. "I must admit I argue with Sister Josephine over those draperies."

He turned to face a short woman on the far reaches of fifty, dressed in a black habit that did little to disguise her plumpness. Her wimple accentuated the roundness of a face marked with laugh lines, full cheeks, round brown eyes glittering with amusement. He had the unchristian vision of an apple dumpling.

"Sister Josephine has a fondness for gloom and doom?" he teased.

She pursed her lips, then burst into a snort of laughter. "I've always suspected as much, but let's keep that our secret." She gave him a slanting glance, conspiring in something. "And here's another: I have a sinful fondness for Braupt's chocolates, but Clara prefers ices."

"Ices," he repeated, catching on. "And where does one find ices in September?"

"Baylor's Drugstore on Commerce Street. His wife is Italian."

"Baylor's on Commerce Street."

"You have a nice smile, Dr. Kincaid," she said apropos of nothing and throwing him slightly off balance. "One isn't supposed to have favorites in an orphanage, but I'm only human. Clara is a favorite of mine, as was Maggie."

He looked at this kindhearted nun and found himself thinking of the mother he hadn't seen since he was four years old: physically the most beautiful woman he'd yet encountered in this life, so selfish and cold inside.

"Mr. Cromwell doesn't smile easily," she said.

"Thank you, Sister," he said, fighting the breathless sensation of a four-year-old boy, racing down the lane after his mother's departing carriage, crying and tripping over his own feet, nearly blinded by tears and the certain knowledge that the shiny black carriage was never going to return.

The next thing he remembered of that day was his older brother Royce gathering him in his arms, his face set in the stern angles of the man he would become, his boy's eyes glistening while he carried his young brother up the lane. Peyton had met them at the foot of the steps. He withdrew a big white handkerchief from his pocket and proceeded to wipe the tears from the face of his youngest son.

We will never speak of this day, boys, he had said.

And nobody ever did.

Gordon turned away and stared, unseeing, out the window. Aurora Hammond, Celeste Kincaid—both of them selfish, faithless women capable of abandoning their own flesh-and-blood children. But where he had had Peyton to furnish a loving home, Clara had had only this orphanage.

God, he wasn't a father.

He *was* a father. But he knew as well as anyone the ease of planting a seed in a thoughtless moment, and that kind of fatherhood was not what Sister Agatha or Mother Bernadette or even Miss Quinn wanted for little Clara. Could he do it? Did he even want to try?

"Ah, here they are," she chirped.

Gordon turned slowly. Clara stood in the doorway, Maggie behind her with her hands resting on the child's shoulders.

Clara was dressed in a blue dress, the hem falling just above black ankle boots on which the polish failed to disguise the wear. A starched white pinafore covered the dress. Her flaxen hair was caught up in a large bow at the back of her head with soft little curls already escaped and framing her face.

If he were to place Gordy beside her, anyone would see the blood tie. Her blue eyes were studying him warily, so like his own eyes in shape and color, with the same confused shadows behind the light.

Clara's wary gaze shifted to Sister Agatha. He waited for something to spark in the child's face, a smile, an easing in the tense manner in which she held her small body. What he saw was a deep intake of breath and her narrow shoulders shuddering as she released it. Maggie pulled her fractionally back, cradling the child against her own body.

So small, so innocent . . . so vulnerable.

The devil take it. Clara was *his*. She was the second chance he didn't deserve. This time he'd do it right, and the deuce with Mother Bernadette. Clara was going home with him.

He realized he was fingering his hat brim, as nervous as a green private before the first battle. He sent a message to his leg to work properly—the confounded limb had a tendency to give way when he least expected it—and crossed over the room. He squatted on his haunches so he was eye level with his daughter.

"I find myself craving Italian ice on a warm day like this," he said. "Do you have any idea where we can find Italian ice?"

His smile felt rigid as she looked at him seriously.

"Baylor's," she said.

"Baylor's it is, then." He pulled his bowler hat on his head and tapped the crown, almost eliciting a smile from Clara. "Shall we go?"

The child slipped her hand into Maggie's. Gordon followed them to the door, stopping just inside when Sister Agatha's hand landed on his forearm. Maggie and Clara continued on down the steps while discussing the pros and cons of taking the streetcar.

"Maggie has always favored the crab cakes at Hauptmann's," said Sister Agatha innocently.

He felt the rumble in his chest and wondered if it showed on the face he was trying to keep serious. "Hauptmann's?"

"Half-block down from Baylor's."

He lost the battle and chuckled as he followed Maggie and Clara.

Maggie sat on the hard bench of the streetcar, irritated beyond measure with the slow-moving traffic, the dirty, crowded buildings blocking the breeze, the jarring calls of the hawkers on every street corner.

A laundry wagon pulled alongside. EMPIRE'S STEAM LAUN-DRY, BEAUTIFUL SNOW WHITE, PEARL OR IVORY FINISH, THE BEST EQUIPPED LAUNDRY IN THE CITY, she read as the two-wheeled wagon stopped, caught in a traffic jam caused by a milk cart drawn by two obstinate mules blocking the intersection. The drivers exchanged eloquent insults and she flinched.

"It went rather well, don't you think?"

She pulled her gaze from the traffic and looked at Dr. Kincaid. He was seated across from her with Clara curled on the seat beside him, her head in his lap while she slept. Faint yellow splotches left by melted lemon ice marred the pristine whiteness of Clara's pinafore, the only one she owned without mended holes.

She reached out to stabilize the packages sliding on the seat beside her. "We're late getting back."

"You're the one who declined to use my carriage," he pointed out agreeably.

"You'll not be buying Clare's favor with your fancy carriages and lemon ices and hair ribbons," she said, her voice lapsing into heavy brogue with the strange emotions battling inside her.

"It's a hired carriage and we bought hair ribbons for all the girls."

His hand, sun-bronzed and looking so elegant with his long fingers and a fine dusting of golden hairs on the back, lightly brushed the white-gold fringe of hair from Clare's brow. The child burrowed a little closer into his lap without wakening. Maggie thought she wasn't going to cry, and in the next instant sudden scalding tears burned her eyes. She looked away.

"Aye, ribbons for the girls and licorice for the boys and chocolates for Sister Agatha. What do you plan to use to bribe Mother Bernadette?"

"I was thinking of a whip but decided her tongue could lash out well enough. What do you think of flowers? Would that work with the estimable mother superior?"

She supposed he might have seen the tears in her eyes and

was trying to tease her into a better humor, and truth be told, it *had* gone well. She'd had as much fun as Clare: laughing with his teasing manners, eating crab cakes and slurping lemon ices, standing forever inside Felan's Emporium while Clare selected hair ribbons for all nine of the girls in the orphanage, and it hadn't even been necessary to tell him he shouldn't give only to Clare.

He'd surprised her with his insight, his gentle yet firm way with the child, his laughing pleasure in a simple little outing. She hated him.

"Do what you will," she said, turning back to stare out the window. She heard something that sounded like a sigh, and felt his warm hand grasp hers.

"Maggie, whether it's me or the Cromwells, you're going to lose her."

She felt as if she were hurtling over a cliff and knew she would never fly. And not even a kind Father Fitz to break the fall this time. She closed her eyes. "Aye, the Lord giveth and the Lord taketh."

And taketh and taketh, she thought.

"By the rivers of Babylon, there we sat down, yea, we wept when we remembered Zion."

"And sure it is you can quote scripture, but do you believe in it?"

"Things happen. I gave up trying to guess why long ago," he said in a voice filled with a strange weariness. She slanted him a glance, seeing again that confused, hopeless look in his eyes.

All had their crosses to bear. What were his? He hid his pains and sorrows well beneath that rogue's charm, but his eyes would give him away. Why was she helping him? She had her own crosses and heavy enough they were.

Her fidgety hands folded and refolded a pleat in her skirt while she battled the confused anger inside her. Aye, it could only be called anger—at Dr. Kincaid for wanting Clare and at Father Fitz for moving to Richmond, and at herself for placing her own heart first.

"Our stop is next," she said, gathering the packages. "Best waken our wee *cailín*."

"I'll carry her."

His movements were unhurried, practiced, and she wondered if his brother had children, for him to know this rare art of moving a sleeping child. But then, maybe it was something he'd learned in doctoring. Clare let out a little sigh as her hands went around his neck and she buried her face in the crook.

They had exited the streetcar and walked half a block before he spoke again. "What does *mó cailín* mean?"

" 'Tis an endearment. *My girl*."

"She likes it. May I borrow it?"

"Do as you will." He gave her a speculative glance as he paused and shifted Clare's weight, but said nothing. She suddenly felt guilty. "I can take her—your leg."

"My leg is fine," he said curtly.

"Pride goeth before a fall," she said, equally sharp.

"Dammit, I'm not going to drop her."

"You'll not curse in front of wee Clare."

"Clar-*a* is asleep."

"Not anymore!"

He tucked his chin, looking down. Clare twisted her head on his shoulder and smiled angelically. "Are you fighting with my Maggie?"

He looked up again and she saw the creases at the corner of his mouth deepen. "Your Maggie seems to be angry with me," he said, turning his attention back to Clare.

"Humph." With all the bad grace she felt, Maggie spun around on the pavement and stalked ahead of them, walking so fast her boot heels kicked up her skirts.

Clar-*a*, as if he'd named her himself. How dare he!

And just where was the grand Dr. Kincaid, father, when wee, tiny Clare was suffering from the colic and Maggie, aye, *Maggie* walked the floor night after night, singing until her voice was gone? Where was Gordon Kincaid, *father,* when wee *Clare* took her first steps, spoke her first words, read her first storybook?

Off to the racetrack he was, or flirting with some empty-headed piece of society fluff like Miss Hays . . . or something worse, unspeakably worse, as with Clare's poor mother.

Clar-*a*!

She drew a shuddering breath and impatiently swiped her eyes with the back of her hand. When she dropped her hand, she saw a tear-blurred Father Fitzhugh standing at the corner. Another carriage was already drawn up in the alley behind Dr. Kincaid's. Father Fitz looked at her gravely, then looked beyond her. Maggie stopped beside him and turned. Dr. Kincaid was strolling with Clare's hand in his own, a full half block behind.

"The Cromwells are here?" she asked, watching the golden man and child.

"Yes." Father Fitz paused. "I'll be in my study, Maggie."

She didn't reply, and soon she heard the rectory door close behind her. She handed the packages to Dr. Kincaid when he and Clare came up beside her.

"You'll be wanting to give out your favors," she said, avoiding his gaze. She knelt in front of Clare. "You are a sight, *mó cailín*, but we haven't the time to fix you now." She brushed back a stray wisp from Clare's forehead, allowing her fingers to linger in the soft, wind-blown curls, then stood.

He too was looking at the child, his face lowered a little, golden hair falling wildly over his forehead, his deep blue eyes intense. She couldn't look at his pain any more than she could look at Clare's trembling chin, so she led the way toward the steps, listening to the sound of them following.

"I trust I fed you enough that you've lost your appetite," he said in his teasing drawl. "And you should be tired enough to be cranky. You will be cranky, won't you, Clara?"

Clare sniffled and Maggie stopped, turning around. He was already on his haunches in front of the child.

"Be brave, little one." He tapped Clare's nose lightly with

his forefinger. "If they give you Brussels sprouts, you can slip them to the dog. If they don't have a dog, hide them in your napkin—it always worked for me."

Clare giggled through her sniffles. He leaned his head forward, resting his forehead against Clare's. The wind blew up, entwining his burnished hair with her white-fire curls, fragile golden threads binding father and daughter.

After a moment, he pushed up, his face registering a fleeting grimace of pain, then held out his hand. Maggie had a sudden memory of an Irish girl in an immigrant shed with a tall, broad-shouldered priest holding out his hand to the frightened child. As Maggie had done on that day, Clare unhesitatingly placed her small hand within Dr. Kincaid's—no, Gordon's—large hand.

This is what it means to trust, she thought. "They will be waiting in the visitors' parlor," she said in a low voice. "I must get Clare a clean pinafore."

He gave her a cynical, one-sided smile, saying nothing. She turned and fled into the orphanage, already halfway up the stairs before she heard them enter and shut the door.

Her footsteps dragged on the way back down. It was only natural that each child in the children's home developed a special bond with one of the caregivers. It was Mother Bernadette's policy that on the rare instances when a child went on a home visit, that special caregiver was not a part of the leave-taking. Maggie knew she should have sent the pinafore down in Sister Josephine's keeping. She was risking Mother Bernadette's displeasure, but Clare was already upset. She'd be there for Clare, giving whatever strength she could.

Maggie stopped outside the door. The parlor was crowded with people and she guessed Mother Bernadette had filled the time while they waited by serving the Cromwells tea. Sister Agatha bustled about the room, refilling teacups and offering sugar cookies.

To her surprise, Mr. Cromwell wore a clerical collar, so he must be a reverend of some Protestant faith. The white cleri-

al collar was the only light touch on either; both Mr. and
Mrs. Cromwell were dressed in heavy black mourning. It
was uncharitable of her, but she thought they could have
lightened their mourning just a smidgen for Clare's benefit.

Clare sat on the horsehair sofa between her prospective
parents, her little feet dangling just over the edge of the cushion, hands primly folded in her lap and her gaze lowered.
Mrs. Cromwell's pose was identical except her black half-
boots reached the floor. But while Clare looked frightened,
Mrs. Cromwell looked cowed.

Cowed by her husband's pronouncements of divine retri-
bution given in just the same tone one employed to discuss
the weather with a stranger. Maggie wished she could see the
mother superior's face, but Mother Bernadette had her back
to the door.

Mr. Cromwell was going on and on about the effects of
vice and moral corruption in a calm, genial voice, giving frequent glances through his wire-rimmed spectacles toward the
window, as if some wicked sinner were hiding in the
draperies. He was just the sort Father Fitz called a holy
howler, amiable, well-intentioned and brimming with sancti-
mony. Maggie shuddered to think of a childhood filled with
that brand of piety.

"Here she is," chirped Sister Agatha, and all eyes turned to
the doorway. The Reverend Mr. Cromwell peered at her
down the length of his long, narrow nose.

Blessed Saint Brigid. She felt like a specimen under
glass. "I've Clare's clean pinafore," she said, stepping into
the parlor.

"Are you the one who taught Clara to speak Irish?"

"Clare speaks English, Mr. Cromwell," she said, tucking
her chin to avoid Mother Bernadette's steely-eyed gaze. Aye,
I'll behave, Mother, she thought.

"And well she should." He pulled out a handkerchief and
wiped his brow. "I've nothing against the Irish, mind you. It's
just that there're so many of you now." He tucked the handkerchief back in his breast pocket, at the same time shaking

his balding head. "The pubs, prizefights . . . all that drinking and wagering, not to mention they breed like rabbits."

"Yes, well, we're not here for a discussion of the ills of the city." Mother Bernadette rose with her usual grace. Maggie saw an apology in her eyes as she looked her way, as if Mother Bernadette—stern, just and kind Mother Bernadette—need apologize for a boor's ill manners.

"I'll take that, Maggie."

Maggie knew what she was supposed to do and did it, handing the pinafore to the mother superior. As she turned to leave, she saw the sinner in the draperies. Dr. Kincaid stood apart from the rest, half-turned from the window, a teacup poised to sip. He gave her a subtle smile over the rim, quick and perceptive.

Dr. Kincaid handed his teacup to Sister Agatha. "Will you see me out, Miss Quinn?"

"Aye."

"Mother Bernadette, Sister Agatha." A golden, aristocratic nod to each as he took his leave. "Clara." Another nod, and he was suddenly grasping her elbow, steering her toward the door.

"Ma-ggie!"

His grip tightened on her elbow as if he, too, heard need in Clare's high-pitched voice. Maggie shrugged out of his grasp, swinging back into the room.

"One hug, *mó cailín,* and then you must go."

She could actually feel Mother Bernadette's disapproval, Sister Agatha's smiling approval, the Cromwells' unease, as Clare's little legs ran across the threadbare carpet. None of them mattered.

She hugged Clare, hard and long, then set her back. "Be a good girl for Maggie. Aye?"

"Aye."

Finally, a smile tugged at Clare's lips. Maggie brushed the last trace of tears from the child's cheeks and stood. Clare crooked her finger, gesturing to Dr. Kincaid. He bent down ringing his head level with Clare's, golden waves of hair against flaxen curls.

"You didn't say good-bye to the Cromwells," whispered Clare.

"I know," he whispered back, and Clare laughed.

Maggie wished she could laugh; it was all she could do to force a small smile. Instead of stopping at the door, she continued on outside with Dr. Kincaid. He stopped at the foot of the steps and she wasn't sure why, but she paused beside him. She felt so bereft of a sudden, and he was so large and warm and strong. He lifted his hand and drew his thumb along the angle of her jaw, catching her chin and raising it a little. Their eyes met, tears threatening in hers; his dark, dark blue and so perceptive.

"I can see myself to the carriage. I was just trying to rescue you before you did something you'd regret," he said.

Loose stones crunched beneath her feet as she stepped back. She held herself very straight and nudged her chin up. "I don't need rescue by you. I—I'm on my way to help Father Fitz pack his books."

The lines at the corner of his mouth deepened and she felt the ground tilt beneath her feet. Oh, Maggie, Maggie, she thought, 'tis the devil himself testing you.

"While you're in there, tell him to put in a good word for me with the mother superior," he said, only half-teasing.

"I'll do nothing of the sort. It's the mother superior's decision to make and she'll make it for Clare's best interest."

"That sanctimonious black crow is not the man to raise Clara." He pushed the hair from his forehead in an impatient gesture. "*God,* having to live with that hypocrisy would be enough to turn any child into a sinner."

"And what will you be teaching her—blasphemies, betting on the horses, fornication?"

"What the hell do you think I am?"

She couldn't take the words back and the last hateful word seemed to hang in the air between them, reverberating with ugliness. She reached out to touch him—she didn't know why—but he gave her a murderous glare and turned away. She dropped her hand and stared at his broad back.

"I don't know what to think of you," she said quietly. He didn't respond and she left him, not stopping until she'd reached the back porch of the rectory. When she was hidden in the shadows, she did stop, adding to her own pain by watching the Cromwells leave with Clare.

Dr. Kincaid watched too, resting his shoulders against his carriage, his arms crossed on his chest; as insolent, aristocratic a pose as she'd ever seen in the Earl of Lachlan. Reverend Cromwell halted and said something to him. Dr. Kincaid responded with only a haughty smile.

Maggie turned then, her leaden feet carrying her to Father Fitzhugh's study. Father Fitz finished placing another thick tome inside a packing box.

"Has she gone, my Maggie?"

"*Wirra.*" The old Irish lamentation came naturally.

He looked up then. "You did not like the Cromwells."

"I can't—I hardly—" She drew a hurtful, hitching breath. "He's a pious, sanctimonious black crow."

Father Fitz moved slowly, folding his tall body into his armchair. "Are you being quite fair, child?"

"No." She sank down on the floor at his feet, leaning her head against his knee. His hand rested on her braid and then moved, lightly stroking with his thumb where tiny wisps of hair escaped at her nape. Clare was going to have a home. Father Fitz was going to be a bishop. She had prayed for these joys to come to the two she loved most in the world.

"I don't—I don't even know why I'm crying."

"Do you not, my Maggie?" he said quietly. "I do."

She stared off into the shadowy corner of the room where packing boxes were stacked, one upon another. His gentle fingers brushed her cheek like the strings of his harp as he swept away her tears.

Chapter 5

Gordon lay still on the rumpled sheets, his chest heaving as he fought to catch his breath. He watched the shadows move on the plaster ceiling and waited for the nightmare to recede. It had been years since he'd dreamed of prison camp, but this time was different. In the strange way of dreams, Maggie and Clara had entered into it.

He sat on the edge of the bed and laced his fingers through his hair. He couldn't believe he wanted his daughter so intensely, but he did.

Clara had worked her way into his heart and went deeper with each trusting look, each childish giggle. For one blessed hour, he had felt alive, brought back to life by the touch of a child's innocence, a woman's barely concealed tears.

He got up and prowled the room, touching crimson bed-curtains, the back of the velvet chair arranged in front of the grate, the single half-burned taper sitting in the middle of a glass dish on the polished end table.

He withdrew a match from the china safe and lit the candle, then rummaged in the bottom of his medical bag until his fingers closed over a framed miniature. He rubbed his thumb gently over his son's face, then set the small portrait on the table. His leg throbbed from all the walking he'd done today, but that pain was so much easier to bear than this scouring sensation of loss and what-might-have-been.

His sister-in-law had commissioned the portrait when Gordy was five, Clara's age now, and the two children shared so many of his own physical traits. Gordy's heart had closed to him long ago, and although the loss left him feeling empty, he understood. His son had no choice because Gordon had given his son no choice.

He needed to walk. He walked to think, to solve his problems. Gordon dressed, then leaned over to blow out the candle. His gaze fell on the miniature and his hand hovered over the portrait, afraid to touch it again. He cupped the candle, blew out the flame and left the room.

Even at this late hour, traffic moved on St. Paul Street. He waited for a cab to pass, then crossed the street and walked a block to Monument Square. He leaned against the iron railing and looked to the Revolutionary War monument rising from the center island. He knew it well; he made a pilgrimage to this square on every trip to Baltimore. It was the only monument he'd ever seen honoring ordinary soldiers, not generals.

The wind came up, scattering leaves at his feet. He looked around at the hotels and commercial buildings that had replaced the bankers' mansions that once ringed this square. The rich had fled to Mt. Royal and the suburbs, leaving the downtown to the waves of immigrants, the Germans, the Poles. The Irish.

And what will you be teaching her?

In all honesty, he didn't know what he could teach his daughter, his children. To abhor war and honor life? But that sounded as preachy and pious as the dour Reverend

Cromwell. Sometimes a man had to take up a weapon to defend the lives of those he held dear.

All morning he'd thought of how he would make it up to Clara, had even toyed with the idea of taking Maggie with them to Virginia to stay as long as it took to ease Clara's way. Even at the risk of another failure, he determined to make it clear to all of them—Mother Bernadette, Father Fitzhugh, Maggie—exactly where his daughter belonged. With him.

He understood, though. Maggie did not know him for anything more than a rogue who fathered bastard children and abandoned them while he entertained himself at the racetrack. He could comprehend that part—ugly as it was—although it hardly made the wound any less painful. He had thought—had hoped—that what he was missing in the skills of fatherhood would be amply recompensed by what he had to offer Clara. Old Riverbend and all that went with it: his name, his breeding, his wealth.

Well, if they did not see it, he would have to show them.

Maggie, will you turn against me now?

He rammed his hands in his pockets and gazed at the pale marble fasces in front of him ringed with the names of dead soldiers. He lifted his gaze to the classically garbed female figure holding up a laurel wreath.

He could lose Clara as he'd lost Gordy. He felt a new and bone-deep chill. Clara wasn't his even now. He had no father's rights to the child. If they gave her to that pompous crow . . .

He would not let it happen.

Chapter 6

Gordon lingered at the rectory gate with Father Fitzhugh, both of them looking across the alley to the play yard, where a dozen or so children ran, skipped, leaped and squealed under the watchful eyes of Maggie and several nuns.

"As much as the children will enjoy a picnic, I feel obliged to warn you, it can be a rather unnerving experience if you're over twelve years old yourself," said Father Fitzhugh.

Gordon turned his attention back to Richmond's next bishop. Father Fitzhugh was indeed a distinguished-looking man, with his thick black hair going silver at the temples, those sharp green eyes. It was his mouth that was wrong for his face, seeming always poised on the edge of a smile. The ladies in the drawing rooms of Great Britain must have wept when Lord Hugh Fitzhugh donned a priest's collar.

Gordon tried to imagine what demons possessed a man, to turn him to the priesthood. A woman he loved but couldn't have? Or perhaps the man had been seeking some sort of redemption, in much the same manner Gordon had sought to redeem his shattered life through medicine.

"What brought you to America, Father Fitzhugh?"

The priest was silent, his gaze fixed on the children's play yard. The sky was a clear blue, cloudless, and the crystalline light shimmered in the morning dew still clinging to the clipped grass of the rectory lawn.

"The children," said Father Fitzhugh finally. "Not those children you see playing over there, but . . . Sometimes I think there are more Irish in Baltimore than there are in Dublin now."

"But you're Anglo-Irish."

"Norman. The first Fitzhugh came to Ireland in 1169. Did you ever hear of the Irish Penal Laws?"

"Can't say that I ever paid much attention."

"The laws were passed after the Orange-Stuart wars," said the priest, then his voice took on a low singsong quality. "No Catholic may bequeath his estate as a whole, but must divide it among his sons, unless one of those sons become Protestant in which case he will inherit the whole estate."

Father Fitzhugh looked down at his shiny black shoes. His mouth curved at one corner. "And so it was that the Fitzhugh's retained their title and estates. In Ireland, religion *is* politics. A wrong is always remembered."

"And avenged?"

"Too often."

"Then you'll be right at home in Richmond, Father."

The morning breeze lifted the edges of Father Fitzhugh's cassock. He raised his dark brows and fixed his searching green eyes on Gordon's face. Gordon shrugged away the unasked question. Politics were his brother Royce's venue, and Royce was welcome to it.

Father Fitzhugh rubbed the back of his neck and cleared his throat. "The sisters will have the children ready by noon tomorrow. You can change here at the rectory if you want to attend Mass first."

"I'll pass. All that preparation I have to handle."

"Afraid of lightning bolts or boredom?"

Gordon smiled and watched Maggie break up an altercation, then kneel down, smoothing the hair from a little boy's forehead as she soothed him. This was a gentle, soft Maggie, so different from the woman whose eyes spit fire while she accused him of . . .

He didn't want to look too closely in that direction. He was guilty of at least one of her accusations; Clara was proof of that.

The breeze caught at her hair, pulling a strand loose, and she raised her arms to pin it back in place. The motion lifted her breasts and caused one dress sleeve to fall back, revealing her bare white arm. She cocked her head slightly as she stabbed the hairpin through the shining black mass of hair.

It was such a simple action—such a womanly action—and he felt something stir inside him. He turned away from the vision to see the priest was studying him.

Father Fitzhugh's expression shifted quickly and subtly. "And you, my friend? Should I be saying prayers for your deliverance?"

Gordon met the priest's pointed question with cold silence.

Father Fitzhugh, no fool, frowned. His gaze shifted to the children's playground and Gordon thought he was watching Maggie playing pitch with the boys. A delivery van rumbled down the road, its squeaking iron wheels momentarily drowning out the noise of the children. Father Fitzhugh brought his gaze back to Gordon, who held it.

"Clara is a special favorite of mine," said the priest in a low voice. "As is Maggie."

They understood one another. He heard the warning in Fitzhugh's tone and tossed it back. "Whatever it takes, Father, *whatever* it takes—my daughter will go with me, not with that pious bastard."

The Saturday market was always the busiest, the overflow spilling down the hill on both sides of the street in a maze of benches, boxes and baskets piled high with flowers, produce and fruit. It was a feast for the senses, bright colors and mingled scents, the thrum of voices in every language of the polyglot city.

Maggie paused in front of a stall. On a neat platform were bunches of mint, watercress, piles of chestnuts and chinquapins and, what appealed particularly, rows of plump, juicy peaches, likely the last of the season. She ran a quick mental inventory of the number of coins in her reticule and her expenses for the remainder of the month. She walked on.

In the distance, the thin whistle of a train rode the sunshine, disembodied from itself, from time. Travelers on a journey to new places, to visit old friends, people she didn't know connected to people and places she would never visit.

Maggie rolled the ache from her shoulders and lifted her chin. She had her connections: the nuns, the children. They were her family now. So why this sudden discontent, this desire for sweet things and new experiences?

She dug in her reticule for some pennies and made her regular stop at the Grummans' stall on the corner of Eutaw and Lexington. She was shoving the half-loaf of bread in her reticule when she looked up and saw Gordon Kincaid on the opposite corner.

His size and coloring made him a man who would stand out in any crowd. Today he was hatless and the sun striking his hair caused it to gleam like a golden helmet, a chivalric knight stepped from the pages of Sir Walter Scott. She felt a strange seizing in her chest and the sensation was frightening, as if she were choking for air. He hadn't seen her yet and she told her legs to move, but they didn't obey fast enough.

"Miss Quinn!" He lifted his hand and waved.

A canvas-covered farm wagon rolled down the cobbled street between them and when it had passed, he was already cutting across behind it. He carried a spray of wildflowers in his hand, asters, black-eyed Susans and fringed gentians with their delicate purple blooms, the last a portent of cooler days ahead. The bribe for Mother Bernadette, she supposed.

"You've saved me a trip back to Saint Columba's," he said, smiling a little.

A single petal had dropped on the sleeve of his cutaway jacket, bright splash of yellow against striped brown wool. He held out the flowers and when she didn't take them, he lifted her hand.

"My apologies, Maggie," he said in a soft voice that was as seductive as the perfume suddenly thrust into her grasp.

"No . . . not you." She swallowed, staring at the pearl buttons on his gray waistcoat. " 'Tis I that am sorry," she murmured. He touched her chin with the backs of his fingers, lifting her face. "About yesterday," she said. "I had no right. It was just seeing Clare . . . and you." How to apologize for the inexcusable? Her voice caught. "Do you understand a little?"

She couldn't tell. His dark, dark eyes were enigmatic and then a faint smile came across his face. He let her go with a whisper of a touch across her cheek. She stepped back, uncertain of herself, of him.

"I think I do," he said. "Friends?"

"Aye."

He smiled then. It was a powerful experience for an almost-nun, to be the focus of that stunning masculine smile.

The crowd lapped around them like a wave on the sand. A woman with two little girls on either side pushed behind Maggie, shoving her so that she had to take a hop-step to keep her balance. He took her elbow in his hand to steady her. He was wearing gray leather gloves, she thought insensibly. The same dove gray as his embroidered waistcoat.

"I'll walk you home," he said.

Her normal common sense flooded back, as did the brogue, a sure sign of her unsettled condition. "Nay. I've another errand and I'll not be taking your time away from you."

"My time is yours," he said, and then the one-sided smile. "And the pleasure all mine."

She started walking and he moved beside her, not touching her elbow, thank you Blessed Mother, but close. She concentrated on where she placed her feet and they walked with silence between them, working their way down the hill. The crowd thinned. Gordon stopped at the last produce stall.

"Hungry?" he asked.

She looked. Peaches, piles of blushing peaches. It was as if he'd been following her through the market, reading her mind. She shook her head to decline, but he was already engaged in conversation with the farm wife behind the bench. The farm wife bobbed her head and giggled a little, reminding Maggie of Miss Hays. Was there no female immune to him and his roguish ways? He reached for a fruit.

"*Nein, nein,*" the woman said, shaking her head and selecting a different peach. "This one for your *liebechen, ja?*"

He laughed; the farm woman laughed. Maggie, understanding just enough German, blushed like the peach.

"*Zwei,*" he said, holding up two fingers of one hand while he reached in his pocket with the other. He handed over four bright copper pennies in exchange for the fruit, then turned around.

"Catch, *liebechen,*" he said, tossing one of the fruits.

Giving a startled laugh, she tried. But one hand was filled with flowers, the reticule dangled from her other wrist and the peach took on a life of its own, bouncing from her palm, against her chest, through a tremble of fingers and blossoms, finally landing with a splat at her feet.

"Oh, Maggie-mine." He drawled the words out, countrified slow. "Whatever shall I do with you?"

He rubbed the second fruit on his coat sleeve and stepped forward until less than an arm's length separated them. He lifted the hand holding the peach toward her, held it within a whisper of her face. Slowly, slowly, his hand drifted downward so that the soft peach fuzz caressed her skin from temple to jaw.

All around her, the world went motionless so it was like a stereoscopic picture: the farm wife frozen with her laughing mouth open and no sound issuing forth, a mule poised with one foreleg lifted. And Gordon Kincaid, his features set in a grave and virtuous severity while he watched her.

She rocked a little and he made no move to steady her. He grinned suddenly, a devastating flash of white teeth and cobalt eyes and temptation slanted only at her.

The world began to turn again, people moving and talking and laughing. Pigeons strutted and pecked at crumbs in the street. A hackney rolled by. The farm wife was laughing. Maggie picked up her skirts and began to walk. She heard a low, masculine sound of amusement and then he was beside her.

"Still friends, Maggie-mine?"

"We cannot be friends, Dr. Kincaid." Oh, why would her *r*'s roll so! She bit her lip.

He chuckled, unabashed. "Not if you're going to insist on calling me Doctor."

He was the devil's own temptation, and Maggie felt the clutch on her heart like a claw grasping for her very soul.

Sunshine beat down on their heads from a sky gone hazy, and the air was thick and still. The few sailboats on the distant river bobbed in the current like a child's plaything. Maggie walked beside him, quiet and bemused. Gordon tilted his head and saw her look quickly away, as if she didn't want to be caught looking at him.

He thrust his hands in his pockets, loosened his stride, and whistled a few bars of "Dixie." A smile came over her face, although she carefully kept her face averted from him.

"So now that we're friends again," he said, "tell me something about Maggie Quinn."

"And there's a fascinating story, Dr. Kincaid. 'Twas just the three of us, Mum and Seamus and me. And then Seamus died and Mum decided to come to America, and it wasn't until I got here that I realized how poor we were."

He waited for her to go on, and after three more paces realized she was done. He laughed. "Maggie, you've told me absolutely nothing."

"Aye, and if it's a long story you're wanting, you'd best talk to a Kerryman, they all have the gift of blarney."

She wasn't wearing a hat today. The sun became lost in her blue-black hair, light and hair both trapped in a tightly braided coil.

She was looking down at the bouquet of flowers; he was looking at her, and neither of them saw the street vendor pushing a peanut cart toward them until it was almost too late. He reached for her arm to pull her out of the way as she made a small gasping sound and reached out. Their hands clasped.

He allowed himself to feel the touch of her longer than was polite or necessary, the tiny, fragile bones, the soft warmth of her skin. Then she slipped her hand away.

It wasn't lust; lust was what he'd felt with Clare's mother. And it wasn't love—no, he was certain of that. Love was what he'd felt for Augusta. Love was youth and laughter and a shared background and making babies together. It wasn't this—whatever this mysterious thing was.

She brushed at her plain black skirts as if she could wipe away his touch. "You needn't go any farther."

He gave her a lazy smile. "I'll tag along."

"Where I'm going is no concern of yours."

"Is Saint Maggie making a call on a special friend?"

She looked up, startled. "What did you call me?"

"Saint Maggie. Does that bother you?" He hoped it did, because she sure as the devil bothered him.

"'Tis only that Neddie calls me that as well." She shrugged. "Come along if you must . . . and aye, it's a special friend we'll be visiting."

Within a block, the environment began to change. Within two blocks, he realized they were headed toward the waterfront. Instinctively, he became the protective male, taking her arm within the crook of his own. A block ahead, a waterman lurched from the doorway of a pub, paused, then reeled down the pavement. Ribald laughter floated out from the batwing doors and then they swung open again, belching out two more drunks.

"You have no business down here," he bit out, coming to an abrupt stop. She pulled away from his hold.

"If you're afraid, you can turn back. I'll not be stopping you."

"My God, Maggie, even the buildings down here can't stand up straight."

"Do not blaspheme around me, Doctor."

Why the devil was she speaking in such thick brogue? Before he could move, she was several paces ahead of him, walking with a purpose that kicked up the back of her skirts, revealing a tantalizing bit of white petticoat and slim ankle. He groaned. He wasn't even a drunken sailor.

"Maggie. Wait."

She didn't. She didn't stop until she was standing only a few feet away from the pub doors. She looked stricken. She turned once in a slow circle, walked over to a lamppost and touched it, looked around again.

"Maggie, what the devil—"

"Neddie." She dropped his flowers to the ground, used one hand to lift her skirts from the spittle and muck on the pavement and pushed open the pub doors. Stunned, disbelieving, he stared at the swinging doors.

"Holy Jesus Christ and all your saints!" Gordon followed her inside.

Maggie peered through the drifting smoke, seeking a face she might recognize from the parish, but the light was too dim to make out features. Careful to hold her skirts above the beer-soaked floorboards, she picked her way toward the bar.

The barkeep lifted one thick eyebrow. "Ma'am?"

She opened her mouth as a hand closed around her arm and yanked her off her feet.

"Neddie," she managed to squeak as Gordon pulled her outside. He didn't stop until they were well away from the barroom doors. He gripped her arms so hard it hurt.

"What were you thinking?" he said.

"You don't understand. Neddie's not here."

"Women—" He placed his palms on her shoulders and

shoved, causing her to step back. "Don't—" Shove. "Belong—" Shove. "Inside—" Shove. "Saloons."

She'd backed herself up against the street lamp. He pushed his wild hair off his forehead with the same impatient gesture she'd seen him employ yesterday. "Do you know what could have—Dammit, Maggie."

She sucked in a quick breath as she saw Jamie O'Connor barreling toward them. He must have been inside the pub. "Jamie, stop!"

She swung her reticule as Jamie swung a strong waterman's fist. Gordon must have seen something in her expression because he turned swiftly and ducked. Her reticule caught Jamie smack against his jaw. She didn't feel overly guilty. A half-loaf of bread inside a cloth bag wasn't much of a weapon.

"*Dhia*, Mary Margaret," said Jamie, rubbing his jaw. "I think you're swinging your roundhouse punches at the wrong man."

Gordon gave him a disdainful glare as if the waterman had just spit at his feet. Gordon Kincaid was tall, broad-shouldered and clearly angry. There was nothing insignificant about him, gentleman or not—but Jamie O'Connor was a workingman, his muscle and sinew hewn from hours on the skipjacks drawing the clam rakes and crab pots and fighting the sea. She didn't want to be the cause of a brawl and didn't want to see either man injured. She only wanted to know what had happened to poor old Neddie. And feared to find out.

Dr. Kincaid finally stepped back. He looked at Maggie, raising one brow in a silent question.

How to explain? *Why* did she need to explain herself to either of these arrogant males? She crossed her arms on her chest and looked at Jamie. "Where's Neddie?"

Jamie tossed his head, flicking the thick red hair off his forehead. He stared at her face for a long moment, and then his face softened and the light in his eyes shifted from anger to something else.

"Neddie died," said Jamie. "My da saw to a proper burial for him."

It was inevitable that the old man would die, especially given the indignities of his sad life, but she felt her heart breaking, and found herself leaning against Dr. Kincaid without the least notion of how she had gotten there. His arm came around her back, holding her gently against him.

"Lucky?" she managed to whisper. He tilted her face up and she looked into his eyes, seeing a compassion there that convinced her he was a fine doctor, a man meant to heal others.

"Maybe he was lucky," he said softly, and she waited, breath held, for him to do . . .

"Maggie."

Her name, spoken so harshly by Jamie, slammed the sense back into her. She swung her head around and saw the anger blazing hot in Jamie's eyes. She stepped back, and Jamie took her arm.

"She was asking after Ned's dog, Dr. Kincaid," he said, and his voice was as thick as Mulligan stew. Flaunting his heritage—*I am poor, and I'm Irish, and still a better man than you.* "If you'll be excusing us, Mary Margaret and I need to speak a few words in private."

Dr. Kincaid lifted his hand to his forehead in a salute as mocking as the twisted shape of his mouth. Jamie drew her toward the pub doors.

"Anywhere but in there," said Dr. Kincaid.

It was a low voice of command and Jamie stopped, but only long enough to toss his words over his shoulder. "She's one of us, although she seems to have forgotten it. She'll come to no harm in my care."

Two oil lamps cast arcs of flickering light through the purple fog of tobacco smoke. Jamie led her around a group of men drinking from tin pails and when one of them nodded to her, she realized they were all men she knew, not just from St. Columba's parish, but from the old life in Killady: Padraig O'Connor, Donagh O'Brennan, the Flannerys.

Jamie rubbed his hands over his face, sighing. "Ah, Maggie, I'll give you up to the Church with a song in my heart if that's where you'll find your happiness, but not to the likes of Mr. Kincaid with his fine and lordly airs."

She leaned up against the rough, knotholed wall and wrapped her arms around her waist. "It's not like that, Jamie. I'm not my mum and he's not Geoffrey Fitzhugh. Dr. Kincaid *wants* his daughter, and all I'm doing is helping him."

"My poor Maggie, always dreaming of that grand, good place to make her own." His face was lost in the smoky shadows, but she didn't need to see his face. She'd known him all her life.

He took a step closer, his scarred workman's hands reaching toward her. "Close your eyes, lass," he said, cupping her face between his palms. "And smell the stench of potatoes dug up black and rotten from a stubble field. Feel the pain of hunger in your belly and the ground beneath your knees, the dirt turned to mud from the spilled blood of our kinsmen. Do you feel it, Maggie? Feel the sob in your own throat as the rope goes 'round your da's neck and the murderin' scum string him up to die, twistin' and turnin' and fighting them to the bitter end when his bladder and his bowels go free."

He dropped his hands and hissed a breath between clenched teeth. "Free! The only freedom we knew was the freedom to die for the land watered for centuries with the blood of our fathers."

She hugged herself tighter around the waist, as if she could keep her body from exploding with the memories. "It's over, Jamie."

"It's never over. Do I need to remind you of more?" he said. "Of your dying mother, keening as her poor home goes up in flames, and the landlord, the nobleman who—"

"*Stop.*" She covered her hands with her ears. "It's done and can't be undone."

He pulled her hands down, and as his blue eyes studied her face, his thumbs drew gentle circles on her wrist. "Your

Dr. Kincaid is not one of us. He's one of *them*. He killed to defend his right to own people, just like Ireland—"

"Ireland!" She wrenched away and gestured with her arm, taking in the barrels and rickety benches and men drinking *poitín* from tin pails. "Was Ireland so grand that you have to re-create it here? Are you so full of the pride that you can't see there was nothing there for us? It's glad I am to be done with the place."

She brushed her palms along her temples, feeling so tired as the anger drained out of her. "Dr. Kincaid wants to adopt Clare, and I want to know that he'll be a good father to her. That's all, Jamie. That's all it is."

Those strange quaking sensations she felt when Gordon Kincaid only so much as brushed her sleeve were nothing but her own uncertainties. She didn't know how to love a man, and thought that a blessing, given Mum's sad life.

"And Jamie," she said, hating the quaver she couldn't control in her voice. "Perhaps he is more like you than you want to believe. Perhaps he took up his guns just like an Irishman: for love of his home. For love of his family."

Jamie gave her back nothing, not even a breath, then he looked over her shoulder and his mouth went thin and white at the edges. Gordon came to a stop so close beside her that she caught the faint scent of sandalwood. The two men exchanged hard looks.

"If you're done, I'll walk you back to the orphanage," said Gordon, his gaze shifting to her face, which she hoped he could not see well in the weak, shadowy light. She stepped aside and would not look at him.

Jamie leaned against the wall and crossed his arms on his chest. "Are you going with him?"

"Aye, Jamie."

Jamie let out a ragged sigh. He gestured with one hand, as if giving her his leave. "Do as you will, Maggie. God knows, you always have. *Dhia is maire dhuit.*"

She moved until she stood so close to him she could smell the sea in his woolen shirt. "Will you look for Lucky?"

His lips turned then in a sad kind of smile. She reached out and cupped his wind-chapped face between her palms. "May God and Mary be with you too, *mó cara*."

Gordon tried for a gentleman's politely bored smile that just wouldn't come, so he gave up and reached in his pocket, pulling out his card case. He withdrew a card and handed it to Jamie O'Connor, careful not to look at the man's face. He knew that look, and knew too that sometimes loving came at too great a cost for a man to bear.

"I'll be at the Barnum Hotel for four more days," he said. "If the dog turns up, bring him by. I know of a good home."

He took Maggie's arm and steered her through the sawdust that lay damp and greasy on the floor, around a wash pail filled with oyster chowder, the boxes and barrels and rough men who openly stared as they made their way through the crowd. The swinging doors of the Skipjack Saloon slapped together behind their backs, cutting the yeasty smell of beer.

"A gentleman should never pry into a lady's affairs, but do you want to talk about whatever was going on in there?"

His words seemed to echo in her silence. A flush blossomed on her cheeks and her stiff white collar moved as she swallowed hard, but she only shook her head.

Her gaze lingered on the lamppost, the vacant pavement beneath, then she closed her eyes and drew a cross with her hand. Her face held such a sweet sadness it made him ache to comfort her, and he almost slipped his arm around her waist before he realized what he was doing. He jammed his hands in his coat pockets.

She looked at him then, her eyes deep, shimmering green seas. "Did you own slaves?"

He couldn't help sighing. "My family owned slaves."

She nodded as if he'd just confirmed all her worst suspicions. So now he had another flaw added to the tally: fornicator, deserter of infants, slave owner.

He was sorting through various weak excuses for the great

sin of the South when she choked back a sound that was almost a sob.

"Gentians." She leaned over and picked up a small purple flower from the bouquet still lying on the pavement. "Mum's favorites," she said, her quiet voice hoarse with pain.

It was then he allowed his arm to slip around her waist, and instead of pulling away, she rested her head on his shoulder.

She had wanted only to return to the orphanage, spend a few moments alone in her room before the evening schedule with the children, but she ended up at the top of Federal Hill with Gordon Kincaid, watching the sun begin its descent over the city.

They had walked the blocks with a silence between them, as if he understood her inability to speak until she had her emotions—her memories—under control. Now he stood with his hands in his pockets, gazing over the river to where the dome of the new City Hall speared the skyline.

She watched an oriole skim across the sky, then leaned over and picked up a fallen leaf, folding it over and over on itself, watching her hands because she couldn't quite bring herself to look at him as she spoke.

"You asked me earlier today about Ireland. . . . We came from a place called Killady in County Clare, the O'Connors, O'Brennans, Flannerys. My da, Seamus Quinn, wasn't really my da, but he was the only father I ever knew and he was a good man who treated me as if I were his own. He was head trainer for the earl's stables, so we lived better than most, in a real cottage on the estate instead of the mud and stone *shibeens* of the other families in the village."

It was strange how memories could be both cruel and sweet. And a soft smile touched her lips at these memories.

"The O'Connors were fishermen, but theirs was a large family with too many to feed, so they fostered Jamie with my da so he could teach Jamie the way of the horses. There were the earl's children when the Fitzhughs visited their estate, but they wouldn't have anything to do with Irish children, so

Jamie and I had only each other, me being Mum's only child."

Some days she could close her eyes and the sweet, loamy scent of peat would come to her out of nowhere, and then the visions would rise up so vivid she could almost reach out and touch them: the reed-choked edges of the Shannon estuary with the curraghs rocking offshore, the stone hedges and potato plots, the fields of the Fitzhughs' estate in every shade of green imaginable where the horses ran free.

She always made herself look around then, at the good nuns who had taken her in, the children, every one of them dear to her heart, and made herself think of this strange country she had fled to as a frightened child. America, so big it took your breath away, full to bursting with life and dreams and promises. And which she loved desperately.

She dropped the leaf and looked at Gordon. He was standing some feet distant, his head tilted to one side, listening without watching her, and she felt a new warmth in her center. It was a wise man who knew when to look away.

She laughed softly. "Jamie brought me a dog one day, said it had followed him home, but more likely it had been carried home, the dog having only three legs. That was our Jamie's way before the troubles. I didn't know then; I thought our life was good, and Mum wouldn't speak of much—oh, she was a fine woman who knew how to laugh and sing and dance away sorrows, but whenever troubles came she didn't want to fight them, only for them to be over."

"Sometimes that's the best way," he said in a quiet voice. "Time passes and life goes on."

"Aye. And Mum always said we enter this world alone and we leave it in the same way, and what happens in between— be it sorrow or joy—is only as good or as bad as we make of it."

And she thought no one had ever died as alone as sweet, sad Deirdre Quinn, coughing her life out on a damp, stinking ship.

"What troubles forced you to leave?"

No, Gordon Kincaid, she thought. I will not share those memories with you when I have never spoken of them to anyone. It would make the fires and the hangings real again, and she could not bear any more of that cruelty.

She forced a small smile. "In Ireland, there are always troubles. Whether hunger or evictions, or simply a bad catch from the sea."

And music and laughter and poets and legends. She loved Ireland and hated it, and would give anything to travel there once more before she died.

Maggie leaned her back against the weathered old observatory, all that remained of the Union fortifications left to languish long after the War Between the States had ended.

She watched Gordon watching her, waiting for her to hand him the words in her heart. The breeze gusted into a wind that blew her skirts against her legs and ruffled his golden hair as he turned to gaze out over the harbor.

"Baltimore must be the ugliest city on the continent." He lifted his shoulders in a shrug. "Maybe the world."

She smiled then at the perceptive man, changing the talk to something neutral. "I thought that too at first, but it's wrong." He turned his head and at his dubious glance she continued. "Baltimore has made a virtue of ugliness, practiced it so long they've raised it to a fine art."

"Ah, Maggie-mine, you should be a Southerner if you can see that silver lining."

"The Irish believe in their myths as well." She laughed softly. "Who else believes in little people who cobble shoes at night and hide pots of gold at the end of rainbows?"

He placed his hand over her shoulder, bracing his weight against the wood, and gazed down at her. He was close enough that she caught the scent of sandalwood and something more, something subtle and mysterious. A hint of a smile touched his lips. "And do you believe in those little people?"

"I might be American now, but I've still got me Irish

blood," she said, turning on a thick brogue. She returned a faint smile. "The *sidhe* are naught but fallen angels, you see."

"*Sidhe?*"

"The fairies."

"Fairies?"

"Aye, but they're known as the Good Folk, and sure it is they're not good enough to be saved," she said. "They are wild and wicked, their chief occupations being feasting and fighting—though there'll be some fine musicians in the lot of them. And wasn't it Carolan, himself the finest of the Irish bards, who claimed to have slept on a fairy rath and forever after the music ran in his head."

He smiled. "Did you sleep on a fairy rath, Miss Quinn?"

"Would you listen to the man, accusing me of consorting with the fairies, and next I suppose he'll be waving a rowan wand and claiming I put a curse of enchantment on his fine self."

He was silent, his dark eyes moving over every feature of her face. "No wonder those children love you," he said finally.

For a moment, she felt so very Irish, filled with that strange admixture of laughter and sorrow that all Irish children took in with their mother's milk.

He looked up and she guessed he was studying the observatory, thinking of its purpose. There was little in the way of peace on the face of this tall, splendid man. She almost reached up to brush the tousled hair from his forehead, but he dropped his arm and stepped away.

"They should tear it down," she said quietly.

"They should leave it forever. A monument to all the politicians."

She thought of her stepfather and silently agreed with Gordon's assessment of the men who spoke so eloquently from the safety of their philosophies that other men were willing to die.

"Your leg? The war?"

"I rode with Stuart."

She supposed he thought that was an answer, and in a strange way it was, although it told her nothing of how he was injured. Suddenly the memory flashed like a thunderbolt inside her brain.

"Kincaid," she said, pushing away from the boards. "The general. You—"

He huffed a small snort. "The Southern general the radicals wanted to hang?" He shook his head again. "Wrong Kincaid. I was a lowly cavalry captain who spent the last two years of the war inside Fort Delaware."

Fort Delaware. The most infamous of the Northern prison camps, as feared in its day as the Rebels' Andersonville. She listened for bitterness or hatred in his voice, emotions the revolutionary Irish prided themselves on, but heard neither. Only a deep weariness for which she both admired and pitied him.

She walked to the edge of the hill and folded her hands behind her back. The wind blew off the water, carrying the tang of the harbor. A twig snapped as he came up behind her. "The Virginia Kincaids," she said.

He made a low sound of amusement. "It was rather refreshing when you didn't recognize the name."

"Your father was the famous senator."

"Grandfather. Peyton was the governor, my brother Royce the general."

"And what will you be, then?"

"A farmer." He paused and she turned so she could see his face. "Maybe a father."

"Fine things, both." She wondered why he didn't say doctor. The compassion was in him so deep he couldn't hide it no matter how hard he tried, but she didn't ask.

He was limned in the fiery sunset, a hot wash of color across his angled cheekbones. It hurt her heart to look at him.

"Who was Neddie?" he asked softly.

She looked away, staring into blood-red eternity over his shoulder. "An old, blind beggar." Her voice caught. "Once he'd been a sailor on the clipper ships, seen the world. China and India, California, and then he went blind and had nothing save an old dog for company."

His hands were on her shoulders, his strong fingers pressing into her skin. "The world is an ugly place, Maggie."

Then he was lowering his head and his lips were against hers, firm, then softening . . . a touch of the night wind and a taste of the sky-fire. He pulled back and her mouth parted as she reached for a breath. He stroked her lower lip with his thumb and she forgot to breathe.

"The world is ugly and most of the men who run it are ugly. Remember that, Maggie."

She blinked. Swallowed. Twisted her hands in her skirt because she didn't know what else to do with them. "Why—why did you kiss me?"

Streaks of amber and coral blazed across the bleeding sky. The awesome brilliance set his hair aflame and was reflected from the water, the stone bridges, the buildings with their glass windows, even the ground at their feet, until it seemed all of heaven and earth were ablaze.

He stared at her, an intense gaze reflecting the sky-fire. He made a rough sound, a strange half-moan. "The world is ugly and harsh, Maggie, but you . . . you are . . ." He pulled her closer, and she felt the weight of his head against her own.

"Maggie," he whispered into her hair.

She stood awkwardly enfolded in his man's arms and heard the pain in his voice. She was only the earthly Maggie Quinn, who couldn't even save herself from temptation. She lifted her arms, placing them around his waist, knowing she was as lost as he.

Chapter 7

Gordon returned just before noon on Sunday with two wagons packed with hay, Miss Hays and a friend he introduced as Drew Fielding. It took almost a full half-hour to load nineteen boisterous children in the back of the two wagons. Maggie watched the first wagon, driven by Mr. Fielding, pull away. Sister Agatha, God bless her pluck, sat on the bench seat beside Mr. Fielding, her wimple fluttering in the breeze.

Sister Agatha turned on the seat and waved, smiling broadly. Billy Kohn stuck his fingers in his mouth and shrilled an earsplitting whistle. Maggie covered her ears with her hands.

A picnic for nineteen orphans and his bachelor friends. Wherever did he come up with these notions? She narrowed one eye, assessing her charges, trying to determine which of them was going to be the first to develop an upset stomach. She took in Dr. Kincaid's white linen suit and turned a laugh into a small cough as he came up beside her.

He held out his hand to assist her into the back of the wagon with her half of the gaggle of giggling children. "I thought we'd go to Druid Hill Park," he said, smiling like a pirate. "You being Irish and all."

"Aye, and I suppose you expect the fairies there to turn this hay into cakes to feed the children."

"All under control, Maggie-mine." He gave her a little shove up. "In you go."

She squelched through the straw, dodging feet and wriggling bodies. Miss Hays, with her big straw hat and lace-trimmed parasol and striped taffeta dress, was already seated on the driving bench. The expression on her face was that of a woman overwhelmed by the confusion. Clare was half-buried under the hay in the wagon bed, scuffling with the other children for possession of a ball.

Maggie stilled them with a nudge of her foot and pulled Clare out from under the straw. She lifted the child over the seat next to Miss Hays. Gordon had come around and was climbing up to the bench. He winked as if to say thank you.

"Better get your fanny settled, Miss Quinn," he said as he released the brake. "This team is a little flighty for a hay wagon."

"My what!"

"Fanny." He made a little clicking sound with his tongue and spanked the reins. The wagon lurched forward. Maggie landed on her fanny. Clare broke into gales of laughter.

Well, what was a picnic without a little silliness? Maggie wiggled a bit, getting comfortable, unlike Miss Hays, who kept looking around as if she feared someone might recognize her.

They pulled up at the Madison Avenue entrance. The large wrought-iron gates were already swung open and the attendant waved them forward. Within minutes, they were pulling to a halt near Druid Hill Lake.

Mr. Fielding's wagon had already disgorged its occupants, and groups of children were running and rolling in a game of tag. Gordon *had* thought of everything, sending a third wagon ahead that must have been loaded with food and big quilts. She recognized his driver, who was in the process of spreading the feast out on one of the quilts. She mentally apologized again. Six adults to chaperone nineteen children should be more than adequate.

Gordon assisted Miss Hays down first, then lifted Clare from the bench, swinging her in a wide arc and causing her to squeal with delight. Watching them together, Maggie felt an ache that was both pleasure and pain. While Miss Hays went ahead with Clare tagging at her heels, he came around to the back of the wagon. Maggie began handing children out to him and soon it was just the two of them left.

He grinned and reached up for her. Caught up again in the effect of that dazzling smile, she didn't move. His hands spanned her waist and suddenly she was flying, weightless, laughing with the same abandon as wee Clare, and this was not Maggie Quinn, virtuous Irish-Catholic girl, but someone she didn't know and didn't trust.

Her feet landed on green velvet turf and he was laughing back. For an instant, she thought he was going to kiss her again, here in front of nineteen children and Sister Agatha . . . and Miss Hays. Instead, he untied her bonnet strings and tossed the cloth hat into the wagon bed. She made a grab for it, missing by an inch, and the pirate grinned again.

"A little sunshine is a healthy thing."

"Aye, and I'll have freckles all over my face."

He tapped her nose with his forefinger. "We'll check later."

"Humph." But she smiled.

The children were running every which way, their shrill voices piercing the stillness. She watched them while she plucked hay straws from her skirt, wishing their lives were always so filled with gaiety, silently thanking Gordon Kincaid.

It was a beautiful day. The leaves on the oaks showed traces of gold and soon the dogwoods and maples would be waving red leaves in brisk fall breezes. On the hills beyond the lake, bunches of chrysanthemums spread and billowed, lavender and white and umber pillows on a green grass quilt.

A party of canoeists was out on the lake, the oars cutting through the water like wooden spears. A mallard glided from around the jetty, followed by his mate, leaving two silvery wakes that rippled and spread and converged. The mallard dived and came up again, sunshine glistening on his wet head so the green feathers shimmered like emeralds.

She laughed with the sheer beauty of it all.

Gordon's voice cut across her laughter and she turned, still smiling. She watched him deftly field a baseball tossed by one of the boys and, one-handed, scoop up Alice as she tripped on a running pass in front of him.

"This was a wonderful idea," she said as she came up to him. "You're going to get caught up in God's good graces in spite of yourself."

He laughed and shoved a plate in her hand. "Fill up and find a comfortable spot. Miss Hays is auditioning today."

His mouth was curved in a teasing smile, and yet she felt his words like a slap. She forced something onto her face she hoped was an answering smile, and took the plate, real bone china with tiny pink roses scrolled around the rim.

She covered the painted roses with fried chicken, potato salad, pickled watermelon rind and tiny cucumber sandwiches and handed it to Alice. It wasn't until all the children were settled that she filled her own plate and joined Sister Agatha and Alice beneath the spreading boughs of a large oak.

She saw Clare, standing momentarily alone and looking their way, seeming uncertain of something. Maggie inclined her head toward Gordon and Miss Hays on the other side of the quilt. After another hesitation, Clare scampered over to join them, settling beside Gordon. He reached over and ruffled her hair, saying something Maggie was too far away to hear, but she could hear Clare's giggle in response. Miss Hays was on his other side, trying valiantly to juggle her plate and parasol.

"Seems a sin for a man like that to be a bachelor all these years," said Sister Agatha, following the direction of her gaze, and her thoughts as well.

Maggie slanted her a glance, seeking some ulterior motive in the innocuous words and seeing only Sister Agatha's sweet, round face. "I believe Miss Hays is going to change that," she said.

Sister Agatha plucked several grapes from the bunch on her plate and handed them to Alice. She plopped another in her own mouth and chewed, her thoughtful attention directed across the quilt. She shook her head finally. "I should think he could do better than Miss Hays."

The lemonade Maggie had been in the process of swallowing burst out of her mouth in a misty spray. Sister Agatha calmly handed her a linen napkin. "Another grape, Alice?" she asked while Maggie hid her laughter in the napkin folds.

Maggie sat side by side with Miss Hays on the bank where the meadow grass gave way to lake water. The gabled structure that was the boathouse thrust over the water like a fanciful gingerbread creation. The breeze off the lake cooled Maggie's face. She rubbed a cheek that was tacky with sweat and dirt against her drawn-up knees. Before them, the men were on the lake, each manning a canoe filled with children. She watched anxiously the one Gordon was paddling. Alice was with him and Alice couldn't swim.

Miss Hays stirred beside her. "He is mine, Miss Quinn."

A tightness squeezed Maggie's chest, a tightness she didn't want to acknowledge. "Do you love him, then?"

"I think I've loved him half my life." Miss Hays twirled the stem of her parasol around and around. Maggie watched the shadow moving on the grass. "Drew and Gordon and my brother all attended the same boarding school. Gordon didn't even know I was alive then, but he does now. I think he's going to ask me to marry him."

"Aye, you may be right." Maggie fiddled with a stem of coarse grass, then plucked it and chewed on the end. The water, rippled gold with sunshine, lapped against the bank. Somewhere, a blue jay squawked.

Miss Hays twisted around. Her pink lace parasol stippled her face with light and shadow. "Even if I'm wrong, he'll never be yours. You're Irish-Catholic. Gordon is . . . he is a Kincaid."

A Kincaid, a Protestant from as aristocratic a family as a nation without royalty could produce. Maggie understood the intended insult; it was in her Irish blood to understand.

She picked another stem of grass and knotted it. "Not him or any other," she said quietly. "I'm going to be a nun, Miss Hays."

Miss Hays's face looked a little foolish in its bewilderment. She glanced over to where Sister Agatha stood on the stone-banked jetty, a child on either side of her as they tossed bread crumbs to the ducks.

"A nun," murmured Miss Hays. And then she smiled.

The music was lovely, not like a pipe organ but gay and twinkling and perfect for the day. Gordon had made some arrangement with the barker that reserved the carousel for their children for a whole half-hour.

Mesmerized, Maggie watched the carousel going around and around; the wooden horses with their prancing legs, their brightly painted tails and manes seeming to fly in the wind. The horses were in three concentric circles, anchored to the spinning platform by poles. The two inside circles bobbed up and down as if by magic. It was a kaleidoscope of color and sound.

"The children will never forget this day," she said to Gordon as she returned Clare's wave and then Alice's. She let out an unconscious sigh. "It looks like so much fun."

"You've never ridden a carousel?" he asked, sounding amazed.

Maggie made a little laughing sound, hiding the tiny ache inside. "And just where would I ride wooden horses?"

"In a park named for Irish sorcerers."

Before she could draw a breath, he had her by the hand, dragging her toward the carousel.

"It's for the children," she said, attempting to disengage her hand.

He ignored her protest and the next thing she knew, he was lifting her to the turning platform. He jumped on after her, grimacing with pain as he took his weight on his bad leg. She reached out to steady him but dropped her hand at the proud, disdainful look that came over his face. His graceful hands grasped her at the waist, lifting her sidesaddle onto the back of a silver horse.

"If you swing around to the outside," he said, "you can grab for the ring."

"Ring?"

"Brings good luck."

Holding her skirts to retain some semblance of modesty, she swung her legs over the gold-painted tail of the horse. His hand steadied her back as she rocked, almost tumbling backward. She grasped the pole and he moved to the horse behind her. He straddled a sky-blue stallion, his legs so long, his feet were touching the platform. Golden hair blew back from his face in tousled waves. She laughed again. Their gazes met and he smiled.

Around and around they went, the world a whirl of fading green trees and blue sky and streaming ribbons of color. The autumn-scented wind caressed her face. She imagined she could feel the imprint of his hand on her back, a lingering warmth that seeped to her bone.

"Grab for the ring, Maggie-mine."

He pointed to a pole that flashed by so fast she barely saw it. As they came around again, he leaned far out, reaching, and snatched something shiny from the top of the pole. Smiling like a cat with cream, he held the object so the sun glinted from it, then tucked it into his pocket.

Too soon, the music and the carousel both slowed, winding down. He was beside her, his hand at her elbow to help her dismount. He held her an instant too long for politeness and then let go. She jumped from the platform and pressed her hand to her chest, as if to keep her heart from exploding.

"Next time, I'll take you riding on the real thing," he said.

Next time. There could be no next time. Maggie stared into his face, into those eyes that held all the mysteries of the universe.

His eyes grew dark. "Walk with me."

"Nay. I must stay with the children."

He looked around and back to her, his lips curling in an ironic smile. "Drew, Sister Agatha, Franklin. Enough to watch them, I should think." Without waiting, he took her hand on his forearm, placing his other hand over her fingers to prevent her from pulling away.

She realized suddenly that walking with him was never awkward. She didn't have to lengthen her steps to keep up; he shortened his stride to accommodate her. She didn't have to watch where she placed her feet; he kept to the uneven turf and gave her the beaten paths. It was the way of a gentleman, and for a minute she allowed herself to imagine she was a fine lady out for an afternoon stroll with her gentleman.

"You should be walking with Miss Hays," she said, reminding him, reminding herself of her proper place.

"Miss Hays is fatigued from the sun."

They shared a smile and the smile would have to be enough. They could never share his daughter, for Maggie was to become a nun, and he was going to wed Miss Hays.

Gordon allowed her to draw her hand away and then allowed her to choose the direction and set the pace. She turned down the stone path leading to the music pavilion. A breeze rustled the crinkly leaves of a crepe myrtle, showering dark pink petals on the pavement in front of them, and a memory stirred at the edges of his thoughts.

His sister-in-law was pushing him in his rolling chair down the hallway. Annabelle stopped at the back door, set the brake and gave him a searching look. He nodded. After a moment's hesitation, she reached for the canes she had previously propped against the wall and held them out to him.

Already, the sweat was creeping down his chest and back, and there was a hard knot of fear in his throat. But he took the canes, gripping the wooden handles so tightly his nails bit into his palms, and pushed himself out of the chair. When he was upright and reasonably steady, she shoved the door open. Gordon hobbled out to the gallery, where his father and brother were lounging in the evening breeze.

He remembered he'd been barefoot and how marvelous that had felt—to be able to feel the cool hardness of the flagstones on the soles of his feet. It didn't matter that his shirt was clinging to the sweat on his skin, making it itch; or that he was carrying more of his weight with his arms than with his legs. All the doctors his father had brought in over the last year were being proven wrong at this moment.

At first the only sound was the leaves of the old crepe myrtle tree rustling and his grunts of exertion. Then Royce gave voice to a Rebel yell so loud and startling that Peyton's face blanched white, but they held still and watched until Gordon made it across the wide expanse of gallery and settled into the chair Royce had vacated. It was only then that Gordon saw the tears rolling down his father's cheeks.

And it was like a dam had been broken because they talked for a long time after that: about how Franklin and Annabelle had worked with him all those months, in secret, until he was ready to show his father and brother himself.

They avoided the subject of the war—that wound was still too raw—but they spoke of the more distant past, and of the future. It was then Gordon shared another secret he'd held close: the desire to study medicine so he could apply the lessons he had learned during his rehabilitation for the benefit of other men who had been wounded in the war. And it was Royce who had argued that as a single father his first priority should be his son.

And now here he was—a doctor. And his only regret was for his son because, of course, Royce had been right too.

He had another chance to be a father, with Clara. If only Peyton had told him. . . . But he had no right to think that way. He understood why his father had maintained his silence on Clara. Peyton had understood that Gordon needed to set himself free before he could turn to Clara.

Annabelle, he remembered, had also stayed with them that hot summer's night, sitting quietly as was her way on the edge of the gallery. She had laughed when Royce let out the Rebel yell and had been the one to bring the lap robe and wrap Gordon's legs when he got chilled. But she hadn't said much that night. It wasn't until he was boarding the train to take up his medical studies that she hugged him tight and said, "Do what you have to do, Gordon. Then, please, come home."

"She would like you."

Gordon didn't realize he'd spoken aloud until Maggie turned her face to him. She had a way of tilting her head and peering through her long lashes that turned her eyes the deep green of a hemlock forest. Her skin was so translucent he could see the blue vein pulsing in her temple.

"And which of your fine ladies would this be, Dr. Kincaid? For some strange reason I can't imagine any of them itching to invite me to tea."

"Stop that." The words came out harsher than he'd intended. He cleared his throat to try again. "Stop saying that we come from opposite worlds and that mine is somehow better than yours, because it isn't."

She had moved ahead of him and now she turned, clasping her hands behind her back. "And sure it is that's how you'd take my meaning. But maybe it's my own pride saying my world is better than yours."

"And which of your worlds would that be?"

The teasing dimple at the corner of her mouth disappeared. She nudged her chin up and began to walk away from him.

He never knew which side she was going to present to him. Maggie, brave Irish lass with dreams in her eyes and memories too painful to share. Or Mary Margaret, quiet convent girl, who behaved as if a man so much as standing next to her endangered all hope of salvation.

And then there was the young woman he thought he was coming to know. That Maggie was generous and kind and loyal, her heart as big and open as her heaven.

He lengthened his stride and came up beside her, careful to maintain a polite distance between them because he wanted to touch her. "I can't help but think you'd like Annabelle as well. In her world, a tea party is a waste of an afternoon better spent down by the river with a fishing pole, a can of worms and a book under her arm in case the fish aren't biting."

"Well, your Miss Annabelle sounds like a most sensible sort, and now I'm wondering why it is you're not pursuing her as our wee Clare's mother."

"Annabelle is my brother's wife."

She stopped, placing her hands on her hips where a wide black cummerbund nipped her waist to the span of a man's hands. She gave him a long, slow look, as if she were taking his measure. "And do your brother and his most sensible sort of a wife live nearby you?"

"Five-minute walk across the pasture."

"Well, then," she said. "I should think that will be good for Clare, to live nearby a sensible lady who might be kind enough to take her fishing of an afternoon."

His heart did a flip in his chest as her words sent so many confused thoughts reeling through his mind. In spite of the slate of moral flaws she'd tallied against him, Maggie was still willing to aid him in winning his daughter. Good.

But he wanted his own family, himself as father. Try as he might, he couldn't fit Rebecca into the picture, especially after today, with her nose tilted into the air, so complacent in her superiority to orphaned children, nuns and Irish peasants.

But Annabelle and Royce—no, they fit in the family portrait far too easily, and he saw himself fading in his own mind's eye back into the shadow father.

"Clare went fishing once. . . ." Maggie wrapped her arms around her waist and looked away from him. "Someone will have to put the worms on her line, though, she's a bit squeamish."

He wanted to tell her he was desperate to take his daughter fishing, to bait her line with bloodworms. He was so desperate to have a family again, he would have sold whatever he had left of his soul. But he couldn't seem to get any words past the dryness in his throat.

He turned and walked carefully away, trying hard to hide his limp. He stopped at the pavilion and spread his hand out flat on the wooden railing. Splayed his fingers wide until he could feel the stretch of skin against the nerves and bones of his hand.

He glanced up and saw that she too was looking at his hand. His doctor's hand, which could perform complicated surgeries, but had never baited a fishhook for a son or tied a ribbon in a daughter's hair.

Her gaze came up, met his, and then jerked away.

She was a study in contrast, in her plain black skirt and long-sleeved white shirtwaist with a stiff, high collar. A grosgrain ribbon the color of pink camellias was tied in a bow just beneath her chin. That tiny, whimsical touch of rebellion made him smile.

"Thank you for the ride on the carousel and the walk in the gardens," she said. "But it's time for me to be returning to my duties with the children." She cast a look over her shoulder. He watched the way the curve of her breasts pushed against the white cotton shirt as she drew in a deep breath.

"It's been a lovely day," she said. "For the children, I mean."

He turned and leaned his elbow on the railing. His smile deepened. "Just for the children?"

"No. . . ." She ducked her head, carefully averting her face. "Not just for the children," she said softly.

He wished he hadn't teased her. Those flashes of vulnerability were an almost painful thing to see. *Don't,* he wanted to say to her. *Don't give me any more glimpses into your heart, because it scares me. It pulls me into a place I traveled through once, and never want to visit again.*

But of course he didn't say anything because he was as vulnerable as she, and a coward at heart. He wanted to reach out and touch her face, to feel the bone and softness of skin beneath his fingers. But he didn't do that either. He curled his hand into a loose fist and flashed his best rogue's smile.

She turned away, but not before he saw the flush stain her cheeks and the sudden sheen in her eyes. He knew she would leave him now for the safety of her children. He had hurt her, and he didn't like knowing he could do that so easily.

When she disappeared around a bend in the path, he thrust his hands through his hair, then tipped his head back and closed his eyes.

Maybe a man couldn't prevent the rushing of his blood. Couldn't stop the desperate need for a woman from coming over him. But he sure as the devil could control his behavior.

He needed Maggie's help in his campaign to win his daughter. That was all. He didn't want her in his life. And yet, and yet . . . there was something about her. . . .

Becca lounged in the shade of a sugar maple, still spotlessly clean, looking exhausted. Gordon tried to think of anything she'd done to cause that level of tiredness and decided she'd worn herself out just observing the children's energy.

The children were wearing down too, many lolling in small groups at the bank of the lake, a few out on the jetty with Sister Agatha, tossing bread crumbs to the ducks. Maggie and Drew were assisting Franklin in packing and loading the supply wagon. Gordon crouched beside his fascinated and fascinating daughter, both of them bent over an anthill.

"Which one is the mother?" asked Clara.

His heart gave a lurch. Maybe any child would ask that question—but it struck sharp into his guilt.

"It's called a queen and you won't see her. She stays safe inside almost all the time." He put his hand on the ground, allowing a number of ants to crawl across the back of his hand. "These are the worker ants, the soldiers. They go out for food and carry it back to feed the nurses and babies inside the colony. If there's danger, their job is to protect the queen and the baby ants."

"No daddy ants?"

This was getting deep. Gordon drew in a breath. "Not in the way you're thinking."

She thought about that, her little brow creasing in concentration. "Kind of like an orphanage with the nuns, I guess."

"Kind of."

He turned on the balls of his feet to sit Indian fashion and drew Clara onto his lap. He felt a pleasurable glow when she didn't resist, instead squirming to get closer. She smelled of watermelon and sunshine and childhood.

"Did you have a good time with the Cromwells?" He was probing and didn't feel the least guilty. He meant to win this battle with the mother superior and knew he was already fighting dirty.

"They didn't have a dog."

"Brussels sprouts?"

She giggled. "No. Peas."

He smoothed her hair back from her brow. It felt good against his palm, soft. "What do you think of Miss Hays?"

Clara looked in the direction of the sugar maple. "She's pretty. Like the china doll at the Cromwells'."

He glanced again at Becca. She was spun-sugar perfection in her pink-and-white-striped dress with puffy leg-o'-mutton sleeves and a big square collar of lace. Her blond ringlets were covered by a white straw hat decorated with pink and white plumes and trailing blue ribbons. She didn't look as much like a china doll, he thought, as she looked like a spoiled, pampered society belle.

Clara tipped her head backward, peering up into his face. "Do you think she's pretty?"

"Umm, I suppose."

Clara twisted around sideways, her legs swung over his knee, her head resting against his sternum. The sun was beginning to drop and the breeze quickened into a wind, chilling the air. He opened his coat and wrapped it over her, drawing her closer to him, keeping her warm and safe.

"When I was a boy, I used to look at the stars in the sky and think if I could only reach up and grab one, I'd get anything I wished for." He rested his chin on the top of her head, wishing he could change some part of the past, the part that placed his infant daughter in an orphanage instead of in his arms. "If you had three wishes, Clara, what would you wish for?"

She was silent. "Anything in the whole wide world?" she said finally.

"Anything."

"A dog."

He realized he'd been holding his breath and let it out slowly. That one was easy enough. She could have a dozen dogs at Old Riverbend. Kittens, ponies, he'd build an entire zoo. "That's one," he said. "Two more."

"To take Maggie to Ireland for a visit."

She'd surprised him with that one, but he remained quiet, waiting for her to elaborate, hoping she would.

"That's why she calls me Clare. My name is Clara, but Maggie always calls me Clare because she's from someplace in Ireland called County Clare."

He thought of his taunting of an upset Maggie just the other morning with his *Clar-a,* and felt petty and small. He understood it was Maggie, herself an orphan in a strange land, who had given his child the love she needed to grow.

"You love Maggie," he said, and it wasn't a question because he knew she did. Clara remained quiet. Maybe children raised in orphanages were afraid to admit to loving. His own childhood had been blessed in so many ways, but he thought he could understand. He drew in another deep breath and held her a little tighter.

"You still have one wish left," he said quietly, wondering if she would wish for a father or a home, the biggest wishes he wanted to fulfill for her.

"I'm saving that one."

Before he could ask her what or why, all hell broke loose.

Chapter 8

Maggie saw it as it happened—saw Sister Agatha turn away from the lake, shepherding several children off the jetty—saw one child turn back, unnoticed, and reach far over the water trying to catch a duck.

"Alice," she screamed, but it wasn't a scream because the sound was caught in the terror closing her throat. Maggie dropped the quilt she'd been folding and raced for the jetty as Alice's head disappeared from sight beneath the murky water.

She hadn't a far distance to go, maybe half a field, yet it seemed to take her forever no matter how hard her legs pumped. She hit the land end of the jetty, dodging children, thrusting off Sister Agatha's restraining hand.

"Alice," was all she said, and Sister Agatha's face went white. Maggie heard the eruption of noise and activity behind her and then she was in the water and heard nothing.

She dived low, unable to see anything in the stirred-up silt. Reeds choked the bottom, wrapping around her arms and boots like the tentacles of an octopus. A death trap. *Blessed Mother, keep her safe until I can find her.*

She didn't know how long she'd been groping, feeling nothing but water and reeds. Her heart pounded against her chest. Fire seared her lungs. Maggie shook herself free from the entanglement and surfaced for air.

She dove again. All she could do was reach, try to find the child by touch. Every movement she made stirred more muck until it seemed she was held imprisoned by mud and slick, grasping water weeds. Her skirts and petticoats floated around her, adding to her confusion and disability. Her head was bursting, heart and lungs exploding, every movement caused a tortuous, lancing pain to shoot through burning muscles. Something kept her going. One more reach through swaying reeds, one more touch of the bottom.

Once more. *Alice, where are you?*

A child's hysterical scream caused him to jerk his gaze to the lake in time to see Maggie disappear beneath the surface.

Gordon thrust Clara from his lap. "Stay with Miss Hays," he said. "And don't move anywhere near that water. Understood?"

Clara looked at him with huge, frightened eyes. "Ma-Maggie."

"Will be fine," he said as he yanked off his coat. "Go." To his relief, the child moved as instructed. "Drew—Franklin," he yelled as he took off running for the jetty.

He was acting on instinct, no time to taste the fear rising in his throat. He reached Sister Agatha, huddled at the land end of the jetty with children clustered around her.

"Alice," said Sister Agatha, her voice hoarse.

A child. God, a child.

"Keep them back." He didn't see her nod or her arms pulling little bodies closer; he was already past them, Drew racing on his heels. They reached the end of the jetty as Maggie surfaced with the youngster in her arms.

He was certain Alice was dead. From the glimpse he'd

gotten, her face was blanched and lifeless. "Can you touch bottom, Maggie?" he shouted.

"The reeds," she said, tossing her head to fling water from her eyes. "They're holding me." He made a motion to go in after the both of them and Maggie called out, "Nay, they'll hold you too."

It was an effort for her; he could see the strain in her face and those damned layers of skirts and petticoats kept wrapping around her legs, impeding movement. Too slow already, when time was critical.

He spoke to Drew, who was leaning over his shoulder. "I'll pass the child out to you." In two strokes, he'd reached Maggie. "I've got her. *I've got her.*"

Maggie looked at him through enormous eyes, her face ashen, her jaw set with determination. She reluctantly released her hold on Alice. He understood. He truly understood the impulse to hold on as if you could squeeze life back into a dead body. In this case, it might work. If they weren't too late.

"Breathe, breathe," he murmured as he passed the lifeless body to Drew. His soaked boots were stone-heavy. He couldn't kick them off and it took too many seconds to heave himself up and onto the jetty, but maybe it wasn't as long as it seemed because Drew was only now laying the child on the ground.

"Maggie," he said to Drew, while already leaning over Alice. "She'll never get out on her own." He put his fingers to Alice's neck for a pulse . . . and felt nothing.

"No." He pressed his mouth to her cold blue lips. "No," he breathed into her mouth.

Water in her lungs. How long had she been without oxygen?

He took her arms and pumped them, then pushed his palms against her skinny chest. He did it again and again, unwilling to accept her unnatural stillness. An innocent eight-year-old girl with light brown hair caught up in two braids tied with red ribbons.

He pumped and pushed while his muscles burned with the tension. He blew his own life into her mouth, hard.

"Breathe," he said, and it was the closest thing to a prayer he'd uttered in a decade. He blew again. "Breathe."

Suddenly her head lolled to the side. She spluttered, coughed, then greenish brown water gushed from her mouth and nose, and she was retching.

He raised her shoulders, cradling her head so she wouldn't choke and to make it easier for her to draw air into her lungs. "Good girl. You're all right now," he murmured.

When she was finally done gagging and retching, he drew her onto his lap, holding her hard against his chest. He rocked her back and forth, squeezing so tight she squirmed. Her hair was parted down the middle and his eyes lingered on the thin white line of her scalp, thinking how vulnerable she was, how fragile the barrier between life and death.

He felt a hand on his shoulder, but didn't look up. Not yet. He was too shaken.

"I've a blanket for her," said Maggie.

The larger world thrust itself back into his consciousness. He heard Sister Agatha's calm voice, and Franklin's deep one, as they reassured crying children; heard Drew's irritated voice dealing with a nearly hysterical Becca. Alice hiccupped repeatedly.

He took Alice's cold hand in his own and looked up. Maggie stood over them. Her wet hair had come undone and hung in a heavy rope over her shoulder. Her eyes looked huge in her white face and her lips had the same bluish tinge as Alice's. Tremors of shock and cold shook her body.

The skinny, shivering child in his arms would be dead, if not for Maggie.

Maggie stepped back, speechless. He must have scraped his face against the stones lining the jetty, as blood seeped from a long cut along his jaw. Wet hair hung wild over his forehead. His shirt clung like a shadow to his chest, defining every quivering muscle. His linen pants were streaked with mud and vomit. He pushed himself up from the ground and gathered a quilt-bundled Alice into his arms.

She watched him carry the child off the jetty as Drew Fielding draped a white jacket over her shoulders. She reached up, touching the lapel. "No," she said, beginning to shrug it off. "I'll not ruin this fine coat."

Gordon stopped and looked back to where they stood. His eyes were still black with that awful emotion. "Wear it," he said in a terrible, angry voice. "God's not going to save you from pneumonia. The jacket might."

Her hands shook as she pulled the jacket tight. Her whole body insisted on shaking and she didn't know if it came from cold or shock. Mr. Fielding placed his hand against her back, a warm, calming touch.

"He doesn't mean it the way it sounds," he said. Maggie was still unable to speak. After a long pause, Drew continued, "We're men, Miss Quinn, and as men, it is our duty and privilege to protect the women and children around us. For Gordon, it's even more. He swore an oath, as a doctor, to do everything in his power to preserve life. That child nearly died."

"But . . . but it was Dr. Kincaid who saved her." She looked up into Drew's face.

"True, Miss Quinn. But actually, if it weren't for you, Alice would be dead."

Maggie's fingers thrummed the harp. Now, when all were safe, nineteen children fed and put to bed, only now did she feel terror twisting her into a nauseated knot. So she came to Father Fitz's study where she wouldn't disturb the children and played her music.

She saw movement and looked to the doorway, expecting to see Father Fitzhugh, finding Gordon instead. He'd changed into Father Fitz's clothes, a pair of black trousers and collarless white shirt, but he bore little resemblance to the priest with his golden hair still tangled and wild, his dark eyes so deeply troubled.

He looked at her with a faint, sardonic smile at his lips. "I thought I sent you to bed hours ago."

"Aye, you did." She thrummed several more notes, softer. "And wee Alice?"

"Sleeping. Right now I'm more concerned about you." He studied her, a physician's serious appraisal, then gave a little groan. "Barefoot, Maggie? You'll be lucky if you don't take a chill."

Harp strings vibrated beneath the pads of her fingers. Barefoot? Aye, but she wasn't going to destroy her slippers by wearing them to cross the alley to the rectory.

Although he leaned casually against the doorpost, he had a taut air to him, a man burning inside and fighting to hold himself in check. She said nothing, only played the harp, hoping the music would soothe his wild emotions.

He turned his face away from her, his cheek against the wood. "What is that you're playing?"

"One of the old slow airs, 'Ar Eirinn.' "

Only because she lifted her head did she see the slight sway of his body, like a strong oak fighting a gale. She dropped her hands from the harp, half-rising to go to him.

"No," he said. "Don't stop."

"You'll sit awhile, then?" She drew a small smile from him.

"Aye, Maggie-mine. I'll sit for a while."

His feet made no sound as he moved across the carpet, his left leg dragging slightly. He settled into Father Fitzhugh's favorite armchair and leaned his head against the cushion, his eyes closed. Maggie returned to the harp, choosing the haunting old airs, poignant melodies that conjured up misty moorlands filled with fairies and the ghosts of ancient kings.

After many minutes, she looked his way. He was watching her as if she were one of the fairies, mysterious and otherworldly.

"You *are* the one who saved wee Alice."

He shook his head, then looked away. "Medical colleges teach a man arrogance. You begin to believe you can outmaneuver death." He nudged a small ceramic nightingale across the tabletop with his finger. "What they don't teach in the books and lecture halls is that sometimes the patient dies in spite of the tricks in your black satchel. And the bitter pain of that failure."

"You would not be the man you are, Dr. Kincaid, if you did not feel that pain. You would not be the man Clare deserves as a father."

He made a strange, low cry that got caught in his throat. "Where was your God today, Maggie? Alice could have died, you could have died. It could have been Clara."

"Aye, but it was none of those things." He made no response. She rose and walked toward him. "Were you not there, Dr. Kincaid? There by the grace of God to blow life into the wee child when none of the rest of us would have known what to do."

"You make it sound so simple." He lifted his lashes, a brief look, yet searching. She placed her hand on his shoulder.

"But it is simple," she said.

He shook his head again, then drew a deep breath that caused his body to shudder as if in a chill. His arms came around her hips and he leaned his face against her abdomen. She wanted to weep for him.

"It will be all right," she murmured.

He made another sound, a strange half-laugh that was buried in the folds of her gown. His arms seemed to tighten around her. Awkwardly, she patted his shoulder. She ached to give him what he needed but didn't know how to comfort a man. He lifted his head.

"Would you play some more, Maggie?"

"Aye, Dr. Kincaid." This small comfort she could give him.

"Would you sing for me?"

"Aye." For you.

* * *

Maggie paused on the pavement, looking up, her eyes following the three-tiered tower atop Camden Station to the highest spire poking into the gray, wan light of a city morning.

"Looks almost like a cathedral," she said.

Father Fitzhugh paid the cabdriver and then took her arm. "A modern-day cathedral dedicated to commerce and industry and too many people in too big a hurry."

She slanted him a glance, uncertain of his tone of voice and even less certain of his meaning. His face gave away nothing this morning, but was a mask, with his set jaw and serious eyes. She waited quietly while he saw to his baggage, and then walked with him outside to the boarding platform.

The wind tore at her hat and she reached up, resetting the long hatpin, anchoring the black cloche more securely. "You will write?"

"I'll write," he said. She bit her lower lip. He fingered his hat and said, "You'll visit me in Richmond?"

"Aye. By next summer I'll have saved enough money."

He started to shake his head and caught himself. They'd had this discussion before, but she would not take his dollars for her own selfish pleasure. People jostled all around them, yet she felt as if the world held only the two of them right now, two sad people, each trying to be brave for the other.

"Last night in the study," he said. "Dr. Kincaid . . . I couldn't help but hear."

She hesitated, gazing at the long line of train cars hitched one after another, seeing instead a bowed, angry man with wild, golden hair and eyes of midnight.

"He—he is so lost, Father Fitz."

"He needs you, my Maggie. He needs your faith."

"He frightens me."

Father Fitz said nothing. Maggie looked away from his searching gaze. She wanted to tell him everything, not as a confession of sins to her priest but as a daughter might seek comfort from a parent. She couldn't, not to Father Fitz or to Mother Bernadette or even to Sister Agatha.

None would censure her for a kiss properly given and received within the bounds of matrimony. She understood marriage was a state blessed by the Church with its own sacrament. She couldn't say it because Dr. Kincaid's kisses were not proper. She hadn't even tried to prevent him when he did and then had wondered—nay, wickedly hoped—he would kiss her again. Prideful vanity and carnal pleasure, sins they might be, but they tumbled inside her mixed with a precious joy that she could not believe was sinful. She felt weak, and afraid of the stranger inside her own skin.

"I cannot help him," she said wretchedly. "I don't know how."

"My willful Maggie." He brushed her hair at her temple. "Pray for guidance," he said quietly. "You are a good woman with much to give."

"But I am not, Father."

She was not good. She was selfishly tied to a child who was not hers and a priest she loved as a mortal father and a man who was the devil's own temptation. She was not good at all.

"Maggie, there are many crossroads in life," he said, smiling at her like she was the lost girl in the immigrant shed. "Sometimes the path that seems most frightening is the path that leads to the greatest joy."

"How do you know which path to take?" she asked desperately.

"It's the not-knowing that makes us human." He drew her into a hug and she rubbed her cheek against the soft wool of his coat. "I'm a priest and perhaps I've been wrong to love you as a father would love a daughter. As a priest, I say to you, do not abandon Dr. Kincaid or wee Clara in their time of need."

"And what would a father say to his daughter?"

Father Fitzhugh's face turned grim. "Be careful, *mó cailín*.

our heart is a precious gift, do not give it to a man who oesn't deserve it."

Maggie stood on the platform for a long time after he was one; stood with the tears wetting her cheeks, listening for he train whistle until long after it had faded.

Chapter 9

Gordon stepped out of the leaded glass doors of the Barnum Hotel, holding the door open for the porter who followed with his luggage. A group of rowdy boys ran down the pavement, calling to each other in Gaelic as they dodged through drifting fog and pedestrians. They passed behind him and one blew on a conch shell. Gordon started at the unexpected noise, then chuckled. It seemed a long time ago, but he'd been a boy once himself.

"Check your pocket, Dr. Kincaid," said the porter, shoving the luggage cart onto the damp pavement. "If the urchins have lifted your wallet, I'll send security after them." He pulled off his cap and ran the back of his hand across his forehead. "Shanty Irish should keep their peat rats in Bogtown where they won't be a bother to decent folk."

"Well actually, I'd like to have that boy's shell horn," said Gordon. "My daughter would like one of those, I think."

The black porter beetled his brows. "You wouldn't want

your daughter touching the thing. No telling what diseases she might catch."

The war might be long over, thought Gordon, but not much had changed in the South. Southern society remained nuanced with layers and mores no Northerner could ever comprehend. The best white families, most now living in genteel poverty, remained at the top of the social hierarchy.

But below them was another kind of battleground where free blacks and former slaves fought to better their lot against the equally strong desires of the whites to keep them in their place, and all of them, white and black, looked on the poor Irish as unwanted competition for scarce jobs.

"Shall I hail you a cab, Dr. Kincaid?"

Gordon fixed his brown bowler on his head and peered through the fog. "No, I think that's my driver turning the corner now." He stepped to the edge of the pavement as Franklin pulled Drew's carriage to a halt. Gordon placed his palm on the fender and looked up. "How's our filly today?"

"Settled, I think. I'll put her through a workout tomorrow." Franklin set the brake and wrapped the traces. "That your luggage, Doc?"

Gordon nodded and stepped back as Franklin climbed down from the driving seat. Every year for as long as he could remember, with the exception of the four years of the war, the Fieldings held a house party before the Dixie Cup race at Pimlico. Every year, the Kincaids attended, even when they didn't have a horse entered. But this year, Royce and Annabelle had stayed home. Annie was pregnant.

He'd always found the party insufferably boring. The guests would stroll out on the lawn with punch glass and lemon cake in hand to watch the children in a game of croquet, the nannies pushing baby carriages down the lane, then stroll back inside to discuss what a fine day it was and what boarding school will your son be attending this year?

All those children, thought Gordon with a sudden wave of amusement, and not a pregnant woman in thirty years. It was as if proper society kept its bloodlines pure through the miracle of immaculate conception.

But this year the party wouldn't be boring. Clara would be there, and if he was lucky, Mother Bernadette would honor his request to send Maggie as chaperone.

Maggie was under his skin, he couldn't deny it any longer. In the days since the picnic at the park, he'd seen her everywhere. He saw her in a slim black skirt and starched white shirtwaist walking away from him. In hair so black it shone blue in the depths of a braid wrapped tightly into a coil.

Today, he thought he saw her coming out of Felan's Emporium carrying a brown paper parcel tied with string, and again in the crowd at Hauptmann's dining on crab cakes and shucked oysters. He thought he saw her pushing a cart of soiled bed linens down the corridor in the Barnum Hotel.

And each time he saw her, in that dizzy moment before he realized it wasn't Maggie after all, he would feel that rush in his blood and the heavy thud of his heart in his chest.

Gordon reached for a carpetbag to toss up on the carriage roof. Franklin and the porter both glared at him, so he set it down and stepped back, mindful of Franklin's concern for his weak leg—the poor man had had to pick him up from the ground too many times in the last ten years—and the porter's concern for proprieties.

No, the truth was, he hadn't seen Maggie Quinn since that night in Father Fitzhugh's study. He'd gone back to check on Alice and Maggie both, worried they'd develop pneumonia or influenza after the chill, but Maggie was already teaching when he'd arrived that first day, and he didn't push the mother superior to call her from the classroom so he could make an assessment of her health. Mother Bernadette had enough nursing experience to recognize signs of illness, and too much womanly intuition.

Because the deeper truth was, the day Gordon Kincaid met Maggie Quinn was the day his comfortable world fell apart.

He heard someone call his name and turned. The street

lamps were already lit and they cast an eerie yellow glow through the drifting fretwork of fog rising off the river. He saw a man coming toward him, leading a dog on a rope leash.

It was the saddest excuse for a dog he'd ever seen. About the size of a spaniel, this mutt appeared to be the color of a dried acorn, although it was hard to tell in the deepening fog, and was so skinny his ribs and hipbones showed stark through the dull, matted coat. When the man stopped, he saw it was Jamie O'Connor. The dog sat at his feet with his head drooping forward.

"You call that a lucky dog?"

"Well, it was our Maggie that gave him the name," said Jamie, *his* head held proud beneath an Irish tweed scally cap, his strong jaw thrust forward. His gaze took in the carriage and the two men who were strapping down the luggage. "I'd take the dog home to my own brothers and sisters if it weren't—"

Gordon was beginning to like this man, so he interrupted before Jamie was forced to admit his family couldn't afford to feed another mouth. "I said I know of a good home."

"Maggie will want to know where this good home will be."

"My daughter wants a dog."

Jamie cocked his head and gave him an assessing gaze. "Your daughter in Virginia?"

"The daughter I'm taking to Virginia. With a dog."

"Aye, well, this isn't a dog to know the difference between a fine brocade love seat and a patch of straw, and I doubt he'll recognize a back door from a front one, and he won't be wiping the mud off his feet before he enters."

"But he was a loyal friend to a blind old man. Lucky will do just fine." Gordon reached for the leash and when Jamie handed it over, he led the dog to the carriage, then lifted him inside. When he closed the door and turned, Jamie was still standing on the pavement, watching. Gordon narrowed his eyes and stared back.

"I gave Maggie a dog once," Jamie said after a moment.

Gordon smiled. "She told me. A three-legged specimen."

"I'm thinking she might have told you how she came by the dog but not as how she came to lose him." Jamie's gaze turned inward and then he seemed to physically pull himself back. "Do you have a minute to walk a few paces with me?"

Gordon nodded. He felt chilled suddenly and thrust his hands in his pockets as he fell in beside Jamie. They were almost of the same height, both broader across the chest than most men, one wearing corduroy pants and a jersey shirt rolled at the sleeves, the other a frock coat and silk ascot. Both of them caught in that strange silence between men who are reaching for a common ground and don't know what to say to one another.

The train whistle blew from the 6:18 departing the Calvert Street Station for Washington. A newsboy walked past, hawking the *Evening Gazette* and chanting, "Jones Fall fire kills seven."

"That's how Maggie's dog died," said Jamie. "In a fire; only it wasn't because he was missing a leg that he couldn't get out. It was because the red-coated soldiers had tied him to the Quinns' only table. Then they set the cottage on fire."

"Good Lord, man." Gordon stopped. "Where was Maggie?"

"Watching. She got away from me and tried to go after the dog, but the fine Lord Geoffrey Fitzhugh caught her and held her back. It was probably the only decent thing the man ever did, because the roof went about then. Then he bought her and her dying mother a third-class ticket and sent them to America to be done with them."

So like his own South. All men carried both light and dark within them. It was the choices they made that determined which force won out and he thought the darkness would eventually claim Jamie O'Connor. Maggie suffused light from within.

"And Maggie's father?"

Jamie stared at a trolley car rattling down the street. A long edgy moment passed and then their gazes locked, head-on.

"Sure, there was one man hanging by his neck from a yew

tree and some would say Seamus Quinn was her true father, me being among them, as he was the man who raised her up from a wee lassie. And there'll be others saying the man who held her back from the fire was the one to give her life."

The revelation should have shocked him, yet it didn't. He remembered that dinner with Father Fitzhugh and wondered why he hadn't seen it then. Black, black hair, astounding green eyes. Height above the norm. Father Fitzhugh was twin brother to the Earl of Lachlan, and he wondered, had the priest wanted him to see? Was that his real purpose in asking Gordon what he saw when he looked at Maggie?

"I shouldn't be telling you this," said Jamie, "except I care about Maggie and I know she'll never tell you herself."

No, she wouldn't, thought Gordon, and something caught in his chest that hurt. He removed his hat and thrust his fingers through his hair, started to put the hat back on, then didn't.

He hated wearing hats and holding the fool thing gave him something to do with the hands that suddenly itched to grab Jamie O'Connor around the throat. And he didn't even know why.

"Maggie says she wants to be a nun," Jamie was saying. "And I think she does, but not because she has a true calling to the Church. God didn't bring her across an ocean to land in a convent orphanage so He could hang wings on her back. She landed in that orphanage because Geoffrey Fitzhugh's twin brother wanted her there. And as much as we wanted to take her into our own family, it hasn't been bad for her. She found peace inside those stone walls. She can mother the children, and I ask you, what kind of man would I be to take her from all that because I want her to be the mother of my own lads and lassies?"

Gordon curled his fingers around the hat brim, tightly. "Why are you telling me these things?"

"Because I've known Mary Margaret Quinn my whole life and I fancy I know her as well as anyone." Jamie's legs were braced wide apart, his chest filled with the air he breathed in.

His face was so close Gordon could see the flaring of his nostrils, the tight creases at the corner of his mouth. The threat in his eyes.

"Don't do to my Maggie what the earl did to her mother," he said. "Fine, rich gentleman you might be, but I would kill you for that."

Gordon sat on the blue leather seat, still as stone, his mind racing. The wet, coal-scented wind twisted the window curtains and plucked at his hair. The sky was dark, the towering buildings darker, and the driving lamps shone a weak yellow light inside the carriage. Gordon saw none of it, felt none of it.

He jumped when something landed on the seat beside him. He looked down as Lucky settled his head in his lap.

"You need a bath, old boy," he said, fondling the dog's ears. He cupped the dog's face and lifted it, then shook his head. "I wonder why she didn't name you Beauty, since you seem to have made a virtue of ugliness."

The thought made him smile. He tried to imagine Maggie as a child. It was a given she hadn't worn dresses of sprigged muslin while she played tea party with a miniature tea service made from real bone china. She probably ran around the stables with holes in her stockings and skinned knees and straw in her hair. And he thought if it weren't for the privations of poverty, such freedom made for a happier childhood.

Hadn't Maggie herself told him she thought her childhood in Ireland was good? But then, his Maggie would always see the rainbow in the clouds.

His Maggie? Just when did that possessive slip into his vocabulary?

The dog lifted his paw and slapped at his hand. Gordon went back to stroking the mutt, unmindful of the mud and stink that would surely ruin his good kid gloves.

"So tell me, Lucky, old boy, just what was Mr. James O'Connor trying to tell me back there—other than the obvious point that he thinks I'm a royal bastard set on seducing the woman he loves?"

So was he? Had he been fooling himself all along that he wanted Maggie only as an aid to winning his daughter when, he had to admit, he'd been aware of her as a desirable woman from the first moment he sat beside her in the concert hall?

The carriage swayed as it took a wide turn, and then they were leaving the noises of the city behind. It was a twenty-minute drive to Drew's estate.

Rebecca would already be there.

Rebecca loved the idea of becoming Mrs. Gordon Kincaid, but she felt nothing for Clara beyond a polite tolerance and his feelings for Rebecca didn't go much beyond a polite tolerance either. What a bleak life for all of them that would be.

He straightened his bad leg, stretching it to the side. His heart was beating too fast and his chest was too tight to breath. And the pictures playing through his mind were those of a woman, head tilted and light dancing in her black hair while her fingers caressed the strings of a harp. A woman with shimmering green eyes holding a child in her arms, his child. Maggie, patting his shoulder while his arms encircled her hips and he buried his face in her skirt.

"God save me, Lucky, old boy," he said, and his voice shook. "I love her."

Chapter 10

The mother superior sat behind her desk. She did not gesture to the chair or ask Maggie to sit, so Maggie stood.

"I'm assigning your teaching duties to Sister Elizabeth," said Mother Bernadette.

Maggie gripped the back of the chair by the top rung. "Why?" She was utterly miserable: Alice's near-drowning, Father Fitz's departure, Clare and Dr. Kincaid. Without teaching to occupy her mind, she would surely go mad. "Is it the accident? I promise I'll watch over my students. They'll not breathe, that I won't know it."

"Do you think me so small that I blame you for an accident, Maggie?" Mother Bernadette waved her hand, as if dismissing such nonsense. "Mr. Fielding has shown great interest in Alice these last days," she said with a smile threatening in her eyes. "Perhaps the Lord works in mysterious ways."

Maggie swallowed, unsure of the direction this conversation was taking. "Perhaps." She looked at the ceiling, the floor, the corner of the maple desk, everywhere except Mother Bernadette's oval face. "Mr. Fielding is unmarried," she ventured.

The wooden chair creaked as Mother Bernadette shifted in her seat. "It's not often that one of our children is wanted by two homes."

This was so sadly true, Maggie could say nothing.

Mother Bernadette sighed. "I believe our Clara is Dr. Kincaid's true daughter. I would like to believe Dr. Kincaid would be a true father. But I will not dismiss the Cromwells' suit until I'm more certain of Dr. Kincaid's commitment."

"Yes, Mother," she said humbly, recognizing the words as a reprimand and accepting them as such.

"Both girls, Alice and Clara, have been invited by Mr. Fielding to visit his estate. You will accompany them."

Blessed Saint Brigid. Her throat went suddenly dry and her palms sweaty. "And Dr. Kincaid?" she asked in a hoarse voice.

"He will be there, of course, as will Miss Hays. Does that bother you?"

Maggie lifted her head. "A little." A lot. "You could send Sister Agatha in my place?"

She watched Mother Bernadette write something in a notebook. She gripped the chair rung a little tighter while she waited. She didn't even know what she wanted Mother Bernadette to say. Even Father Fitz had asked her not to abandon Clare and Dr. Kincaid in their time of need. But she remembered his other words, the earthly words: *Do not give your heart.*

Mother Bernadette set her pen down and closed the notebook. "I could and I will if the assignment is too much for you. I chose you because you're not a nun and will be less conspicuous as a houseguest, both girls are fond of you and I have no doubt you'll see to their welfare while they're there."

Maggie's heart was pounding. A thousand thoughts possessed her, none of them she could put into words. Suddenly she realized how contemptible she was, putting her own fears above Clare's needs and Alice's chance for a home. She drew a deep breath and then relaxed her sweaty grip on the chair. "I'll do my best, Mother."

"I never doubted that." Mother Bernadette allowed a small smile, then she leaned back in her seat, her hands clasped together at the edge of her desk. "I've given a great deal of thought to a conversation I had with Father Fitzhugh, and come to the conclusion we've all done you a grave disservice, out of kindness maybe, but a disservice nonetheless."

"It was no disservice to give me a home."

"And you have no debt to repay by dedicating your life to the Church," said Mother Bernadette with steel in her voice. "You must experience something of the world before you make your decision to leave it. That is the other reason I chose you to accompany the girls to the Fielding estate."

Maggie narrowed her eyes against the glare of the sun through the window, nearly shivering at the memory of a golden-haired man with dark, troubled eyes; remembering how she had felt when his arms went around her.

After a pause, Mother Bernadette said, "When you return, I'll make my decision concerning Clara's future."

"And my future?" asked Maggie, keeping her voice low to hide the trembling inside her.

"Only you can make that decision." Mother Bernadette looked at her gravely. "I pray that when the time comes, you make it for the right reasons."

Maggie tried to explain to the two children that they were on a home visit, stressing the *visit,* but they would not understand. There was a wild elation in them, already spinning daydreams of fathers and homes of their own filled with puppies and kittens and china dolls. She knew Clare had already made her choice; not even a five-year-old female could resist the man with his charming winks and roguish smiles. From Clare's perspective, when put up against the dour Reverend Cromwell, Dr. Kincaid was a hands-down winner in the father sweepstakes.

It hurt a little, to have been the most important person in Clare's life, and now, and now . . . She would not think such selfish thoughts.

The estate house she saw from the coach window was large, three stories of white-painted brick, a symmetrical box in its form with long windows on either side of a large door. The Palladian windows and fanlight over the wide entrance reminded her of Castle Lachlan. The door stood open and she saw Mr. Fielding coming down the half-circle stairs. She leaned over and straightened Clare's hair bow, Alice's collar, and then the coach door was opening and Mr. Fielding was offering a hand.

"Ladies," he said genially. "I trust the trip was not too unpleasant." He gave Maggie a smile and lifted first a wiggling Clare, followed by a more sedate Alice, from the vehicle. Maggie exited on her own.

It was pure joy to breathe in clean country air. She turned around slowly, just looking, imagining how wonderful it would be to wake up each morning and look out a window to see nothing but lawn and trees with the sun peeking over distant hills. She had lived with nature for a backdrop once, long ago when Ireland with its mists and moors and green, green turf was still home.

The girls were already racing, their little boots crunching the white pebbles on the drive. She opened her mouth to call to them, but Mr. Fielding stopped her with a touch on her elbow.

"Let them be for now," he said indulgently. "It must feel good after being cramped inside that carriage."

"Aye, Mr. Fielding, but—"

"No buts and no Mr. Fielding," he said. "You're my guest as well as the girls, so I expect you to call me Drew and you will be Maggie. We don't stand on ceremony at Burleigh, I'm afraid."

He was a kind man, she decided. Not an elegant aristocrat like Gordon Kincaid, but handsome in that rugged, wind-off-the-sea manner of American males. She did feel out of her element, and had a sudden wish she'd let the mother superior send Sister Agatha in her stead, but she could tell he was sincere.

"We've a large number of houseguests expected—the races, you know, and the house party was planned before the mother superior gave her permission for this visit," he was saying, "so I must apologize for the accommodations."

"I'm certain whatever you've set aside for us will be more than adequate."

He laughed and scooped Alice into his arms. "For this little lady and Clara," he said, grinning back at Alice, who had wrapped her skinny legs around his waist and was leaning backward, trusting him not to let her fall. "They'll be off the old nursery with all the toys that survived me and my sisters' childhood. It's you I'm worried about; I'm afraid all we had left for you was the governess's room, and Alice tells me you grew up in a castle."

"As a stableman's daughter. We lived in a thatched-roof cottage behind the stables."

"Ah, the sweet smell of the stables."

"I trust you built upwind of yours?"

"Maggie, my dear, you are going to be a most refreshing houseguest," he said, laughing and setting Alice back on the ground.

Clare squealed then and Maggie looked over to see flaxen curls flying as the child raced across the lawn. Gordon was strolling in their direction with Miss Hays on his arm, both of them dressed as if they'd been riding. Miss Hays wore a stylish habit the color of primroses with a smart little hat angled on her sausage curls. Maggie self-consciously brushed her hand down the front of her plain black skirt. She nudged her chin up and exchanged a small smile with Drew.

Gordon shook off Miss Hays in time to catch Clare as she flung herself at him. He hefted her in the air and she squealed again. Maggie could see his rakish smile from across the lawn. Clear afternoon sunlight set his hair aflame.

She felt dizzy, as if she were the one being swung around

and around, not wee Clare. She didn't know who she was or what she was doing here.

He set Clare on the ground, taking her hand in his own as she wobbled a bit, and they began walking toward the drive. How could she have forgotten in a matter of a few days how improbably beautiful he was, how potently, elegantly male?

"I'll have a maid show you to your room and send the luggage up," said Drew, grasping her elbow and guiding her toward the house. "You take your time getting settled in, maybe treat yourself to a nap before dinner. We'll take the girls on a tour to entertain them for a few hours."

"But—"

Gordon had stepped directly in her path. Maggie's gaze traveled from polished riding boots, up the long length of tight camel britches and fitted blue woolen jacket. He didn't say anything, and when their eyes met she saw a peculiar tautness to his face, dark midnight eyes—no pirate smiles for *Maggie-mine.*

She pushed at a lock of hair that had come loose during the confinement with two active little girls inside the carriage. The whole braided coil seemed in danger of unraveling, but in her current state of agitation, she couldn't think what to do about it.

"No buts," said Gordon in that terrible, stern voice. "You look like death warmed over."

Hell's bells, thought Gordon. From the look Drew just shot him, he must have sounded like the complete ass he knew himself to be. But she did look awful; shadows under her eyes so dark they looked like bruises, pale, translucent skin, and he'd swear she was going to start shaking any second now.

Her quick gaze went to Rebecca, still clinging to his forearm, and a blush warmed her face before she nudged her chin up and looked him full in the eye. And it all happened in the space of time it took him to draw in a breath.

Damn. He'd bungled it, and bungled it good. Practiced all morning how he was going to approach her, how to recover from falling apart in front of her. Thought up scheme after scheme to dump Becca, who was clinging to him like a leech, so he could greet Clara and Maggie alone when they arrived. In one stupid outburst, he'd blown it all.

"Maggie," he said, softening his voice. She was already on the front steps. She stopped, one trembling hand lifted and pushing ineffectively at a lock of shiny black hair that wanted to escape and blow around her face.

"It's all right, Dr. Kincaid," she said, her voice thick with the brogue, a sign he was beginning to recognize as deep emotion. "I'll unpack and then come for the wee *cailíns*."

He wondered if any other man had seen the vulnerability she hid beneath that strong, upthrust jaw, but when he glanced at Drew, he knew he was not alone—which made him think of James O'Connor giving her up to the nuns because he loved her—and a wave of possession came over him so strong he almost staggered.

"Maggie," he said, one more effort. She followed the maid without a backward glance.

"We'll be somewhere around the stables, Maggie," said Drew to her retreating back.

"Aye."

Too late, he stepped away from Becca, shaking off her possessive grasp on his forearm. Rebecca patted the sausage curl that hung beneath her plumed hat and looked at the children. Her she-cat smile faded.

"If you'll excuse me, gentlemen," she said, "I think I'll retire to my room for a nap as well."

"Of course, Rebecca," said Drew in a dry tone of voice. "Come along, little ladies. We've a new litter of barn kittens."

Silently, Gordon took Clara's hand and followed Drew.

He lasted ten minutes and then left Clara with the others, playing with the kittens. He climbed the stairs to the third floor, his mind jumping from concern over Maggie's health, to his own frightfully impolitic behavior, to displeasure with the accommodations assigned her, on the third floor with the children and servants. It wasn't his home and there was nothing he could do to alter the situation, but he didn't want her thinking she was consigned to servant status and feared she'd jump to that erroneous conclusion.

She had dismissed the maid and was unpacking the girls' clothes. He leaned against the doorjamb, watching her as she worked with her back toward him. He wanted to step into the room, take her in his arms and tell her he had been a sorry ass, then kiss her until she was breathless to prove his point. She must have sensed his presence, because she spoke first.

"You've bought the girls dresses," she said in an even tone that might mean anything.

"It wasn't meant as a bribe. We wanted them to feel like they fit in with the other children who'll be here."

She was silent a moment. "It was kind of you, then."

A little less Irish in her voice; he took that as a positive sign. She turned. He didn't know what he expected to see, the severe, convent-raised schoolmarm or the brave Irish lass with hurt in her eyes.

He saw only Maggie, with her head tilted slightly, exposing the pale curve of her neck between stark white collar and a sensual upsweep of shiny hair. She was backlit by the sun pouring through the window so that gold motes played against her black hair and dusted her skin, a vision that exploded inside him, almost sending him to his knees with the force.

While he stood in the doorway paralyzed with lust, she withdrew a little navy blue dress from the carpetbag and shook it out. "And isn't it a lovely room," she said, slipping the dress onto a hanger and walking to the clothes cupboard. "All pale blues like the sky and pink like when the morning sun hits the mist."

He pushed himself away from the doorjamb, giving a slow perusal to the children's room, seeing a very ordinary room with nothing of pink mists and blue skies. On the far wall, the connecting door to the tiny accommodations she'd been assigned stood open.

"Your room," he said. "It's only until—"

"Enough is as good as plenty, Dr. Kincaid. 'Tis more than I'm used to, with such a fine view of the meadow where the horses are running."

More silver linings. She could probably find that fool pot of gold at the end of the rainbow. And he still hadn't apologized or set his mind at ease on those awful black circles under her eyes. He stepped into the room. She actually jerked backward. He swallowed a curse and tamped down his lust, taking her by the hand and drawing her to the window.

"Sore throat?" he asked, tilting her head back with his hand. Sunlight glinted gold in her eyes as she shook her head. "Headache? Body ache?" He stroked the ridge of her cheekbone with his thumb. No fever. "Chills?"

Her throat convulsed as she swallowed. "Healthy as a horse."

"Someone once told me 'tis a sin to lie."

She began to smile, then lost it as her mouth twisted down instead. She held the back of her fisted hand hard against her mouth and blinked rapidly. He drew her into his arms and she stiffened, as taut as one of her fiddle strings.

"What is it, angel?" he asked quietly.

"N-n-nothing."

She felt even better in his arms than in his imagination, warm, lusciously soft and feminine, and smelled faintly of jasmine and little children. He rested his chin on the top of her head and that was good too. She was tall enough that he didn't have a permanent crick in his neck when he tried to look at her.

She was miserable.

"Umm, nothing except Father Fitz, Clara—and a bastard who goes by the name of Kincaid. Maybe my girl has had a little too much on her mind these last weeks?"

"Clare is your girl and Miss Hays is your—your—"

He lifted her face with his thumb. Irish eyes, so very green, sable-lashed. His own eyes followed the arch of her brow, the curve of facial bone and full, moist lips. She was a

woman, all sensual curves. She was Maggie, with all the irre-
sistible allure of the night sky, and he felt himself falling,
down and down into nothingness the way it happens in
dreams.

He would have stood there forever in a free fall, but she
broke it with those decadent black lashes masking her eyes
and a defensive turn of her head.

"I haven't proposed to Miss Hays, Maggie. She's nothing
more than a friend."

"That may be, but she is expecting your proposal and you
know you need a mother for wee Clare."

He let her go and she stepped back, not looking at him but
watching her hands twisting together in front of her waist.

"I did. I do. But I've been thinking maybe you were right
after all. Maybe the woman I choose for Clara's mother
should be the same woman I'd choose for a wife. A real
marriage."

"I never said—"

"You didn't have to say it." He smiled faintly. "Your eyes
speak volumes, Irish."

Her skirts made a soft swishing sound as she turned away.
He stepped forward one step, not allowing her such an easy
escape. He lifted his hand and placed it on her shoulder, just
resting, a subtle restraint and an insinuation of something
more.

"Your doctor is sending up a dinner tray and his special
herbal tea. Miss Quinn will sleep the sleep of the angels
tonight while the two bachelors practice fatherhood." He
gave her shoulder a gentle squeeze. "Tomorrow, Dr. Kincaid
and a rested Miss Quinn will start over. Fair enough?"

For far too long, he had dared not hope for anything, and
now he stood here, hoping for it all. But if he were to tell her
that, she would only cloister herself away from him. He had
to win her trust first.

First her trust, then her love, and then her hand in marriage. His name alone would shelter her from some of the

bigotry she faced so bravely. Hell, he'd use his physical strength if need be.

To everyone else, even her little orphans, she was *my Maggie*. He was going to take Maggie Quinn and make her *his*.

Chapter 11

It was a soft dawn with a fine misty rain cloaking the track at Pimlico. Maggie turned her face up to the sky, loving the touch of raindrops on her cheeks. She felt herself transported in time and miles, back to a childhood filled with misty mornings in a verdant land where sleek running horses were pampered like kings.

She thought her middle name might better be *guilt,* her being here at the track with Gordon and Drew while the children slept tight in their beds at Burleigh. But the appeal had been so great, it hadn't taken an excessive amount of cajoling on Gordon's part for her to accept his invitation to this morning's workout.

The grandstand, painted a whimsical shade of violet, was empty of all but a few spectators. At this early hour, with no races scheduled until tomorrow's big stakes, the atmosphere was tranquil. People moved in and out of the drifting gray mists, wraithlike, their voices muffled by the rain.

"Warm enough?" asked Gordon. He placed his hand at the small of her back.

"Aye, 'tis a fine rubber coat you've loaned me," she teased, glancing down at the worn, cracked garment that hung from her shoulders like a tent.

"Enough is as good as plenty." He gave her a teasing wink. She laughed. He steered her toward the white fence rimming the oval, where several men leaned against the rail, watching the horses while sipping coffee from steaming tin mugs. Drew moved over, making room for her next to him. Gordon stood tall, like a solid wall behind her.

She rested her elbows on the rail, her chin cradled on her curled hands, watching the horses cut through the mist on their morning workout. Her pulse seemed to pound in time with the thundering hoofbeats as the excitement mounted in her.

Sleek, powerful Thoroughbreds, their hooves flashed like silver scythes, spewing up clumps of mud from the boggy track. The jockeys in their peaked caps appeared absurdly small, each bent low over the streaming mane of his large animal.

"Which one is yours?" she asked, speaking to both men.

"There's Reckless, just now coming around the oval," said Drew, pointing to a chestnut who was running full out, straining every muscle and sinew. "Put your money tomorrow on my Reckless."

Gordon's hand landed on her shoulder. "Don't listen to him. His odds were five to two last time I checked," he said. "Put your money on Shenandoah."

"What a lovely name," she murmured.

"It's one of the old traditions at Riverbend that the women name the foals. My sister-in-law named this one." He was quiet for a moment, then said in a low voice, "Maybe you'll name the next one."

The wind blew up, bringing with it not the scent of the rain and the turf but of the man behind her, a scent of maleness and danger and temptation. The ground vibrated beneath her feet as horses thundered by in front of them. She remained still, frozen in place by a hand resting lightly on her shoulder and words already dissipated into the morning mists.

After a while, he said, "Would you like to walk back to the shed row?"

She found her voice. "Aye," she said, and was surprised to discover that her legs still worked as they should.

The area where the horses were temporarily stabled was a scene of concentrated activity. Steam from the horses' flanks rose in the cool air as they were unsaddled and walked. Trainers crouched low to the wet ground beside still giants, gentle hands checking fragile legs and hocks for strains and bruises.

Metal clanged against metal as somewhere a farrier fashioned a shoe. The smells she breathed in were the old ones, of horse sweat and sweet hay and crushed grass. The scene was a vivid picture out of her childhood and her breath caught in her throat. She was so intent on watching the activity, she almost planted her boot in a pile of steaming horse dung.

"Watch your step," said Gordon, reaching out to assist her.

He didn't let go of her arm and she knew she should pull away, but she didn't. She saw Franklin trailing behind a bay being led in, his head bent as he studied the bay's gait.

"Franklin's your trainer!" she said.

"Franklin's my everything." Gordon's face grew serious. "Before the war, he was a slave on a neighboring estate, one of those places that fulfilled every nightmare the abolitionists preached from their pulpits. He's a good man, despite that hell, and knows his horses. I'd be lost without him." He reached out and brushed the hair at her temple. "Could I get you some coffee to warm you up?"

"Sounds nice. Could I walk with your trainer?"

His lips turned up in a half-smile. "Go ahead, Irish. I brought you here to enjoy yourself."

He gave her a wink again before walking away. When he

returned, she was holding Shenandoah's halter while Franklin crouched down, oiling a hoof. She patted the mare's muzzle and smiled at Gordon as he approached.

"She's a fine filly, m'l—"

Blessed Saint Brigid, she bit it off just in time. *M'lord,* as if she were the little girl addressing the earl. If he caught her mistake, he ignored it.

"She's got heart," he said in an easy drawl. "But I don't like running her in the mud—she pushes herself too hard." His gloved hand reached out and stroked the mare's neck. It was a gentle touch, a caress. "She's too valuable a mare to waste her in a track fall."

Watching him, the emotion playing across his face, Maggie decided the horse's value as a brood mare might happen to be a secondary concern to the man's compassionate nature. She thought the better of him for that. "Will you scratch her, then, tomorrow?"

Gordon squinted up at the sky. The mist was thinning, the sun threatening to break through. "No need to decide now," he said. "We'll see what the morrow brings."

"This gal knows her horses," said Franklin, pushing up from his crouch. He pulled a red bandanna from his hip pocket and wiped his fingers.

"She grew up at the Lachlan estate in Ireland," said Gordon. "Her stepfather was head trainer there."

"I'll be," muttered Franklin, jerking his head around to study her. "They had a three-year-old took the Irish Derby and Epsom Downs back in . . . '59, I think."

Maggie nodded. "Caprice. He was my da's pride."

A wide, nearly toothless grin broke out on his face. "So, you going to tell your new friend Franklin your da's secret to winning?"

Maggie pressed her face against the mare's neck, rubbing her cheek on the damp, sleek hair, drawing in the hot scent of powerful horse. The mare turned her head, staring at Maggie out of large, intelligent eyes, then nuzzled her nose into Maggie's neck. Maggie laughed, patted the bay and stepped back.

"She told me she wouldn't be minding some milk and fresh eggs in with her oats tonight. A dinner like that before a race gives a girl heart, you see."

"Eggs," muttered Franklin. "Who'd ever guess fresh eggs?"

"I think we can trust her," said Gordon, winking at Franklin while he passed her the coffee. "Unless she's already wagered a month's salary on Drew's Reckless."

"It's a cinch tip," said Maggie, holding back a silly smile. She took a sip from the tin mug and choked, grimacing and shuddering. "Sugar!"

"Well, of course. I saw you put three sugar cubes in one small cup of coffee that night at Father Fitz's dinner," said Gordon, taking the tin mug back.

"That was because you . . . you . . ."

He was watching her face, looking somewhat aggrieved, and then he broke into that sudden, dazzling smile. "Do I make you nervous, Irish?"

She looked away, glancing around at Franklin's checkered cap, at a sparrow perched on a fence rail, a groom leading a sweating horse. She licked her lips, tasting the cool rain. When she looked back at Gordon, his dark eyes were focused on her mouth and he wasn't smiling anymore. She fought the urge to lick her lips again.

Her heart was racing like one of the fleet-footed fillies. It was as if she were floating somewhere just off the ground with no familiar earth beneath her feet. She stepped back and turned away, suddenly afraid—not of him, but of herself.

"I'll drop down here tonight before the party," she heard him say to Franklin, and then he was beside her, his warm hand once again at her back. "We have some children waiting on us at Burleigh, don't we, Maggie?"

She nodded and fell into pace beside him, carefully watching where she placed her feet.

Several hours later, she found herself leaned up against another paddock fence, watching Gordon lead Clara around on a spotted pony. Alice sat on the top rail beside her, awaiting another turn, while at her feet, old Lucky lounged with his tongue lolling out of his mouth. A groom led another pony into the paddock. Maggie smiled at Drew as he came up and leaned against the fence beside Alice.

"I wish I could play today, little lady, but I'm afraid I can't," he said, putting his arm around the child's waist. "There's another pony saddled up, though, so you don't have to take turns."

Maggie jerked her head away from whipping pigtails as Alice swung her head around.

"Really?" Alice's smile was so big, so real, Maggie's heart gave a sudden pitch.

"Really," he said, taking Alice by the waist and setting her over the fence. "Go on," he encouraged with a slight nod and matching smile. Alice scampered away, her pigtails flying behind her. Drew's hand reached down, his fingers working the brown ruff on old Lucky's neck while both of them watched the groom lift Alice to the pony's back.

"You've a big heart," said Maggie softly.

"Old Lucky here, you mean?" He chuckled. "I think Gordon plans on shipping the mutt home to foul up the bloodlines in his brother's retrievers."

"I was speaking more of wee Alice. I've never seen her so carefree." She gave a tiny laugh. "Timid, shy Alice. Look at her now, riding the ponies, laughing. 'Tis a miracle you've worked this past week."

His face grew serious. "You've got it backwards, Maggie. That day at the park, watching you and Sister Agatha with those children . . . shoot, it made me realize just how selfish a man I've been. Then when that child almost died . . ."

He leaned his weight on his forearms and lifted one booted foot to the bottom rung. "She's done something to my heart I can't explain, but I want to give her the moon just for the pleasure of seeing the smile on that serious little face."

"Mother Bernadette won't hold it against you that you're unmarried. Not many of our children are wanted by good, loving homes and it's the children's happiness she really places first in her own heart."

"I can only hope."

Maggie hoped that would be true for Clare as well. Drew tipped his head and slanted her a glance. "I've got a stable full of riding horses if you want to ride this afternoon."

"I haven't ridden since I was twelve years old."

"It's not something one forgets."

"Maybe not, but I haven't suitable clothing for it all the same."

Gordon was leading the spotted pony toward them and she smiled again as she returned Clare's wave. Her smile dimmed when she saw Miss Hays working her way across the back lawn, holding the hem of a turquoise riding habit just at her boot tops and dodging the children's croquet balls as if they were steaming horse droppings.

"I can probably rustle up something from the trunks in the attic," said Drew. "Might not be the height of fashion, but it would be serviceable."

"What fashion?" asked Gordon, coming within hearing distance.

"Maggie needs a riding habit," explained Drew.

Gordon gave her an appraising, very male look. "Did you pack something for the dinner dance?" he asked.

"I've nothing suitable for a dinner dance."

"That green dress you wore for the concert would do. Didn't you bring it?"

She shook her head.

"My Maggie doesn't dance," announced Clare from the back of the pony. Gordon turned his head toward his daughter. He lifted one brow. "My Maggie's going to be a nun," said Clare. "I don't think nuns are allowed to dance. That's why she sent Jamie O'Connor away when he came courting— 'cause she's going to be a nun. Nuns can't get married either."

Gordon turned his head back. Their gazes locked and for an instant she thought she saw a vulnerability in his eyes, but it was gone so fast she couldn't be certain. Then that sudden, flashing smile lit his face. "That true, Irish? Jamie O'Connor?"

He drawled the poor man's name out so slow she thought it might be next Friday before he reached the last syllable. She pushed away from the fence. "Jamie O'Connor is a fine, hard-working man, Dr. Kincaid. You'll not be making fun of him."

If Gordon recognized her temper rising to a low boil, he ignored it and her both, directing his attention to Drew. "Can you send someone back into the city?"

"Green dress?" said Drew with laughter tingeing his voice.

"You got it."

"Gordon?" It was Miss Hays's voice and there was a whine in her tone.

Maggie thought she saw Gordon's shoulders droop, and for a sinful second she was overcome by spiteful pleasure at his misery.

"You promised to take me riding," said Miss Hays in her little-girl's manner. She hesitated, tilting her head to the side while she studied Clare. "I suppose we could take the child with us," she said dubiously.

Clare's happy expression crumpled and she tucked her chin as her little hand reached out to fist in the pony's mane. Maggie allowed a heartbeat for Gordon to say something, anything, to Miss Hays, but he was looking at his daughter, reaching for Clare's hand, maybe to pat it, maybe to lift her down.

"The child has a name," said Maggie as she clutched her skirts in her fists. "It's Clar-*a*."

She swung around, heading toward the back lawn, where the children of other houseguests were squealing in a game of croquet. She'd taken three strides when she stopped and swung back. "And she's not *Irish*."

As a parting shot, it wasn't much, but it eased her boiling temper to a slow simmer.

According to Letty, the green dress was suitable for the races, totally unsuitable for a dinner dance.

"I've my gray silk," said Maggie. She went to the clothes cupboard and pulled out the simple dress, then held it in front of her body. Letty shook her head, clucking a little so she sounded like one of the hens in the chicken house.

"Don't you have anything—you know—" The maid's hands fluttered just above her ample bosom and finally landed on her own shoulders as she pantomimed a low-cut, off-the-shoulder gown.

Maggie smiled. "No. Nothing like that," she said, returning the gray silk to the closet. "I'll just eat my dinner with the children and be the happier for it."

Letty's forehead creased in a thoughtful frown. "Hold that gray one up again."

Maggie sighed a little, then humored the older woman, who was being so kind to both her and her young charges. Letty stood with one arm across her waistline, chin propped in the other hand. Her soft brown eyes studied Maggie for a long minute. Suddenly her face exploded in a grin.

"Mr. Fielding has five sisters, you know," said Letty as she turned for the door. Maggie watched her leave, wondering what Mr. Fielding's sisters had to do with gray silk dresses. Twenty minutes later, she found out.

Letty bustled back into the tiny room with a gown draped over her arm. She held it up in front of her and the material cascaded to the floor, shimmering like moonlight—a silvery creation with metallic threads interwoven in light gray silk to create a fall of light and prisms. Maggie gasped, her fisted hands going up to her face.

"I can't wear that! Whatever were you thinking?"

Letty's smile broadened as she withdrew one hand from beneath the folds of material. "I was thinking these pearls in your hair would be perfect."

She was an impostor, the cottager's daughter dressed as a princess attending the castle ball, but Maggie knew silvery gowns and strings of pearls did not change the woman inside.

Drew Fielding was more than a kind man; he was a saint, altering his seating arrangements so she was placed as his dinner partner. With his subtle aid, she made it through seven courses, each with a different wine, and dessert. Not that she ate much; she was too worried she might spill something on a dress that must have cost more than she would earn in a lifetime.

His table was long, seating all twenty of his houseguests for dinner. Gordon had been placed far down the other side between Drew's sister and Miss Hays. Once, she made the mistake of looking down the length of the damask tablecloth to discover his intense, cobalt gaze fixed on her. She was careful not to look that way again.

It seemed as if a hundred faces crowded the drawing rooms now, with more and more carriages rolling up the graveled drive. Drew had excused himself and was standing with his sister in the large entrance foyer to receive his guests. Maggie wandered into the drawing room, where most of the furniture had been removed and the thick Persian carpet rolled up for dancing. The musicians, partially hidden in an alcove, were tuning their instruments.

The large room shimmered in the illumination from the shiny crystal and brass gas jets. Sterling candelabras with a multitude of branches, each holding a lit candle, had been placed before every pier mirror and in the window niches, reflecting the brilliance a thousand times over.

She assumed flowers must be the fashion this year, as most of the women seemed to be festooned with ribbons of real hothouse blossoms trailing down their skirts. In a strange reversal of practicality, artificial flowers adorned their elaborate coiffures.

A set was forming for the first quadrille. She watched the dancers while a bittersweet ache filled her heart, remembering the country dances of her childhood, her grandfather stomping his foot in time with his fiddle while Mum whirled on a carpet of grass with partner after partner. A quadrille wasn't so different from a country dance, she thought.

She couldn't seem to pull her gaze away from Gordon. That ache squeezed her chest again as he drew Miss Hays into a graceful circle in time with the music floating from the alcove. The shimmering light played in the always tousled waves of his hair, etched the strong angles of his face.

"I'll be free in a few minutes." Maggie started and then looked up into Drew's rugged, kind face. He smiled faintly. "I don't believe for a minute you can't dance," he said as he held out a glass filled with a pale gold liquid. She took the glass as he continued, "You'll join me in a dance set when I can escape from the door?"

"Maybe. I—I—"

"No maybes." His smile faded. "You're my guest, Maggie," he said. "A most welcome guest in my home. Remember that."

She nodded and then lowered her lashes, studying the bubbles rising to the top of the glass. He touched her elbow gently and then he was gone. Once again, she was by herself in a roomful of people who moved around her as if she were as invisible to their eyes as the servants who carried silver trays laden with punch glasses through the crowd.

Another set was forming. Her heartbeat quickened when she caught sight of Gordon, alone now and circling the dancers in that sauntering, slightly hitching stride that was uniquely his own. He was headed toward her.

She set her glass on the marquetry table beside her and whirled around, making for the door like a titmouse escaping a tomcat. Her heartbeat slowed when she glanced over her shoulder to see if he followed and discovered he'd been waylaid by a fat little man with a mustache that reached all the way to his side-whiskers.

She spotted a window alcove off the main hall and ducked into it. She walked over to the long window, gazing out onto the side lawn, where couples strolled, illuminated by the soft glow of Chinese lanterns.

Idly, her fingers rubbed the rich velvet draperies that were cut fashionably long so they puddled in a half-circle on the parquet floor. She thought the nuns could probably fashion three dresses for little girls just from the amount of blue velvet wasted on the floor.

"The dancing is in the drawing room, Miss Quinn."

Maggie's eyes rolled, then she squared her shoulders and turned around to face Miss Hays. "Aye."

Miss Hays tossed her head, causing her ringlets to bounce. "Oh, I forgot," she said in a silky voice. "Nuns aren't allowed to dance." Her skirts rustled as she took several steps, stopping at a small inlaid table that held a collection of porcelain figurines. She picked up a shepherdess, rubbing the figurine with her gloved fingers. "I think Gordon is going to propose tonight."

Maggie swallowed down the sudden pain that wrenched her all the way to her toes. "I'm sure you're right."

Miss Hays tilted her head, slanting Maggie a glance from beneath her gold lashes. "I suppose you know he wants to adopt that child you're so fond of."

"And will you be making a good mother for wee Clare?"

Miss Hays lifted one ivory shoulder in a shrug. She turned a little and rearranged the figurines so the shepherdess stood beside the shepherd. Next, her white-gloved hand moved a small lamb to a position beside the paired shepherd and shepherdess. Maggie wanted to look away and couldn't make herself look away.

A knowing, self-satisfied smile lifted one corner of Miss Hays's mouth. "In case you're ever invited to a dinner party again, the little fork placed at the top of your dinner setting is for the fish course," she said.

Maggie turned back to the window, feeling as deflated as wee Clare. She wouldn't run, no matter how much she wanted to escape back upstairs with the children.

"I'll remember that, Miss Hays. It was kind of you to tell me."

"Oh, think nothing of it. An Irish immigrant couldn't be expected to know." She paused. "Miss Quinn, you know nothing of Gordon's world. I can at least teach the child manners."

Maggie longed to lean her head against the cool glass but kept her shoulders stiff and listened to the light sound of Miss Hays breathing, waiting for the next sting from the woman's nettled tongue. Instead, she heard the swish of silken petticoats as Miss Hays left the alcove, followed by a rich masculine voice coming from the hallway.

"Becca," he said, sounding surprised. "Have you seen Maggie?"

"No, Gordon. She must be hiding somewhere," said Miss Hays with a whisper of laughter in her voice. "They're playing a waltz. My favorite."

She didn't have to see them; she could imagine Miss Hays's fluttering eyelashes and the little gloved hand going to his forearm. Maggie leaned her forehead against the glass and listened to their footsteps until the sound was lost in the music.

Gordon went through the familiar rituals, making the idle party chat that had been bred into him. It took little of his concentration to make himself pleasant while his feet executed the dance steps to the strains of the orchestra. He cast another searching glance over his shoulder as he led Becca into a turn.

He couldn't find Maggie.

He'd seen her only twice since dinner. Once from halfway across the room when she'd whirled as if fleeing from him and he'd been stopped by old man Gearhart searching for tips on tomorrow's races; the second time when Drew led her out at the top of a country dance. Every man's head had turned to follow the vision of stately Maggie dressed in swaying moon shadows and starlight. Drew had been fielding good-natured jokes and pointed questions ever since. But Maggie had disappeared.

He felt like the stupid prince in the fairy tale who'd lost his fairy princess, except he didn't even have a slipper in his possession to help run her to ground. Not to mention he couldn't extricate himself from Becca, who'd attached herself to his side as if they *were* married.

He didn't want to hurt Becca's feelings—she'd been throwing herself at his feet since she was fourteen—and he'd been the kind friend of her older brother, gently discouraging her. He could kick himself for giving her the small encouragement she needed to jump to visions of wedding gowns and trousseaus.

He'd bitten back so many pointed, caustic remarks in the last hour, he wondered why his tongue wasn't bleeding. Becca moved closer in the execution of a glide, so close he could feel the stiff whalebone in her corset against his body. Gordon stepped back a proper arm's length and smiled down at her. "Your slippers are going to be worn through."

She batted her lashes. "No matter. I love dancing with you."

All the pretty words froze in his throat. This was the wrong woman in his arms and if she couldn't grasp that from his subtle signals, he'd have to be blunt. The music swelled and came to an end. He stepped back another step, for the first time in all his years in a ballroom failing to offer his arm to his dance partner. He bowed slightly as she reached for him.

"If you'll excuse me, Becca," he said, imitating a gentleman. "I'm going to look for Maggie."

Becca's nose wrinkled. "Maggie! It's about time that immigrant took the hint she doesn't belong here."

Damn him for a fool. He grabbed Becca by the arm, pulling her out of the drawing room, dodging bodies and questioning looks until he had her outside on the gallery. He made himself let go when what he wanted to do was squeeze her arm until he inflicted bruises.

"What the hell did you say to her?"

"No-nothing." Becca stretched herself like a cat against him. "I only told her . . . just mentioned . . ."

Gordon peeled her arm from around his neck, ignoring the wide-eyed, pouting look on her face. He stepped back, disgusted with her, with himself. "Mentioned what, Becca?"

"That you were going to propose to me tonight."

A stillness settled into every line of his body. "I took you to a concert, a picnic with two dozen children, and on both occasions Maggie was there," he said in a hushed voice. "Every other minute we've spent together has been at your instigation. If you expected a proposal from that, I'm sorry, Becca, but you were jumping to conclusions."

"But I've loved you forever, Gordon. Since I was a little girl—before you ever married Augusta." Becca leaned forward against the railing as a hysterical giggle came out of her throat. "I've waited for you all these years, waited for you to get over losing her."

She turned suddenly, her hands gripping the rail behind her. "Can't you see that woman's all wrong for you? She's—she's not like us."

"Thank God for that." He looked away, over her shoulder to where Chinese lanterns shed a flickering light on the manicured paths. "Maggie loves my daughter," he said quietly. "If there was nothing else to her—and there is much, much more to her—I'd love her for that alone."

For a long minute the only sound came from the music drifting through the windows. Becca pushed away from the railing. She looked up, gazing at him as if she thought he might speak. He had nothing to say, so he looked away again.

"I'm not dancing anymore tonight, thank you," she said woodenly. "I've a headache coming on."

"Yes." He stepped back another step and bowed. "I'm sorry, Becca."

Her petticoats rustled as she moved past him, through the open door, where she vanished in the crush of milling bodies.

Gordon stood alone on the gallery, her wooden voice echoing in his brain.

Gordon pushed open the door to the nursery, softly so as not to awaken the children. Alice and Clara, each in a narrow bed, slept soundly. Letty sat in a deep, tufted armchair beside a shielded lamp. She sat up straight when she saw him.

Maggie, he mouthed.

Letty came to the door. "She's come up twice to check on

the children." A shadow of sadness seemed to pass across Letty's face. "She's not downstairs dancing? She looked such a vision, I thought . . . hoped . . ."

"I'll find her." He closed his eyes. "I'll find her."

"Yes. Do."

Gordon moved slowly toward the stairs, trying to hide the limp.

"If it helps any, she took her fiddle with her the last time—said she was going to play. I just assumed she meant with the orchestra."

His hand curled around the wrought-iron balustrade. "Thank you, Letty. That does help."

The sounds of the party filtered up to the second floor, the buzz of voices and shrill laughter, the wafting tones of the instruments. He stopped in his own room, not bothering to turn on the gas or light a candle but moving through the shadows to the window.

He gazed out over the back lawn of the Burleigh estate, wondering where in the rolling meadows she was hiding, worried she would take a chill in the cool night air, scared witless she might have run away altogether. A woman alone, at night, in unfamiliar terrain.

Maggie wouldn't run, especially when she thought her orphans needed her.

A cloud drifted in front of the full moon, passed on, and he saw it then, the white-peaked roof of the summerhouse set in a dip of ground near the river. Far enough away that she might feel comfortable there, safe enough to play her violin.

No one saw him as he left the house by the rear. He crossed the back lawn and topped a small rise. His chest tightened when he heard the haunting sound of a solitary violin. He followed the sublime notes all the way to the summerhouse. He saw her in profile then, standing in the middle of the circular pavilion, her head tilted over the violin.

He stopped in his tracks, arrested by the picture of Maggie sketched in moon glow, dressed in folds of starlight, her hair piled high on her head and threaded with lustrous pearls. It was a pagan vision: black hair and white shoulders, tall, slim body clothed in draping lengths of shimmering silvers and pale, lustrous gray. A Druid priestess within an ancient stone circle, calling the gods with her haunting music.

Slowly, slowly, his feet carried him the final distance and up the single step—inside the circle, drawn inexorably by a green-eyed sorceress.

His shadow touched her first and she missed a note, then recovered herself while her fingers tightened on the bow. He stopped just behind her, slightly to one side, so close she could see the shiny tips of his leather dancing slippers. He stood for a long time—tall, brooding male, saying nothing. Her music slowed, quivered, then stopped, suspended in the stillness. Maggie dropped her arms, the violin dangling against her knee. She could not move or speak or even breathe.

He reached out and took the violin from her trembling hand, then the bow, laying both on the built-in seat. He clasped her by the shoulders and turned her. She looked up into his face—this man with all the golden beauty of the archangels, this man who was mystery, and pain—and deep, wondrous joy.

"Dance with me," he said.

"Nay—"

He placed his finger against her lips, silencing her. He took her hand into his own and his arm circled her waist. She moved from necessity as he took a step and pulled her into his motion.

Their music was the chirp of crickets and soft night breezes, the whisper of a man's breath and a woman's heartbeat. Their ballroom was lit by stars and moonbeams and it was theirs alone.

The universe spun all around her, and she shivered. He pulled her closer into his warmth. For a moment, his leg pressed against her hip and she felt the heat and hardness of his body, then he took another step and they parted.

She breathed in the scent of a man's clean sweat, and the perfume of an enchanted, mystical night. Tears stung her cheeks. When had it happened, this love for a man she must not love?

"Maggie," he murmured into her hair. He slowed, another turn, a glide . . . and then he stopped.

She was shattering into a million pieces, an exploding star, falling, falling, falling through the endless night sky. She hid her face in the tucks of his dress shirt.

He touched her chin, lifting her face so she had to look at him. The faintest of smiles touched his lips as he brushed the moisture from her cheeks with his thumbs.

"What did she say to you?" he asked in a quiet voice.

Maggie stepped back, a safer distance. "That the wee fork is to be used for the fish." She took another step and turned away from the tender light in his eyes. "You must promise me you'll see to Clare . . . because . . . because . . ."

"Because Becca is too selfish to be a mother." He closed the distance between them, placed his warm hands on her chilled, bare shoulders. "I guess *you're* going to have to marry me."

"Wherever do you come up with these notions?" she said, desperation creeping into her voice. "You cannot marry such as me."

He lowered his head and she felt his breath against her nape, then his lips against her skin. She shuddered down the entire length of her spine.

"Why not?" he said,

"Earls do not marry the cottier's daughter."

"This isn't Ireland."

"Nay, but 'tis the same anywhere. And I am Catholic, you are not."

"Dammit, Maggie. Do you think I care about forks and fish—do you think Clara cares?"

He wouldn't let her escape. He was missing an important point she needed to make, but she lost all ability to think as he rained kisses across her bare shoulders. His arms came around her body, his fingers skimming beneath her breasts.

"You must stop." She batted at his hands. "What you are doing is wrong."

He gave a soft laugh, his breath moist against her skin. "No, Maggie," he said, his hands moving, cupping her breasts.

Blessed Mother, he was touching her where no man had ever touched and . . . and she liked it even as she feared it, the strange heat and quivering sensation moving, swelling inside her.

"Nothing has been this right in years," he said.

His hand moved up to the bare skin above her bodice, then slipped inside her gown. His thumb grazed her nipple through the thin fabric of her chemise and a jolt of pure fire raced through her. She sucked in a breath.

"I want you," he said, his voice low, urgent. "I need you."

"You've gone mad," she moaned.

"You want me," he murmured into her ear.

"Nay. 'Tis wrong, wrong."

"You don't know what you're saying." He turned her in his arms. "Kiss me, Maggie. Kiss me and then tell me we're wrong."

He loosened his hold as he lowered his head, as if he knew she wouldn't move away. His lips grazed hers, feather-light, a whispered kiss while their breath mingled together. His tongue moved over her lips, tasting, and then he drew on her lower lip, nipping, teasing. Her mouth opened and she learned in an instant what had gone before between them was nothing.

His tongue thrust deep inside her mouth as he pulled her tight against him. He enveloped her, his arms, his heat, the ardent pull of his hard body. Her hands fluttered at her sides, straining to touch something that was not him, but there was nothing except moonlight and shadows and man. He grabbed her wrists, pulling them up to his shoulders.

"Hold on," he murmured into her mouth.

A strange ache flooded her body. She moaned softly and leaned into him. His arms came around her, holding her tightly, and she clutched at his shoulders, but it wasn't enough.

She was lost, helpless. Drifting somewhere beyond place and time, where even the angels trembled.

He pulled back and gazed down at her—eyes of midnight, lit with stars. "Breathe, angel," he murmured.

She drew in a breath that hitched and made her shudder. He smiled, a slow smile filled with a warmth and tenderness that caused her knees to go weaker. He smoothed her hair with his hands, over and over again, the same motion she would use to soothe a child.

"Don't say anything," he said softly.

As if she could speak, or even think of the proper words: No and no . . . and you must not give me your kisses . . . and I cannot, must not, love you.

She lowered her eyes. He lifted her chin between his fingers and bestowed a quick, chaste kiss on her parted lips. Her voice was still lost, swallowed in the infinity of the night sky. He gave that soft, deep-toned laugh again and wrapped her arm around his.

"One more dance, inside where everyone will see us," he said. "Then, and only then, I'll let you escape."

Even if she sprouted wings, she could never escape. He owned her soul forever. Owned it because she'd given it to him freely.

Chapter 12

The rain began before dawn, a cold, pounding rain that turned the fields to quagmire. Gordon prowled the breakfast room, his mind jumping from Maggie to today's race and back again. He was pouring his third cup of coffee when Drew joined him. Candlelight flickered on the silver urn as he lifted it and poured a cup for Drew.

"Will you run Shenandoah today?" asked Drew, taking the cup and saucer from his hand, then taking a seat at the table.

"Haven't decided. Letty tells me this will end before ten and the sun will be hot and bright." He smiled faintly. "Something to do with enough blue in the sky to make a Dutchman's britches."

Drew laughed as he added cream to his coffee. "Believe her—she's always right."

Gordon paced another length. "Shenendoah's odds are good. If I scratch her, I lose my stake, but dammit, the fool horse put the fear of God in me when she stumbled that one time."

"Well, my odds have improved. Reckless is a mudder." Drew stirred his coffee, watching the motion of the silver spoon as he drew endless circles in the dark liquid. "Maggie?" He looked up. His amber eyes narrowed. "Was she all right last night?"

Gordon pulled out a chair at the opposite end of the table and sat. He rubbed his face with his hands, then leaned back, meeting Drew's hard gaze. "I don't know. Becca got her claws into her somehow and Maggie's not one to say much."

Drew lifted his cup and blew into it, then took a swallow.

"I asked her to marry me," said Gordon.

"Maggie or Becca?"

"Dammit, Drew."

The cup made a clinking sound as Drew replaced it in the saucer. "What answer did you get?"

Gordon grinned. "She turned me down flat."

Drew returned the grin and then let it fade. "Becca's here for several more days. Watch her, Gordon. A meaner hellcat you'll never want to see."

"Becca?" He was beginning to realize Drew was right. She'd lashed out at Maggie, unprovoked, from the very first introduction, and she'd struck low when she did.

"Becca," repeated Drew. "There's a reason she's a twenty-seven-year-old spinster, and it has nothing to do with those china-doll looks of hers."

"Are you telling me I'm a stupid man who escaped by the skin of his teeth?"

"Something like that."

"Why didn't you tell me before?"

"You were so determined to get yourself shackled again, you wouldn't have listened." A maid carried in a platter of ham and eggs. Both men waited until she'd placed the tray on the table and left, then Drew spoke in a somber voice. "Maggie? Is she just another means to get Clara?"

Drew's question hurt, yet it had started out exactly that way. Somewhere between handing his card to a prim, buttoned-up schoolmarm and now, he had caught those glimpses into her heart he told himself he didn't want to see. And fallen in love.

What a funny thing love was, the way it crept up on a man, blindsiding him. And what fools men were, to think they could choose to love, when it was love that did the choosing.

"No. Not at all." Gordon felt the need to pace more than the need to eat. He pushed back from the table. Thoughts and emotions and memories clattered inside his head and twisted inside his gut. Augusta and Gordy. Maggie and Clara. For whatever reasons, he'd botched it the first go-around. He had a second chance. Few men got a second chance.

"Gussie's been dead over ten years now," he said, amazed he was speaking thoughts men never discussed. "It's odd how you forget, Drew. Things you thought you'd remember forever just slip away, lost."

He slanted a glance at his longtime friend. Drew was buttering a biscuit, not looking at him, just listening.

"I loved Augusta, but what I remember was different from what I'm feeling now. With Maggie, it's . . . it's . . ." His voice failed, inarticulate, unable to come up with a word or phrase to explain what had happened to him last night.

"Less Sir Walter Scott and more Shakespeare."

Gordon stopped suddenly and looked at Drew.

Drew's lips curled in a humorless smile. "We Southerners tend to gloss over our realities in favor of our romanticism. Honor and valor, we'll win this war in thirty days, our slaves are happy. Bullshit. But we wanted to believe it. If we'd read less of Scott's chivalric knights and more of Shakespeare's tragic kings . . ."

Drew shrugged one shoulder, dismissing his musings. "You and Gussie were little more than kids, a war gathering around you," he said. "We all went through it. Everything was mist and romance in those early days, even the idea of the war itself."

Gordon peered through the window into the slate sky weeping sheets of rain. Odd, but the July dawn after the smoke cleared at Gettysburg had looked just like this one.

Only then he'd been flat on his back in the mud, unable to move, certain he'd be dead before nightfall.

"Turned out a bit differently, didn't it?" he said quietly.

"We grew up. The whole damn country grew up."

Gordon felt a strange pressure at the back of his eyes, a tightening in his chest. In three years of a wartime marriage, he'd spent maybe three weeks as a husband to Gussie. Enough time to father a child she bore alone, too little time to foster a marriage. Augusta hadn't grown up; she'd died from a fever and would be forever young in his memories. But he hadn't died, and for the first time in ten years, it felt good to be alive.

Drew swallowed the dregs of his coffee and pushed away from the table. "Do we ride out to the track and drown on the way, or take the carriage and get stuck in the mud?"

"I'm a decent swimmer."

Drew slung his arm over Gordon's shoulder in a gesture reminiscent of their more debauched days at the University of Virginia. "You're one lucky bastard, even if my horse is going to beat yours today. Maggie's a winner. If I'd seen her first, you wouldn't have a chance."

There was friendship in the words and more, a subtle warning. "Hands off, buddy." Gordon slapped Drew on the back. "She's all mine."

A man could be forgiven his foolish notions, watching the beautiful horses go through their paces; momentarily forget the frightful fragility bred into the running giants. Some people said a good racer was born to run, but he'd always harbored the fanciful thought the best racers, like Pegasus, were born to fly.

From the backstretch rail, Gordon watched Shenandoah come around the oval. She was inside, pulling ahead in a pack of four, a dark shadow cutting through the rain like a ghost rider of ancient lore.

A good horse, she had the heart, the speed, the intelligence of a winner. She was giving it her all this morning, sensing the charged anticipation in the air, as aware as the touts lining the fences that the race was today. In this last workout before the meet, he could see his jockey, Rufus, holding her back.

They flashed past his position, Shenandoah, Drew's Reckless, the colt from New York favored in today's big stakes. The thrum of their hooves on the sodden ground seemed to meld with his heartbeat. His filly led by a nose. They turned the oval and the jockey leaned fractionally forward, easing the bit, and Shenandoah crossed the finish a full length ahead.

He met Franklin back at the shed row as Rufus brought her in. Plumes of steam blew out of the bay's nostrils, wreathing around her head. Gordon ran his hand over the sleek coat, down her shoulder, to the hock that had been injured in her last mud run. Cool to the touch, no swelling.

Franklin spat onto the ground. "So, what's it gonna be?"

"She's in top form," said Rufus from behind him.

The bay turned her head, staring at Gordon from those intelligent brown eyes. Pleading, he thought. He remembered the night she'd been born. It had rained that night too; a thunderstorm that was blowing up a whirlwind outside the birthing barn while he and Annie and Royce crouched inside, watching the mare's heaving breaths as she struggled to give birth to this foal. Shenandoah's dam had been the first brood mare he'd bought for his own stables; this filly, the first to be born at Old Riverbend in over fifty years.

He'd touched that spindly, wet foal as she took her first breath and felt something miraculous, a jolt as electrifying as the lightning crackling in the night sky.

Gordon straightened. As always in wet weather, his injured leg throbbed. Rain sluiced off his hat brim, running down beneath his open collar. "We scratch. Get her inside and rubbed down."

Franklin stared at him over the filly's broad back. "She could take home the winnings in this field."

"She could break a foreleg."

Franklin pursed his lips, spat one more time. His check-

ered hat was so wet, it was almost flat on his head. A sudden
grin split his face. "She ain't happy and Rufus ain't happy,
but you just made me a happy man."

Gordon returned about the same time the sun broke through
the clouds, announcing he'd scratched his horse and would
play host to all ladies interested in attending the races.

Maggie could hardly bring herself to look at him, though
he did nothing to indicate he remembered that wanton kiss,
or his foolish proposal, or even the dance they'd shared. He'd
treated her with the same gentlemanly courtesy he displayed
toward the Fielding sisters and Miss Hays and all the other
houseguests.

Only once, over one lady's shoulder as he was helping her
into the carriage, did he give Maggie his pirate look—that
swift smile with laughter filling his dark blue eyes. She'd
flushed all the way to her toes and turned back inside.

She didn't attend the races, choosing to stay with the children and help with the party Drew had planned for them
while the adults were away. He'd brought in clowns and
buckets of homemade peach ice cream and arranged pony
rides across the back lawn.

Miss Hays hadn't attended the races either, but she had a
headache and kept mostly to her room. Maggie thought even
the servants were grateful for that small blessing.

Maggie was upstairs, helping Alice change out of the new
party dress that was probably ruined with peach ice cream
and grass stains, when she heard the carriages returning.

"Do you think Mr. Fielding's horse won?" asked Alice, as
her head whipped around toward the window.

Maggie rubbed her cheek where the braided pigtail had
snapped across her face. "Maybe, Alice, and if we can get
you dressed you can be running down the stairs to find out."

"Hurry."

She took Alice by the shoulders, turned her around and
managed to tie the bow at the waist in spite of the child hop-

ing up and down. "Go," she said, tapping Alice on the bot-
om.

Alice went like a shot. Maggie followed, laughing.

Most of the returning guests had assembled on the side
allery where they could see the children, who were still in-
olved with Mr. Toggle the clown and several ponies. Alice
vas tearing across the lawn toward Drew, who had such a
leased look on his face, Maggie assumed his Reckless must
ave performed well.

Gordon already had Clare, holding her propped on his hip.
'heir gazes met over her head. His smile turned warm. The
reeze ruffled his hair, blowing a lock across his forehead
nd adding to his devilish charm.

"Did you win? I know you won!" said Alice as Drew
cooped her into his arms.

"We won, little lady. You're my good luck charm."

Maggie was looking at Drew when she heard Clare's
oice, loud as a clarion call.

"If my daddy's horse had been running, he would have
von."

Silence. An instant, heavy silence. She imagined she
eard her neck creak in the oppressive stillness as she turned
er head. Gordon stood with his daughter in his arms, his
ody suddenly taut and his eyes wary.

Father and daughter, their sculpted faces so close together—
golden waves of hair, those long-lashed eyes slightly lifted at
he outside corner. Their impossible, God-given beauty.

It was there, plain as plain could be.

"It's true," said Clare, who was probably the only person
naware of the tension vibrating in the atmosphere like
lucked fiddle strings. Clare whipped her head around,
earching until she found Maggie, who was stunned motion-
ess just off the side gallery. "Miss Hays told me, my Maggie,
nd it's all right, really."

Maggie glanced to the gallery, where Miss Hays rested
asually against the white spindle railing. Miss Hays

straightened, a small, vicious smile lifting one corner of her
mouth.

A wren hopped from one wrought-iron table to another,
pecking at cake crumbs. Bright balloons swayed against a
backdrop of trees and sky. Little commonplace things that
seemed so sharp all of a sudden.

Gordon's face was set hard, his eyes gone black. He flicked
a glance at Miss Hays, then cupped Clare's head with his
palm and brought her face gently forward against his shoulder. His graceful fingers brushed through the child's curls.

"You mean it's all right that I'm your daddy?" he asked in
a hushed voice.

"Uh-huh." Clare lifted her head and gazed into her father's
eyes. "And that Maggie is my mother. That was my third
wish. I always wished Maggie was my mother. Would you
marry her if she wasn't going to be a nun?"

The bright blue sky went gray as the blood drained from
her head in a sudden rush. Rocked by both the falsity and the
cruelty of what Miss Hays had put into Clare's head, Maggie
still managed to stand steady. She just couldn't seem to control her hands, fisting and unfisting in her skirts.

She blinked rapidly, terrified she was going to cry. She
hung immobilized in another silence that seemed to grow until it became a thundering in her ears. Somebody came up beside her and grasped her arm. It took her a moment to realize
it was Drew.

He and Gordon exchanged a look she couldn't fathom, but
Gordon gave an almost imperceptible nod. "Hush, princess,"
he said to Clare, pushing her head against him once more.
"Miss Hays hasn't been totally honest with you, but we'll
talk about this later."

"You'll honor me by being my dinner partner tonight,
won't you, my dear?" said Drew in a tone so normal she had
to blink harder to hold back the tears.

He squeezed gently on her arm and Maggie went with him
through the mob of houseguests, some scandalized, some
merely curious, all staring at her as if she wore a scarlet letter.

her bosom. He stopped as they came abreast of Miss
ays. Maggie stared blindly ahead.

"I believe Gordon has a few words he wants to say to you
fore you disappear," Drew said. "If this were his house, I'd
ow him the privilege of asking you to leave, but since it's
ine, I'm going to be selfish."

Miss Hays tilted her head. "Isn't it true?" she said in her
tle-girl's voice. "I'm certain I didn't misunderstand Gor-
n; it's the child who misunderstood. He didn't marry you,
iss Quinn, because you're Irish and Catholic." She shook
r head. "And all these years you've hidden his daughter
om him—but then, she is a bastard, isn't she?"

"Enough, Becca. That's a jealous lie and you know it." Al-
ough Gordon stood somewhere behind her, Maggie heard
e tightening in his voice, the leashed fury. He stepped for-
ard, near enough that she felt his body's heat.

Drew was squeezing her arm so tight it hurt. When he
oke, it was in an explosive hiss between clenched teeth.

"You'll be gone within the hour, Rebecca, or I'll throw
ou out personally."

nce inside, Gordon reached for Maggie. She shot him a
ok of such quiet despair, he let his arm drop. The woman he
as going to protect with his name had just been publicly
hipped by connection with that very name. If Rebecca
ays had been a man, he'd beat her to a bloody pulp.

"I'm sorry, Maggie. It's my fault," said Drew. "I should
ve asked her to leave this morning."

Maggie didn't seem to hear Drew. She lifted her lashes
ad met his own gaze. Light shimmered in the moisture fill-
g her eyes. "Clare," she said in a voice that quavered out of
er control. "You will explain to my wee Clare?"

"Maggie." Gordon reached out again and she backed away.

"I need some time. Oh, Blessed Mother." She turned and
arted climbing the stairs, moving slowly at first, gripping
e banister and pulling herself forward. She made a choked
ound that tore at his chest and then she was flying up the

steps with a sudden burst of speed that sent her boot heel flashing.

He exchanged glances with Drew. "Can you put someone outside her door so Becca doesn't get to her again?"

"Yes," said Drew. "You talk to your daughter. I'll do whatever I can to limit the damage."

Gordon kept his daughter on his hip and watched Maggie's feet disappear beyond the first landing. Two females needed him right now and he was torn as he'd never been torn in his life. I did this, he thought. To both of them.

Clara was sniffling in his arms. Maggie clearly wanted some time alone. Clara first, then.

The house was too damned crowded.

He pushed open the door to the conservatory. No one else was in here. He carried Clara inside, walking over to a stone bench sheltered by a giant rubber plant. He sat on the hard granite with his daughter in his lap.

God, how to explain your sexual transgressions to an innocent child?

"I am your father, princess." He brushed her hair back from her face. "Maggie loves you dearly, but she is not your mother."

Clara peered at him seriously from dark blue eyes. "Do you know who my mother is?"

He nodded. "A pretty lady who isn't here. When you get older . . ." He stopped, looked over her head at the shiny green leaves of the rubber tree, brought his gaze back.

"I wasn't there when you were born, Clara. For important reasons you can't understand yet, your mother couldn't keep you. She cared enough, though, that she left a message with the mother superior—it was a picture I had given her." His arms tightened around the child. "I want you, princess. I want to take you home with me and really be your daddy, to love you for the rest of your life."

"But M-M-Maggie." Her little chest heaved and then she buried her face in his shirt.

He felt himself crumbling inside as his daughter wept and

hiccupped against his chest as if the whole world were too miserable a place to be borne. Sometimes it was, but he wasn't going to tell her that small truth. She'd learned enough of misery in her five short years and the blame for that could be laid squarely on his shoulders.

"I want Maggie to go with us too," he said, stroking her back.

Clara lifted her head. Something defiant seemed to glimmer behind the teardrops. How courageous she was, a small child, abandoned and raised in an orphanage, yet she could stand up for what she wanted. *It's all right.* Damn, it wasn't all right, but he'd do his best to make up for the wrongs he'd done to her.

"Maggie isn't a nun yet," he said. "I asked her to marry me last night. I think now she'll say yes."

He didn't believe he was making false promises to his daughter. What Becca had said were outright, vicious lies, but she had made certain they were made publicly. Maggie's reputation was in ruins. She had only two choices now. Enter the convent or marry him.

Or marry James O'Connor, Irish waterman.

No, he wouldn't let that happen.

"When you were little, did any of your wishes ever come true?" asked Clara in a small, quivery voice.

"A few." He leaned his forehead against hers. "Are you making that third wish now?"

"Uh-huh."

He'd make it come true. He had to. They both needed Maggie too desperately for him to fail.

Maggie left the summerhouse and followed the path down to the riverbank. Tightly packed seed balls hung from the limbs of tall sycamores, their branches reaching far out over the water. She huddled against the mottled trunk of one of the forest giants, watching a bittern wade at the shoreline, listening to his deep, booming call.

The drifting sounds of people from the lawn had ceased

long ago. The light would soon be gone. She knew she couldn't stay here forever. She would have to go back soon, back to her young charges. Back to . . .

Not yet.

She walked a ways upstream, picked up a pebble and tossed it into the river. The pebble made a small splash and disappeared beneath the surface. Tiny waves rolled out from the center, spread in ever-widening circles until they too disappeared.

A twig snapped beneath the tread of someone's boot. Maggie leaned over and picked up another pebble, tossed it into the darkening water. Gordon approached her and draped a shawl over her shoulders. Her hand shook as she reached up and fingered the fringed edge.

"Maggie," he said, and pulled her into an embrace.

It was sinful to want this so much, but she could not help herself and could not find God to help her.

She allowed his arms around her, taking succor from his strength because she couldn't find her own. After a long minute, she looked up into his face. "You talked to wee Clare?"

"Yes." He let her go and looked away from her, over the river. His profile was hard and sharp, tense. "I've pulled some strings and got a special license. We can be married tomorrow."

"I cannot marry you!" She turned and walked away, two paces. "I cannot," she whispered vehemently.

"You have to. I'm the cause of this; I won't let you face it alone."

"There's nothing else to be done. I'll leave first thing in the morning. Sister Agatha can come stay with the girls and I'll go back to my teaching. Now that Clare knows, Mother Bernadette will surely let you have her. You need never see me again."

"You won't have a job to go back to," he said, and she couldn't miss the anguish in his voice. That alone convinced her it was true. She swung around. Not this too. Soon she would have nothing left of the safe life that she had known; the life of peace she had struggled so desperately to build after fleeing Killady.

"Wh-what do you mean?"

"The talk will follow you. Some of these guests have daughters in that school. If you think your word is going to carry more weight than their money, you're sadly mistaken."

With the setting sun at his back, his face was nothing but shadows, yet she could feel the tension in him. It was palpable, like a scourge against her skin.

"Dammit, Maggie, the story of the virgin birth just isn't going to wash on this telling."

"But I'm not Clare's mother!"

"People believe what they want to believe and it's usually the worst."

She collapsed against the trunk of a tree. The bark felt scratchy even through the layers of cloth on her back.

"I'm going about this all wrong." He pushed a breath through his teeth. "I *want* you for my wife. Clara wants you for her mother. Forget everything else." He moved so he stood in front of her, so large, so much a man. "Help me make a family, Maggie."

She looked into his face. It hurt to look at him and she could not make herself look away. Love was not supposed to be this way, so hurtful your belly was twisted in knots and even your bones ached with the pain. The wind blew up and she shivered.

He held out his arm. "Come on, you're cold. Let's get you inside."

Wordlessly, she placed her hand on his forearm. He covered her fingers with his other hand, protecting her from the wind. They walked up the path, past the summerhouse.

"Clare's mother, you could not marry her?" She felt his muscles tighten beneath her palm, but he said nothing. "Did you not even love her, then?"

He stopped. "No. And I have no idea how she felt toward me."

She pulled away and hugged the woolen shawl tight against her chest. "But you made a child with her."

"Yes. All I can say is that I'm ashamed. I can't go back and undo it. I don't even want to go back and undo it. That moment of what you call sinfulness produced Clara. Can you honestly say that child is wrong? Wronged, yes . . . but not wrong." He took both of her hands in his own. "Maggie, forgive me enough to marry me."

" 'Tis not my place to judge you or forgive you. You must look to your own faith for such."

A faint smile curled his lips. "Is that a yes?"

Wretched Miss Hays, who had loved him so twistedly it turned to hate, and wee Clare's mother, who had given up the babe from her womb. And him, with his rogue's eyes looking at her now, smiling and pleading. She knew the righteous path and yet she was no wiser, no stronger than either of the other two women.

She hugged her waist hard and all the pain she felt in her belly sounded in her voice. "You are asking me to give up my soul for you."

"I'm asking you to give me a chance to prove I love you," he said quietly. "Nothing more."

When he took her hand, she didn't withdraw it. They walked together for several paces. The wind was blowing so strong now, her skirts were snapping around her ankles.

"Do you know anything of Catholic teaching?" she asked as they topped the hill and the house came into view.

"A little." He sounded wary. "Why?"

"I know naught else but my faith. To marry you is to spend the rest of my life in sin."

"I can't swallow the idea that a marriage performed by a clergyman is invalidated by some man wearing a pointy hat in Rome. How many gods do you think are floating around up there? How many pearly gates?"

He stopped and bowed mockingly. "Pardon me, ma'am," he said, sweeping his arm. "Do you wish entrance at the

Catholic gate or the Hindu? Perhaps you're a Swahili, in which case, there is no gate."

He turned his head and gazed out over the river, his eyes narrowed against the wind that was whipping his hair.

"You are mocking me."

"I'm mocking the conventions, the rules built by men, not gods. What I'm offering you is my love, my daughter, my . . ." He hesitated, as if meaning to say something and thinking better of it. He turned back and grasped her shoulders. "Everything of mine is yours. It's the best I can do. I can't promise eternal salvation. All I know is the here and now, and that I want you with me."

She looked over his shoulder to the Fielding house, where yellow light was beginning to beam from the windows as the servants went about lighting the gas jets. "And the other rules, the ones made by the gentry? Do you not understand the cost to be paid?"

She looked into his eyes and saw no comprehension there, only an impatient waiting. And how could he understand, anyway? He was to the manor born, while she . . . she was not.

"I am a poor Irish immigrant," she said simply.

"And this is a nation of immigrants, Maggie."

That bone-aching pain rose up in her. She took his arm when he offered it, silently, because all her words and explanations had fled. What had always been so simple was now so complex, as complex as the man walking beside her, who was altering his pace for her, covering her hand to protect it from the cold.

The worst of it was, he almost made her believe it really was simple. A man and a woman and love, a different kind of salvation. Her heart wanted to believe this new faith, but she knew a woman's heart was a treacherous thing.

In Ireland, Maggie had learned what happened to a poor woman who got caught with a child in her belly and no wedding ring on her finger. She saw what happened to Seamus

Quinn, who had taken that woman and her child into his heart and his home, then turned to the Brotherhood for the passion that was lacking in his marriage. And she saw what happened when the constabulary came to Killady to punish.

Maggie learned the terrible price to be paid, and she carved those lessons into her heart. The gentry were ruthless in guarding the castle walls. You did not enter the gates through the grace of marriage, you were born inside.

Sometimes, though, even now, Maggie would wake in the middle of the night with a hollow, heavy weight around her heart. In the silence of those dark hours, she would remember the rocking of the ship, a wasted woman lying on a hard, narrow berth and a pair of loving hands pressing a jeweled rosary into her own.

" 'Twas a gift to me from your father," her mother had said. "Forgive him, forgive me for loving him. He was such a splendid man, you see."

"Please, tell me his name," Maggie had begged.

Mum died with her secret held close. But Maggie wasn't blind and was no longer a child. She could look in the mirror and see herself, black hair, green eyes, a woman taller than the norm. She could look in the mirror and see the bastard daughter of Geoffrey Fitzhugh, the twelfth Earl of Lachlan.

Chapter 13

"*L*etty will be staying with the girls," he said as they walked up the steps. "Your things have already been moved to one of the bedrooms on the second floor."

Miss Hays's room, thought Maggie, barely suppressing a sigh. "Why?" she asked.

"Because you're not the governess."

He walked with her up the stairs and down a hallway papered with blue-and-white-striped silk. He stopped at an open door halfway down the length.

"Wear the green dress for dinner," he said. "I'll knock on your door in an hour."

A maid was in the room. The girl dipped her head and knee in a curtsy. "I've aired the bedding for you, ma'am, and built you a fire in the grate. If you'll be needing anything more, just ring this bell," she said, gesturing to a braided pull near the white marble mantel. "Would you like me to pour your tea?"

Maggie shook her head. "I'll be fine."

When the girl reached the door, she stopped and cast a shy glance over her shoulder. "We've been saying, those of us belowstairs from the old country, how it's that happy we are to be serving one of our own."

For a moment, Maggie almost smiled, until the full import of the maid's words hit. "I don't even know your name to say a proper thank-you."

"Moira."

"Thank you, Moira."

The maid nodded and reached for the doorknob. "Moira?" The girl looked over her shoulder again. Maggie's hand fluttered up to her collar and she could feel the heat of a flush on her neck. "What does Mr. Fielding call you?"

"Are you asking me if he's one of the rich folk who call us all Bridie?" Maggie nodded and the girl said, "He's not that sort, ma'am. He calls me Moira."

"And Dr. Kincaid?"

A look of surprise flashed across the girl's face. "Why, he asked me my name, he did. Just like yourself."

They shared a smile, and then the maid left. A blue and white china tea set sat waiting on a wooden cart. Maggie lifted the teacup by the handle. The china was so thin she could see the dark wood of the tester bed through it.

She walked over and stood in front of the fire, wrapping her arms around her waist and watching the flames curl around the logs. Her throat felt scratchy and a headache was beginning to grip behind her eyes. The flames flared and jumped as a gust of wind tore down the chimney.

She thought it strange, yet somehow appropriate, to be condemned for a sin she hadn't committed, staring as if mesmerized at licking flames.

And my future? she had asked Mother Bernadette. And the reply, as always with the mother superior, had been the truth: *Only you can make that decision, Maggie.*

If she found the courage to follow her heart against the strictures of her Church, what then? Gordon claimed that America was different from Ireland. But he viewed the conventions from within the safety of the castle walls. Would his world shun her? Would they ostracize him for breaking the rules? And would he come to hate her for bringing that cost down on his head?

She felt so alone all of a sudden, and destitute and terribly afraid.

The knock came in exactly one hour. She opened the door to see Gordon with Clare's hand clasped within his. Clare was dressed for bed in a long nightgown covered by the pink-and-white-striped robe Gordon had bought her.

Maggie was uncertain of the etiquette required under these new circumstances. She stepped back from the door, not inviting them in, waiting for him to make the decision. His mouth twisted in a sardonic smile that made her feel like he was reading her mind. He nudged Clare forward and then leaned against the doorframe, placing himself not quite in the room, not quite in the hallway.

Maggie knelt down in front of Clare and brushed her hair back from her forehead. Clare looked up into her father's face. They shared a grin and he nodded slightly.

"We brought you something." Clare pulled one hand from behind her back, holding out a small box tied with a green ribbon.

Maggie's hand trembled as she took the gift. She stood and looked questioningly at Gordon.

"Open it," he said. She untied the bow and lifted the lid. "Brings good luck," he said, then nodded to Clare. "Give Maggie a good-night kiss and I'll take you back upstairs."

Speechless, Maggie knelt again for a sloppy kiss. She held Clare tightly for a long minute and then let her go.

"I'll be down for you in ten minutes," he said, and took his daughter's hand, pulling the door closed as they left.

Maggie sank into a heap on the floor, her knees too weak to stand. It wasn't an expensive gift, but it signified so much more.

Grab for the ring, Maggie-mine.

He was challenging her to be brave enough to lean over emptiness, reaching for something shiny. But the token was more than a challenge. That day in the park and a giddy ride on the wooden horses. He remembered. Maggie bit at her lower lip. Slowly, her thumb rubbed the shiny brass ring.

Gordon took Clara back to the nursery, stayed his promised ten minutes, during which he read both girls a story, then stayed another ten before going for Maggie.

After seeing Rebecca Hays into a departing carriage, he and Drew had closeted themselves in Drew's study. The arrangements were made, a marriage license obtained through Drew's services as a county judge, church and pastor reserved for eleven o'clock tomorrow. Rings were procured with almost the same ease; one of the houseguests owned a jewelry store in Baltimore.

Maggie had dressed in the green gown for dinner. He hadn't been at all certain she would, half-fearing she would plead a headache and hide out in her room. He didn't know how to treat her, how to penetrate through the subtle barricade she'd erected around herself. With time, he could woo her with sweet words, small gifts of flowers and sheet music, morning rides and afternoon walks.

He didn't have time. She hadn't mentioned it and he wasn't about to remind her, but she had other avenues open besides marriage to him. The convent. Jamie O'Connor, standing on the sidelines, watching and hoping for her to turn to him.

Gordon couldn't allow her anywhere near that convent-cum-orphanage until his ring was on her finger. He could wrap her in a cocoon as tight as those convent walls at Old Riverbend; ease her into his world slowly so she would feel that safety she needed. And maybe Jamie was man enough to threaten to kill for her, but he wasn't man enough to make her love him back.

He turned down the hallway leading to her room and nodded to Mr. and Mrs. Cannaught as they passed by on their way to the double oak stairs. God, his heart was pumping so fast, as though he'd been running. And hadn't he been running for years?

Always away: from family, from opening his heart to the danger of loving. But now he was running toward living again. There were no more choices to be made, nothing left to do.

But make her love him back.

The crystal lusters on the wall lamps tinkled as a door opened next to him. He caught the scent of dusting powder and violet sachet and then saw Lydia Gearhart step into the hall, followed by her husband. Lydia smiled, one hand reaching out to stop him.

"She's a lovely young woman, Gordon," she said. "So fresh and wholesome. If you can convince her we're not all hateful creatures like Miss Hays, she'll make a wonderful mother for your son."

Years of practice enabled him to manufacture an answering smile, but he couldn't have spoken a single word through the tightness that grabbed his throat.

His son. Gordy. He should have told Maggie about his son while they were walking. He'd almost told her, then bit back the words. She was so frightened by it all, the haste, the vicious slander. He had to tell her about Gordy, but he needed the proper time, when he could explain the . . . the constraint that defined his relationship with his son.

The clock in the foyer chimed the half-hour. Harold Gearhart took his wife's elbow. "Come along, dear," he said. "The young man has some courting to do and my throat is dry."

Gordon stepped aside, allowing them to pass. For so long, his life had been nothing but empty time stretching endlessly before him. Now it was rushing like a freight train down a steep grade with the brakes gone. He had courting to do. He had secrets to reveal.

Now. There wouldn't be a better time than now. Gordon lifted his hand and knocked on her door. He heard the rustle of silken skirts and then the door opened. Maggie lifted her face and looked at him.

Damn, she'd been crying.

Maggie stared at him, waiting for him to smile. She needed him to smile. She was twisted inside out with fear and mortification over things she hadn't even done and things she wanted to do . . . the thought of walking down those stairs, into his world, facing his friends . . . she was close to physically ill. And he still wasn't smiling.

"Are you ready?" he asked.

"Aye."

He moved smoothly, taking her hand in his own and pulling her forward. He reached around her and closed the bedroom door.

He lifted his hand. Feather-light, his fingers drifted down, tracing a line from her temple to cheek, caressed the corner of her mouth. His hand turned and her lips opened with the delicate touch of his thumb stroking her bottom lip.

He gazed at her from beneath those golden lashes. "I forgot to mention one thing before."

"What?"

"This." He bent his head and brushed soft kisses at the corner of her mouth. His breath was warm and caressing against her cheek. She made a sound in her throat, both protest and longing. He laughed softly.

"You mustn't." She placed her palms on his chest and pushed, terrified someone would walk down the hall and see them coupled in this carnality. It would be seen as proof of her alleged sin.

"Ah, but we have our first disagreement." His hands stroked up and down her arms, his mouth a sulky curve. "I feel I must."

"Someone will see us," she whispered frantically.

He looked first over one shoulder, then the other in an exaggerated gesture. "Not a soul around. Every man here kisses his wife at least once a day anyway. It's the done thing, I'm afraid."

"I'm not—"

Her protest was swallowed in his throat as his mouth covered hers. His grip tightened on her arms. With a subtle movement, he had her back against the door and she was trapped with his hard body pressing against her, his mouth drawing on her lips, her tongue, the very air she needed to breathe.

She was drowning in him, more trapped in his heat and long length than she'd been trapped in the water weeds. Only the fear she felt now was so much different and mingled with a pleasure so intense, she thought she might suffocate from it alone. He pulled back suddenly, leaving her breathing hard and raggedly.

"Chin up, Irish. You've nothing to be ashamed of."

He stared at her with that grave, tender curve of his lips she'd first seen last night. Maggie lifted her chin. He took her elbow in his grasp and guided her down the stairs. And into his world.

She made it through the dinner with Gordon's quiet support on one side and Drew's presence on her other side, both men wearing expressions that seemed to dare anyone to make a comment on Miss Hays's false accusations. Now the ladies had been excused to the drawing room while the men lingered over port and cigars. She was on her own.

Maggie hesitated just inside the door, watching the other women for clues. Drew's sister, Emily Brewer, caught her eye. Emily inclined her head and then touched the back of a chair with so much gilt on the frame, it absolutely glowed. Maggie crossed the room and took the seat while the other ladies milled in small groups and settled on the divans.

Coffee, Americans and their coffee. She longed for a cup

of tea, but accepted the tiny demitasse cup of coffee from Emily Brewer and balanced it in her lap. She cast indirect looks at the other ladies.

Mrs. Cannaught, with a face like a dray horse. She wasn't usually friendly, but she was sitting on the divan next to Mrs. Gearhart, who was kindness itself. Mr. and Mrs. Gearhart made an interesting pair, him so short and round like a fine little pigeon while she was inches taller and as skinny as a fence post.

There were the two Ormond sisters, all frilled and curled. Maggie couldn't read their signals; they hadn't been cutting, but they had yet to speak to her either. The one with the curliest hair had an eye for Gordon Kincaid. Maggie couldn't blame her; the man was so beautiful he ought to be framed and hung in a museum.

Maggie sipped on black coffee and listened to the buzz of conversation, thankful no one was addressing any comments her way. She wondered how long she was expected to sit here before she could politely excuse herself. If she were home, she'd be tucking the last little child into bed about now.

After today, that life was lost to her. Unless she took her vows. Nobody cared about a nun's reputation so long as she was pure and chaste once she entered the order.

A nun or a wife.

She longed for Father Fitz and his wise, loving advice, Mother Bernadette and her good sense. But it was her life, and the decision hers alone.

When the time comes, I pray you'll make it for the right reasons.

"How did you meet Dr. Kincaid?"

Maggie started, almost dropping her cup and saucer. It was Mrs. Cannaught. Maggie took a deep breath.

"When he came to the orphanage." No, that wasn't a good answer. Mrs. Cannaught's brows lifted. "He was to give a speech at our fund-raising concert," Maggie elaborated. It wasn't quite a lie and she'd confess if she could find a priest willing to take her confession after tomorrow.

"Are you telling us he just happened to discover he had a daughter in that place?" Mrs. Cannaught hissed a little between her teeth. "Come, come, Miss Quinn. We aren't fools."

"You will have to ask him how he came to know about wee Clare. I do not know the answer."

Mrs. Cannaught lifted her cup, her upraised pinky drawing an arc in the air as she sipped.

"Drew has talked about little else since that picnic in the park," said Emily. She walked over and stood behind Maggie's chair, placed her hand on the high gilt back. "He was very impressed, Miss Quinn. With you, and with the other sister, what is her name?"

"Sister Agatha."

"Yes, that's it."

"But you are not a nun. Or am I mistaken?" Mrs. Cannaught's eyes held malice even though her tongue was silk.

"I am not." Yet.

"I can see how a convent might balk at that prospect."

The subtle barb hit and stung deeply. Maggie blinked back sudden tears. She opened her mouth to deny, but the words got caught behind the lump in her throat, and she shut it.

"The child is yours, isn't she, Miss Quinn? We can all tell she is by the way she follows after you. And you've got—"

"The child is mine."

All heads turned to the door. Maggie closed her eyes briefly and sagged into her chair. She looked at Gordon standing in the doorway. His expression was severe, his eyes dark as midnight.

"Maggie loves Clara and Clara loves Maggie. That's what you see and that's all you see," he said, coming into the room. His left leg dragged as he crossed the thick carpet. He stood beside her chair. "Two people in the world know the identity of Clara's mother. Miss Quinn is not one of them."

She could feel the tension arcing between Mrs. Cannaught and the man standing beside her. "If you care to delve a little more deeply," he said in a smooth voice, "perhaps we can

swap names. You first, Savanna. Who was your latest lover?
And your husband doesn't count."

Mrs. Cannaught sputtered. "I never—"

"Now, now, dear." Mrs. Gearhart reached over and patted
Mrs. Cannaught's knee. "My Harold . . ." She looked around
innocently. "Harold never lies to me," she said, as if that were
an explanation of something.

"Because he knows what a treasure he got when you married him," said Emily Brewer with laughter in her voice,
breaking the tension. "Letty sent a message that the girls
wanted Miss Quinn to read them a story. Perhaps you'd be
kind enough to walk her upstairs," she said to Gordon.
"You'll need to light a candle for the third-floor hall."

He reached for Maggie's hand and pulled her up. Emily
took the cup and saucer, exchanging a small wink with the
gesture. Instead of the proper hand on forearm, Gordon kept
her hand grasped within his own. He slanted her a glance,
nudging his chin up slightly. Maggie followed the hint and
lifted her lashes.

"I have asked Miss Quinn to marry me," he announced as
more of the men filed into the room. "I had asked her before
Rebecca Hays spread any of her vicious lies, asked her because I want nothing more in this world than to spend the rest
of my life with Maggie Quinn. If I'm a lucky man, by this
time tomorrow night, she'll be Mrs. Kincaid."

He turned so he was facing her. "Forgive me, angel, but I
need to prove a point."

He kissed her. He kissed her soundly. Bells seemed to be
clanging inside her head. He was solid and imposing and
heated. While his arms surrounded her, she ached with embarrassment and agitation. She felt lost and bare when he let
her go.

Only then did she realize the noise she heard was laughter
and some hand-clapping. He reached down and laced his fingers through hers, covering her hands with his palms.

Maggie-mine, he mouthed only to her.

Perhaps he was right about this land called America.

Maybe here, it didn't matter if one was born Catholic and the other Protestant, one poor and the other rich.

Maybe love was enough to break down the walls and let happiness in.

Chapter 14

*M*aybe love wasn't enough. Sunlight poured through the opened window, striking the gold crucifix of Mum's rosary, momentarily blinding her with the brightness. Maggie moved away from the bedroom window, turning her back to the sight of God's beautiful morning.

She wanted her church. She wanted to step into the shadowed box and make her confession to the priest seated on the other side of the screen. She'd never thought of herself as becoming any man's wife. To take her wedding vows, unshriven, without the wedding mass and a priest's blessing . . .

She didn't have to marry Gordon. No one was forcing her. She could return to St. Columba's, help the nuns with the orphans until the next class of postulants. Take her vows. Become a bride of Christ.

Lose Clare. Never see his quick, rakish smile at her again. *Oh, Blessed Mother, what do I do? What is right?*

The gray silk rustled and pooled on the floor as Maggie

knelt. She closed her eyes. Her fingers worked the rosary. "I believe in God the Father . . ."

"Damn." Impatiently, Gordon yanked at the black ribbon bowtie. He lifted his chin and watched in the mirror as he retied the fool thing. He stepped back and studied the man in the mirror, unhappy with what he saw.

He should be dressed in formal tails, dark blue, finely tailored frock coat at the very least. Not this country day wear. He was getting married, dammit.

It hadn't been this way the first time. Then, there had been a courtship, a huge, formal wedding with hundreds of guests, followed by dancing under the stars. A bride he was confident would show up at the altar.

This time, the haste, the secretiveness—the devil take it, his own family wouldn't be at the church, didn't even know he was getting married again. It all seemed so furtive, when what he wanted to do was shout from the rooftops: *Maggie is mine!*

But Maggie was not his, might never be his.

He still hadn't told her about Augusta or Gordy.

He should have told her last night when he walked her back to her room, but the glimmering moisture in her eyes as he gave her a chaste kiss on the cheek stopped him. One more burden laid on her shoulders and he was certain she would convince herself by sunrise not to go through with the marriage. It was a risk he hadn't been willing to take.

He heard a scratch at the door. "Come in," he said.

Drew entered, followed by Emily. "The carriages are out front," said Drew. "You sure you want us to take both girls?"

Gordon fingered his tie and managed a small smile. He looked at Drew. "For various reasons, I haven't told Maggie about Augusta." He paused, swallowed. "Or Gordy."

Drew stared back at him, whatever he was thinking hidden behind an impenetrable mask.

"I'll tell her on the way to the church, Drew. Even I'm not that much of a bastard."

"We'll meet you at the church, then."

And after I tell her, he thought, there might be a wedding. And there might not.

She gripped the balance strap as if her life depended upon her hold on a narrow strip of leather. Gordon sat across from her, his gloved hands in his lap, legs angled off to the side. His own thoughts were in turmoil as he struggled to come up with the proper words to tell her he'd been married before, had a twelve-year-old son by that marriage.

She stared out the window. The carriage passed through the gates of Burleigh and began a winding tour down rutted country lanes. Amid the clink of harness traces and the low resonance of the team's hooves, the carriage lurched, then smoothed. She gripped the balance strap harder.

It was only a short distance to the little country church. Now—get it over with. He drew in a hard breath. "Maggie, there's something I have to tell—"

"I must tell you first." She swung her head around. Her eyes were huge and brilliant green set against her white face. "My Mum . . . she was not married to . . ." She paused, blinked her eyes and drew on her bottom lip. "Mum . . . my father . . ." She turned her head back to the view from the window.

"Maggie." He reached across to take her hand, his heart beginning to ache for her, for Clara, for himself. He couldn't tell her he already knew, but he had to convince her it didn't matter. She scrunched her body tighter into the corner of the coach and in that instant he understood so much more.

He withdrew his hand, settling it back on his lap. Damn him for a fool, but she feared his touch not because she was convent-bred, but because a man such as himself had so wantonly used her mother, then discarded both the woman and the child he had created. He silently cursed Geoffrey Fitzhugh, the Earl of Lachlan.

She fingered the rosary that she wore around her neck. It was a work of art, wrought from fine gold, beads of jade and lustrous pearls. An expensive piece, a prince's ransom in the matched pearls alone.

"Mum was fevered when she was dying, might be she didn't know what she was saying." Maggie turned her head and looked at him. "This," she said, lifting the gold crucifix. "She gave me this and said it was a gift to her from my father. It was the only time she said anything—that my father was a fine man, but she never gave him a name."

"Your mother must have been very brave and very generous."

"Aye, she was that. And very sad." A bar of sunlight slanted across her face, highlighting the strong bones that gave her face so much character.

"Why would you think that would matter to me anyway?" He laughed, an ironic little sound. "Clara is my daughter, remember."

I too am a bastard, he thought, but for Gordy's sake I can't confess that yet. Later, when she was his wife. He would tell her then, hold her in his arms and confess one last sin for which he wasn't culpable but which had burned in his gut for most of his boyhood.

"It would matter to your friends," she said in a low, breathy voice.

"Maybe. Some of them anyway." The truth was a painful thing. "*Friend* is the wrong word to describe anyone who—"

Her chin came up, quivering nonetheless as she proudly fought back tears. He moved suddenly and sat beside her, taking her hand and pulling it into his lap. "I need you. Clara needs you. Now that her parentage is no longer a secret, she needs you more than ever. You know how cruel people can be."

"She has you."

"She needs both of us."

The carriage wheels turned, bringing the white clapboard church into view. He heard Clara and Alice, their high-pitched voices filled with excitement as they caught sight of the coach. Gordon's hand gripped hers more tightly as the carriage rolled to a halt. His heartbeat accelerated. Now, he had to tell her now.

"Maggie," he said. "Before we—"

The carriage door opened. Drew peered inside, then held out his hand to assist her. Her gaze lifted to the church and then she sank back against the leather cushion like a frightened rabbit seeking a burrow. Drew's hand dropped and he looked at Gordon, lifting one brow in question.

"Take the children inside," said Gordon quietly. "Maggie and I are going for a short walk."

He waited until Drew had ushered Emily, Letty and the two little girls through the church doors, then assisted Maggie from the carriage. Her reluctance to leave the safety of the vehicle was palpable. He was relentless, tightening his grip on her gloved hand, subtly coercing her until she moved.

He kept her hand in his own, walking across the churchyard with no set destination in mind. They came to an iron fence enclosing the cemetery. She stopped, tried to withdraw her hand. He resisted.

"I cannot marry you," she said, turning her face up. "You are a stranger to me. I know naught of you or of your world."

He drew in a long breath, mastering his own rising panic. *Tell her now,* said his conscience. *Don't. Later, after she's yours,* whispered his fears.

A future without Maggie, raising Clara on his own when he knew nothing of being a father. Gordy, already lost to him, lost forever without her to guide him, to show him the way.

Four short weeks ago, his life had been barren, himself so accustomed to the bleakness he never even thought about it anymore. Maggie had changed that, reawakened his heart. He could not lose her now.

He manufactured a smile. "You know I love you."

"Nay, I know only your sweet words and your wicked smile."

His experience was broad, but he found it wasn't broad enough to soothe the fears of a virtuous Irish-Catholic girl. A young woman he wanted desperately in his life. He was re-

duced to begging, so he begged, but he was still a man, so he
tried to hide the pleading behind a slightly sarcastic tone.

"If I said your heart is precious to me, would you believe
me, or call it only more sweet words?"

She made a choking sound and turned her head away. He
lifted his hand to smooth her hair, changed his mind and let it
drop. He wrapped her arm in his own and began walking her
toward the church, not allowing her to withdraw. Implacable.
He wouldn't force her to stand at the altar beside him, but he
wasn't going to make it easy for her to get away either.

Maggie slanted him a glance. His expression was grim, his
profile set hard, his eyes narrowed. He held her arm wrapped
around his own, trapped tightly against his body. His stride
was so long, she was forced into a run to keep from falling.

He headed directly for the church doors.

Her heart was fluttering inside her chest like a bird dash-
ing itself against glass. Her skirts became caught around her
ankles as he pulled her rapidly up the steps. He didn't pause
when she nearly tripped, didn't even glance at her.

"Gordon, please."

He pushed open the church door and drew her over the
threshold, through a small foyer and a set of louvered swinging doors, into a small sanctuary. Abruptly, he let her go.

"Decide, Maggie," he said in a merciless voice, then
walked up the center aisle.

His tall body was a black shadow in the dimly lit interior.
His stride was even; whatever strength it took, he managed
to disguise his limp. Her hands twisted in her skirts as she
watched him. He walked past the rows of wooden pews, no
more than twenty feet, and stopped in front of the chancel
rail. A black-robed parson already waited, prayer book in
hand, a little deeper in shadow in front of a wooden altar.

Drew slipped out from the first pew, turned and looked at
her, then moved to a position beside Gordon. On the other
side of the aisle, Letty sat between the two girls. Gordon
turned halfway and smiled faintly at his daughter. Clare

whipped around, her knees in the pew as she leaned over the wooden back.

"Maggie," she said loudly, a broad grin lighting her face.

Maggie clutched her hands around her waist. Gordon turned his head, slanting her a look. Their gazes met—instant, silent communication. He stood with his body held stiff and proud—proclaiming to the world he'd made his choice—and stood at the front of the church waiting. She could turn and walk out the door, no one would stop her; or she could join him.

"Maggie?" Clare's voice, uncertain now.

Letty reached over. "Sit, little one," she said, pulling Clare back into the pew. "Hush, now."

Maggie strode up the aisle, the sound of her boot heels echoing in the nearly empty church. She didn't look to the right or left and didn't stop until she stood beside Gordon. He took her hand in his own and led her up the one step to the altar.

His voice—that rich, seductive voice that always resonated through her blood like music—repeated his vows with quiet strength. Then it was her turn, the short, balding Episcopal priest peering at her through rimless spectacles.

Her voice quavered pitifully as she followed him: "I take thee, Gordon Alistair Kincaid, to be my wedded husband, to have and to hold from this day forward—" Stronger, aye. "For better or worse, for richer for poorer, in sickness and in health—" She lifted her lashes and looked at the beautiful man who was mystery and her heart's aching need. "To love, honor and obey, till death us do part, according to God's holy ordinance—" He squeezed her hand as she stumbled over those words. "And thereto I plight thee my troth."

He gave her that beautiful, slow smile, and then he was handing a ring to the minister, who blessed it with a prayer. Gordon took her hand, working her glove free, and slid a wide band onto her finger. The ring was smooth and warmed from his own body's heat. Tiny diamonds sparkled between three square-cut emeralds.

The parson recited a prayer so familiar and another, unfamiliar one, but the words were all swimming together in her brain anyway. Then they were kneeling together, Gordon Kincaid and Maggie Quinn, in front of an altar, and the priest stood in front of them, his hands upraised in blessing.

". . . that you may so live together in this life, and in the world to come you may have life everlasting. Amen."

She was married, Mrs. Gordon Kincaid.

Chapter 15

Maggie sank down into the deep cushions of the nearest settee while Gordon stood at the mahogany desk, registering for their room at the Barnum Hotel.

She hadn't cried when she hugged wee Clare and Alice or accepted the goodwill of Drew and Emily and Letty. She'd breathed deeply and blinked her eyes and managed to hold back the tears throughout the nearly silent ride into the city.

Gordon must have sensed her battle, because he'd said nothing, only grasping her hand within his own and gently massaging it. After a while, he'd entwined his fingers with hers, a gesture she found suggestively intimate in spite of the two layers of gloves separating their skin. Now the treasonous tears were again pushing at her chest and stinging the backs of her eyes.

He turned from the registration desk and came toward her and she allowed her gaze to travel up the long and splendid length of him. He belonged here, amid the gilt and rich carpets and highly polished wood. How long would it take him to realize she didn't?

He smiled a little as he held out his hand. She took it, her knees were so weak, she probably couldn't stand without his assistance. They followed a bellhop up a wide, curving staircase to the second floor and all the way down a long corridor. The bellhop unlocked a door at the end, pushed it open and handed the key to Gordon.

She stepped into a sitting room done in rich blues and gold. Her eyes swept over the furnishings: polished tables, fluted crystal chimneys over the gas jets, a white marble fireplace with gleaming pier mirror above. Beyond, a door sat partially open and she could see only a bed, a very large bed, hung in the European fashion with royal blue bed-curtains. She heard him speaking to the bellhop and then the door closed. Gordon came up behind her and placed his hands on her shoulders.

"Is it regret or fear?" he asked.

She turned and looked at him. "A little of both."

He gave a small laugh. "Honest Maggie. You'll shame me into a man yet."

As he had done with Clare, he cupped her head in his hand and brought her face gently against his shoulder. She thought he brushed a kiss into her hair.

"Tomorrow, we'll face the world and I'm going to make you listen to a confession of my own. But you've given me back my life, Maggie." He set her away, took her hands into his own and held them against his chest while he gazed steadily at her.

"I'm going to leave you alone for a few hours. I need to send a telegraph to my family telling them my good news." He smiled, as if the thought pleased him. She hoped the information would please them, feared it would only dismay them.

"Franklin is shipping Shenandoah back today," he said. "I'm going by the train station and then will run some errands. While I'm gone, I want you to take a nap. I'll leave instructions at the desk for a bath to be brought up. A tea tray. . . . Pamper yourself for a while and then I'll pamper you later. Fair enough?"

She wanted nothing less than to be alone with her doubts and fears. She nodded.

"I'll lock the door. The maid will announce herself before she comes in with the tray."

She still hadn't found her voice when she heard the key turn in the lock. She was left alone in a room that smelled faintly of sandalwood, with no company except her own dark thoughts. She walked over to the window, drew aside the heavy drapes and watched until she saw him come out on the pavement. His hair was blowing in the breeze, richly burnished gold with the glow of the afternoon sun. He hailed a cab, climbed inside and was gone.

Maggie let the drapes drop closed and roamed the sitting room. She touched the curved back of the settee, her fingers drifting over the griffin carved into the frame. The maid brought a tea tray, lingered for a few minutes, giving her shy, knowing looks that caused Maggie to blush profusely.

When the maid left, Maggie settled on the settee—she couldn't bring herself to walk through the door into the bedroom. She smoothed her gray silk skirts over her legs, then folded her hands in her lap. Sunlight glanced off the diamonds in her wedding band. She touched the stones. Mrs. Gordon Kincaid.

She loved him.

For how long, she didn't know. But she knew she had been loving him while riding that carousel and walking down the flower-strewn path. She went to the Fielding estate, and she loved him then.

She would love him until the world came to an end. Her safe world *had* come to an end. And now she stood poised on the threshold of a world she didn't understand, didn't even want. Except that he was in it.

I must tell Mother Bernadette I am married, she thought, and Father Fitzhugh.

She tried out words in her head: *Mother Bernadette, you have been like a mother to me, but there was not time to tell you before. I am Mrs. Gordon Kincaid because a woman told lies about me and Clare, so he rescued us and I let him because I love him, you see. It is not a proper marriage in the laws of the Church and my soul is imperiled. But my heart was already lost. I made my choice, dear Mother, and I chose a family. Pray God, I can do good in this life that frightens me so.*

Maggie walked over to the small secretary and pulled open the center drawer. She withdrew some gilt-edged stationery and an ivory pen, then sat in the chintz-covered chair.

Firelight sent huge shadows against the high ceiling. Maggie leaned back in the tub and watched the shadows dance in and out and around the ornate plasterwork. She was careful to avoid looking at the bed, so huge and central in the room. It brought too many heated thoughts, too many fears.

She might have spent the last fourteen years of her life in an orphanage run by nuns, but her first years were as a country girl. There was a similarity in the mating habits of sheep and pigs, dogs and horses. Surely God, in His wisdom, had designed men and women in much the same manner.

Maggie lifted the sponge and squeezed water between her breasts. She could see her heart pumping like a wild thing in her chest. The water had grown cold; she was as naked as the day she was born. And Gordon should be back soon.

Her skin prickled with the cold as she stood and reached for one of the soft towels. She'd brought the package the bellhop had delivered into the bedroom but hadn't opened it. Now she tucked the towel around her and walked over to the velvet-cushioned bench at the foot of the bed where she'd placed the box.

She reread the note that had accompanied the gift:

My dearest Maggie,

A package accompanies this note, a small token of my feelings. The maid has been instructed to take your clothing for laundering tonight. Send it all, Maggie-mine. Tonight, you dress only in the new as we begin our life together. Humor me, I aim only to please you.

Your husband,
Gordon Kincaid

She touched the stiff gold bow, then carefully removed the wrapping—it was much too pretty to be used only once. Her breath eased out in a sigh when she lifted the lid. She stroked the lustrous satin, not emerald green, but a rich, dark green she couldn't describe except as the most beautiful color she'd ever seen. She lifted the gown and drew in a very deep breath.

The front was cut low, nothing except skinny straps to hold it on her body. It had no neckline, would barely cover her breasts and the material was held together down the center front by ribbons. She laid it beside the box and searched through the tissue paper. Surely there must be a robe, something decent to cover herself with.

Nothing but tissue paper.

She had nothing left of her own. Their bags hadn't been brought up and she'd naively followed his instructions and given everything, even her chemise and drawers, to the maid. The towel wasn't a viable option. She'd be struggling with every movement to hold it around her.

There was nothing to do but try on the gown. She lifted it over her head and the satin was just slithering over her hips when she heard the key turn in the lock. Blessed Saint Brigid, he was back.

She heard his voice and more footsteps, the clatter of china and trays. She gathered from his words and the sounds that he'd ordered a dinner for them to eat in the room.

The gown fell all the way over her, draping her in deep, rich sensuality. She took a step and realized the material was slit on the sides all the way to her hips. Her throat went dry. She couldn't look at herself in the mirror. It was bad enough to glance down and see the swell of her breasts above the plunging neckline.

"Maggie?" he called from the other room.

She heard the hitching tread of his footsteps and turned her back to the door, clutching her hands over her breasts as if it might help. The door opened. She waited, breathless, for him to say something. Her knees began to tremble as the silence lengthened.

"My Irish sorceress." His voice was low. She feared she'd hear laughter in his tone, but what she heard was a thousand times worse. It was that deep, rich timbre that resonated through her, a sound that was both heat and seduction.

"Will you join me in the other room for dinner?" he said.

"Gordon, I—you—" Her tongue fumbled over words she couldn't even find. Suddenly he was behind her, not touching her, only his imposing body standing so close to her nearly naked one.

"Courage, Irish," he said softly. His arm came around her, a champagne glass clasped in his hand. "Try some of this. It might help." She took the glass, still unable to make herself turn and face him. His finger traced lightly down her exposed back. She couldn't control the shudder that raced through her.

"Nothing's going to happen tonight without your permission," he said. He removed his hand and when he spoke next, his voice was businesslike. "I'll be waiting in the sitting room. Don't take too long or the duck will get cold."

Gordon removed his coat and tossed it over the large box he'd carried in with him. Inside the box was a thick chenille robe. If she didn't come out on her own, he'd relent, but he was counting on her courage. Hoping, anyway.

He undressed down to his trousers and then donned his own dressing gown, belting it loosely at the waist. If he was going to have to try and eat while looking at her wearing a nightgown he'd chosen simply to torment himself, she could look at the hair on his chest. Of course, the sight probably would only add to her fright.

He was playing dangerously. In all his years of bedroom games, he'd bedded only one other virgin—Augusta. As he looked back on it, she'd been little more than a child out of the schoolroom, a Southern girl bred to submit to her husband. No one had bothered to mention to her she could find pleasure in the coupling. She'd been terrified and he'd been an overeager ass.

He wasn't an impatient, ruttish boy any longer, and Maggie . . .

Ah, dear Maggie. Passions simmered inside her. It was there in the way she met his kisses, unschooled and ardent, the way her body cleaved recklessly to his own. Tonight, he'd be the teacher. He'd teach her how her body could sing as wondrously as her voice. And he'd drown himself in her music.

He was pouring himself a glass of champagne when he heard the bedroom door open behind him. He turned. God, what fool said she wasn't beautiful? She was a woman to die for.

Chapter 16

He wanted her to walk, had had visions all afternoon of tall, stately Maggie walking across the room to him wearing that gown, her long legs bared by the slit up the side. She was standing in the doorway as if her feet were glued to the carpet.

Gordon poured her another glass of champagne, just enough to ease her tension. He held out the glass, coaxing her to come to him. He smiled, just a little. "It's customary to drink a toast to the bride, but I never drink alone."

Her face was so serious. Her eyes reflected the color of the gown, dark, dark green. She moved stiffly, like a woman going to her execution. His smile wanted to broaden, but he managed to keep his face set, until he got a glimpse of those legs, and then he couldn't hold it back. Long, slim and shapely, and provocative as hell draped in rich green satin.

She stopped an arm's length away from him, met his gaze briefly and then swept those sinful lashes downward so they cast shadows on her cheeks.

He held out the champagne and she took it. "A toast to my beautiful bride," he said, lifting his own glass. "May you have no regrets."

She lifted her gaze again. A faint smile played at her lips and then she took a small sip from the glass.

"Gordon . . ." Her fingers twisted the crystal around and around. He occupied himself at the little table, lighting the candles, giving her time to find the courage to say whatever it was she needed to say.

"I know naught . . . I mean . . ." She looked away at the fire, the table, the ceiling, everywhere but at him. "In an orphanage run by nuns . . . a convent school, a girl doesn't . . ."

He reached out and took the glass from her hand. "We eat next," he said matter-of-factly. After setting both glasses on the small round table, he pulled out her chair and gestured. "Crab soup is a favorite of mine and you can't get it anywhere like in Baltimore."

She seemed at a loss for words, but her face had relaxed into a hint of a smile. He decided that was encouraging. He took his position close beside her and proceeded to serve up two helpings of soup. "Roast duck, new potatoes in parsley butter, fresh green beans—nothing exceptional, but I hope it suits."

"And sure, isn't it a lovely meal."

He felt absurdly proud hearing her words, as if he were Saint George and had managed to slay her a dragon instead of simply ordering up from a hotel kitchen. He picked up his soup spoon.

"The blessing?" she said.

He lifted a brow. "Are you intent on saving my soul?"

"I shall try very hard," she said seriously.

Honest Maggie. He had to swallow before he could speak. "You shame me, angel. I'm afraid I need you more than is safe for any man to need a woman."

She looked down at her hands, still folded in her lap. "Aye," she said softly. " 'Tis much how I feel toward you."

His heart gave a sudden lurch. Not once had she said she

loved him; he didn't even expect her to say those words. But this—this was so damn close.

"I would like to say the blessing tonight."

She lifted her head, her lips hinting at a smile, and nodded.

"Dear Lord," he began quietly. "Thank you for the food we are about to receive. But even more, I give thanks for this gentle, kindhearted, spirited woman who has become my wife. May I become worthy of her with Thy blessings. Amen."

When he looked at her, he saw a tremulous smile at her lips. He handed her a linen napkin. "Eat your soup, Irish. It wouldn't do for the doctor's wife to be suffering from malnutrition."

He kept up an easy discourse while she ate her soup and by the time she was done, he'd coaxed some answering conversation from her. He had no interest in food. This hour was for taking in the sights and scents of Maggie.

As he watched, her tongue stroked her bottom lip unconsciously. Slow heat began to dissolve and flow in his loins. He imagined himself rising and standing behind her, letting down that glorious mass of hair so it would fall free in a shimmering cascade to the floor, running his hands through the black silk tresses. Imagined unfastening the first two of those silk ribbons and baring her breasts to his eyes . . . but the night was still young.

When the duck was gone, he selected a ripe strawberry from the fruit tray and dipped it in the champagne. He held it out and the strawberry passed from his fingers to her mouth. His thumb brushed her lips, catching a drop of red juice. A low sound came from deep in her throat.

Her hands fluttered and twisted in her lap, as if she instinctively recognized the subtle intimacy in the act of accepting food from his hand.

He touched her cheek, gently forcing her to look at him. Her throat convulsed as she swallowed. She closed her eyes, hiding the sensual green shadows behind thick black lashes. He leaned forward and kissed her.

She stiffened and he thought for an instant she was going to push him away, but her arms went over his shoulders as her lips parted. He delved deeper, tasting champagne and tart berries and Maggie. His hands stroked down her neck, reached lower for her breast, and he stopped himself. He pulled away from the kiss slowly, with little nips and teases at the corner of her mouth. She was breathing rapidly.

He stood and held out his hand. "Come sit by the fire with me. We need to talk."

She looked at him then with such a bewildered expression that he almost laughed. He pulled her up and led her to the plush sofa in front of the marble fireplace. She sat stiffly, with her knees together, her hands gripping the gown between her breasts. He sat next to her and put his arm around her shoulders, subtly forcing her into a more relaxed position against him. Yet he could feel the tension in the tautness of her muscles.

"Sometimes I forget that you didn't spend your entire childhood inside that orphanage," he said. "Your first twelve years were spent on a stud farm."

She nodded against his chest. He stroked her bare arm with his thumb, gently, up and down. "And did you ever watch the stallions servicing the mares?"

She was silent for a long time. He felt her breath on his chest. "Nay," she said softly. "But I heard them."

"And it frightened you."

More silence, and then a whispered assent. He moved his hand and brushed the hair at her temple. "I've stood in the stud barn watching it, angel, and I'll tell you that the sight is beautiful, violent, frightening and arousing all at the same time. But it has nothing to do with what happens when a man and a woman join."

She gave a faint little giggle. "And next he'll be telling me the Immaculate Conception was not a miracle at all."

He smiled at her bravery. "Well, there are certain similarities, I must admit." He tilted her face up. "Maggie, I can sit here and give you a doctor's explanation of . . . consumma-

ion," he said, choosing the less graphic word at the last moment. "But I think, given the fact you already have some
idea, the better thing is for you to trust me to guide you
through it, show you how a man and woman . . . join together." He brushed his thumb across her bottom lip and her
mouth opened.

He was dizzy, desperate with wanting her. He shifted her
back against the cushions and kissed her. The kiss was long,
beginning slow and gentle then turning urgent. And she gave
back to him in moist, whispery sighs, the thrust of her breasts
against his chest, her hands molding his back.

He shifted his hands, undoing each of the ribbons on her
gown, touching her breasts as they were revealed, her belly,
between her thighs. And when he was done, he raised back so
he could look at her. Her eyes were wide and dark, her mouth
bruised and trembling.

He stood and held out his hand to her. "Now, Maggie."

One minute Maggie was in his arms being kissed, and the
next, she was standing beside the bed in a room lit by firelight with his hands loosening her hair. He fanned the braid
open and then his fingers were lifting through her unbound
hair, spreading it, letting it drop down her back.

"Beautiful, so beautiful," he said in that rich, resonant tone
that vibrated through her blood. "My beautiful Maggie."

Then he was removing his pants and removing her gown
and kissing her, and somehow she found herself in the bed
with his long length stretched beside her. Instinctively, she
turned in to him. He made a low sound and she felt the vibra-
tion against her chest.

He rolled her onto her back and leaned over her. His gentle hand brushed her cheek. "If I frighten you, say stop and
I'll stop." He laughed deep in his throat. "God only knows
how I'll manage, but I promise you I will."

She didn't know who she was—not virtuous Maggie
Quinn, for virtuous Maggie Quinn would never reach up and
cup his face in her hands, asking without word or thought for

another kiss. But she wasn't Maggie Quinn now, she was Maggie Kincaid, and her husband answered her silent plea and lowered his head to kiss her.

His mouth took hers as his hands moved over her skin creating flashes of fire everywhere he touched; and his hands were everywhere, her hips and thighs, a tickling line from her throat to her navel, her breast.

He moved, his mouth suckling at her breast and his hand dropping lower, between her legs, up and down the inside of her thighs, tangling in the soft curls between her legs. She heard little whimpering sounds and realized they were coming from her.

She writhed as his fingers probed into her most intimate place. He shifted, raising her hips in his hands, and his mouth was where his hands had been, tasting her. Oh, Blessed Saints, he must not, she must not. She turned and twisted, reaching to push him away, but instead her hands grabbed his shoulders, pulling him closer. She burned and ached and wanted something desperately.

"Yes, yes," he breathed into her. He added his finger to the sensations his mouth was creating and then she heard nothing as an explosion rocked her body, splintering her into thousands of tiny white lights.

He came up over her, his arms around her, holding her trembling body together. "Yes, yes, my beautiful Maggie." He kissed her, little breaths of kisses all over her face. "Yes, yes," he whispered as his hands moved back to that exquisite spot of torture again.

She moaned, immediately on fire even before the last flames had died. He shifted over her—held her tightly as he eased into her, stretching her to fit him, creating an aching pain. She fought to hold back her sounds as he pushed himself deeper, creating pain at the same time he soothed her with kisses, until he gave one mighty shove and she cried out.

"Oh, Maggie, Maggie," he said as he kissed away her tears. His voice ached as if it hurt him too. More soft kisses down her throat. "Only a little while—soon."

His breathing was tight and shallow. He held himself over
er, perfectly still, with only a faint tremor in his arms. His
ace, that beloved, beautiful face, watching her from dark,
eated eyes. Slowly, pain turned into a fullness. She let out a
ttle sigh as her muscles released the tension.

He raised back and entered her again, renewing the pain.
he clutched at his arms, suddenly afraid.

"Relax, angel," he murmured against her ear, and her
vhole body shuddered, not from fear but from the sensation
f his breath on her skin. He nibbled her ear lobe and waves
f delicious sensations rushed through her.

He turned his head and kissed her, kisses so quick and
ard she couldn't quite catch his mouth with her own. She
aught his face between her hands, stilling him, and her
highs tightened around his hips. The movement caused a re-
ction; she felt him flex inside her and the answering re-
ponse of her muscles tightening around his thickness. His
reath hissed between his teeth.

"I can't control this much longer." He smiled, but there
vas strain in the effort.

She felt her eyelids go heavy, slumberous with a female
ower she'd never imagined. "Show me. Please."

He began to move, slowly at first, a gentle thrust and with-
rawal that had her aching for more. Hesitantly, she re-
ponded, her body lifting to meet his, and he quickened the
ace. He reached down to the place where their bodies
oined, rubbing his finger against the spot where his tongue
ad touched her before. She felt herself spiraling out of con-
rol, intent only on that sensation of burning pleasure where
is body met hers.

He gave her no mercy now, even when she bucked against
is hand in an effort to escape the fierce onslaught of sensa-
ion. The heat built until it was almost exquisite pain and then
e hurled her further into the spiral, thrusting harder, deeper
nside her in a way that made her cling to him and cry out in
a pleasure so strong and fundamental she couldn't control it.

This was Gordon inside her, thrusting, withdrawing, thrusting again. Gordon, cradling her in his arms. Gordon, whom she had doubted, loving her. And that final thought freed her from the last of the bonds holding her back. She opened herself to him fully: her mouth, accepting his tongue, her hips accepting his penetration, her heart, accepting he loved her as much as she loved him.

The heat coiled inside her, growing stronger and stronger and when the explosion finally came she arched wildly beneath him, her body shuddering as her hips continued to pump herself against his hard thickness. She heard her own cries and didn't care.

He grasped her hips, his fingers biting into her skin, and shoved himself hard into her, then his head flung back and a long, low sound tore out of his chest. He gave one final thrust and she felt his life flood into her while his body jerked and shuddered within her arms.

He collapsed on top of her and she held him, stroked his back and shoulders. He nuzzled his face in her neck.

"*My* Maggie," he said.

She turned her head and brushed her lips where his pulse throbbed in his throat. She could feel his heart beating against her own. He rolled and pulled her with him, his arm cradling her in his warmth. Her body was weak, totally spent, yet she felt safe, enfolded as she was by his strength.

His lips brushed her forehead. "I'll make myself into the man you deserve. I swear it, Maggie."

"*A mhúirnín.*" She pressed closer to him and buried her face in his chest.

His warm breath ruffled her hair. He stroked her hip, a gentle motion that seemed to guide her into sleep. His breathing slowed and deepened.

His low voice barely penetrated through her drowsy, sensual haze when he said softly, "What does *á mhúirnín* mean?"

She struggled, half-conscious and drifting. His hand was so warm, so soothing on her skin, and she was already sliding into darkness. Her lips formed the words, but no sound came out. *My love.* It was her last thought before sleep claimed her.

* * *

She slept in his arms, as trusting as a child. His fingers tangled in her hair, smoothed it, tangled some more. Gordon eased away from her and got up.

She sighed a little but didn't awaken as he gently cleaned her with a damp washcloth. When he was done, he lowered himself next to her and drew her back into his arms.

His wife.

He'd fallen in love again, a different love that was already deeper than anything he could have imagined. He'd tricked her—no, not quite a trick, but a subtle pressure—using her love for Clara to coerce her to marry him. Reprehensible.

For tricks, he'd used every trick in the book of seduction to get her into his bed tonight.

Passionate Maggie. She'd given herself, wholly and trustingly, until the trick was on him, sorry bastard that he was. He could walk away from the games he'd played before, but he could never walk away from Maggie. Not because of what he'd done to her, taking her virginity, but because of what she'd done to him. She'd taken his heart—and his soul too, he feared.

He hadn't even told her he had another child, a son she would have to deal with. He couldn't begin to guess what Gordy's reaction would be when he discovered his father had a new wife, he had a little sister and Maggie, dear Maggie, was to be mother to both.

Somehow, tomorrow, he'd find a way to tell her. She would have every right to hate him.

He held her hard against his chest and fought back sleep—he wanted to make this real, make this last. Tomorrow, it may be only a memory.

A cacophony of city noises floated up from the street below. Gordon stood on the balcony, disinterestedly watching the flow of traffic in front of Monument Square as he sipped on a morning cup of coffee. He heard the bedroom door open and stepped back into the sitting room.

"I thought you'd sleep late this morning," he said. She was dressed in the chenille robe he'd left at the foot of the bed and managed to look seductive even in that. Evidently, she'd been awake long enough to braid her hair in two long plaits.

She smiled uncertainly. "You are dressed to go out."

"I have some patients I want to see one more time before I go back to Virginia." He didn't say it, but he wondered: Would she be traveling with him and Clara, or was last night going to be the extent of their marriage? One wildly passionate night. He walked over to the tea table where the tray he'd ordered earlier waited. "Coffee or tea?"

Her uncertain smile faded into apprehension. "You do not want me with you, then?"

He looked away from her. Acting on assumption, he poured her a cup of tea, then added milk. Get it over with, he thought. She wasn't going to understand; he had no right to expect her to understand. She came forward slowly and took the cup and saucer from his hand. She looked from the milky tea up into his face, her green eyes filled with hurt. Damn.

"I told you yesterday I had a confession to make."

"Aye, you did."

He raked his fingers through his hair, then looked steadily back at her, meeting the confusion and pain in her eyes. "I was married before, Maggie. During the war. I have a son by that marriage."

The porcelain cup rattled against the saucer. She stilled the clatter with her free hand against the rim of the cup and carefully placed the set back on the silver tray. She was worrying her lower lip and he wanted nothing more than to kiss that worry away. He turned on his heel and went back to the window.

"And your wife?" Her voice quavered on the last word.

"She died." His left hand clenched and unclenched at his side. He made himself stop by grasping the damask draperies. For a long time, he listened to the sound of her breathing.

"You could not tell me before?" she asked in a small voice.

"I tried yesterday, in the carriage. Before that—I don't know, everything happened so fast and it just never seemed to be the right time." He turned and leaned backward, resting his palms against the sill, watching her. "Stupid of me, I know."

She shrugged one shoulder, said nothing. He waited, half-hoping she would come to him, making no move to go to her. He would not beg or coerce her. Not now, not ever again.

Golden light bathed her face as she moved through a shaft of sunlight, her steps slow, apparently aimless. She stopped at the back of the settee.

Gordon's hands tightened on the sill. Mingled emotions surged through him—self-reproach, dread, even anger. To be judged and found wanting for himself, that he could handle. He had made his own conclusions on the matter: Guilty as hell. But to be condemned for Augusta and Gordy—no. There was no sin in having married and produced a child, only in not speaking of it before now.

When she said nothing, he pushed himself straight, hiding the wince of pain brought on by the abrupt movement.

"Your clothing has been returned, laundered," he said. "The brown bag that was beside the robe." He walked to the door, paused with his hand on the knob. "I'll order a carriage and wait in the lobby. Twenty minutes. If I don't see you, I'll know you've made your decision."

The only sound as he left was the door quietly closing.

It took her longer than twenty minutes. She wasted the first five simply absorbing the knowledge he'd left her standing alone. By the time she'd dressed and pinned up her hair, Maggie expected him to be gone.

She'd fallen asleep last night thinking of herself as his wife, the woman he loved enough to marry even though she was an Irish-Catholic immigrant and he was a Kincaid. But she must be honest with herself now. He hadn't married her for love, but from kindness or guilt or the need for someone to mother his children. Or maybe some mixture of all three.

But not for love.

Her hand gripped the railing hard as she descended the stairs. If he was already gone, she would walk the city and try to sort through her muddled thoughts. If he waited, she didn't know what she would do.

Maggie saw him immediately as she entered the lobby. He stood near the door, gazing blankly at the street. A bar of sunlight slanted across him, casting his face in half-light and shadow.

Her footsteps slowed and then halted. He'd waited, but she didn't know what that meant any more than she understood her own tumultuous emotions. Seeing him brought a sudden awareness of the enormity of what she had done. And what she had allowed him to do to her.

He turned his head a little and their gazes met. His taut expression didn't alter. Without conscious thought, her feet started forward, carried her across the lobby. She stopped with a distance between them, a rift as wide as his deception.

He sighed and looked away, then brought his midnight eyes back. She saw nothing there, no light, no shadows, nothing of his thoughts.

"My wife?" His voice was flat.

"I stood beside you yesterday and made a vow before God. For better or worse."

He smiled faintly but was wise enough not to make any more false promises. He offered his arm. Maggie took one step forward and placed her hand. Her wedding band caught the sunlight, glittering diamonds and glowing emeralds. She bent her head and looked away.

Chapter 17

G ordon reached for the carriage door, then pulled back. "This is a special case," he said. "Will you just bear with me?"

She had no idea what he meant but nodded in agreement. He climbed out of the carriage, then turned to assist her. A flock of speckled hens scratched and cackled at their progress through the yard. A worn-looking woman came out on the front porch, wiping her hands on a calico apron as they approached the sagging steps.

"How's our boy doing?" he asked, holding out the wicker basket they'd bought just hours ago at Lexington Market and filled with food purchases.

"The leg's good, but come in and see for yourself." The woman brushed a straggle of fine, graying hair from her cheek, then took the basket. "What have you done this time?"

Gordon sent Maggie a sidelong glance, a warning of some type. "Nothing," he said. "Just an overabundance from

Burleigh's gardens this year. Couldn't stand to see it go to waste."

"You don't fool me for a minute, Dr. Kincaid," said the woman, and then she smiled a weary smile. "But I'll take it, and thank you." She looked from Gordon to Maggie and back again.

"My wife," said Gordon. "Sadie Jenson."

"Well, it's about time. You've been single much too long." Sadie's smile became genuine and she gestured toward the door. "Come on through. He's sitting out back watching the redwings harvest the last of the corn."

Gordon laughed and followed Mrs. Jenson into the small house. Belatedly, Maggie realized she was to follow. The house smelled of fresh bread and pine soap. They passed through a small parlor into a kitchen. Gordon stopped there, placing his black satchel on the table. He opened the satchel and removed several bottles.

"Expectorant, some morphia—use that sparingly," he said as he placed each bottle on the table. Mrs. Jenson nodded without questioning. Maggie began to understand this was a ritual they had gone through before. "I took it upon myself to see Dr. Lewis," he said. "The arrangements are for him to come by here at least three times a week. You let me know if he doesn't."

Moisture shimmered in Mrs. Jenson's eyes. Gordon glanced at her, started to say something and then didn't. He pulled out three large brown bottles and set them beside the others.

"Valentine's Meat Juice, fresh from Richmond. Should be enough to get you through a couple of months."

"Yes," said Mrs. Jenson in a small voice. Absently, she stroked the yellow oilcloth. "A couple months. . . ."

Gordon's boots sounded dully in the silence as he moved around the table. "Sometimes a patient's wife needs some medicine of her own," he said, putting his arms around her and drawing her into a hug. "Best medicine in the world."

Mrs. Jenson made another small sound and rested her

cheek on his chest. Gordon patted her back and caught Maggie's eye. She saw the shadows moving in the dark, dark blue, the tense lines back in his face.

Mrs. Jenson stepped away and straightened her shoulders. "Go on out back. I'll join you in a minute."

Maggie hesitated as Gordon moved past her and pushed open the door. "Mrs. Jenson, can I—"

"Just need to compose myself. I'll be fine after that."

"Aye, then," said Maggie softly. She pushed open the kitchen door and walked out into brilliant sunshine. As her eyes adjusted to the light, she saw the two men sitting beneath a misshapen oak. Beyond them, a flock of redwings cavorted over the cornfield, flashing brightly colored epaulets.

She heard the door slam, then Mrs. Jenson came up beside her. They stood in silence, watching the two men.

"You wouldn't guess looking at him that he's a famous man," said Mrs. Jenson after a moment.

"Famous?" said Maggie weakly.

"Went all the way to London last year to give a talk to the medical society there on those fake limbs he designed. I forget how many patents he holds on those things, not that I understand it much anyways. All I know is the one Cal wore fit, and it worked. Your husband's factory puts them out by the bushelful." Mrs. Jenson lifted the corner of her apron and patted the lingering traces of flour from her hands. "You haven't been married long, have you?"

"No." Maggie watched a gray cat prowl at the edge of the cornfield and then slip into the shadows between the rows.

She didn't know anything about his factory, his patents, his fame as an orthopedic specialist. She was beginning to understand that she knew almost nothing about him.

"I expect this will be their last visit," said Mrs. Jenson in a low voice that caught at the end.

Gordon leaned forward with his elbows on his knees and bent his head, as if listening to a secret. As they watched, he raised himself back, an easy grin on his face. He said something that caused the other man to laugh. The laugh turned into a fit of coughing. Gordon reached in his pocket and pulled out his silk handkerchief, holding it to the other man's mouth. Bright spots of blood appeared on the yellow silk.

"My Calvin was your husband's sergeant during the war," said Mrs. Jenson. "Cal got himself shot at Chancellorsville, couldn't get away from the fires burning the woods. Your husband went in and got him. Course, Calvin lost his leg, but he always said that didn't make no never mind. Doesn't speak much about that time, but he'll tell anyone it was your husband that saved his life."

"And this time he can't."

"No. Consumption—it runs in Cal's family."

The redwings rose en masse, their distinctive *kick-a-poo* cry filling the air as they wheeled against the deep blue sky.

"Perhaps I should wait in the carriage," said Maggie, reluctant to interfere with the two men or impose herself on the saddened, weary Mrs. Jenson.

"No. Cal will want to meet you. He always said what the doctor needed was a good wife." Mrs. Jenson laughed self-consciously. "I do run on so, just listen to me. . . ."

Gordon looked over and gestured for her to join them. He rose as she approached, made the introduction, and then indicated she was to take his chair. A brown shawl blanket covered Calvin's lap and dropped to the ground. Even so, it was evident his left leg had been amputated just below the hip.

They talked for a while about the harvest, the weather, inconsequential things. At some point, she realized Gordon had stepped closer to her, and then felt his hand lightly on her shoulder. She looked up. Their gazes met and his face softened. She resisted the urge to reach up and touch his hand. She couldn't. She had to remember his perfidy.

"You two visit a minute," he said. "I want to step inside and see if Sadie will let me sample her cornbread."

"You go on, Cap'n," said Calvin, giving Maggie a slight wink. "This little wife of yours is safe with me."

"No woman is safe with you, Cal."

Both men laughed and then Gordon took off for the house.

"They're going to talk about me," said Calvin when Gordon disappeared inside. "They think I don't know I'm dying, but you can't fool an old soldier like me. Stared death in the face before. This isn't much different."

"It's not an easy thing to talk about, but if it were me as your wife, I'd be wanting to share my fears. Perhaps it would be wise for you to tell her you know."

He looked at her from tired brown eyes, and surprised her with a smile. "Gordon himself has been needing a wife for years. I think maybe he found a good one."

"It's not that kind of marriage." She plucked at a loose thread on her shawl, avoiding his gaze.

"You listen to my advice this time," he said. "All he needs is someone who cares, been needing it for like to ten years now."

She looked up. "And sure it is we all need that."

She saw her husband then, standing near the back of the house watching them. His tall body was silhouetted by bright light against a blue backdrop of sky.

He rubbed the heel of his palm hard against one cheekbone. He seemed to sigh and then started forward. She looked away before he realized she'd seen his emotion.

He was a complex man. Maybe even an extraordinary one. And she wanted nothing more than to get away from him now. Far, far away. To someplace safe where, maybe, she could make herself stop loving him.

Mother Bernadette pulled a pair of reading glasses from a ribbon around her neck and settled them on her nose. She lifted the top sheet of paper. He'd had a lawyer draw up adoption papers; Clara would bear the name she should have borne since birth. The other document was the marriage certificate. And at the bottom was the envelope addressed in Maggie's handwriting to Mother Bernadette. He could only imagine what sentiments were expressed in that letter.

Gordon pushed himself out of the uncomfortable armchair and prowled the visitors' parlor, listening to the shuffle of papers as Mother Bernadette went through the stack. He'd already explained that Clara knew he was her father and obtained a verbal agreement that this adoption should proceed without delay. The other matter he'd left for her own discovery.

"So you married our Maggie," she said with a small sigh in her voice. "Because I said Clara needed a mother?"

"No. If that marriage certificate read Rebecca Hays, you'd be right. Not Maggie."

"I'd feel better about this if she'd come with you."

"I wanted to spare her the explanations."

"Then explain, Gordon."

Gordon stopped in front of the mantel. He reached up and touched the long glass prisms on the candleholder, causing them to tinkle like chimes. He turned and leaned one shoulder against the wood frontispiece.

"Rebecca skewered her with lies in front of I don't know how many people, things that would ruin any woman's reputation. I'd already asked Maggie to marry me, but I don't know that she'd have said yes without Becca's impetus."

Mother Bernadette pulled the glasses off, carefully folded the arms and tucked them beneath her cowl. "Maggie knows she could have returned here."

"She couldn't have continued teaching. A few of those guests were parents of students in your school."

Mother Bernadette opened her mouth to interrupt and Gordon shifted impatiently. "You know how subtly it works," he said. "All it takes is one or two women who consider Rebecca a friend and Maggie an outsider. Savanna Cannaught for instance. She couldn't resist sinking her claws into Maggie. Her husband's bank controls business lines of credit. A few cautionary words from banker to businessman, and suddenly there's a father standing in your office threatening to remove his daughter. That father may or may not believe the lies against Maggie; it doesn't matter as long as he believes the monetary threat against himself. Enough fathers and your school is in jeopardy. We're not talking morality, or at least not the kind of morality they claim to espouse, and you know that as well as I do."

"You paint a bleak picture, Gordon."

"But not a false one."

She sat for a moment, staring at her hands in her lap. "No," she said finally. "I would like to argue that point, but I can't. Maggie still could have come back, though. She was well aware we wouldn't turn her away." She leaned forward and lifted her teacup, took a sip, then replaced it on the saucer. "Knowing Maggie—"

"Don't jump to pie-in-the sky conclusions." Gordon returned to the chair and sank into it. He shook his head. "Whatever she felt, I bungled it by not telling her about Augusta and Gordy until this morning."

"Oh, Gordon," she said softly, the disappointment apparent in her tone. "Why?"

"I was already guilty of so many moral flaws in her mind—how was I supposed to tell her I have a son I hardly know?" He leaned back and spread his fingers wide, giving her a one-sided smile. But that smile cost him. "There you have it in a nutshell. Dr. Kincaid is the world's biggest coward."

"Maggie took the news hard?"

"She was devastated," he said slowly. "I fully expected her to come back here as soon as I left to make my rounds. Why she didn't, I don't know."

"That won't do, Gordon. There's too much at stake. Clara, Maggie—you and your son—four lives are entangled in this now."

Maybe five, he thought. The possibility certainly existed. "It's not me," he said. "I never expected to feel this way again about anyone. I'd give her the moon and the stars on a silver platter if I could."

"Then reach for them," she said. "Fight for her."

"Fight for her." His lips curled in self-mockery. "What right have I to fight for her? As soon as I know she's not with child, I'll let her go. I know that's what she wants."

"Young fool."

Gordon closed his eyes. He wasn't so young anymore, but *fool* certainly hit the mark.

"Let me explain something to you about your wife," she said. "Maggie came to us as a twelve-year-old child who brought with her little besides her memories and her faith. Has Maggie spoken to you about the events that caused her family to flee Ireland?" He shook his head—he saw no need to elaborate on Jamie O'Connor—and she said, "If she ever does, consider it a monumental gift, because none of us, not even Father Fitzhugh, have ever been able to extract a single word from her on the subject."

"What's your point?"

"Bear with me, I'm coming to that. We know what she witnessed through Padraig O'Connor recounting the story— I won't go into details because that is Maggie's privilege if she so chooses." For a moment Mother Bernadette became lost in her thoughts, then she shrugged. "Father Fitzhugh reached through her grief with his harp, the songs of her homeland. In many ways, Maggie's salvation has been in her music. But even once she began to respond to us, there were never any words from her to ease that burden I knew she carried inside. And being the hard woman I am, I determined to make her talk about it."

She huffed a small breath, her lips almost smiling, then said, "I failed. Sister Agatha believes all the world's sorrows can be addressed more easily in a kitchen, so she took the child to the rectory kitchen where it could be just the two of them, ostensibly to teach Maggie how to make sugar cookies, but of course the goal was to get the child to talk about Ireland.

"And now the point I'm trying to make. Sister Agatha got no further than any of the rest of us, so she sat the child on her lap and point-blank said: *We're not leaving this kitchen until you tell me what happened in Killady.* And Maggie's response?"

Gordon shrugged. He couldn't even begin to guess.

Mother Bernadette placed her reading glasses on her nose, then unfolded the letter from Maggie.

" 'In Ireland,' " she read in her uppercrust Philadelphia accent, " 'we have a saying. The things that cannot be explained are either miracles or mysteries, and they both have to be taken on faith.' "

Her starched habit crackled as she let out a deep sigh. She lowered the paper to her lap. "That was what she told Sister Agatha fourteen years ago, and even then, I envied that child the strength of her faith. In all these years, her faith has never faltered. And if I were to read you more of this letter, which I will not do, as Maggie wrote it to me in trust . . ." Her mouth softened at the edges. "I would be revealing that now Maggie feels her soul is imperiled by marrying outside the canons of her faith. All this might seem silly to you, but it has always been tremendously important to her. No matter what else she said in this letter, that alone tells me her feelings for you are strong."

Maggie had tried to tell him just that about her Church and he hadn't really listened. "Is that what you believe?"

"That she loves you or that she's doomed herself to eternal damnation?"

He smiled caustically. "They may be one and the same."

"We've had these kinds of discussions before and you don't need to hear it again." She paused. There was a warmth in her ice-blue eyes that didn't appear often. "You really should have been born a Catholic," she said. "I've never met a man as hard on himself as you are."

The statement didn't deserve comment, so he let it pass. She leaned over and set Maggie's letter on the table in front of her.

"What I believe is that Maggie searched her heart and made a conscious decision, and given her history, I will say unequivocally that she chose the more frightening path. Now *you* have a responsibility, to your wife, your children. Yourself." She waved her hand. "Put the religious issues aside. They'll solve themselves if and when you and Maggie solve this issue of trust. What do you want from this marriage, Gordon?

He almost laughed. Himself a bastard son, deserted by the mother who bore him. And as good a father as Peyton had been, giving him his own name, loving him in his Old World manner, it hadn't been enough to fill that hole in his chest. He never felt good enough, worthy enough of his father's love.

And the women who mattered had a habit of leaving him. Celeste, the mother who didn't want him. Augusta, the young wife who died. And now Maggie, the woman who mattered most.

Already he was losing her.

"All I have ever wanted in my life is a family. That's all, not wealth or fame, just a family."

"You have one, Dr. Kincaid. Now make it work."

He looked at the shadow slanting across the floor. "How?" he murmured.

"Take her home, Gordon. And when you get there, show her how much you love her."

Chapter 18

*M*aggie stood on the swaying iron platform. The last salmon fingers of sunset colored the clouds just above the treeline. She was dressed in a new traveling suit of gray-blue worsted wool trimmed with black velvet piping, and the wind whipped the skirts around her legs. The train wheels turned, *clickety-clickety-clack-clack*.

It had been hard, saying good-bye to the nuns and the children, knowing she might never see them again.

So many had come to see them off: the sisters and all seventeen of the children left at the orphanage; Drew, clasping Alice's hand in his own, the child laughing as she shared her excitement with Clare while Drew joked with Gordon and promised to come stay with them for the New Year's Day fox hunt.

There was so much confusion in the send-off that it was only after she had hugged Alice that Maggie looked up and saw Jamie O'Connor standing off to the side and alone.

Their gazes held for one taut moment and then he stepped

back. She was married now, and perhaps a married woman should seek her husband's permission before conversing with a single man, but Maggie didn't look at her husband. She walked the distance to Jamie, who watched her come until she stood in front of him, and then he looked away at the personal railway car on the siding.

His mouth curved into a slow smile. "It's a fine life you'll be living, Mrs. Kincaid."

She glanced at the huge maroon car that would take her via Harpers Ferry and on into Fredericksburg, arriving in her husband's hometown about this time tomorrow. Four rooms, even a kitchen and piazza, if she were to believe Gordon's explanation to Clare, and she could see the iron piazza jutting at the end of the car, so she supposed the rest was truth. She couldn't imagine such luxury.

"Aye, 'tis a wee bit different from third-class steerage." She tried to smile and almost succeeded. "I'll be Clare's mother, Jamie." Her voice trembled slightly. "And Dr. Kincaid has a son. He's twelve . . . and he'll be needing someone to care for him and . . ."

"And those are fine things, but it's you I'm thinking about. Will you be happy, darlin' Maggie?"

"Aye," she said, but feared it was a lie.

"And you know, surely, that if you need anything, all you have to do—"

"No, don't say it." She lifted her shoulders in a small helpless shrug. "He's my husband, Jamie."

He took a step away from her. He looked at the gilt letters scrolled on the railcar: RIVERBEND ESTATES. He took off his tweed cap and she saw that his fingers were white on the brim.

She wanted to say to him: *I'm sorry, James O'Connor, for all the wrongs I have done you. I didn't know it could hurt this much, to love and not be loved in return.*

He faced her again and she saw his eyes fix on something over her shoulder. Maggie turned, slowly and carefully, as if she were afraid of falling. She had fallen so far already. Gordon's eyes, intense and blue, fixed on her, and then he was standing so close she could smell the spicy soap he'd used for shaving.

"Jamie came to say good-bye," she said, the color rising warm on her cheeks.

"You must stop and visit us if you're ever in Virginia," said Gordon, and she could read nothing within his mannerly voice. He took her arm. "We have to go, I'm afraid. Clara is already boarded."

"*Dhia is maire dhuit*," said Jamie softly. She tried to return the blessing but her throat was too tight, so she didn't. Jamie drew a deep breath. "You were always a grand lady, Mrs. Kincaid. Don't you be forgetting that."

He held out his hand to her, and her eyes filled up as she took it—then she was watching him walk away from her. Her final farewell to the old country. And she did not know this parting could be so hard either.

The train whistle blew as she hugged Sister Agatha, who patted her on the cheek and whispered, "I knew he could do much better than Miss Hays," which caused her to smile even though the smile trembled.

The engine hissed steam as she looked into Mother Bernadette's oval face. "Mother," she said, and her voice cracked over the word she meant in all its many meanings.

"We have a saying in Philadelphia," said Mother Bernadette, her face so serene, her blue eyes so knowing. "God never closes a door that he doesn't open a window."

Maggie tried to smile again, but her eyes blurred instead so that she stumbled as Gordon took her arm within his own, folding his gloved hand over hers. He led her away. No, toward . . .

Toward the private railcar that would take her into the unfamiliar territory of his Southern life. She walked the boarding ramp, arm in arm with her husband. All around them, people laughed and shouted in excitement. The whistle shrilled again and smoke gusted from the iron stack.

We are walking together, she thought, as husband and wife—together, but not speaking.

And now she stood on the iron platform alone, the wind tearing at her hair. The scenery rushed past in a blur of a run-down shack at the edge of a twisting dirt road, a Negro boy on a long-eared mule, dark groves of hardwood forests. The last rays of the sun lingered for one golden, shimmering minute and then the sky turned gray as the long night began.

The platform swayed as the train wheels turned, *clickety-clickety-clack-clack,* and the wind caused tears in her eyes.

"Do I really have a brother in Virginia?"

"Yes, princess. And a cousin too." Gordon sat on the edge of the berth and brushed the curls off Clara's forehead. He was taking his daughter home with him. He'd won. One battle anyway. He leaned over and kissed the spot where his fingers had touched.

"It's time to get some sleep," he said. "We've a busy day tomorrow too."

Clara clutched her rag doll against her chest. She looked at him with wide blue eyes. "My Maggie's sad."

"I know, Clara. Sometimes leaving is very hard."

In the confusion of nuns and children and passengers boarding, he hadn't seen Jamie O'Connor until Maggie walked toward him. Gordon wasn't going to dwell on why Jamie had come to see her off, or what words they'd shared before he joined them. His one thought had been to get his girls on the train and headed home.

For a moment at the train station when Jamie had spoken in Gaelic, he'd thought Maggie would leave with the Irishman instead. He paled to think of it.

"I love you, princess," he said, whispering the words as Clara had fallen asleep that fast. And he realized then how long it had been since he'd spoken those words to anyone. Hard words for a man to say, because they made him so vulnerable.

He got up slowly so as not to awaken Clara and went to the dressing room, where he changed from his traveling clothes into a lounging robe, carefully hanging his day wear in the ingenious little pantries and closets so Maggie would not feel this was her wifely duty. *Show her how much you love her.*

He went to look for her, but he paused at the door to the smaller sleeping berth and looked at his daughter snuggled with a raggedy, homemade doll in the lower bunk. He spent a long, sweet moment suspended in the train's gentle rocking, watching his daughter sleep.

He'd won the battle with the mother superior for possession of his daughter. He thought he had even won his daughter's love. But the real battle would be for Maggie.

When he finally stepped into the parlor, he was surprised to see that the sky outside was as gray as the velvet curtains at the train windows.

Maggie was in the small kitchen, washing their supper dishes.

She'd removed her suit jacket and her white shirtwaist was pocked with dark splotches where she'd splashed water on the front. The slim skirt hugged her hips and swayed at the hem with the train's motion. Evidently the wind had made a shambles of her coiffure as she stood on the platform, for now her hair hung in a thick black braid down her back.

He went to her and took her hand from the water, turning it over. He rubbed his fingers down her wet, reddened palm. He could see the rapid pulsing in the blue veins of her wrist.

She looked up at him, her eyes so deeply green and troubled. He wanted to say, *I love you,* and take her to the big bed in the sleeping compartment to prove his words, but that wasn't enough. And yet, there weren't any other words to tell her what was turning his blood to smoke.

"And who would believe hot and cold running water in a train car," she said in that way she had that was both teasing and vulnerable.

"You don't wash dishes anymore, Mrs. Kincaid." He rubbed his thumb on the back of her hand, feeling each separate, slender ridge of bone. Her hand was trembling. God, what had he done to her, to them? How could he make her believe in him again? Trust him enough to love him back?

He gripped her shoulders and set her gently away from the sink. Her head tipped back. Her cheeks were flushed, her eyes deep green pools, and he could see nothing in them but the reflection of himself.

Show her how much you love her.

He took her hand and led her into the parlor. "Sit down, Mrs. Kincaid."

She sat in the blue velvet chair near the window, using the arm to support herself as she folded into the seat. She rubbed her neck where the pulse beat above the high lace collar of her shirtwaist. She looked at him, then away. "Gordon, I—"

"Hold the thought, Irish," he said. "Let me pour you a cup of tea first."

He had only tonight. Tomorrow they would arrive in Fredericksburg. His wealth, his position, his name—they were all the wrong weapons to use in this battle to win his wife's trust.

All he had left were words. They were not sweet words, or pretty ones. But they were his truth.

Gordon handed her the cup of tea. He tried to smile but couldn't manage it, so he turned away and lowered himself into the chair across from her. He picked up the book he'd read to Clara while Maggie battled her fears alone on the piazza. He thought of pouring himself a brandy. His throat was as dry as sedge. He set the book aside.

"Her name was Augusta," he said.

Maggie's gaze flashed up to him, then down again to her hands, watching her finger move around and around the rim of the teacup. A small frown creased her brow.

"She was seventeen, I was twenty," he said. "Both of us too young, but the war had just begun and marriage seemed the thing to do, rather than wait. We had four days together before I left. First Manassas was ten days later. Wars aren't conducive to building a marriage, but we were lucky in some ways. She stayed at Riverbend with my family and I was in

Virginia with Stuart, so we managed to get a night together here, an hour there."

Marriages were made in the sharing of the chores that filled a day, a moment of spontaneous laughter, a flash of anger, the meeting of eyes over the dinner table. He'd never been really married to Augusta. The war saw to that.

"Gordy was born in '62," he said. "A month before the Battle of Fredericksburg. I wasn't there until a week later, but we camped nearby for much of the winter . . . so in spite of the multiple horrors of that campaign, those days turned out to be the best we had. I saw her the last time for an hour, just before we pulled out for Lee's move into the North. What turned into Gettysburg."

"Where you were wounded."

Her eyes had gone darker, fixed on his face now. He smiled, but the smile cracked in forming and became something else. He looked away from her, out the window that framed a sky that had turned the deep blue of twilight.

"Actually, we almost missed the whole thing. By the time we hooked up with Lee, the battle was two days old. One night's rest and we were sent deep in the enemy's rear to harass them on their retreat. At the same time Pickett's men were going down to everlasting fame on Cemetery Ridge, we were engaged in a worthless saber fight with Custer. We suffered about two hundred casualties. I was one of them, left on the field for dead."

God, how he had fought to live then. It had seemed so very important, to live long enough to get back home, not knowing he would have no home to return to.

He stood, to prove to himself that he could, and his bad leg trembled, so he walked. To prove to himself that he could.

Her head was bent now, showing the black braid at the nape of her neck. "But you were not dead," she said softly.

"Right, but I was out of the fighting for the duration, not subject to exchange because of Royce's guerrilla command." He ran out of car length to pace, so he stopped and stared out the back window at the dark shapes of trees rushing past.

"Gussie was still in the thick of it," he said. "Fredericksburg had been devastated, starvation was more than a thought that winter."

"Aye, I remember the Famine in Ireland." Her voice was so soft, laced with nuances of painful memories.

He turned and leaned his shoulders against the wall. "I suppose you do," he said quietly. He waited in case she might say more, but she only tucked her chin and contemplated her hands folded together in her lap. He returned to the chair across from her.

"Peyton stayed at Riverbend but sent the women and children away," he said. "Annie eventually ended up with Royce, hiding out with his command up in the mountains. Gussie and Gordy went into Richmond to stay with her father. She was helping in the Richmond hospitals, where she contracted typhoid. Only twenty years old and too weak from malnutrition to fight her way through it."

"Gordon—"

"Let me finish, angel," he said, lifting one palm. "At the time," he continued, "I was half-dead myself from what was probably typhus. Mother Bernadette brought me the news. I wanted to die, but Mother Bernadette, being the woman she is, wouldn't allow that self-pity."

He didn't see her move, but she was somehow kneeling in front of him and had taken his hand between hers. God, his chest was so tight it was squeezing something up into his throat and he could hardly push the words through.

"For ten years, I walked around dead inside. But now with you, Maggie . . ."

He would never know if she leaned into him first or if he reached for her. But somehow, her hands were in his hair and he was sliding out of the chair and onto his knees, and his lips were brushing her temple, while her breath was soft and moist on the curve of his neck.

"Gordon," she said, her voice breaking over his name.

He cupped her face, so soft and warm and wet against his palms. "Please, angel, don't cry."

She turned within his embrace and gave him a tremulous smile, and then she gave him more, and when her mouth opened to him, he laid her beneath him and took the forgiveness she offered.

Chapter 19

"*Y*ou haven't asked a single question about the home I'm taking you to, Maggie. Aren't you curious?"

"I know 'tis large. You cannot be poor and own a train car with a name printed on the side."

Today he was so acutely attuned to her that he could see the anxiety shading her eyes. He was beginning to sense the slender core of pure steel in her. She wasn't the silent, emotionally bereft child Mother Bernadette had spoken about. She was a woman with the kind of quiet courage to walk beside him into a world she knew nothing about, and had many reasons to fear.

"The train car is a convenience I share with my brother," he said, intentionally downplaying the factor of wealth involved in such ownership. "Riverbend has a history going back through generations of Kincaids, and like all land holdings, its size and prosperity ebbed and flowed with the abilities of the man at the helm. Peyton doubled the acreage when he married Royce's mother. He built her a large house as a wedding gift—we call it the Big House—and it's where we lived all the years I was growing up. That house, and the land from his mother's family, belongs to Royce now, or rather, to Royce's wife. But that's a story Annabelle will have to share with you."

He thought how Annabelle would sense immediately all the many reasons he'd married Maggie. Annie would be the friend his wife needed, had probably never known. Instinctively, he knew Maggie's values placed a far higher premium on friendship than on financial wealth. One tended to learn true values in the crucible of fire. Maggie's trials had been different from his own, but no less intense.

"Just after the war," he continued, "Peyton deeded the original land, and the house his grandfather had built, to me. We're a close-knit family and are inclined to think of the land in its entirety as Riverbend still. For convenience sake, when we need to make a distinction we call my portion Old Riverbend and my—our—house the Old House."

"And your brother in his Big House is very near, close enough to walk."

"Five minutes if you go across the pasture," he said, remembering touching on some part of this conversation that day he'd walked with her in Druid Hill Park. Was that the day it had begun for him, the intense love he felt for this woman? "A little longer walk if you take the river path."

She nodded. Her gaze was very clear, yet somehow distant, as if she looked backwards into her own past to all the things and people that had been taken from her when she was too young and helpless to have any control over her own life: her mother, her home and country, the very center of her identity as the daughter of an earl. But she had him now as her bulwark against adversity. There was power in the name *Kincaid,* even among the social elites. She didn't know it yet, but he'd given her that power when he gave her his name, and given it to her gladly.

The September skies waxed blue, and black-eyed Susans grew thick in the meadow along the creek where Clare was playing with her rag doll. Gordon leaned back on one elbow, watching his daughter, while Maggie packed the remains of their picnic lunch in the wicker hamper.

He felt sated and languid, and pleased with himself for the idea of bringing his girls on a picnic while they waited at Manassas Junction for the train cars to be switched to the RF&P track. It occurred to him suddenly that the battlefields were just beyond sight, but the ghosts had been vanquished by the sun, and he thought this day was turning out to be near perfect.

Maggie wiped a plate of India china with a cloth and stacked it in the hamper. "Will you tell me about your son?"

One corner of his mouth quirked. He suspected that although she professed no interest in his land or business concerns it wouldn't be long until she was poking into the household arrangements, butting heads with him over how the children should be raised, schooled, managed. The thought of a Maggie secure enough in their marriage to argue with him made him feel weak with delight.

"I meant to tell you about Gordy last night. Something wonderful happened and it slipped my mind."

He was desperate to tell her about his son. Maggie, with her compassion, her love for children, was the key to bridging the terrible chasm between himself and his son. Maybe, dear God, maybe they *could* be a family.

"Gordy was named after me, but it was too confusing, so he's stuck with that moniker for now. I hardly know my son. This is an explanation, Maggie, not an excuse."

He sat up and wrapped his arm around one knee. "When I came home, it was to a ruined land no one would recognize," he said. "Royce was in prison, the gallows still a real threat. Annie was pregnant with their first child, Peyton had grown old. Myself . . . I was an invalid stuck in a wheelchair."

Maggie had twisted the dish cloth up into a knot in her hands. He watched the muscles tighten in her pale, slender arms. He had forgotten what it was like to watch a woman perform a small homely chore and feel the need come over you when you least expected it. He shifted and pulled the wicker hamper closer, stowing the glasses as he talked.

"Gordy was two, and of course he didn't know who the angry stranger was. I frightened him and he scared the wits out of me—a single father who couldn't even get himself from the bed into the chair. Annie had already become the mother Gordy needed. When Royce was given amnesty and came home . . . it was just easier to let them become his family."

"Perhaps you're being a little hard on yourself," she said softly.

"Perhaps. The truth is I would have been a lousy influence on any child at that time in my life. So angry and bitter. Royce had a family, was willing to make Gordy part of that family and I convinced myself my son was better for it being that way."

"But you missed him."

"Perceptive girl," he said. "I told myself I'd be his father after I got my medical degree, but when that day came, I looked at my son and realized it was too late."

"It's never too late."

"It won't be easy, Maggie. I've done nothing to earn his trust and it's just going to be worse coming home with a wife and little sister for him to accept. But I'd like us to try."

"Aye. We must."

Strands of hair had come lose from her upswept hair and feathered her neck. He thought how he wanted to run his lips along the long, white arch, from the knob of spine to that sensitive place behind her ear.

"And your Virginia," she said, her lilting voice rolling the *r*. "Will you tell me about her as well?"

He gestured with a sweep of his arm. "This is Virginia."

"Aye, but is it your Virginia?"

It was a question he understood, and didn't want to answer. He took the cloth from her hand and set it in the hamper, then closed the lid. "Tell me about your Ireland."

For a minute the only sound was the gurgle of the creek and the whisper of the breeze through the tree branches, then she said, "My Ireland . . . sure it is a place of beauty, and great sadness as well. There's a legend of the ancient kings of Ireland, of when they lost everything on the surface of the land and knew their time was over. They went sideways into the western sun to a place called Tír na nÓg, a place of eternal youth where they built their new kingdom of pearl and silver palaces in the hollows of the hills. Every Irishman believes it is there, but none have ever searched for it. We Irish like to dream our dreams, but we do not like to test them, for when we lose our dreams, we are as lost as those ancient kings."

"You'll understand this land, then, Maggie." He placed his arm over her shoulders and drew her closer against him. "That creek is called Bull Run. If you walk a mile or so down the bank, you're on the MacLean farm, and the Manassas battlefield. Sadly, that's Virginia. An accident of geography, I suppose, but the eastern war was fought here in this stretch of land between Washington and Richmond; four long years of armies clashing in some poor farmer's cornfield. The scars on the land have faded. The people?" He shrugged. "I don't know. Maybe it will take generations for the trauma to heal, maybe not."

She looked up. "Would it have been better to win?"

"No," he said on a soft exhalation of breath. "It ended properly, one nation with a definitive end to slavery. Maybe one day it will even be one people. But it was a matter of pride then, and remains a matter of pride. We Virginians were used to going on the conceit we were the *nation,* cradle of presidents and patriots. Now? Well, now we have to pretend there's glory in the ashes of defeat, so we build our own legends and myths and look backwards to a time that was always better. A time that never truly existed except in our illusions."

He turned his head and rested his cheek on her hair while his gaze traveled over the meadow, the trees showing traces of gold at the edges of the leaves, the blue-gray mountains rising softly against the deeply blue sky. The creek water capered over stones and a meadowlark called.

"You love it," she said.

I love it, he thought, accepting the pain of that. He lifted her face with the intent of declaring his love for her but found himself looking into green eyes brimming with moisture. "God, you understand, don't you, Maggie?"

"Heaven help me, but I do."

There was a timbre in her voice he recognized as something akin to fear, but then he was kissing her and Clare's laughter sounded over the breeze, and nothing else seemed to matter because his wife was kissing him back.

Maggie followed Gordon and Clare to the iron platform of the railcar, feeling as overwhelmed and misplaced as she'd felt on a gangplank in Baltimore Harbor so many years ago. Gordon lifted Clare in his arms and disembarked. Maggie hesitated. He held out his hand.

"Come on, Irish," he said in a soft voice that made her think he could see her heart fluttering all over her chest. When she still could not make herself move, he set Clare down and reached up.

His strong, gentle hands spanned her waist, and after he had lifted her down, his hands lingered. His thumbs rubbed just below the swell of her breasts and she felt her nipples go taut and aching. Her legs, covered with new silk stockings and lacy white drawers, quivered as if they were naked.

He jerked his gaze away from her face and drew in a deep breath. And then he laughed. "I think you waved that rowan wand and put a spell of enchantment on me."

He made her smile. She ducked her head and looked away. Slanting shadows lay across the tracks of the Richmond, Fredericksburg and Potomac Railroad. Warm, damp air blew off the river and carried the noises of the busy wharves. They had traveled all day to get here; the sun was beginning to drop behind the white cupola that rose over the freight depot across the tracks.

Her eyes swept over the crowd gathered in front of the ticket office, where two men stood on a raised platform. One

white-haired man with a great hawk nose was waving his
arms and speaking to the group, but she wasn't interested in
listening to him. She was searching for a man who might be
Gordon's brother, but she saw no one remotely resembling
her husband.

Her heart stopped fluttering and sank. She was an unwel-
come trespasser, an Irish-Catholic wife. She slanted a glance
at Gordon, seeing his face go taut as his own gaze swept over
the gathered group, then across the tracks to where a group of
black men stood.

"Be still, Clare," she said, avoiding her husband's eyes by
attending to Clare's disheveled appearance. "We'll not be going much farther now."

She looked up from retying Clare's hair bow as Franklin
approached. He stopped in front of Clare and gave her a
gummy grin before kneeling down.

"So this is Ole Riverbend's new miss," he said. "Got us a
couple ponies there, but you might be too pretty a little thing
to be messing around with a dirty old pony."

Clare hopped from one foot to the other with enough energy to dislodge the hair bow again. "No, no, Daddy's teaching me how to ride." She looked up at her father and
Gordon's face softened as it always did when he looked at his
daughter. "Right, Daddy? You'll let me ride the pony. I'll
wash it and feed it and—"

"We have to get there first, princess," said Gordon, breaking into her effusive promises. He looked at Franklin as the
trainer pushed up. "Where's Royce?"

Maggie couldn't tell if there was an undercurrent of anger
in his voice, but his face had once again taken on that hard
look.

"The general's waiting at Riverbend. Miz Annabelle was
feeling poorly today and you know how he gets."

"Yes, but I understand," he said. "We'll stop there first.
Did you bring a wagon for the baggage?"

"Brought Cyrus along. I can drive you back in the

brougham or stay here and make sure the whippersnapper does the job right."

"First let me find him. I bought some new luggage for my girls that neither of you will recognize." His gaze swept down the long line of cars and the milling crowd as passengers disembarked and were met by family and retainers. "Why don't you wait here with Franklin," he said, bringing his gaze back to her. "I'll take our girl with me and let her walk off some of this excitement."

He reached down as Clare reached up and their hands clasped, bringing another tender curve to his mouth. He looked to the man speaking to the crowd and seemed to hesitate.

"Old man Pettigrew stirring up trouble?" he asked.

Franklin shrugged. "The man carries a heavy load."

Gordon's eyes narrowed. "Nobody makes him carry it. He sure as hell wasn't the only one who lost sons in the war."

The wind seemed to die at that moment and she clearly heard the speaker's exhortations. "The Fourteenth and Fifteenth Amendments may stand forever," he cried in a deep, rumbling voice. "But we must—we *must*—make them nothing more than dead letters in the statute books."

Gordon's mouth twisted. "Election season in Virginia. It's madmen and fools and better left alone." He paused, then said, "We won't be long. Stay with her, Franklin."

She watched her new family walk away from her. Gordon was nattily dressed in a double-breasted gray frock coat accompanied by gray-and-black-striped trousers, a white shirt with high collar and a black ribbon bow tie. He walked down the rail siding in that long-strided, slightly hitching way he had, with his small daughter's hand clasped firmly within his own. She suddenly felt very alone.

She tipped her head back and gazed at the deep blue sky. She half-turned and studied the red dirt road that curved around a weeping willow tree. The speaker was stirring the crowd into rustles and rumbles with something about a

Union League, the ignorance of black voters and the purity of white blood. Maggie was careful not to look at Franklin, but she couldn't help the question.

"What is it all about, Franklin?"

He huffed, then lifted one muscled shoulder in a shrug. "Well, you're the white missus, and I'm the colored help. You'll do best to remember that it's all right for you to be seen giving me orders, but not talking-like. I can come in your kitchen to deliver something, but you don't ever let me through your front door. In that kitchen of yours, there'll be a special cupboard where you keep the old jelly jars, and on a hot day, you can offer the nigger some cold lemonade, just as long as you're careful to serve it in the jelly jar and not in the glasses the white folks use."

"Oh, Franklin, why?"

"All kinds of ways to win a war, ma'am. Some around here ain't quit fighting the last one." Franklin pulled his checkered cap from his head and rubbed the back of his hand along the pewter-gray hair at his scalp. "I shouldn't be talking out of turn here, Mrs. Kincaid. But you're new to the ways here and although your husband's a good man, he tries hard not to see what's around him."

Maggie bit her lip and looked off to a large oak tree that dipped its broad leaves in the warm, damp breeze. She felt as if she were about to cross some invisible line, once again venturing into a realm of dangerous men and secret societies, a place that always ended darkly, with the weeping of women and children.

"Pettigrew is running for the legislature," said Franklin "He might believe what he's saying over there; in fact, I think he does—him losing just about everything he had when them Yanks came through here in '64. But the other man up there—the one that looks like a monkey in a frock coat. That's Moulton Johnson, and he's just pure evil. You stay as far away from him as you can, and that won't be hard—your husband can't abide him."

"Aye, I'll remember that."

And then she saw Gordon and Clara returning, and her heart seemed to leap in her chest. Gordon had shortened his stride to accommodate Clare's little legs. He was looking down at his daughter as Clare almost skipped beside him, and Maggie's lips curved, watching them together.

A woman stepped out from the crowd, and Gordon's stride faltered so that Maggie thought for a moment that his leg was going to give way. But then she saw his gaze lock with the woman's and hold tautly, until the woman looked down at Clare.

Go up to her, speak, do something, she thought, for if he did, she would know the woman dressed in lilac and lace with a smart leghorn hat over her honey-blond hair was not Clara's mother. And then her heart could start beating again.

The woman lifted her gaze; Gordon tipped his hat, and the whole thing from the time his stride faltered to now was a time of a breath, and an endless eternity.

And then he was coming toward her, closer, so close she could see he was looking hard at her. Something flashed in his eyes—a sort of wild and desperate wanting—and without moving, she felt utterly and hopelessly lost in the mysterious depths of that look. But then Franklin spoke, and what she had seen, or thought she had seen, was gone.

"I'll go help Cyrus load the wagon."

"Do that," said Gordon. "And stop at the Big House. If Annie's not well, my place might not be ready for us."

"Will do, 'cause it ain't ready and my Dulcie's not going to let you bring your bride into a dusty house." Franklin tipped his gray head toward Maggie. "Welcome, ma'am. Gonna be nice having the doc's wife at the Old House. Been lonely too long."

"Thank you, Franklin," she said, blinking against a sudden push of tears.

Gordon took her elbow. "Come on. Let me get my girls home."

He led them to a shiny blue brougham with the top folded back. Gordon lifted Clare onto the leather seat, then assisted Maggie. He walked behind the carriage to the driver's side. The well-oiled springs didn't even sigh as he climbed in.

"Ready?"

"Aye." She made herself fold her hands calmly in her lap. "Who is Dulcie?" she asked.

"Franklin's wife. His whole family works for us, Dulcie as housekeeper. Cyrus is their eldest son. He's got his father's magic touch with horses. Phoebe, our cook, is married to Cyrus. Phoebe's mother cooks for Royce. Have I lost you yet?"

He looked at her, his eyes glistening from reflected sunlight, or excitement or happiness. She had to look away. Her own emotions were so unsteady and she didn't know how to act anymore, but she was certain of one thing. She would not spoil this homecoming for him or for Clare.

"Give yourself time," he said softly. "You might find you like being lady of the manor."

She thought that doubtful but said nothing to contradict him. She wondered if, in his house, there was a separate kitchen cupboard filled with old jelly jars. And she knew she would change that if it were so. If she was Mrs. Kincaid, lady of the manor, it would not be the manor Franklin described.

They traveled down twisting country lanes, past fields planted in winter wheat and rolling hills still verdant green. The rich scent of the river permeated the air. Amid the stands of young oak and loblolly, dogwood trees shot crimson color against the gathering shadows. It was a beautiful, tranquil land. She tried to picture it as he'd described it to her, denuded of forests, ravaged and bloodied by the campaigns of two armies, and failed.

He turned down another road and she suddenly saw the skeleton of what must have been a grand house. Now it was a burned-out shell, collapsed in on itself, the charred remains choked with tall weeds and twisting morning glory vines. A sapling sprouted from a crack in front steps that led the way to emptiness. Only the three brick chimneys stood tall, as if in prideful contempt of defeat.

The sight triggered memories and she actually heard fire snapping through thatch, felt the searing heat of flames against her skin and the fear twisting her belly. Forgotten echoes sounded in her head: horses screaming as smoke drifted into the stables, Mum's wailing lamentations, the clash of sabers and scuffling of heavy boots as the soldiers dragged her stepfather away.

She pushed the memories back, reburying a past that could not be changed. Gordon looked over as she sighed and their gazes met over Clare's head. She'd seen the photographs after Antietam and Gettysburg, carnage horrifying even in black and white pictures that lacked the sound and scents that gave true scope to any experience. He'd been so courageous to share some of those memories with her last night.

"The same would have happened to Riverbend if Peyton hadn't stayed through the worst of it," he said in a low voice. "As it was, Old Riverbend, our house, was used as a Union hospital after the Wilderness campaign. You'll still see the scars, since I haven't done much to fix the place up over the years. You can refurbish to your heart's content." One corner of his mouth lifted in a teasing smile. "You can change the name too; it'll be less confusing."

"You have not lived there, then?"

He shrugged. "I just rattled around in all that space. Spent as much time in the Richmond house as I did here and ended up staying with Royce more often than I stayed at my own place."

"You are close to your brother. . . ."

He studied her face and she looked away from his scrutiny.

"Yes, I am, but . . ." He reached over and touched her knee. "My brother can be frightening, Maggie, although if what Franklin was telling us is true, there's a good reason for Royce not meeting us like I expected. And I'll admit I'm worried."

"I'm being foolish."

"No, no." He paused, glanced down at his daughter and then back to the road. "Annie's in the family way," he said. "She's never had an easy time of it, never carried a child to term, and the last miscarriage nearly killed her. Royce gets beside himself. She might have a hangnail, she might really be having problems. It's hard to say until I talk to her."

"Are you her doctor, then?"

"No. It's too close a relationship and she needs someone with special knowledge in gynecology."

"Perhaps I can be of some help to her," said Maggie.

"I'm sure you will. Annabelle will love you. I have no doubts on that."

She was silent for a while, half-listening to him answer Clare's stream of questions, worrying her hands in her lap. He pulled the team to a halt at the top of a rise. Before them, the Rappahannock rolled in streaking ribbons of brown and gray as it executed a lazy bend.

Gordon drew Clare onto his lap. "Over there, princess, on the top of that bluff," he said, pointing in the opposite direction. "Old Riverbend."

Maggie looked to the tallest rise where he pointed. She drew in a long, quiet breath. The house was still a distance away, visible through an arched stand of trees. A graceful home, large even from this range, with tall, round columns supporting the double verandas.

Painted white, it shone in shades of salmon and pink, reflecting the light of the setting sun. It was an eerie, magical vision, like seeing Tír na nÓg rising from an enchanted mist awaiting the next banquet of the ancient kings.

" 'Tis beautiful," she murmured.

"It hasn't been a real home for anyone since Peyton built Riverbend, almost fifty years now. We'll make it a home again."

She looked into his eyes, seeing none of those confused, hopeless shadows that used to haunt him so. He brushed his hand down the back of Clare's head, smoothing her hair, and shifted his gaze again to the mystical house on the hill. "Our home, Maggie."

She loved him. She loved Clare.

She was terrified.

Chapter 20

The Big House, Gordon had called it. Well, it was that, three stories in the center and two stories in each of the wings, with a long gallery and more of those white columns.

Maggie felt as if someone stood behind each of the tall, dark windows, staring out with a malevolent eye at the brougham rolling up the lane. The wheels crunched onto a drive of crushed shells and she saw the malevolent eyes were waiting on Riverbend's front gallery.

She would never have taken this man as Gordon's brother. Royce was dark where her husband was fair, his hair cut long and the rich brown of plowed earth. His face was stern and harshly elegant.

He held his lean body in a rigid, soldier's stance with one hand resting on a boy's shoulder. The boy bore such a strong resemblance to Clare, Maggie knew he was Gordon's son. Neither one moved or even smiled as Gordon set the brake and jumped down from the brougham.

The two men exchanged a hard look over the harness

traces and then Gordon came around, assisting her and Clare from the carriage. Even Clare had grown silent.

"Where's that Irish fire?" said Gordon.

Maggie nudged her chin up in a display of courage she didn't really feel. She took Clare's hand, waiting with mounting apprehension for one of the men to make a move.

A small woman came out on the gallery, followed by a girl about the same age as Alice. The woman paused, her gaze fixing on Clare, then shifting to Gordon, and her mouth curved in a soft smile as she started forward toward the steps.

"Annabelle." The general's low voice commanded a halt.

"Silly man," she said. She stopped beside her husband, leaned up on her toes and kissed his cheek. "There," she said, patting the spot she'd just kissed. "Now smile."

The general's face softened as he watched his wife move down the front steps. When Annabelle came closer, Maggie saw a woman of delicate beauty, large brown eyes, ash-brown hair piled loosely on her head so stray wisps of curls escaped and framed her face. Annabelle held out both hands and Gordon clasped them, then kissed her cheek.

"Charming as ever, Annie-girl," he said, finally smiling himself.

"Impossible rogue as usual," she said teasingly. "You've been gone too long but I'll forgive you if you'll introduce your wife and this beautiful little girl."

"This beautiful little girl is Clara Kincaid, age five, a bundle of energy and never-ending questions." He looked down at his daughter. "Say hello to your Aunt Annie, Clara."

Clare smiled shyly and executed a poor approximation of a curtsy. Annabelle knelt down in front of the child. "My daughter, Hope Ann, is nine. I think you're going to be great friends. We'll let her show you all around tomorrow. There's a new litter of kittens out in the barn and your Lucky got here a few days ago. Would you like that?"

Clare looked up at Maggie, her blue eyes once again shimmering with excitement. "Would it be all right, my Maggie?"

"Aye, wee Clare. Tomorrow."

Annabelle lifted her hand, which Gordon grasped, assisting her up. She rubbed the top of her rounded belly while an apologetic smile formed at her lips.

"It gets a bit difficult after a certain point," she said, directing her words to Maggie. Maggie smiled back, immediately taken with this woman's kindness. "And you must be the young woman who captured our rogue's heart." Annabelle held out her hands again. "Welcome, Maggie. I've been awfully lonesome waiting all these years for Gordon to find himself a wife so I could have a friend living next door."

When Maggie took her outstretched hands, Annabelle pulled her subtly forward. "Don't mind the stiff men on the gallery," she whispered. "Royce would like us to believe he's a tiger, but the sad truth is, he's nothing but a tabby cat—leaves all the really nasty jobs to me."

While Maggie was choking back a startled laugh, Annabelle withdrew her hands and ducked her head just a little.

"Like this one," she murmured. Annabelle lifted her head, turned and leveled a glare at the two males still standing on the gallery. "Gordy," she said in a tone that Mother Bernadette would have admired.

The boy looked up at his uncle. Royce dropped his hand from Gordy's shoulder and nodded. Maggie knew with a certainty that Gordon hadn't exaggerated his estrangement from his son. The past five minutes and that questioning look to the wrong man were proof of the enormity of their task.

Gordy came down the steps, moving with an adult's stiff formality instead of a boy's energy. He was tall for his age, all elbows and knees, his hair slightly darker than Clare's and tousled over his forehead. He stopped in front of his father and held out his hand.

"Welcome home, Father."

Maggie had a thousand thoughts and tried to convey them to her husband with a look: *Ruffle his hair, yank him into a hug and hold him while he squirms. Do something to break that stiffness, even if it makes him cry.*

Gordon's hand clenched at his side and then he lifted it, taking his son's in his own, but they were like two strangers meeting.

"Son," he said. They dropped hands. "Your new sister, Clara," said Gordon, "and my wife, known as *my Maggie* to most everyone." He looked at his son, his dark eyes intense. "Perhaps you'd like to call her Maggie for now."

Gordy glanced first at Clare and the faintest of smiles touched his lips. Then he jerked his jaw into the air and glared at Maggie, as if challenging her to find the least little thing likable about him. She could love this frightened boy, she thought. Maybe she already did.

"A pleasure to meet you, Gordy," she said, holding out her hand. He looked at her outstretched hand but made no move to take it.

"Welcome, Mrs. Kincaid," he said solemnly.

Maggie walked carefully up the three steps, across the flag-stone gallery and through the green double doors toward the room Annabelle called the second parlor.

She stifled a mad urge to break into a child's chant: *First parlor, second parlor, third parlor, more*. Maybe she could chant in Gaelic and garner herself another disapproving frown from the general.

It was indeed the general's voice that she heard coming from the parlor as she came down the hallway. For a moment she stood hidden by the heavy gold portieres, looking in on this family that had become her family.

Annabelle was seated on a medallion-backed brocade sofa with her daughter beside her. The men were in matching wing chairs angled around an Oriental chest that held an elaborate silver coffee service. Whereas Royce looked comfortable, almost sprawled in his chair, Gordon looked like he needed to pace, but his daughter had him caught by sitting on his lap. Gordy was sitting on the piano bench, staring at his father.

She felt dazed and disoriented, as if plucked up by a

whirlwind and then set down in a place she would never understand.

Annabelle had called their supper an informal affair, and sure, the food had been plain enough, sliced country ham and candied sweet potatoes, green beans and tomatoes from the garden, all of it served at a damask-covered table on translucent china with more solid plate silver than she had ever seen in her life.

Throughout the entire strained meal, the males had glowered at one another while Annabelle tried valiantly to pretend this was normal behavior and Maggie herself sat stiffly watching Gordon to be certain she picked up the proper fork. By the time it was over, her stomach was in knots and she excused herself for a walk in the garden, turning down Annabelle's offer to accompany her when the general fixed her with one of his hard glares.

Maggie patted her hair and smoothed her bodice so she wouldn't look as frayed as she felt, and the general noticed her then. He rose like a gentleman, and even managed a touch of a smile.

"Come in, come in. We were just discussing whether or not to form a search party for you."

He had a fine way of inserting insults into his manners, she thought. She came into the room, very carefully, as if she were treading on ice.

"Hope Ann saved you the best seat," said Gordon. "I'd get up like a gentleman should, but our little girl has me grounded." He sent her a swift wink and she knew he meant it as encouragement. Blessed Saint Brigid, did it show on her face, this dazed, dizzy sensation?

As she took the seat on the sofa beside Hope Ann, Royce reached in a brass-hinged humidor and withdrew a thin cigar.

"Put the disgusting thing back," said Gordon. "There are ladies present."

Royce lifted one dark brow. "Really, brother? My wife doesn't mind." He tilted his head at Maggie. "I fear my tongue was tied all through supper, as I couldn't decide what to call you. Mrs. Kincaid certainly won't do."

"Maggie will be fine," she said, and lifted her hand. "Please, go ahead and smoke. It is your home, after all."

"And so it is, Maggie. So it is."

Annabelle let out a small sigh, causing her husband to pause in the process of cutting the tip from the cigar. He looked at his wife and the hard glint in his silver eyes visibly softened. Wordlessly, he returned the cigar to the humidor.

"Well," said Annabelle brightly. "If I could play that piano decently, we could have ourselves some musical entertainment. I'm afraid I'm sadly lacking in that lady's talent, and poor Hope Ann inherited her mother's ten thumbs. Do you play the piano, Maggie?"

"No."

Gordy plunked the middle C. "My mother played the piano," he said. "She would play for my father when they were courting."

"I'm sure that was lovely," said Maggie. She covered one hand in her lap with the other to hide the trembling. She wanted to look at Gordon, but was afraid of what she might see, so she didn't.

Gordy swung his long legs around on the piano bench so he was facing her. "My mother was a Raleigh. Her mother, my grandmother, was a Randolph, which means she was related to the Carters and the Lees. Did you ever hear of Robert E. Lee? He was almost as good a general as Uncle Royce."

She looked at the general. For the space of a breath, he smiled at her. She nudged her chin up. They had their pride. She'd give them a taste of pride, and she'd give it to them in her best Irish voice.

"And sure wasn't it me own mother who was of the clan O'Brian, her great-grandfather times twenty being the great Brian Boru himself, the first High King of Ireland, and himself descended from the greatest warrior of them all, Cú Chulainn."

She smiled then, caught up in the absurdity of sparring with a twelve-year-old boy who was so wrought with nerves he couldn't keep his foot from tapping the floor.

"And true enough, wasn't Cú Culainn's greatest battle fought over a cow," she said, and saw Gordon's face relax.

Hope had been watching her cousin with a small frown pinching her face. But now she fixed her attention on Maggie, and her mouth turned up in a shy kind of smile. "Would you tell me that story sometime?" she asked.

"Aye, 'tis one of Clare's favorites."

Gordy plunked a chord, then ran a trill up the keys. Maggie suspected he played the instrument quite well, but for some reason was embarrassed by that accomplishment. Almost as if he were privy to her thoughts, he lifted his hands from the keys and reached for one of the framed pictures sitting on the piano top amid a collection of dried flowers.

"Gordy," said Annabelle, and there was some type of warning in her voice.

The boy turned his head, careful not to look at his father, still sitting with Clara in his lap, her head tucked against his chest as he stroked her hairline.

"I'm sorry, Aunt Annie," Gordy said, carefully returning the framed picture to its place on the piano. "I didn't realize I wasn't supposed to look at my mother's picture anymore."

"Gordy!" Annabelle's sharp tone cut through the sudden silence, but Gordy had turned his dark eyes hard on Maggie.

I will not try to take her place in your heart, she wanted to say to him. But the words got stuck somewhere deep in her throat, because for all the truth of them, she did want him to make room in his heart for her too. And he was looking at her as if he knew it, and resented it.

Already she was failing her husband. So many ways she was bound to fail him; she knew nothing of running grand households or serving fine dinners, but in this one thing, the matter of his son, she had honestly believed she could be . . . a mother to his son, help Gordon make his family whole. And then maybe Gordon would find it in his heart to truly love her for that gift.

She wanted Gordon to say something, but when she looked at him, he was staring at the portrait with the look of a man who listened to a memory rather than a present reality. She made her eyes go wide in an effort to hold back tears.

"Uncle Royce never lost a battle," said Gordy suddenly.

"Tell me, Royce," said Gordon, his fingers still softly brushing Clare's forehead. "However did you manage to win every battle and still lose the war?"

Royce laughed. "I'm a man of many talents. Isn't that right, Annie-girl?"

"None of which are visible tonight," said Annabelle in a tart voice. "That poor child is falling asleep. Let me show you to your rooms, Maggie. I, for one, have heard about as much as I can take."

Annabelle stood, using the sofa arm to push herself up, and her husband saw it. His face hardened, and his eyes grew shadowed. Annabelle looked away, as though she couldn't bear to meet those tarnished eyes.

"Please, sweetheart, when you get to the top of the stairs, would you follow the doctor's orders?" he said, and there was a timbre in the general's voice Maggie hadn't heard all evening.

There was love in the words, and a quiet desperation too, and she suddenly realized she had been so caught up in her own fears that she'd missed the eddies going on beneath his brusque exterior.

"And if I had done that all evening?" said Annabelle to her husband, her hand gently stroking her mounded belly. "What would you have done then?"

"I would have cooked up a dinner of hardtack and spoiled bacon and made Gordy eat every last bite."

Hope giggled and he flashed her a grin, then his eyes went back to his wife, and his mouth curved in the most tender of smiles while the love burned in his eyes. Annabelle's face flushed as she held his gaze, and for a moment Maggie forgot to breathe, she wanted what they shared so desperately.

"Show your aunt to her rooms," Royce said to his daughter. "So your mother can get the rest she needs."

Hope Ann linked arms with her. "Clara can sleep with me, in case she gets scared. Mama and her cousin used to do that all the time when they were children."

"And isn't that a kind thought," said Maggie. She held out her hand for Clare. "Come along, *mó cailín*."

Clare slid down from her father's lap in a tangle of ruffled white petticoats and cotton bloomers.

Gordon laid his palms on the chair arms, as if to push himself to his feet, although he remained seated, his narrowed gaze fastened on his son.

"I'll be up in a minute," he said.

His mouth was set tight, but she could see the hurt anger in his eyes. She thought his pain ought to ease the aching tumult in her own heart, but it didn't.

They were both of them dreaming of that grand, good place to make their own. Only neither one of them knew how to find it.

Gordon watched his wife and daughter leave the room with his sister-in-law and niece, and almost wished he could escape with them. He considered himself a patient man, but right now the anger lay very close beneath his skin, and he knew it would erupt at the smallest additional provocation.

He forcibly relaxed his grip on the chair arms and took several deep breaths as his brother went through the ritual of lighting that smelly cigar and his son ran trills up and down the piano keyboard.

His oh-so-polite, oh-so-obnoxious son.

It had taken every ounce of control he possessed to keep himself from lashing out at the boy, and he restrained himself only out of consideration for Maggie's feelings. He'd have a scene with his son, just as soon as his blood settled—and another with his brother later—but he wasn't about to force Maggie to be a part of either one.

Royce stretched his legs out in front of him and released a plume of smoke from his throat. "I'm doing as well as can be expected, brother, thank you for asking."

"Why ask? I knew you would tell me."

"What's that? Must be my hearing," said Royce, smacking his ear. He grinned. "All those cannons firing in all those battles I won. Does bad things to a man's hearing."

"Pull the bait in, brother. I'm not biting."

Royce lifted one brow in that arrogant way of his, then shrugged. "Can't blame a man for trying."

Gordon ignored his brother and focused his attention on his son, who was trying to sidle out the door. "Gordy, I want you to bring me that picture from the piano."

Gordy stopped and turned so his back was against the gold-flocked wallpaper, his head nearly level with the swag tail draping the doorway. God, he was growing up, edging on being a man.

Gordy's lip curled. "What picture would that be, Father?"

Gordon bolted from the chair so fast his bad leg nearly buckled beneath him. He limped to the piano and picked up the wedding portrait, waving it at his son. "This one. The one I remember as having two people in it. And dammit, I was there when it was taken, and you weren't."

"Can't fault the boy for looking at a picture of his parents," said Royce.

Gordon swung around and pointed a stiff finger at his brother. "For once, you stay out of this." Royce drew on the cigar, saying nothing. Gordon turned back to his son.

"I'll never fault you for looking at a picture of your mother. I *will* fault you for the cruelty of your conduct tonight. If you've got the moral courage to walk across this room after what you just did and face me like a man, I will give you this picture—simply because it should rightfully go to you and now is as good a time as any. You can look at it to your heart's content, as long as it never comes out of your room."

Their eyes locked for a moment in challenge, then the boy broke. He walked across the room and reached out. Gordon withheld handing it over.

"I will not ask you to apologize to Maggie because she's sensitive enough to recognize it would be a forced apology. But you will apologize to your Aunt Annabelle, your sister and your cousin. Do we understand one another?"

The boy drew in a breath, his shoulders stiffening, his mouth clamping tight. Gordon wanted to shake him. God help him, he wanted to hit him, his only son.

"Will you strike me, Father?"

Gordon tossed the picture to the piano bench and flinched himself when it landed with a loud clatter in the suddenly silent room.

"No, son. But I ought to. My father would have done so to me."

And Royce, if he hadn't been taking such perverse pleasure in the tension that had eddied around them all this evening, would not have hesitated to physically reprimand the boy under the same circumstances.

A father's right? A father's duty? Whichever, Gordon could see in his son's bowed shoulders that he'd already hurt the boy, just as he meant to do, and now he couldn't bear it.

He sighed, and turned on his heels, catching Royce watching them through narrowed eyes. Royce tucked his chin and looked away. Gordon spied Clara's rag doll on the floor by the chair, so he walked over and picked it up.

"You'll move into the Old House with us as soon as it's ready," he said to Gordy, and waited for his son to object.

Gordy had settled on the piano bench, his elbows on his spread knees and his hands clasped between his legs as he studied the pattern in the Oriental carpet.

No objection, which could mean anything, the most probable being that the boy was waiting until he'd gathered all his ammunition. Gordon didn't have the heart for another argu-

ment anyway. The only sound as he walked across the room
was the exhalation of breath as Royce puffed on his cigar.

"Father?"

Gordon stopped at the doorway and turned. Gordy didn't
even bother to lift his head.

"She might be your wife, but she'll never be my mother."

The bedroom door stood ajar, spilling a wedge of light into
the hall. Maggie poked her head into the room.

"The wee *cailíns* are asleep," she said to Annabelle, who
was already tucked into her own bed, looking small and
childlike herself propped against piles of feather pillows in a
huge four-poster bed. "Is there anything I can be getting
you?"

Annabelle patted the ivory counterpane. "Come sit and
talk a minute. That is, if you're not too tired after all that
traveling."

Maggie gathered her skirts and walked into a room that
smelled faintly of lavender sachet.

"I apologize for being such a poor hostess, deserting you
with the children like that. It's doctor's orders, you see."
Annabelle laughed, surprising Maggie, for the laugh was so
like her own mum's, frothy and light, and the light sparked in
Annabelle's dark eyes. "I'm afraid I pushed my poor husband about as far as he's willing to go."

Maggie sat at the edge of the bed. It felt strange and somehow pleasant to be doing this. As if she were back at the orphanage, sharing a bit of gossip with Sister Agatha.

"Your husband is not happy about his brother's marriage."

"I can see how you would get that impression. Royce was
in fine fettle tonight." Annabelle searched her face until Maggie wanted to look away, but she didn't. Annabelle said,
"What he put you through downstairs was rude and unnecessary, but it had nothing to do with Gordon Kincaid's marriage
to anyone."

"You don't have to explain." Maggie waved her hand, her
face flushing.

"It's not you. And it most certainly is not because you're Irish, so put that thought out of your head right now. I'm to blame for part of Royce's behavior," said Annabelle. "He gets so worried with these pregnancies, it turns him back into *The General*."

This last was said in such a deep, ominous tone, Maggie had to smile. Annabelle's eyes grew warmer.

"Mostly it's Gordy he's worried about," she said quietly.

"It's time for Gordon and his son to know one another."

"Past due, I should say." Annabelle smoothed the coverlet over her rounded belly. "Royce thinks he has to protect everyone: me, the children, the workers on the estates. He's protected Gordy so long now, he's lost sight of the fact that Gordon is the boy's father." She stared steadily into Maggie's eyes. "Gordon's not blameless here."

"Perhaps, but he had good reason to feel afraid."

"You're a lioness when it comes to your cubs, aren't you?" Annabelle chuckled. "You'll do fine here, Maggie. We just have to give the men time to work through their manly pride. Those two brothers are closer than any I've ever met— sometimes that's wonderful and sometimes it's pure misery to be around—but believe me, they'll work through this."

"I know naught of men, 'tis a mystery to me how they think."

"You and half the human race." They shared another smile, then Annabelle looked away. "Gordy . . . Gordy knows right from wrong, and he knew he was wrong tonight. I would have stopped him, Maggie, but I was afraid it would only make the whole scene more embarrassing for you. I owe you another apology, and I'm giving it."

Maggie studied her hands, working at the cuticle of one nail with her thumb. She felt that awful light-headed sensation again, and her mouth was so dry she couldn't even swallow. "The picture was his parents' wedding portrait?"

"Yes, it was." Annabelle stared at a nosegay of flowers inside a bell jar that sat on top of a tall mahogany bureau. "Augusta has been dead a long time," she said finally. "Gordy doesn't remember her. He knows only what we've told him over the years. She was a sweet young woman, flighty sometimes, always kind. She died much too young, but she died, like so many others during those years."

Maggie felt a tight band of misery crushing her ribs. Her eyes were scratchy and sore, as if she wanted to cry. And maybe she did, but she didn't know who to cry for.

"Royce and I were married a few months before their wedding. Unlike us, they never got the chance to make a real marriage out of their union." Annabelle smoothed the fall of lace at her wrist. She drew in a deep breath and let it out slowly. "Don't let a ghost come between you, Maggie. It's the last thing Gussie would have wanted for her family."

"You knew her well, then?"

"I did, but that's neither here nor there. We'll get to know each other too. I love Gordon like a brother and I can see already that you've done something to reach through that fog he's been floundering in for too long."

Annabelle took her hand again, and their fingers were curling together, resting on the white satin counterpane.

"With the doctor's orders imposed on me now, I won't be much help to you in fixing up Old Riverbend or introducing you to the ladies of the county." She made a tiny grimace as if that thought were unpleasant. "I will help any way I can with Gordy and Royce. You married Gordon, so he's your problem."

"Aye," said Maggie, feeling something warm and sweet pass between them. She had an ally—she thought she might have a friend. "I'll be letting you and that wee babe you're carrying get some sleep. Can I be bringing you anything first?"

"No, just hand me that book on the nightstand."

Maggie stood up, retrieved the thick, leather-bound book and gave it to Annabelle. "Good night and God bless."

Annabelle looked as if she were going to say something and then thought better of it. She fanned the pages of her book and then smiled again. "A wedding gift came for you yesterday from a Father Fitzhugh in Richmond. It's in the library for now, until you get settled into your own home."

Father Fitz. He had gotten her letter and sent a gift of love. Maggie could hardly speak, so she nodded in acknowledgment.

"I'm glad you're here, Maggie."

"Thank you, Annabelle."

"Call me Annie. Annabelle always makes me feel like I'm talking to a stranger or someone who's angry with me."

"Aye, then . . . Annie."

A horse whinnied as Gordon pulled the door open and entered the stables, immediately drawing in the scent of hay and harness leather. Momentarily blinded by the shift from night to the light of the barn, he still heard the ominous click of a gun hammer being cocked.

"Dammit, Royce, since when did you start carrying a revolver in the stables?"

"Since Clarence's shop was set on fire."

Clarence, one of Riverbend's former slaves, the best blacksmith between Richmond and Washington—and Royce's closest friend since they were boys together. Royce stepped out from the shadows, holstering a Navy Colt as he moved.

"The Klan's back in action in the county," he said in his low baritone voice that seldom showed any emotion.

"Then I'd suggest you put aside your politics, at least until Annie's through this pregnancy."

A shadow passed across Royce's face. "Christ, I want to. I have, to a large extent," he said. "Passions are running hot over the Mechanics Union. I threw my support behind them and now that it's more than theory . . ." His voice trailed off.

"Craft guild, or voting union?"

"Some of both."

"All black?"

"One hundred percent."

So that explained old man Pettigrew's electioneering at

the train depot. And Moulton Johnson flanked him throughout the entire harangue. Johnson was about the meanest white son-of-a-bitch in the state; he'd damn near whipped Franklin to death when Franklin was still one of his slaves. If there was a Klan resurgence in Spotsylvania County, Johnson was probably responsible.

Gordon leaned up against an empty stall and crossed his arms loosely on his chest. "You've had threats."

Royce stopped, slanted him a glance and then returned to his task. The clang of metal against metal sounded as he shut the last gate. "Don't say anything to the women."

Gordon leaned his head back. Dammit, he'd brought Maggie into a hornet's nest. A brother who'd spent the evening glowering at his new sister-in-law, a son who could be counted upon to shoot her with verbal darts until she bled, and now the damned Klan, with their hooded robes and burning crosses.

"I'll take my family into Richmond," he said, making an instant decision. "You can let me know when this all blows over."

"Running, brother?"

"At least one of us has some sense."

To his surprise, Royce made no comment, only walking past him and stopping when he came to the opened doors. For a moment, Royce stood silently, staring out into the stable yard. "This time, I'd go with you," he said quietly. "Even if it meant losing all this to their torches."

"Annie?" Gordon moved through the hay scraps to stand beside his brother.

"She's not supposed to travel, not supposed to get out of bed, even." He shook his head. "Damn, what will I do if . . ."

"Royce." Gordon felt the anger drain out of him. He lifted his hand and placed it on his brother's shoulder—only an instant, letting it drop when he saw the brightness of his brother's eyes. "Dr. Levin? What provisions have you made to get him out here when the time comes?"

He knew it was small consolation where Annabelle's condition was concerned. She had a history of premature labor and no one could guess when labor would begin or how severely. Dr. Levin's practice was in Richmond, hours away by the cars, but he was the best in the state.

"He's guessing another eight to nine weeks. Plans are to have him come out here then and stay for a while." Royce barked a harsh laugh. "Like it worked the last time."

Three years ago, when Annie lost the fetus at four months while her doctor and Royce were both racing from Richmond to Fredericksburg. She would have bled to death if Gordon hadn't happened to be there at the time.

"She's already past that danger period," said Gordon, trying to ease his brother's fear. "If Levin says eight weeks, he's pretty confident she's gotten beyond those problems. Maybe this one will work. She carried Hope almost to term."

Behind them, large Thoroughbreds shifted in their stalls. Somewhere in front of them, a nightingale was singing. It was peaceful, the tranquillity he'd loved in those years before the war, that age of youthful innocence when anything seemed possible. Older and wiser now, he knew the tranquillity was an illusion easily shattered. Annie's health. The Klan. Royce's damned politics.

"I'd like you to stay," said Royce in a low voice.

Gordon recognized how much that admission cost his older brother, but his own passions were running hot. "You should have thought of that earlier. You've been a royal bastard since we got here. Why should I stay?"

"You hurt Gordy. You sent him a telegraph, dammit. He never even got to meet the woman before you married her."

"So take it out on me, not on her."

Gordon fought the sudden urge to plant his fist in his brother's gut by walking away from temptation. Annabelle's roan jumper lifted her head over the gate, giving a low whinny. He turned his steps to the stall and stroked the mare's neck.

"Is anyone exercising this horse?" he asked as he opened the gate and entered the stall.

Royce walked over and leaned his shoulder against the oak slats. "Gordy takes her out."

"I want my son back," said Gordon.

"What if I don't want to give him back?"

Gordon ran his hand down the mare's forelegs. He slanted a glance at his brother. "Toss me the curry comb."

Royce remained motionless except for a twist on one side of his mouth. "I said, what if I don't want to give Gordy back?"

"Nothing wrong with *my* hearing. Now toss me the curry comb."

"What's the point in brushing down a horse who hasn't been ridden since her last rubdown, other than it gives you an excuse not to face what you don't want to face?"

Gordon raised up. "It'll keep me from breaking your arrogant nose. And as much pleasure as that would give me, I don't think Annie would thank me for ruining that pretty face of yours."

To his surprise, Royce laughed, and there was real amusement in the sound. "Remember the night just before the war when you thought I'd been my usual reprehensible self, so you stepped in to protect her and we ended up fighting on the lawn?"

"And Annie ended the fight by nearly unmanning you."

"A man has to love a woman who has more balls than he does."

Royce started to laugh, but the sound became caught in his throat. He rubbed his face hard with his palms. "Christ, Gordon. What am I going to do? Every day, my wife gets bigger with a child she wants desperately, and all I can think of is this baby is going to kill her. And now Gordy . . ."

He kicked hard at the dirt floor, causing the mare to jerk back. Gordon soothed the mare and watched his brother swing around, pace several lengths of the barn, then walk slowly back through the alternating light and shadows. Royce stopped just inside the stall, leaned over and picked up a long piece of straw and pulled it through his fingers.

"I know Gordy is your son," he said, his voice once again under control. "Sometimes I like to forget that fact, and you've made it awfully easy over the years for me to forget."

"I thought it was best for my son. You had legs that worked, a wife to mother him, a daughter for him to grow up with." Gordon parted the mare's mane, then smoothed it. "I've got to try, Royce. Maggie loves children, even obnoxious ones." He tried to laugh, but couldn't. "Gordy will be a man soon. I'd like him to know he has a father—that I'm his father—before it's too late."

"I was itching to take a strap to him when you asked him to bring you that picture."

"Why didn't you?"

"Because you're his father. And you handled it better anyway." Royce tossed the straw to the ground. "I'll get you that curry comb if you really want to brush down a horse. I'd rather have a snort of sour mash."

Gordon gave the roan one last pat and came out of the stall, latching the gate as Royce extinguished the lanterns. They met at the big stable doors. The moon shed a soft wash of silvery light on the back lawn. A minute of silence passed, filled with the chirruping of crickets.

Royce swung the stable doors closed. Together, they started across the barnyard, but Royce angled his steps toward the paddock fence instead of the house. Gordon shrugged and followed. His plans for the rest of the night did not include getting drunk with his brother anyway. Royce was leaning forward with his arms on the top rail.

"Clara isn't an adoption, is she?" he said when Gordon came up beside him.

"She is and she isn't."

"Aurora?"

Gordon said nothing. Royce let out a sigh.

"Aurora's back—visiting her brother Moulton."

"I saw her at the train station."

And nearly fallen flat on his face, the shock had been so

profound. In that instant of eye contact, he'd known that she knew, and everything about him had frozen.

After giving the matter some consideration, he was fairly certain Aurora's fear of reopening a scandal that had long since died would keep her away. In due time, Clara deserved to know who her birth mother was, even the circumstances of her birth, but she was too young yet to deal with such moral ambiguities, and Maggie was too uncertain of her own place in his life, his heart, to be confronted with a former lover now.

He wondered how long Aurora planned on staying. Moulton Johnson was years older than his sister and had had guardianship of Aurora after their father's death. Gordon had always suspected she'd rushed into an early marriage with Leland Hammond not from love, but from an intense desire to escape her brother's control. Moulton Johnson was a bloodless, cruel man. Aurora would not want to tarry under his roof any longer than refined manners dictated. With any luck, he thought, she'd be leaving tomorrow.

"When are you going to tell me the whole story?" asked Royce.

"When you decide to treat my wife like she's a welcome member of the family."

Royce laughed again. "Your wife spit in my face— figuratively, of course—but when she told that story about the Irish cow, she was telling me I could take my pride and shove it up my southern parts. I damn near applauded."

"God, but you're an arrogant ass."

"Yeah, and your wife has grit. You did good, little brother, and I'm man enough to apologize to both of you." Royce turned and leaned on his elbows. "So tell me how you got so lucky."

Royce carried the scent of the stables. It blended with the other scents of an early autumn night, of fallen leaves and mown hay. Gordon was seized with old memories, remembering the hero worship he'd felt as a boy for this older brother, the countless times Royce had rescued him from a scrape or taken the whipping from Peyton for him.

By damn, he'd always been there, as brother, as friend. Even, maybe especially, with Gordy. And now he was giving Gordy back. Royce didn't have to say the words; it was understood.

Which left the responsibility squarely on his own shoulders, which was where he wanted it, and yet, and yet . . . his son was not some inanimate object to be passed back and forth at will. He was a boy with a sharp mind, injured feelings, and he had tossed down the gauntlet tonight.

A new sound drifted from the Big House, the sound of an Irish harp and an angel's voice singing in Gaelic. To the accompaniment of his wife's soft music, Gordon told Royce the background as he knew it for Clara, followed by the reasons for the haste of his marriage.

"Well, hell, brother," said Royce when he'd finished. "You know I damned near ruined my own marriage. Guess I'll stand back and let you make a better job of your own."

Gordon looked at his brother's face: the hair gone prematurely gray at the temples, the silver eyes that were Peyton's, the dimpled smile that was uniquely Royce's own.

They were so different, and had always looked at life through opposite ends of a telescope. He felt a sudden, deeper kinship at this moment, a meeting on some kind of common ground.

"She sounds like an angel," said Royce. "I had no idea what the purpose of that thing was when it was delivered yesterday."

"Father Fitzhugh's harp," murmured Gordon, silently thanking the priest for that loving gesture. The wind was cool against his face. Leaves rustled beneath his boots as he started back to the Big House.

Royce came up beside him. "So, will you stay?"

Gordon drew in a deep breath and let it out slowly. Maggie was an immigrant from a Catholic background, almost as despicable in the Klan's rabid thoughts as the sin of being born black. But then too, Annie could easily die in a medical emergency.

"We'll stay," he said.

They were Kincaid men, and it was deep in their bones and their blood. Kincaid men stood together to protect the women and children dependent upon them.

Gordon leaned against the pilaster and watched Maggie playing the harp. Her fingers were long and slender, graceful in motion as they plucked the strings. She sat with her head bowed slightly. The fire cast red shadows on her black crown of hair.

She looked up, catching sight of him. He held out his hand. Wordlessly, she rose and crossed the room to where he stood, placing her hand into his.

"It's a magical moon. Would you walk with me?"

"Aye." She ducked her head a little, slanting him a glance from those green eyes, somehow managing to look shy, innocent and seductive all at the same time.

He led her outside and down the path to the river. The moon was fully risen, shining so brightly they didn't need a lantern to see their way. At the riverbank, the water lapped gently against the sand in tiny, silvery waves. They paused, both of them watching moonlight dance on the slow-moving water.

"Did you talk with your brother?" she asked in a voice as soft as the night.

"I think he understands a little better now."

He longed to share the whole conversation with her but didn't. On that one matter, he agreed with Royce. There was no point in frightening the women with mention of roving bands of night riders who might or might not show up at Royce's doorstep.

"Seems his problem was a combination of fear for his wife, which makes him an ogre to be around, and concern for Gordy."

He felt her sigh and turned her to face him. "You never

cease to amaze me, Irish. When I'm itching to smash two hard male heads together, you disarm them both with a story." He touched the corner of her mouth when she smiled. "Did what's-his-name really fight a battle over a cow?"

"It wasn't a battle so much as a war, and only a blathering fool would war over a cow," she said. " 'Twas the Donn Cuailgne, the Brown Bull of Cooley, and wasn't it Mother Bernadette herself who once told me no lady ever uses the word *bull* when *cow* will do nicely, thank you."

He laughed. "Did the estimable mother superior wash your mouth out with soap?"

"Confession. Father Fitzhugh was hearing confessions that day. He tried not to give himself away, but I always recognized his laugh. I had to say five Hail Marys for penance and later he took me for a lemon ice at Baylor's."

She was smiling at the memory, while he was resisting the need to yank her into his arms and hold tight. He looked over her head to where moonlight filtered through the branches of a lofty pine. He wanted to say so many things: *You were happy there, and I'm sorry for taking you away from the people and places you love, but I need you so much, and I want you to love me and I'll make you happy here.*

But of course he said none of those things, because he was selfish and only a little bit sorry, and a man driven by the fear he might yet lose her to the convent.

He took her hand and started walking along the footpath that wended its way upriver. Her skirts rustled as they walked, melding with the sigh of the breeze.

"Where are we going?" she asked.

"You and Clara and I will go there tomorrow, but tonight it's just the two of us. I wanted to share it with you first."

She smiled faintly. " 'Twill be dark."

He glanced up. "A lover's moon."

She ducked her head and he guessed she was blushing. Within a few minutes, he was guiding her through the overgrown ornamental garden and up the flagstones set into the rise.

Old Riverbend, built just after the Revolution, rose before them with all the graceful lines of the period, etched by starlight and moon glow. He felt a resurgence of all the old pride in his heritage that had disappeared with the war. More than that, he felt proud he could give her this beautiful home, proud he could support her in this style.

She stopped. "It's a grand house."

He heard all the unspoken words, the self-doubt in her voice. "We'll take it slow, Maggie-mine." He opened his palms and smoothed her hair, over and over again. "We can't hide from them, they'll be dropping calling cards as soon as the word gets out that Dr. Kincaid brought a wife home with him. But I promise you, they're just people. By this time next year, you'll be wondering why you were so scared of the old biddies."

She made a small sound of disbelief. He took her hands in his own and held them out to the side. "Look at you. A princess, a fairy princess. Just wave that rowan wand. You can turn Mrs. Pettigrew into a toad if you like. You'll win the eternal goodwill of half the county."

Her lips twitched as her sense of humor gained ground against her fears. "Could I wave it at your brother instead?"

"Aye, and wouldn't that be a grand idea," he mimicked

She laughed softly. He brought her hands together and up to his lips, kissing the backs of her fingers. He was so damned lucky to have found her, and with a daughter he never knew existed.

Gordy.

No, he would not lose Maggie by gaining his son. He could not allow that to happen, for without her his life would not be worth living.

She was peering at him through those long, dusky lashes, a shy smile at her mouth. He pulled her closer and kissed the smile from her lips, then lifted her in his arms.

"What are you doing?"

"Carrying my bride over the threshold."

Through the door, up the stairs to a room draped in moon

shadows. Kissing her mouth, her body in his arms—in his bed.

Home.

He took her with all the urgency he felt, not wasting time on leisurely preliminaries, claiming all that was his. She wrapped her arms around him, pulling him down to her with an urgency that seemed as desperate as his own.

Chapter 21

*I*n the days that followed, Gordon spent as much time with her as he could, trying to ease her into her new roles as wife and mother and lady of the household. He wanted to believe she needed him, and so he was there.

But as the leaves changed into brilliant color and the nights became cool, he knew life must settle into a normal pattern, and he had ignored his medical practice for too long. He resumed his schedule in the office; the children settled into their schedule with schooling, and he trusted Dulcie to quietly step in and support his wife if problems developed at home while he was gone.

Gordon attached his second cuff link as he descended the stairs. He was dodging his way through the scaffolding from the renovations when Clara and a wet, smelly Lucky barreled past him.

"Whoa, princess," he said, grabbing her by the shoulders and bringing her to a halt. Her white pinafore was streaked with grime, her curls tangled around a drooping satin bow and a large splotch of red mud trailed down her left cheek.

He wondered if his nose was twitching as he tried to appear stern rather than laugh. "Aren't you supposed to be in the schoolhouse with Hope and Gordy?"

She gave him a dimpled smile. "Mr. Patton let me and Hope go early because we did all our spelling and Gordy didn't consummate his verbs."

"Didn't what?" He reached up to feel his nose, hiding the intent of the maneuver behind a scratching motion.

"You know—his Latin. Gordy hates Latin."

Gordon didn't know whether to laugh at his daughter or search out his son for another reprimand. "Is Gordy conjugating his verbs now?"

"Uh-huh."

"Yes, sir."

"Yes, sir." Her small fingers twisted in Lucky's wet ruff. "Can Lucky and I go now? Dulcie promised us gingerbread."

"Where's my Maggie?"

"Out by the laundry house."

Lucky was gathering to shake. Gordon decided to let them go before he looked like his daughter. He'd indulged himself this morning, spending time with Franklin and the horses and then lingering over his morning coffee with Maggie. He didn't have the time to change his clothes again. "Get yourself cleaned up first, then the gingerbread."

Bright sunshine greeted him as he stepped out onto the back terrace. He shrugged into his frock coat and took another minute he didn't have to watch his wife, radiant even surrounded by a cloud of dust as she pounded the carpet runner with a broom. He suspected a part of her glow came from pregnancy; in the six weeks they'd been married, she hadn't yet had her menses. The thought only added to the brilliance of the day.

He took a deep breath, taking in the aroma of fresh gingerbread along with the mingled scents of a sun-filled autumn morning. What the heck, he was already late. Gordon followed the spicy aroma down the breezeway to the kitchen.

Hot, damp air hit his face as he stepped into the summer kitchen. Dulcie stood by the worktable, her whole upper body rocking as she vigorously polished a silver coffee urn. But his attention focused on Dulcie's daughter-in-law, Phoebe, who was just now lifting a pan from the big oven in the new nickel-plated stove. Steam wafted up from the brown bread.

"I thought you told me that contraption would never work," he said as Phoebe turned to set the pan on an iron trivet. "Smells heavenly in here."

"Weren't nothing wrong with the old cast-iron stove." Dulcie slapped his hand away as he reached to pinch a taste of gingerbread from the top of the loaf.

He tried for a boyish grin. "Please, Dulcie. It's a long day ahead of me and you know the children will eat it all before I get home."

Dulcie laughed and went back to polishing the silver. "We already cut you some squares from the first pan, Doctor. It's wrapped up in that red huck towel on the table there."

He placed his hand over his heart. "Dulcie, Dulcie, you've saved me again."

"Ain't you late for the office?" She craned her head over her shoulder and gave him a grin.

He hefted the towel-wrapped bundle, still faintly warm to the touch, and walked to the doorway. He stopped as he caught sight of his son ambling across the back lawn.

Maggie paused in her work and blew a sharp breath upward. She smiled and rolled her shoulders as she caught sight of Gordy. Gordy shoved his hands in his pockets and didn't smile back.

"Are you done with your Latin?" asked Maggie, bravely holding her smile.

Gordy shrugged. "Mr. Patton let me go to get something to eat."

"Aye, then, if you're going to the kitchen, would you stop by the springhouse first? Phoebe needs a crock of butter."

"Yes, ma'am," said Gordy, and stood without moving, only staring at his stepmother, who managed to keep smiling although the smile was cracking at the edges.

"Come here, Dulcie," said Gordon quietly. He heard the rattle of cutlery and then Dulcie stepped outside the kitchen door.

"Humph," she said, viewing the tension-ridden pair.

Maggie gripped the broom handle tighter. Gordy's head lowered, his jaw thrusting down so he looked like a young bull preparing to charge. Even from across the lawn, Gordon could feel his son's intransigence, a tactile thing like the heat in Phoebe's kitchen. After another tension-charged minute, Gordy swung around and headed back across the lawn in the direction of the schoolhouse, the opposite direction from the springhouse.

Maggie took a breath so deep her shoulders moved. "Gordy, Phoebe baked you some fresh gingerbread."

The boy stopped and turned slowly. "Thank you, ma'am, but I'm not hungry anymore."

Maggie nodded, the boy turned and resumed his amble across the lawn as if he hadn't a care in the world and only then did Maggie allow her shoulders to slump. Gordon controlled the strong desire to go after his son and shake him until his teeth rattled. He would, but not until his anger cooled, and not in front of Maggie.

"Is it always like this when he thinks I'm not here?" Gordon asked in an undertone aimed only at Dulcie. "Or is it sometimes worse?"

"The boy don't ever talk back, if that's what you're asking. But he ain't exactly what you'd call a gentleman either."

Maggie propped the broom handle under her arm, then ducked her head and rubbed her temples with her fingers. A cow lowed in the pasture, and the sun continued to beat down brassy and warm, but the day no longer seemed so brilliant.

"Why doesn't she tell me these things?" he said, and

didn't realize he'd spoken out loud until Dulcie gave another snort.

"What's the missus supposed to say? Gordy's real careful to never do anything wrong, he just don't ever do anything right either. He'll bait her with a question about Ireland, then roll his eyes when she answers, or ask her if the Pope is related to God, or some other such nonsense, then wink at Clara when the missus tries to explain her religion. The worst is when he gets to talking about Miz Augusta, like her family done hung the moon, and the boy don't know hardly nothing about his mother and didn't ever talk about her before. He's just doing it now to needle the new missus."

Dulcie pursed her lips, then huffed again. "You want to ask me another question, I'd say if the boy was mine, I'd give him a good lickin' with a willow switch. Not that you asked."

He handed her the wrapped gingerbread. "Have Franklin put that in my medical bag. I need to talk to my wife."

Maggie had gone back to pounding the carpet runner that was hung over a strung line. With each whack of the broom, a puff of white plaster dust filled the air and settled on her skirts.

She must not have heard him approach, since she jumped when he called her name. When she turned, she was managing another smile, as if that scene with Gordy hadn't happened. She leaned the broom against the carpet and rolled her shoulders.

"You don't need to beat the carpets," he said, placing his hands on her shoulders and kneading some of the ache away. "That's why we pay all this help."

"Aye, but the job will be finished sooner if I do my share."

She used the back of her hand to mop a trail of dirt across her brow. He leaned forward, brushing a kiss on her dust-coated forehead. He looked into her eyes for a moment, waiting for her to say something about Gordy, but she didn't.

"Did you see our daughter?" he asked.

"I was hoping you wouldn't." She laughed softly. "They were fishing in your brother's carp pond."

"I also saw Gordy directly disobey an order you gave him."

She jerked her gaze up, her eyes brilliant green and startled, then she turned away. Her movements were slow as she wiped her hands on her skirt, then reached for the broom.

"Mr. Patton is having some problems with Gordy," she said. "He asked me to tell you and have you stop by the schoolhouse."

"I'll stop on my way in to town and talk to Mr. Patton. Gordy will get more than a talking to."

She stood looking in the direction of the river, but he didn't think she saw the sun glinting off the surface. Her gaze was focused inward, to a place deep inside her.

"He doesn't trust me yet, you see," she said in a quiet voice. Her cheeks were flushed and the skin below her eyes appeared smudged with bruises. "A child gives love only after it is earned, and you earn it in little things. Give me time, Gordon. If you . . . if you whip him over some little thing like . . . like what you just saw, he will think I told you, and I might never earn his trust."

"How about respect, Maggie? Let's try for some simple respect."

"Please, Gordon."

"He's my son, Irish."

"Aye, he is that." She tucked her chin, averting her face, as she went back to pounding dust from the carpet.

He watched her for a minute, then realized she considered the conversation at an end. He thought he ought to say something more but didn't know what it was, so he left her and went to the stables, where Franklin had already saddled his horse.

Gordon stopped by the schoolhouse, had his talk with the tutor, then took his son outside for a different sort of lesson. He was halfway to town before he recognized his colossal mistake. He'd slammed the woman he loved with her two greatest insecurities.

My son, and *Irish*.

* * *

By late morning, Maggie was indulging herself with a second cup of tea while she pored over the household ledgers. The amount of money Gordon had budgeted for refurbishing the house had struck her as preposterous at the time they undertook the task. Now she was appalled at how fast the dollars went.

Whenever she brought up the issue with suggestions for cutting the expense, he only laughed and told her not to worry. Not to worry, when they were spending more in a day than she used to earn in an entire year!

She looked up as the door opened. Dulcie stood in the entrance, balancing a small silver salver in one hand.

"Are you home for callers, Mrs. K?"

"Oh, my." Maggie's heart dropped. She'd managed to avoid all these social obligations she didn't understand, using the household as her excuse. Annie had warned her the ladies would soon start showing up on her doorstep, but she'd pushed that worry aside. They were here now and Gordon wasn't available to guide her through this social quagmire.

"What happens if I decline?" she asked, having learned that Dulcie had more understanding of the proper procedures than she ever would.

"They'll come back one more time. If you decline the second call, you've as much as told them you don't wish to have social relations with them."

"Not wise."

Dulcie smiled faintly. "Not wise. But you could put them off this time."

Maggie chewed on the end of her pencil, considering her options. "I'll see them."

She'd startled Dulcie with that, she could see. Dulcie held out the tray, presenting two calling cards. "Where should I show them? The drawing room's filled with scaffolding."

Maggie took the two cards and read the names. Mrs. Pettigrew and Mrs. Neal. Mrs. Pettigrew would be some relation to the man she'd heard making his speeches the day of their arrival.

The morning room glowed like the ornamental flower garden, with the heart of the sun shining through the leaded glass to caper over the flowered chintz upholstery and pale yellow walls. This and the dining room were her only choices due to workmen crawling over every other downstairs room.

"Here, I suppose."

Dulcie cleared her throat and peered down her broad nose. "Them two are old warhorses."

"You think I should wait for my husband."

"Not my place to say." Dulcie compressed her lips.

"Fifteen minutes and they're gone. I may as well get it over with."

Dulcie inclined her head and left. Maggie didn't understand the sudden coolness in Dulcie's behavior. Either Dulcie disapproved of the two women or she feared Maggie was going to disgrace the household on her first trial. Since Dulcie had spoken of them as old warhorses, Maggie decided it was the callers who were the problem, not her. Just as she arrived at that self-serving conclusion, the door opened.

"Mrs. Pettigrew and Mrs. Neal," announced Dulcie.

Maggie rose to greet her guests. "Please," she said, gesturing to the reupholstered armchairs grouped near the fireplace.

"It's such a pleasure to see Gordon fixing up this place," said Mrs. Pettigrew as she settled her bulk and bustle into one of the offered seats, giving herself the appearance of a hen struggling to lay an egg. "It's been in his family for generations, you know."

"Aye," said Maggie, reseating herself on the spindle-backed chair near the writing desk. "I'm Mary Margaret, but everyone calls me Maggie."

"Yes, well, you've been quite the topic of conversation, Mrs. Kincaid, what with Gordon remarrying after all these years to a stranger. We haven't even seen you in church on Sundays." Mrs. Pettigrew glanced around the recently renovated room. "I might be a busybody like everyone claims, but it wouldn't be neighborly of me if I didn't point out that you've got a certain station in life you have to uphold. You could still the tongues by coming to church."

Maggie kept her voice calm, determined not to make a disaster of this first encounter with society. "My husband is not a churchgoer."

"All the more reason for you to show him the way. Augusta came from a good family. He always attended church with her when he was home on leave."

"You are a busybody," said Mrs. Neal in a surprisingly deep voice. "That's not why we came today, Maggie. I fear we're here begging because we need a Kincaid on our Confederate Memorial Committee and we can't ask Annabelle due to her . . ." She cleared her throat. "Umm, delicate condition."

Maggie brushed at the smudges of dirt that stubbornly clung to her fingernails. "I'm . . . I fear . . ." She looked up, prepared to admit her ineptitude. "I know naught of committees."

"Augusta wouldn't have hesitated. Are you a Yankee, Mrs. Kincaid?" asked Mrs. Pettigrew sharply.

Maggie chose to ignore the repeated references to Augusta Kincaid, guessing Mrs. Pettigrew's intent was to vex her. Through Annie's stories—and what a dear friend Annie had turned out to be—Maggie was coming to feel a sad kind of tenderness for the young woman snatched from her family by an early death.

"I was a twelve-year-old immigrant when the war began," she said. "I didn't choose sides then and the war is over now."

"For some of us, it will never end," said Mrs. Pettigrew pointedly.

For an instant, Maggie slipped backward in time to a smoky neighborhood pub in Baltimore, and heard Jamie's rough voice: *It's never over, á mhúirnín.*

Why wouldn't the world allow those who wished peace to find it?

"I will speak to my husband about this."

"You must show your husband the way. It's expected of Kincaids to take a leadership role in the county. The general has let us all down with his Republican politics. Annabelle is ill. Your husband has been avoiding his responsibilities for years. It's up to you, Mrs. Kincaid."

There was some type of veiled threat in Mrs. Pettigrew's words, but Maggie couldn't really decipher it. "I'll speak to him about that also," she replied noncommittally.

"Your accent?" said Mrs. Pettigrew. "Is it Irish?"

Mrs. Neal reached over and patted her arm. "Now, now, Agnes, does it really matter where Mrs. Kincaid grew up?"

"It mattered to me." Maggie swallowed around an ache in her throat that felt suspiciously like tears. "I'm Irish-born, Mrs. Pettigrew, and I'll not apologize for it. Three years ago, I took the Oath of Citizenship for this country and I'm proud of that too."

Dulcie appeared in the doorway, her dark face expressionless. "The workmen need you in the main parlor, Mrs. Kincaid," she said. "An emergency."

Maggie rose hastily. "Is someone hurt?"

"An emergency," repeated Dulcie. "I'll see the ladies out."

"Aye." Maggie turned to her guests. "You'll excuse me?"

Mrs. Neal smiled and nodded. Mrs. Pettigrew was staring at Dulcie. Maggie hastened to the door, pausing with Mrs. Pettigrew's voice.

"Are you also a Catholic, Mrs. Kincaid?"

Maggie exchanged a quick glance with Dulcie, then turned to face her tormentor. "Aye, I was raised in the Catholic Church."

"We won't be needing you on the committee after all." Mrs. Pettigrew rose and gathered her reticule. "Come along, Mrs. Neal."

Maggie stepped back and let Mrs. Pettigrew pass. Mrs. Neal paused in front of her, reached out as if to touch Maggie's arm, then withdrew the motion.

"She lost three sons in the Late Unpleasantness," said Mrs. Neal.

"I understand," Maggie said beneath her breath. And sadly, she did.

Mrs. Neal plucked at the lace jabot around her throat, looking as if she wanted to say something more, but then she simply nodded and followed Dulcie. Maggie turned and stared blindly out the window. She was still there when Dulcie returned.

"How about I bring you a nice cup of tea?" said Dulcie.

Maggie started. "Oh . . . nay. I must go to the parlor."

"I'll bring you the tea."

"There wasn't any emergency?"

"Old warhorse should have been shot years ago," said Dulcie emphatically.

Maggie crossed her arms over her waist. There was such a wild shaking going on inside her, she thought she might scream or burst into tears.

"I heard Gordy come in," she said, trying to make her voice sound calm. "Why don't I get the children and we'll have a picnic in the apple orchard."

Dulcie picked up the silver salver, her starched petticoat crackling as she moved. "You just asking for more heartache."

"Maybe, Dulcie, but pack the hamper anyway."

Dulcie left without another word. When Maggie went up to Gordy's room, she found him sitting in the window seat, gazing out over the horse pasture with his arms wrapped around his bent knees. He turned his head as she knocked on the open door, and gave her one of his deep blue frowns.

"Since you're done in the schoolroom," she said, "and it's such a beautiful day, I thought we might all have a picnic in the apple orchard."

"I have to conjugate my Latin. Thank you anyway, Mrs. Kincaid."

Maggie drew on her lower lip and her gaze fell to the plush medallion carpet. "If you change your mind . . ." she said, her voice trailing off. She looked up. Gordy was staring across the room at a wedding portrait framed in dark wood that sat on his bureau. She said nothing as she pulled the door gently closed.

She had a picnic in the apple orchard with Clare and Dulcie. Afterward, she let Dulcie put Clare down for her nap and walked to the Kincaid family cemetery. She opened the wrought-iron gate and stood for a moment in front of the newest grave, saying a prayer for the soul of Peyton Kincaid.

She drew a cross, then sat on the clipped green grass and wrapped her arms around her knees as she studied the white marble headstone over the grave of Augusta Kincaid. She pressed her face hard into the bones of her knees, but she couldn't keep herself from crying.

The bell chimed as the front door opened. Gordon glanced up from his correspondence, irritated with the interruption. He'd seen his two scheduled patients, local men who had continuing difficulties with their amputations.

He was trying to catch up on the medical reports he'd let slide this past month, the correspondence with the general doctors who saw to his far-flung patients, and the persistent requests from colleagues to give speeches and take a more active role in the formation of medical societies and colleges.

Gordon laid down the pen, pushed back his roll chair and went into the front room. Clarence was staring through the window into the quiet street beyond. Clarence, just Clarence, during his long years as a Kincaid slave. He'd taken Annabelle's maiden name as his surname when freed, becoming Clarence Hallston.

Gordon had often wondered if that action was a rebuke to the Kincaid family who'd held him in bondage or a sign of respect for Annabelle. He'd never been able to decide, and probably it was some of each.

Clarence turned at the sound of footsteps, his face grave. "Been an accident down at the tobacco warehouse," he said. "Ben Higgins."

Ben Higgins, thought Gordon. Black Republican, brave enough to have run for Congress years ago, up to his ears in the voting arm of the black Mechanics Union now. No, he didn't want anything to do with this.

"You know I don't treat general patients. Why didn't you go for Chatham or Norris?"

"Norris is out of town and Chatham won't see him." Clarence stared at him, his eyes wide and unblinking. He was a big man, dark-skinned, with strong, bulging muscles hewn from years at a stone forge. He held himself with a taut alertness, understandable for a black man whose smithy shop had been burned to the ground by Klansmen.

Gordon returned the stare while something akin to fury rose in his chest; fury with the medical man who rode in night mobs and refused to treat black patients, fury with his own brother for his active role in Republican politics and even fury with this black man who expected him to take a stand.

"Dammit, Clarence. I've got a wife and children. Don't suck me into this mess."

"I've got a wife and children too." A hard, calculating look came over Clarence's face. "I reckon you're just scared to do what's right."

"You're damn right." Gordon tried to put a cutting edge in his voice. "I served my time, paid my penalty. Live and let live is my new motto."

"Yeah, well, Ben ain't gonna live unless a doctor sees to him."

He could feel each separate breath he drew; felt that old idealism upsurge with each indrawn breath, felt it ebb with each exhalation. The issue shouldn't be politics, it was medicine. Years ago . . . this was why he became a doctor.

"Where is he?" he asked.

"Been taken home already."

Maggie had resurrected his heart, restored his pride. Gordon turned to get his medical bag, saying a silent prayer to Maggie's God. *Protect us. Protect her.*

Chapter 22

Gordy Kincaid wasn't thinking about conjugating Latin verbs as he walked among the willows and scrub pines that draped the footpath along the Rappahannock. He was thinking he could be mounted on his horse, Colonel, riding the estates with Uncle Royce if his father hadn't gotten some bee in his bonnet this morning and come full gun into the schoolhouse.

A whipping wasn't much—Uncle Royce had whipped him harder for less—it was being forbidden to ride the estate that was eating at him.

He was stuck with the women for a whole week, like he was some little boy. If Father would just look at him, he'd see he wasn't a child anymore. Why, damn, he was twelve years old now. Gordy flushed a little and looked around, as if someone—Maggie—were leaning over his shoulder, reading the cuss words in his mind.

Maggie. She'd changed everything.

So Father was happy, any fool could see the change. Part

of him liked that, liked the new man who whistled in the morning and laughed instead of yelled when a wet dog put a paw in his lap. Part of him hated Maggie because she'd done what he'd never been able to do: make his father want to stay home.

Criminy, even Aunt Annie liked her. If he didn't love Aunt Annie like she was his own mother, he'd have to hate her for that treason.

Gordy squatted down on his haunches and studied the black droppings that lay scattered like lumps of coal over the pine needles. A deer had been by here. He poked a dropping with his finger, rolling it over. It was warm, still fresh enough to smell.

If he could ride, he and Uncle Royce could go deer hunting, kill themselves a big buck for smoking. He wondered if Maggie had ever tasted venison. She sure didn't know much about smoking meat, that had been obvious during the hog butchering.

Gordy looked up, squinting against the sunlight pouring through the tree branches. The trees were thick here, but they thinned out further ahead, where Aunt Annie said the Confederate soldiers had camped during the war. Sometimes a boy could find real shells still buried in the ground there. He'd have to warn Clara about that. He didn't want her getting shot up by some long-forgotten Confederate bullet.

He surprised himself by liking the kid, even if she was a girl. He'd always thought Hope was enough girl to have constantly hanging around asking girl questions. But that wasn't fair either. Hope wasn't really a girly-girl. She could catch more fish than any boy in the county, climbed a tree as good as he did and usually beat him in footraces, although he always acted like he'd just let her win. He was better with a shotgun, but he was a man, so he was supposed to be better.

Even Hope liked *my Maggie*. Just yesterday, he'd wanted to go fishing and Hope stayed behind because the Maggie-woman was teaching her how to play that stupid harp. He'd been stuck with Clara and had had to put the bloodworms on her hook over and over again while she chattered and scared all the fish away. He'd finally just given up in disgust.

The breeze picked up, stirring the branches on the thickets and trees. He heard the snap of a dry twig and whirled around.

Maggie.

She smiled at him like she always did. He didn't smile back, like he never did.

"Are you fishing again?"

Stupid question. Did she see any fishing pole in his hand?

"No, ma'am."

She sighed and looked out over the water. Her hands were crossed over her waist. He liked that. He'd learned that gesture meant she was in a flap over something, that and speaking with a lot of Irish in her voice.

He didn't want her happy. He wasn't happy, so why should she be happy?

She brought her gaze back to him. "I found a patch of late daisies," she said. "Would you like to pick them and take them up to the cemetery?"

Gordy opened his mouth, but his throat got all dammed up with something lumpy and nothing came out, not even air. She reached for him, smoothed his hair back from his forehead.

"I'm sorry," she said, and the Irish was thick in her voice. "You'll be missing your mother, then, and I've made you sad. 'Tis not what I meant to do, Gordy."

It wasn't missing his mother. He didn't even remember his mother. He didn't know what it was, but it was burning hot in his chest and stinging the backs of his eyes. He blinked a few times. She was kneeling down now, poking through the underbrush.

"What's this?" she asked, probably trying to change the subject.

Gordy looked and an evil thought took form, so wonderfully evil, he didn't even feel like crying anymore.

"That's a special ivy. Grows real thick down here by the

river. My father always liked that ivy the best. Aunt Annie uses it in her table decorations because my father likes it so much."

She peered at him over her shoulder. "Would you help me pick some, then?"

Shoot, why not? For some reason, the stuff never made *him* itch.

"I thought I'd take you into Richmond for a few days. I've a patient I need to see and you could visit with Father Fitzhugh," said Gordon as he sliced into a fresh-baked pumpkin pie. "Want some pie, Maggie?"

Maggie shook her head. She couldn't eat; it was all she could do to sit without squirming and screaming. She twisted her hands in her lap, trying in vain to soothe the itching fire that was driving her mad. Her hands and forearms, even her legs from the top of her boots up to her knees—fiery itching, like a million mosquito bites. She'd worn gloves to the table trying to hide the blisters that were forming.

Gordon peered at her over the floral centerpiece she'd spent an hour trying to arrange before he arrived home. He hadn't made any comment about the lovely green ivy trailing over the ceramic bowl. His blue eyes narrowed.

"What's wrong? You haven't eaten a bite of dinner."

She manufactured a smile. "I fear I'm not especially hungry tonight."

Gordon pushed back his chair and came around to the far end of the table where she sat. He touched her forehead with the back of his hand. She almost felt feverish but said nothing.

He reached for her hand, making no comment on the oddity of wearing gloves to the dinner table. She matched his silence as he peeled off the glove.

"God Almighty!"

"Gordon," she said weakly.

"Maggie, where were you today?"

"Here, down by the river. Why?"

"Don't you know poison ivy when you see it?"

Maggie didn't look at Gordy. She didn't look at the pretty ceramic bowl with the trailing ivy. She twisted her head, erasing the vision of her puffy hand where the little blisters had turned into large watery swellings.

"Gordy, tell Dulcie to mix up a boric acid solution for your mother."

Maggie looked up and met Gordy's eyes, so like her husband's eyes except the son's still held those bewildered shadows. She waited, knowing what was coming.

"She's not my mother," he mumbled as he pushed back his chair. She watched him lift his gaze to the flower centerpiece.

Clare wiggled in her seat. "I'll go, Daddy."

Gordon looked from one child to the other, his own face unreadable. "Now, son," he said.

Gordy shot her a quick glance. Wondering, she supposed, if he should admit the truth to his father or gamble on her silence. She withdrew her hand from her husband's clasp. "You'll not be wanting to catch it from me."

"No, for some reason, the stuff has never bothered me or Gordy. You're a different story with that tender Irish skin of yours." Gordon shot a glare across the table. "*Now,* Gordy."

Gordy moved, pausing at the doorway to glance over his shoulder. She met his gaze and said nothing. He turned his head away.

"Clara." Gordon waited for his daughter to look up. "It makes me very pleased that you and Gordy get along so well. But in the future, you will act like a young lady and not intercede when I am exercising my duties as a father. Do you understand?"

"But Daddy—"

"Listen to your father, *mó cailín*. He wants only what is best for you children."

"But Gordy . . ." Clare bit on her lower lip, then said, "He doesn't mean to be mean. Really, he doesn't."

Gordon's face turned harsh. "The boy's acting like a monster and it's going to end," he said. "He's got everything a boy could want and he damn well better start appreciating that fact."

"Gordon," murmured Maggie.

He shook his head, let out a slow breath. "All right, Irish," he said finally. He glanced at his daughter. "You may be excused, Clara."

Gordon eased the child's chair away from the table to assist her. Clare moved slowly, folding her napkin and setting it beside her plate before standing. "Does it hurt?" she asked. "Your hands, I mean."

Maggie shook her head, wordless with the depth of understanding in this small child.

" 'Tis a sin to lie," said Clare.

Maggie would have choked if her throat hadn't felt cottondry. Beside her, Gordon stood with an utter stillness, almost as if he feared to breathe.

Clare's gaze shifted from Maggie to her father and back again. Her hair was a fuzzy cloud of sparked light as her head moved. "I always dreamed you were really my mother." She paused, hesitantly biting at her lower lip. "Now that you and Daddy are married, could I call you Mama, like Hope does with Aunt Annie?"

Maggie held out her hand, palm up. "*Mó cailín.*"

The child moved, her small, warm body suddenly pressed hard against Maggie's side. Gordon stood beside them, one hand gently stroking his daughter's hair, the other resting on Maggie's shoulder. Maggie swallowed the ball in her throat and said, "You are the best daughter a mama could wish for."

Clare eased back. Her dimples were deep, dark shadows on her cheeks. "Does that mean I can stay up another hour?"

Gordon laughed, a sharp, startled sound as if he'd surprised himself with amusement. "No. A kiss for Mama, and then off to the nursery."

Maggie was aware of Gordon studying her as she exchanged a caress and whispered warning with Clare, but she kept her voice low, trying to keep the confidence between the two of them. "You must give your brother time, wee Clare. Maybe he will never feel as you do, and that is his right. Do you understand?"

She looked over Clare's head. Gordon was still watching them. She could read anything—or nothing—in those dark blue eyes. When Clare moved to him, he leaned over and gave her a tight hug. "Mama and I will be up later to tuck you in," he said, dismissing the child.

As the child disappeared into the shadowed hallway, he said quietly, "She's something special."

"Aye, she is."

He pulled a chair up beside her and settled into the seat. "Let me see the other hand." His face was directed downward, so she saw only his sharp profile and the light playing in his hair. Gently, he peeled away the second glove. "I can't allow my son to treat you with that kind of insolence, Maggie."

"You cannot force your will on him. It would only serve to make him resent me more."

"How can he be so obstinate?" Gordon looked up. His mouth was a thin line. "You are everything he needs."

"It's Gordy's place to make that decision, is it not?"

"You'll come to me if it gets worse?"

"Aye," she said, while determining the situation must become grave indeed before she would make that mistake.

Gordon undid the button at her cuff and rolled up the sleeve. The same large, watery blisters covered her forearm. Maggie clenched her fists until her nails bit into her palm in an effort to resist scratching at the pained skin.

His face was grim as he laid her hand back in her lap. "Anywhere else?"

"My legs."

He blew a breath between his teeth. "You're going to be a sick little puppy for a week or so. I'll have to take you on a nature walk and point out this stuff."

"I think I'll remember." Maggie nodded toward the flower

centerpiece as Gordy came back into the room, Dulcie trailing behind him. "I picked it today because it looked so pretty on the ground, I thought it might look pretty on the table."

Gordy turned on his heel and fled.

Chapter 23

*G*ordon paused by the rustling leaves of the crepe myrtle at the edge of the back gallery and pulled on his riding gloves. The chase was to be launched from Riverbend's stable yard, wet this morning with a heavy dew and churned into mud by the shod hoofs of blooded horses and the polished boots of their owners.

It had been a cool night, but now the early sun glared through a mounting bank of pewter clouds, lifting a mist along the riverbank that settled in the dips of the pasture. The morning promised both an unseasonable warmth and a summerlike storm before the day ended.

He hated the fall ritual of fox hunting in the Virginia hills. But it was tradition that the Kincaids host the opening hunt of the season and Royce wasn't about to leave Annabelle for the event, so Gordon would do his duty and take Royce's place.

More than that, he'd discovered Maggie's sheer joy in riding. Maggie was still inside the Big House, and he wasn't about to forbid her the pleasure of the ride after she had so quietly, and bravely, stepped in to assume Annabelle's hostess duties.

But he'd be damned if his pregnant wife was going to spend a morning going hell-for-leather over fences and hedges chasing a fox from the back of a horse.

Over two months into their marriage now, and he was certain Maggie was pregnant. He wondered if she knew enough about a woman's physiology to recognize the signs or if he was going to have to tell her.

He saw Franklin leading Annie's roan jumper from the stable and stepped off the porch. By the time he'd worked his way through the gathering crowd, exchanging pleasantries and comments on the threatening weather, Franklin had brought Gordon's own Firenza out of the stable and both mounts were saddled.

Gordon lifted the stirrup to Maggie's sidesaddle and laid it over the seat, then tugged hard on the cinch. It was a habit left over from his cavalry days.

"You know what you're doin', Doc?"

Gordon looked over his shoulder. "Want to explain a little?"

"You know what I mean. Seeing all those folks in the shanties. Klan's riding again."

"You heard anything?"

"I'm a colored man. They ain't gonna tell me their secrets."

Gordon eased the stirrup back down. Here was what he'd spent years trying to avoid; now he was knee-deep in the mess but found he couldn't back away. His pride was in this. The health of the county workforce was in this. He'd incorporated the shanties in his rounds and had found scurvy in a population of sharecroppers. Dysentery, tuberculosis, rickets. It was unconscionable.

He patted the mare's neck and looked over her back. Moulton Johnson had arrived in a party of three that included his sister and Doc Chatham. Johnson's whiskers splayed out from his concave cheeks, hence the name "Monkey Johnson" he'd discovered during his doctor rounds through the black community. Gordon had laughed when he first heard the derisive handle, but the blacks of the community also feared this wiry little man, with just cause.

He set his jaw and looked away. Johnson was dressed in a scarlet coat and wearing a brass horn around his neck, which meant he was master of the hunt. Perhaps Johnson had ordered Aurora to attend; such a display of power would not be out of character. Perhaps, and more worriedly, Aurora had chosen to be here.

Whatever the reasons, Mrs. Aurora Hammond was not accompanied by Mr. Leland Hammond. Johnson's duties as hunt master would keep him busy; Aurora's husband was nowhere in sight. Process of elimination left Doc Chatham as her escort for the morning. Gordon had no more respect for Chatham than he had for Moulton Johnson. He wished Leland were here.

If he was a praying man, he'd pray for the heavens to unleash that threatening torrent now, then everyone could go home; one little fox would gain a week's reprieve, and next Friday the First Families would gather on the old fairgrounds to launch the kill, then reassemble for brunch and whispered gossip at someone else's estate house. Gordon Kincaid and his family would ignore the whole tasteless affair.

Gordon said, "You sure you want to be whipper-in this morning? Johnson is hunt master."

Franklin was performing the same check on Firenza's saddle girth. "The general's paying me a whole day's wages for a morning's work."

A man had the right to earn his living with dignity, which meant making his own decisions. Gordon nodded. "Put a guard in our stables at night. No firearms. We'll save the horses if the Klan shows up, but I don't want one of my workers hanging for shooting a white man."

Franklin stepped back from the horse and lifted his cap. He rubbed a knuckle along his hairline as his gaze surveyed the crowd. "You told the missus you're riding into trouble?"

"No, and don't mention it to her. She's having enough problems with Gordy."

She'd been sick for two solid weeks with the worst case of poison ivy he'd ever seen. He had a nagging suspicion Gordy was somehow responsible, although neither Gordy nor Maggie had said anything to him.

"Dulcie said Miz Pettigrew gave the missus a hard time when she came calling."

Gordon paused in the motion of gathering Firenza's reins. There was an intimation in Franklin's manner that went beyond his words, not fear exactly, but a sense of warning. He lifted one brow in question.

"Something about the Confederate Memorial and the missus being Catholic and all," said Franklin.

Maggie was holding back on her problems with Gordy and now this too. He could never find the words for the questions he thought he should ask her.

She didn't trust his words anyway, so he had given up trying to tell her what she meant to him, and tried to show her with his actions instead. But sometimes he would catch her looking at him with such longing in her eyes, and it would feel like a knife in his chest because he knew she didn't comprehend that, without her, he was a man set adrift without an anchor.

Gordon turned his head, searching for old man Pettigrew, seeing only his son, Chauncey, and Chauncey's wife. Chauncey was a friend of long standing, had served as a groomsman at his wedding to Augusta and ridden with Royce's guerrillas during the war. He wasn't Klan, but his father could be.

Gordon mounted his restive stallion as Gordy picked his way through the throng toward him. Gordy's gray gelding was high-stepping with the charged atmosphere, and the boy's face was ruddy with his own excitement at riding in his first hunt.

Gordon grasped the mare's lead when Franklin held it out. "You watch what you say today," he said to Franklin.

"I know when to keep my mouth shut, Doc. You worry about taking care of the missus." Franklin waved his hat and called out to his son, who was gathering the hounds from Royce's kennels. Gordon turned Firenza and rode forward to meet his own son. Gordy eyed the roan trailing behind him.

"She won't like that sidesaddle," said Gordy, looking all too pleased with the thought.

"She's not jumping fences today," he said tersely, and reached for the old canvas army canteen Gordy was opening. He passed the canteen beneath his nose—water—and handed it back to his son. "Stay away from the eggnog in the silver punch bowl," he said, and Gordy grinned.

"Uncle Royce has been too busy helping your wife set up the buffet to spike the eggnog yet."

Gordon held back a sigh. Always *your wife* or *Mrs. Kincaid,* with an occasional lapse into *Clara's mother*. He hadn't expected the task of winning his son to be easy, had prepared himself for the rebellion against the father who hadn't been there. Never had he suspected the boy would be capable of such polite maliciousness against Maggie, the openhearted woman whose blend of laughter and compassion attracted children like lead filings to a magnet.

"And stay away from Moulton Johnson," he said to his son. "Even if it means missing out on the kill."

Gordy glanced in the direction of the gate, then shrugged. At that moment, a hush seemed to settle over the yard; even the wind ceased rustling the leaves of the oak trees as everyone present turned to gaze at the Big House.

Maggie had come out on the gallery. She stood alone, framed between the white marble columns. A pink stain flushed her cheeks as she pretended absorption in the act of drawing gloves over her inflamed hands, and he felt that odd combination of possessiveness and protectiveness roll over him in waves.

Even after all this time, he couldn't get his fill of looking at her. She was dressed in a riding habit the color of the russet leaves, with a white linen ascot wrapped around her long, slender neck. Her hair shone like lacquer beneath her silk hat and was piled in some manner that enhanced the arch of those strong bones that gave her face such character.

"Who is she?" asked a female voice at his side, and he jerked his head away from the vision of his wife to look into the limpid blue eyes of his former lover.

"My Irish wife," he said, surprising even himself with the vehemence in his tone.

Aurora smiled faintly. "They're not staring because she's Irish, Gordon. They're staring because her beauty is so strikingly different from anything they're used to. She flat out takes their breath away."

"She flat out takes my breath away." Gordon shifted his weight as Firenza tossed his mane and backstepped. Maggie was still on the gallery, but was looking in his direction, so he lifted his hand and waved. She smiled, but didn't wave back.

He handed the mare's lead to Gordy. "Go help your mother," he said, and glared at the boy, daring him to voice the refrain. Either the glare worked or Gordy was too excited over riding in his first hunt to bother. He took the lead without comment. Gordon waited until he was beyond hearing distance, then he edged Firenza closer so the two horses stood flank to shoulder and he was looking into Aurora's face.

"Why the hell did you come this morning?"

"Paste a suitably bored smile on your face or you're going to undo all my hard work," she said, then looked to the gallery and let out a small sigh. "I'm not here to make trouble for your family, Gordon. I'm here because Moulton is master of the hunt and if I had stayed away, everyone would be talking about us again."

"Why do I think there's more than unselfishness in your lovely gesture?"

Aurora tucked a flyaway curl behind her ear with a small hand encased in a black kid glove. Somewhere, his mind registered the fact she was dressed all in black, but if she were in mourning for Leland, she wouldn't be at a fox hunt. Except that Clara might be here, and he felt something like fear roil up sour in his throat.

"I need to explain it all to you," she said. "And if our daughter is here, I'd like your permission just to see her. That's all."

"Clara is Maggie's daughter, let's get that straight between us right now." She ducked her head and looked away. Firenza pranced and snorted. He drew the reins in as his mind raced through possibilities. The issues had to be faced and dealt with, that much he knew.

"After the hunt breakfast," he said. "I'll meet you in Royce's study. Until we talk, you stay away from my daughter."

She formed the word *Clara,* as if tasting the name on her tongue, but before she actually answered his ultimatum, a sudden bright smile came across her mouth, one that didn't reach her eyes. When he turned his head, he understood the cause of her expression.

Moulton tipped his black hat to his sister, then looked to where Franklin was gathering the hounds. "I see you've turned that worthless nigger into a whipper-in."

Gordon gave a pointed look to the riding crop Moulton held casually across the front of his saddle. "You touch one hair on Franklin's head this morning, and you'll answer to me."

Moulton's flat nose sniffed the air as if offended. "The sport this morning is red fox, not craven nigger."

A warm gust of wind tore across the yard, scuttling damp leaves and causing Firenza to shy. Let the heavens open now, thought Gordon, before I grab Monkey Johnson by the scruff of the neck and only antagonize him further. He had to consider his family's safety and Johnson was probably the Klan's leader in the county.

Gordon made a motion to tip his hat to Aurora, remembered he wasn't wearing a hat and turned it into a nod. "You'll excuse me," he said. "I must see that my wife is safely mounted."

Royce was leading Annabelle's mare across the yard, so his son had somehow managed to avoid another direct order that pertained to his stepmother. Maggie didn't seem to see her brother-in-law. She was still alone on the gallery, watching Gordon with his former lover.

He nudged Firenza forward, picking his way through the crowd. She was too far away for him to see her eyes. But he loved her, so he knew the pain she couldn't quite hide any longer was in those winter-green eyes.

And he—the man whose heart beat in his chest with a love so strong it sometimes paralyzed him with fear—he had hurt her again.

Maggie stood with her riding boots planted on the edge of her brother-in-law's gallery, trying desperately not to look to the edge of the yard, and failing.

Gordon sat his horse with the long-legged grace of a born horseman, looking elegant in buff breeches and a black hunting jacket. As usual, he was minus the silk top hat the other gentlemen sported, and his hair shimmered a thousand shades of gold in the pale morning light. At his side was a woman on a bay gelding. She was dressed in a black kersey riding habit instead of lilac and lace, but she was the same woman who had stepped out of the crowd at the train station.

Maggie imagined herself gathering her skirts and walking through the crowd of Virginia's First Families to join them. *How pleased I am to meet you,* she would say, a brave smile on her face, and then, *Are you Clare's mother, and if so, why did you give the beautiful little* cailín *away?*

She might have found the courage to do such a thing, if it didn't matter so much.

Gordon lifted his hand and waved at her. She tipped her head and smiled, but she didn't wave back.

This morning was her first outing in society. It was tradition, according to Annabelle, that the Spotsylvania Hunt Club always launched this first fox hunt of the season from Riverbend's yard. So she had come, for Annabelle, who could not perform her duties as hostess due to her pregnancy, and for the Kincaids, who had a position to uphold.

That, and because of the opportunity to ride. All her love for horses had come back to her in these weeks in Virginia's horse country, and, she thought as well, the skills of her childhood. She had amazed even herself with the giddy joy of galloping full tilt across vetch fields, through knee-high meadow grasses and stands of loblolly pine along the river.

Royce led Annabelle's roan jumper into the yard. Maggie gathered the heavy skirts of her riding habit and walked down the steps to meet him.

"Up you go," said Royce, giving her a boost.

The roan snorted, blowing a cloud of steam. Maggie wrapped her leg around the front pommel and carefully adjusted her skirts. The general smiled up at her, as he did so often now.

"What is it about Kincaid wives that you hate riding sidesaddle like proper females?"

"And sure if the man himself were to try such a thing, he wouldn't be asking the question," she said, turning on her best brogue.

He laughed, and a dimple appeared in his cheek. "I'd break my neck," he said, pulling out his drawl like taffy. "Which is what's going to happen to you if we don't lengthen that stirrup, and then Gordon will break my neck for me."

He was already adjusting the stirrup, but she was watching Gordon ride toward her. Gordon was frowning, and she wondered if she had made some social faux pas, or if it was something the lady had said to him causing that hard look on his face.

"Yes," said Royce in his low voice, and when she looked at him, she saw he was gazing at Gordon. She clenched the reins tightly in her gloved hands. Royce said, "It was a scandal, Maggie, and if Aurora had stayed away this morning, the scandal would be back on everyone's tongue and that would have been worse for you, believe me."

She nodded stiffly. "And why didn't he marry her, then? There would have been no scandal, and Clare . . . wee Clare . . ." She found she could not finish the thought, let alone the words.

"She was already married. Gordon went to Texas for a few months. Aurora's husband took her to Philadelphia, then eventually to London. No one knew she was pregnant, Maggie. But if Aurora had stayed away from this hunt on her first visit back in all this time, and if Gordon were to avoid her this morning, then the tongues would wag and the speculation on Clara's parentage would be open."

She stared at the chestnut hair curling over his white collar. He turned his head and then she was looking into light gray eyes that held an unusual warmth.

"It can't be easy for you, and I doubt that it's any easier for her, but I know Gordon's doing the right thing for you and Clara." He smiled as Gordy rode up beside them and reached for the bridle as the gray gelding sidestepped. "You look out for your mother this morning."

"Father will—"

"Of course he will, and so will you."

A man in a red jacket lifted the brass horn that hung around his neck and blew a wailing call. She recognized him from the train station as well, the man who looked like a monkey in a frock coat who had stood beside Mr. Pettigrew. Gordon rode against the crowd as they moved toward the gate, heads bobbing, saddle leather creaking, excited voices lifted up into the gray morning mists.

Gordon drew up beside the family group. "What's Moulton Johnson doing here?" he said to his brother.

"He's master of the hunt this year. Nothing I could do about it if he decided to show up, which he did, and I'm as surprised as you are."

Gordy's horse was prancing and snorting, as anxious as the boy to be off with the hounds. Gordon pulled his gaze from the lane ringing hollow with the horses' hoofbeats and smiled at his son. "Go on. Just stay clear of Johnson."

Gordy turned his horse and followed the yelping hounds.

Gordon looked at his brother. "I can stay. . . . Annie."

"If Annie needs you, I'll send someone out." He waved his hand. "Go on. Enjoy a morning ride with your wife." He laughed and stepped back. "I've got to uphold the honor of the Kincaids and go spike the eggnog."

The river lay below them like a curling pewter ribbon braided with dark trees. A white mist rose from the ground, swirled into eddies by a warm, damp wind that was pungent with the mingled scents of horses and decaying leaves and honeyed ham baking in the kitchen.

Gordon reached to turn her mare, then touched his heels to Firenza and Maggie was riding beside him through the gate, down the lane bordered with flaming oak trees and onto the red dirt road.

Gordy was already off the road and into the vetch field, riding beside Aurora. Aurora turned her head and spoke to the boy, then reached over and touched his arm as he answered, and Gordy didn't jerk away from her touch.

Maggie felt heat sting the back of her eyes. She slanted a glance at her husband. He too was watching his son. A muscle ticked along his tightly clenched jaw.

The hunt master cheered out, "Tally ho," followed by three quick bleats of his horn. The riders ahead surged into motion: Aurora's bay next to Gordy's gray, stride for stride across the field of vetch and into the woods beyond.

"Maggie!"

The wind rushed against her face; her blood roared in her ears. She heard another shout behind her and the pounding of hoofbeats coming up hard. It was Gordon, she knew it, and she urged the mare to go faster.

An overgrown hedge loomed ahead of her, coming up fast in space and time. The mare's muscles bunched and flowed, not hesitating, and then they were lifting again, soaring . . . landing with a squelch and shower of turf, and then the nare's stride opened again. She looked back over her shoulder and saw Gordon had closed the gap, taking the same hedge with a foot to spare.

Maggie brought her horse down to a walk. The hounds brayed in some distant wood, chasing the fox. Gordon had chased after her. She wondered what she was chasing.

The sun broke through a hole in the clouds, shooting a beam of light across stone steps leading nowhere. They were in the clearing surrounding the charred manor house. There were no other people here. Only tall grasses and twisting morning glory vines and the ghosts of defeated Rebels.

She stopped and waited for her husband, whose face was dark and taut with anger. Something like anger burned hot inside her too, so intense it was making her stomach roll.

"Didn't you hear me? Dammit, Maggie, what were you thinking?"

She breathed against a sudden wave of dizziness. "She is Clare's mother."

"Oh, angel." He shook his head, his mouth softening into that tender curve. "Is that why you took off like that?"

She looked down at her hands, feeling another roll in her belly that eased up into her throat, and dizzy, so dizzy.

He hissed an expletive and swung down from his horse so suddenly the stallion snorted and shied. She didn't see him move, couldn't see anything but fog lit with stars. His hands gripped her waist. He lifted her down and she leaned into him . . . so dizzy, and her body felt clammy and cold.

"You didn't know, did you?" he said. "Here, sit down before you faint." He eased her to the ground and pushed her head forward over her knees, then massaged the back of her neck.

"I'm sorry," she said after a minute filled with the rush of blood in her head. "I thought the poison ivy was healed."

"You're pregnant, Maggie."

Her breath backed up in her throat. She laid her palm flat against her belly, splaying her fingers wide, trying to touch the miracle of new life. To make it real. She wanted this so much, she had feared even to pray for it.

She risked a look up at him. His heart was such a mysterious thing to her and his face was holding his secrets close.

"And does it please you?"

"It pleases me greatly that we're going to have a child together. It hurts me that you have to ask."

His hair whipped around his face in damp, tangled waves. He placed his hand over hers, his thumb stroking her wrist. A raw and powerful thing surged through her, a yearning so fierce it left her aching and fearful.

"We're going to be a family, Maggie."

Then he was leaning his head to kiss her, and she still didn't know if he loved her, or only the idea that she carried his child.

The riders stopped as the horns blew two long blasts, the ritual call of the stint. The hounds had lost the scent. Gordy was glad. He wanted the fox to get away.

In twos and threes, the riders gathered at the edge of another wood, steam rising from the horses' flanks as they waited for the dogs to pick up the scent again. Before them, a wide, tussocked meadow unrolled, dipping distantly down to the gray Rappahannock and rising beyond in the same yellowed grass, with low hedges and white rail fencing and another stand of young hardwoods beyond.

Gordy looked through the group, searching for his father. He saw Mr. Johnson, dressed in the hunt master pinks, and Chauncey Pettigrew, who smiled at him, and Mrs. Hammond, who lifted one black-gloved hand and gave him a little wave.

She'd asked him about Father and Father's wife and lots of questions about Clara, so many it made him uncomfortable. He hadn't known how to escape and felt relieved when father's friend Chauncey had ridden up between them. After that, Mrs. Hammond had kept her distance.

The day that started out promising excitement had turned edgy with a different thing, something he couldn't put into words, but felt threatening somehow. And like a little boy, he wanted his father to make the threat go away.

But he didn't see his father. He hadn't seen Father or his wife since early in the hunt. He turned Colonel and wandered away on his own.

He'd been courting Father's displeasure from the instant he'd arrived home with his new wife. Gordy knew it, and still couldn't make himself stop. He pushed back the guilt. Maggie had been real sick with poison ivy and she hadn't even squealed on him. If it had been any other woman, he'd have to like her for that alone.

He followed the bend in the road, then turned on to the old Pettigrew place, riding through a stand of chestnut and into the weed-choked clearing. The grounds were said to be haunted by the ghost of Willis Pettigrew, who had come home after the first battle of Manassas minus an arm and both eyes. The story went that he'd burned to death when the Yankees set the house on fire, but Uncle Royce said that was a lie: Willis Pettigrew had used his good arm to put a bullet through his brain.

He didn't remember Father as an invalid any more than he remembered his mother. But for the first time ever, he realized Father had made hard choices, and lived with the consequences.

He wondered if Father had ever considered taking a gun to his head, and if he had, what made him decide to choose life instead. Gordy thought he must finally be growing up, learning the choices a man made all led to consequences.

He saw a flash of motion in the corner of his eye and went still. The red fox had seen him first—crouched on a pile of stone that was shadowed and webbed with green ivy. The fox's rusty pelt was thick for the coming winter, his black ears pricked forward, his brush drooping long and low behind him.

Gordy stared into bright eyes of jet that stared back at him, and he had the strangest sensation the fox was begging him not to call the *halloa* that would give him away.

The fox crept out of the shadows, his belly low to the ground. Then he whirled and dashed over the stone steps and across the clearing, disappearing into the heavy underbrush with a flash of white-tipped tail. And with every step he took, he left a spoor for the dogs to follow.

Gordy let out the breath he'd been holding, and it was then he saw that he hadn't been alone with the fox, after all. Maggie stood in the shadows cast by the brick chimneys. Gordy looked at his father's wife, and she stared back at him, and something as charged as the storm-scented air seemed to pull him forward. He didn't think he'd nudged Colonel, but the horse was walking through the tangle of vines, and he was allowing it. He was looking into her eyes and couldn't make himself look away.

"You did not call the dogs," she said.

He shrugged. "Doesn't seem to be much sport in it."

It wasn't like hunting game for the table. There was honor and dignity in that kind of hunt. This . . . this was cruelty spiked with violence, twenty starved dogs purposely set against one small fox by men tippling whiskey from silver flasks while they waited for the scent of blood.

She was holding several small purple flowers in her hands, looking at them now. Her hands were covered by gloves, so he couldn't see the inflamed skin.

"You never told Father," he said, hating the way his voice cracked. Something painful and trembly was rising in his chest. He swallowed and tried again. "Why?"

"It would have served no purpose for either of us."

She hadn't smiled even once since their eyes met over the fox, and she wasn't smiling now. He thought she might cry and he didn't know what he'd do if she did.

A man would take the consequence of a wrong act. A man would apologize. God, he wanted to apologize; he just couldn't force the words through the tightness in his throat.

* * *

His suspicions confirmed by the perpetrator, Gordon stood motionless behind his son's horse. The atmosphere was so fraught with tension, neither his wife nor his son had heard him come back from watering the horses. A heavy disappointment replaced his anger when Gordy remained silent.

Maggie was holding those purple flowers, gentians, her mother's favorites, and she was standing amid the charred remains of a house destroyed by soldiers. Maybe she didn't even realize his son had failed to make a proper apology. Her eyes were so distant he thought she must be an ocean away.

He dropped the reins to the ground and deliberately stepped on a twig as he moved forward. Gordy whipped his head around. He stopped beside Gordy and rested his hand on his son's knee as he sat on his horse, not looking at him but at Maggie, who was standing with her head bowed within the tumbled ruins of the Pettigrew house.

"Some men are pure evil," he said. "Moulton Johnson is one of those. And then there are the bitter men. Old man Pettigrew lost three sons in the war, this house, his fortune, and maybe that's enough to break any man."

Gordy's knee was trembling beneath his palm. He squeezed, just a little. "But maybe it's only an excuse to quit, because there are others who lose everything—*everything,* son—and still manage to hold on to their dreams. Those are the people we should admire. They've earned nothing less than our respect." He lowered his voice. "You are looking at one of those people, Gordy. I can't ask you to love her, but you will respect her."

He left his son breathing hard behind him. Crumbled brick crunched beneath his boots as he walked to his wife. He gently pulled the fading purple blossoms from her grasp and tucked them in her side pocket.

"Come on, let's go, angel," he said softly as he slipped his arm around her waist.

She looked up at him. Her eyes were dark and haunted, her face leached of color. He wanted to tell her he knew, but she hadn't trusted him enough to share her past, so he had to wait until he'd earned her trust.

She stumbled once as he led her to the mare. Gordy's gaze followed them the distance, but he looked away as Gordon boosted her into the saddle. The hounds began to bay, crying out that they'd flushed the covert and picked up the scent. Someone shrilled, "Halloa," followed by three quick notes from the horn.

The blood sport was about to reach its inevitable conclusion. He regretted the necessity of subjecting Maggie to the spectacle, but this was one of those hard choices.

The boy had perpetrated a malicious action against an innocent victim, and violated all sense of honor in his failure to own up. He was a Southern boy; well, let him witness firsthand the blood and gore and stink of the violence that stained his birthright. Gordy wasn't going to be allowed to slip away.

Maggie wanted no part of the kill, but something icy gripped her husband and he would not allow her to find her way back alone. His profile was hard and sharp. He sat ramrod straight in the saddle, staring ahead. She could hear Gordy's ragged breathing from the other side of him.

"Back up, Maggie," said her husband in that cold, angry voice. "You don't have to watch." But without turning his head, he reached for the gray's headstall, staying the horse when his son tried to back away.

She was held spellbound with a horrid fascination anyway. The fox had scrambled up the leaning trunk of an uprooted pine tree. He was off the ground, just beyond the reach of the surging, snapping dogs, but he was clearly trapped, and frozen in fright. Those small black eyes were shining, his beautiful tail dragging along the tree trunk.

"Let the dogs go, boy," shouted Moulton Johnson. He raised up in the stirrups, brandishing his riding whip. "I said, let the dogs have him, damn your dirty stinking nigger hide!"

Gordon shifted his coat back, revealing the butt of a revolver at his waistband. Maggie went cold. She did not know this man at all.

Franklin turned his head so he was looking their way and his gaze seemed to catch with her husband's. After a moment, he touched his checkered hat with his thumb, then rode into the middle of the pack of leaping, braying, snarling dogs.

Franklin cracked his whip over his head and she couldn't tell if he was inciting the dogs to a higher pitch of excitement or trying to force the hounds back from the uprooted tree. For an instant, she thought the dogs were going to back away, but then Moulton Johnson cracked his riding whip, Gordon reached for his gun—and the terrified fox lost his grip on the mist-dampened trunk.

The white tip of his beautiful tail flashed, then he let out a piercing cry as the first set of jaws clamped his throat, and she looked away as he completely disappeared beneath the pack of dogs scrambling over one another in their maddened effort to reach the fox.

The horn blew, sounding one long keening note.

Johnson's face was mottled red above his chin whiskers. "Kill him, boys," he cried, brandishing the crop. "Kill him, kill him!"

Gordon released his grip on the gun butt, settling his coat to hide the weapon. "Hear Mr. Johnson, son?" he said in a voice devoid of any emotion. "Foxes mate for life, you know, which means somewhere in these woods is a vixen who might very well starve this winter."

Gordy made a small sound in his throat. Maggie's eyes ached, as if she might cry. He was punishing Gordy for something, and the punishment seemed to her as cruel as the fox's death. She backed her horse away, and when she stopped, she saw Aurora watching them, a small frown drawing a crease between her honey-colored brows.

The air was fetid with a miasma of decaying leaves and feces and blood as Franklin whipped the dogs in, their long white jaws stained with red splotches.

The clouds parted and a beam of sun shot through. Maggie
tilted her head back and let the warmth wash over her. This
day that should have been filled with joy—she was going to
bear her husband a child—had become a different thing, violent and sad. It made her feel cold from the bones out.

Moulton Johnson rode toward them, brandishing the fox's
tail in one gloved hand. It was no longer beautiful—a wet,
matted mass of fur that stank of blood and death.

He drew up in front of Gordon and silence settled over the
clearing. Johnson swung the tail in a slow arc. "Which of our
virgin hunters deserves the brush? Your wife, or your son," he
said, and there was malice in his smile.

"My wife has no use for the filthy thing," said Gordon.
"Take it, son." Gordy couldn't even bring himself to look at
the matted stump of fur. His throat worked as he swallowed.
His father said, "*Take it, son.*"

No, she did not know this cold, angry man. She didn't like
him either. Maggie nudged the mare forward and reached for
the brush. Gordon stopped her by holding out his arm.

"Son, do you want to be a man?"

Gordy reached out and took the gruesome brush. Maggie
looked down, and saw the blood dripping from the stump
onto the polished black toe of his riding boot. And when she
looked up, she saw his eyes glistened with unshed tears.

Maggie cantered into the yard. She kicked her foot from the
stirrup and jumped down from the saddle before Gordon had
even reined in beside her. She was shivering, and the air
wasn't even cold. If she could get to the heat of the kitchen,
maybe she could get warm.

"Go with your mother, Gordy. I have to speak with
Franklin."

Maggie didn't look at her husband or his son. She didn't
wait for Gordy. She wanted to run, but forced herself to walk
through the yard, filling now with returning riders. She heard
running footsteps behind her.

The gallery was coming closer and Royce stood there

waiting. She picked up her skirts and walked faster. Gordy was beside her now. She heard his quick, panting breaths but didn't look at him.

"Master Kincaid."

It was Moulton Johnson's voice, as silky smooth as his white ascot. She stopped and shot a look at Gordy. Two bright spots of color stained his cheeks. They both turned, and she nearly gasped at what Johnson held in his hand.

For an instant, her gaze met with Aurora Hammond's, who was standing beside her brother, then Aurora ducked her head and looked away. A man Maggie didn't recognize stood at Johnson's other side.

Johnson's mouth wore a thin smile. "You forgot your trophy," he said. "And your father wanted you to have the honor."

Gordy's face blanched. Maggie took the brush from Johnson's outstretched hand, careful not let her fingers come in contact with his. The second man smiled at her between his long side-whiskers. He was a big man, barrel-chested and close enough for her to see his eyes were brown. He rubbed one finger beneath his nose, as if offended by the air he was breathing. She made herself turn and walk slowly away.

"The bogtrotters are getting to be as big a problem as the coloreds."

Maggie stumbled. Johnson barked a laugh. "I watched them hang a nigger next to an Irishmen down Savannah way. That Irishman's face turned as black as the nigger's, couldn't tell one from the other except the nigger's hair was kinked."

Her teeth were chattering. She would not turn; they wanted her to turn so they could see her reaction. Walk forward. . . . Royce was on the gallery greeting the returning hunters.

"Kincaids don't take kindly to threats, sir."

She whirled around. Blessed Mother, Gordy was brandishing a knife. She clenched her jaw to stop her teeth from chattering and walked back. To her horror, Aurora was watching her.

Johnson nudged the man next to him. "Did you hear any threat, Chatham? I thought we were talking about the colored problem."

His mouth twitched as he watched her. His eyes held the same glint she'd seen as he shouted at the dogs to *kill, kill*. She slipped her arm over Gordy's shoulder, feeling the hidden trembles.

"Come along, *mó cara*." They walked several paces before he ducked his shoulder and slipped away. She slanted him a glance. "Can you make it inside to the water closet?" she asked softly. His throat worked hard as he shook his head. "And sure there isn't a soul behind the smokehouse."

His chest heaved before he took off running. Maggie followed more slowly. She carefully laid the fox tail beside the stone block, then covered it with leaves. She leaned against the smokehouse wall until the sounds of retching ceased. When Gordy came around the corner, she held out her lace-edged handkerchief. He shook his head and wiped his face with his own.

"Thank you, Gordy."

He cleared his throat. "I owed you something, Mrs. Kincaid."

There was nothing on his face at all, nothing. One minute, she had dared to hope: he had allowed her to touch him, if only briefly, and had stood bravely in her defense. But the chasm had not been fully crossed.

"Aye, then, get yourself some honey tea for your throat," she said, and watched him walk away.

She dug a hole to bury the fox brush and when she was done, she wiped at the hand-stitched kid glove Gordon had given her just this morning, but the fox's blood wouldn't come out. She peeled off the glove and buried it too, and only then realized she had opened the wounds from the poison ivy, and the palms of her hands oozed blood.

Chapter 24

*O*utside, the pewter clouds of early morning had turned black and ominous, broken in patches by a foul yellow light. Some of the guests had already left, hastening to get home before the storm hit. Others still milled about the downstairs rooms, engaging in conversation while they polished off the last of the champagne. Someone was playing the piano in the second parlor, singing an off-key lover's duet.

Maggie knew she was expected to stand between Royce and Gordon just inside the big green doors and bid each guest farewell as they took their leave. She was not skillful in small talk, and everyone would be staring between her and Gordon, speculating on their marriage, on Clara's parentage, and she really didn't think she could bear another moment of that.

Maggie stopped suddenly just outside the heavy gold portieres, unable to take one more step.

"Maggie? What's the matter?"

Her brother-in-law's face wavered in front of her. Maggie

blinked several times. "I don't know if I'm going to faint or throw back my head and howl at the moon."

"Please howl, dear heart. If you faint, I'll have to catch you and then Gordon will get the wrong idea and have to hit me, and I really don't want to furnish these boors with that much entertainment. They've already consumed all my champagne." Royce tilted his head toward the wide, curving staircase. "Go up and share your news with Annie. I'll make the appropriate excuses for you."

"Gordon told you," she said, and she didn't know how she felt about that, but Royce was smiling so his dimple showed and that made her feel warm inside. Then his face turned serious.

"It will all work out, Maggie. By the time your baby is born, we'll have whipped Gordy into line, I promise you."

But you can't make him like me, she thought. She only nodded and turned to the stairs, forcing herself to walk slowly when she wanted to run.

She was halfway up the staircase when she heard Gordon call her. She went back down the stairs, slowly.

"Are you feeling all right?" She nodded. He studied her face for a long time. He was holding his gray kid gloves in one hand and drawing them through the other. "I told Aurora—Mrs. Hammond—that I'd meet her alone in Royce's study. I wanted you to hear that from me."

Such a weight came over her that she couldn't move or breathe. It didn't matter that he was Clare's father, and the other woman, her mother. She, Maggie, was the one who had loved the child always.

For duty's sake she should keep silent, but Clare needed someone to speak for her—yes, it was for her Clare she would speak, not for her own selfish heart.

"You must do what's best for the child, she's only fi—"

"Dammit, Maggie, give me credit for some sense."

He gripped her hand hard just above the pearl button on the ecru lace gloves she had borrowed from Annabelle. Then he looked at what he was doing and sucked in a sharp breath.

"Your hands are bleeding," he said.

"I buried the fox tail." She curled her fingers over her palm and shrugged. "The shovel handle, I suppose."

"What a good-hearted woman you are." He looked almost as if he might smile, then shook his head instead. "It seems I'm always apologizing to you for something. You must get awfully tired of hearing it."

"I believe you mean it."

And she did believe she knew that much of his heart. He took her hand gently within his own and they climbed the stairs together.

Before her marriage, she had never suspected the intimacy of walking hand in hand with a man. She wondered if Aurora had walked beside him like this, and had her legs known such trembles, had her heart raced and her breath deserted her?

At the top of the stairs, he stopped. "I'm saying it again. I'm sorry, but I have to settle this with Aurora."

She felt like a marionette on strings, being yanked and pulled to dance through a life she couldn't seem to control any longer. She thought he must be able to hear the wild beating of her heart, but she tried to school her face.

"Aye," she said, and walked down the hall toward Annabelle's dressing room on legs that felt as stiff as old harness leather.

She found both little girls already there when she pushed open the door. Hope Ann was sitting on the floor beside her mother's chaise with her arms around her knees and Annabelle's hand resting on her shoulder.

Hope Ann looked up and the frown creasing her brow turned into a smile. "Can we go downstairs now?"

"And wasn't it your own father who said you would wait until he gave you permission?"

"Did you drink champagne, Mama?" asked Clare.

Maggie looked at the child who called her Mama so easily. Clare was sitting near the damask-draped window, a biscuit in one hand and laughing mischief in her eyes.

Maggie gathered the heavy skirt of her riding habit and

knelt in front of Clare. Her tongue felt thick and dry. All her life, she'd found it so easy to talk with children, and now, when it seemed to matter most, she didn't know what to say.

She pulled her handkerchief and wiped strawberry jam off Clare's cheek. "Why don't the two of you go into Hope's room and play a game of jacks," she said finally. "Aunt Annie is needing her rest."

Clare jammed the last of the biscuit in her mouth, then joined her sticky hand to Hope's outstretched one. Neither she nor Annabelle spoke as the two girls left the room, Clare hopping from one foot to the other, like playing hopscotch.

When Maggie looked at her sister-in-law, she saw Annabelle's gaze fixed on the doorway where the two children had disappeared. Her lips were curved softly, but a small, worried frown pinched her brows. Maggie knew her sister-in-law tried hard not to show her fear, but she couldn't always succeed.

"I'm going to have a baby." She hadn't meant to blurt out the news like that.

Annabelle turned her head, with a real smile now. She held out her hand and the spill of white lace at her sleeve dropped back so Maggie could see the blue tracery of veins at her wrist.

Their fingers interlaced and Annabelle said, "I'm so glad. Our children will grow up together." She closed her eyes and swallowed so hard her throat moved. Her hand dropped to the lap robe, twisting the material suddenly into a knot so tight her fingers whitened. "If something happens, if I die having this baby—"

"Blessed Mother, don't speak that way."

"No one will let me speak of it, but it could happen—my mother died just like this—and I have to know Hope Ann won't be left to find her way alone. Her father, as much as he loves her, won't be able to give her the . . . teach her . . ."

Annabelle was crying now, making no sound, just the spill of tears from her dark brown eyes running in a stream down her face. "You'll look out for her, won't you, Maggie? Please, I need to hear it."

Maggie knelt and wrapped her arms around her sister-in-law, breathing in the scent of lavender. "You know I will."

Annabelle's hands came up and fisted against her back. "Heaven help me, I'm so frightened for my family."

Maggie stared over Annabelle's head, brushing one hand down Annie's soft hair, watching dead leaves fall from the oak tree outside the window. She felt as if her heart had been cut open too.

Annabelle pulled away and wiped her cheeks with the back of her hand. Maggie got up and went to the bureau, pulling open the top drawer. She handed Annabelle the clean handkerchief.

"I never cry," said Annabelle, wiping her cheeks again. Her oval face was too pale, and she appeared to have lost weight when she should be gaining. As if she were giving all her strength to the baby nestled inside her body.

"And sure it is I can't always hold the tears back when I should."

"What a fine pair we are."

They shared a smile, then Maggie picked up the silver-backed hairbrush that lay beside Annabelle on the chaise. She carried it over to the dressing table and sat on the plush velvet stool. A light knock sounded at the door. She looked in the mirror, and her gaze collided with Aurora Hammond's.

"I came to see you before I left, Annabelle," said Mrs. Hammond, stepping just inside the room without waiting for an invitation. "To wish you well."

Maggie stared down at the dresser's linen runner with its crocheted borders and embroidered tea roses.

"I'll take your words at face value," said Annabelle, and Maggie had never heard such curtness in her tone. "As long as you leave now."

Aurora made a small laugh. "You're right, of course. I wanted to talk to the other Mrs. Kincaid."

Maggie swung around on the stool. Her stomach felt queasy and she tried to keep the shakiness out of her voice, but she couldn't control the brogue. "And what is it you're needing to say, Mrs. Hammond?"

She could hardly make herself look at the woman, for when she did, she wondered. She was a married woman now, so she knew the way a man's hand touched a woman's body, knew how two bodies cleaved together. Had he looked into those pale blue eyes as they joined together and created Clare; had he held her tightly in his arms after the joining?

"My brother," said Aurora on a gust of breath and throwing Maggie off center, as her own mind had been wandering down more intimate paths.

"I don't think you realized that was a threat this morning in the yard—Doc Chatham and Moulton, I mean. Moulton is Grand Dragon of the Klan in Virginia. I don't know exactly about Dr. Chatham, but I think he's Cyclops for the local Den."

Maggie wasn't surprised to hear Annie's gasp when her own lungs were reaching for air. "Why are you telling me this?"

"Because I need you to understand, about me." She turned pleading eyes to Annabelle. "Please, can I speak honestly to you both?"

Annabelle shot her a look. Maggie shrugged one helpless shoulder, then turned her attention to tracing the monogrammed *A* on her sister-in-law's hairbrush.

Aurora said, "I married Leland when I was sixteen so I could get out of my brother's house. What happened later, with Gordon . . . well, it happened, but I wanted you to know that I did everything I could for the daughter Leland wouldn't allow me to keep."

Aurora saw Clare's rag doll lying beside the tapestry footstool, and her face seemed to crumple. She walked over and picked up the doll. "I remembered the nun Gordon was so fond of was from Philadelphia," she said as her hands smoothed the doll's white apron. "I hired a Pinkerton man who traced her to Saint Columba's in Baltimore. It seemed like a sign—an orphanage—so I sent my baby off with a portrait Gordon had given me."

She walked forward and held the doll out. Maggie's hand shook as she took it. Aurora said, "Perhaps you recognized Gordon from his picture?"

Maggie clutched the doll between her breasts, her thumb gently stroking the yellow yarn hair as jagged pieces fell into place. Peyton Kincaid's generosity to St. Columba's. A child residing there who might be his granddaughter.

So many lives manipulated by unseen hands.

"I never saw the portrait," she said.

The children's high-pitched laughter floated down the hallway from Hope Ann's room. Maggie moved a crystal scent bottle and carefully set the limp doll on the vanity top. She stared at the black button eyes, the mouth of red threads stitched into a permanent smile, the grass stain on one white linen cheek that wouldn't wash clean.

"I won't make trouble for your family. I just wanted to see Clara . . . to know that she's happy. I leave to go back to London tomorrow. Alone." Aurora laughed again, and this time the sound was touched with wildness. "Perhaps when Clara is grown—married—Gordon will allow me to meet her."

She paced to the black-lacquered changing screen painted with red and gold dragons. Her hands opened and closed at her side. "I haven't spoken to Gordon yet, so maybe I'm wrong, maybe he's changed and will forbid even that."

Maggie didn't know. She'd seen another side to Gordon this morning at the kill, a hard-edged anger so determined she had almost hated him for it. She braved a glance at Annabelle. Annabelle's hands were folded over her stomach and she was staring hard at Aurora's back. "Just where is Leland now, Aurora?" she asked.

"He's dead."

Maggie let out a deep, shaky breath. Her sister-in-law asked the question that was closing her own throat up tight.

"If Leland died, why did you leave that dear child in an orphanage?"

Aurora turned, her face bearing a dark, haunted look. "I came as soon as I was free."

Maggie breathed. She breathed again. She got up and walked to the window that overlooked the river bluff. The wind had picked up. A fat drop of rain splashed the glass.

She could feel the tears wet on her cheeks, and she wasn't able to stop them. "When did you come?"

Aurora tried to laugh again, but pain rang clear in the sound.

"The day I first spoke with Mother Bernadette," she said, "was the same day you married Gordon."

Maggie's steps were slow as she walked out on the back gallery. The wind gusted, sweeping dead leaves and sending them skipping across the flagstones.

She pretended not to notice Gordy, who was sitting at the edge of the gallery near the crepe myrtle tree, whittling a stick with his knife and pretending not to notice her.

And wasn't that the way of it? His father was closeted inside the study with Clare's mother, and as much as she loved the child, Maggie knew she didn't belong in the room with them either.

She walked to the opposite end of the gallery, away from the boy she couldn't reach with her Irish stories and songs, her Irish heart. She listened to the sounds of the last guests leaving from the front of the house, and watched fat raindrops hit the ground and shatter.

A pain wrenched her chest, so sharp she thought it might cleave her in two.

One day. One short day in God's vast expanse of time, and Gordon could have married the woman he'd joined with to create Clare. A Southern lady who could run Confederate Memorial Committees and wouldn't be an embarrassment to his son.

Thunder rolled, and lightning pierced the clouds. The day

darkened to twilight gray. The wind tasted of river sand and cold rain and charged electricity.

Someone came up beside her, standing so close her skirts whipped against his pants leg. She stepped away and looked into a long face with nut-brown chin whiskers and dark eyes. Dr. Chatham. Her body went numb with cold.

Moulton is Grand Dragon of the Klan in Virginia. I don't know exactly about Dr. Chatham, but I think he's Cyclops for the local Den.

She cut a swift glance down the gallery, but Gordy had disappeared.

"So, Mrs. Kincaid," he said, pulling a fat cigar from his pocket as his eyes bore into her. "You didn't think much of our little fox hunt."

She shrugged. "There didn't seem to be much sport in it at all."

"Well, there's sport, and then there's sport." The doctor shook his head, then clicked his tongue against the roof of his mouth. "What you don't understand, Mrs. Kincaid, your Irish blood making you a foreigner in these parts, is the nigras are sport. One or two get uppity, we remind them of their proper place, and everything settles down the way it's supposed to be. They understand us, we understand them, so there's the sport."

He lifted the cigar, rolling it between his fingers. "It's the white folks that don't belong here who make the trouble— every now and then, we get us a Jew or a Catholic who just plain don't understand that our nigras are happy. Then they go stirring them up, telling them to vote when there isn't a nigra alive with the intelligence to cast a ballot."

He clamped his teeth down into the butt of the cigar and looked her up and down. "Am I making myself clear, Mrs. Kincaid, or do I have to spell it out for you?"

He was a big man, and he loomed over her. Trying to intimidate her with his size and strength. He did frighten her, but her own anger was suddenly a stronger thing. She nudged her chin up and glared back at him.

"And sure you'd better spell it out, as me poor Irish brain is having trouble following your fine Southern self."

He had the effrontery to laugh. "Feisty one, aren't you?" He leaned his head closer, and his eyes narrowed into thin slits. His mouth turned mean. "Your husband seems to have forgotten who he is since you got your vixen claws into him. Now, you can either go back where you came from, or we can make him sorry. Is that clear enough for your bogtrotter's brain?"

"You can't tell me where I will or will not live," she said through stiff lips. "I'm an American citizen just like you."

His face went wine red, and his chin whiskers quivered with the expulsion of his hot, angry breath. The fear of him built in her chest, in her throat, behind her eyes. She backed up, reaching behind her for the porch column, as if it might give her a safe haven.

She pressed her palms against the cold wet marble; watching him, watching his hands and his eyes until she thought the sight of him would be burned on her vision forever.

"Go back where you came from." He tossed the cigar into the pounding rain, then turned and walked away.

She hugged herself, pressing her elbows hard against her waist, as if the effort would keep the fear from exploding inside her. The wind made a keening sound, and the heavens opened. She sidled around the column and stepped out into the storm. Thunder rolled again, followed by another crack of lightning.

You can either go back where you came from, or we can make him sorry.

Where had she come from? Ireland, long ago, fleeing the reprisals there. Then, for the longest time, she'd found a home within the safe walls of St. Columba's. She came to Virginia from St. Columba's, as the Irish-Catholic wife of Gordon Kincaid.

How would they make him sorry?

She slipped on the wet grass, falling hard on her hands and knees beside a final patch of Michealmas daisies. She yanked a clutch from the sodden ground and lurched back to her feet.

She stopped at the family cemetery, jerking open the wrought-iron gate so hard the metal ripped the lace gloves and tore into her palms. She dropped to the ground in front of Augusta's marble headstone.

The wind snatched at her hair, blew sheets of gritty rain against her face. Her fingers scrabbled a hole that filled immediately with rainwater. She shoved the stems of the daisies into the hole, tamping mud to hold them in place.

She said a prayer for the dead, then made the sign of the cross. Already the wind had torn the daisies from the ground and flung them against the iron fencing. She felt the burn in her eyes and then the letters on the gravestone began to slide together.

She swiped the tears and the rain from her face.

"It should be you here in my place, Augusta. I cannot touch your son's heart, no matter how hard I try, and Dear Blessed Mother, I fear I have only hurt our Gordon."

Gordy sat on the wooden deacon's bench outside the closed door to Uncle Royce's study. He could hear the murmur of voices on the other side, but not the words. Father was in there with Mrs. Hammond, and Uncle Royce had told him they were not to be disturbed.

His boot heel clicked against the marble floor as his knee jiggled up and down. He slid a sideways glance down the central hall. Uncle Royce still stood by the front doors, talking with Mr. Johnson. No, not talking; they were staring at one another from opposite sides of the double doors. Uncle Royce's face held no expression. Mr. Johnson looked amused at some private joke.

Click, click, click. Gordy fisted his hands together over his bouncing knee, holding it in place. He wanted to slam his palms on the closed door, but he couldn't. Father was already angry with him.

Criminy, he'd left Maggie alone on the back gallery with

Dr. Chatham. Maybe he should go back. But Doc Chatham was such a big man, at least double his own weight. Father could stand the other man down, but Father kept talking.

He heard footsteps coming down the hallway, too heavy to be Maggie's. A blow of rain suddenly beat a hard and rapid tattoo on the roof. The person turned the corner and he saw it was Dr. Chatham. His heartbeat kicked into a gallop.

Chatham stopped directly across from him. He craned his head and peered through the opened doors as if he couldn't believe it was raining during a thunderstorm.

"Well," he said. "It's a good thing we brought the covered landau for the lady." He straightened and looked at the study door, which suddenly opened.

Gordy jumped to his feet, thankful he didn't have to think of something to say to Dr. Chatham now. Mrs. Hammond stepped out. Her eyes were red, like she'd been crying. He understood. Something was stuck in Father's craw today, something cold and hard, like he didn't care anymore if he hurt someone's feelings.

Dr. Chatham took the lady's elbow. "Come along, my dear."

Gordy waited until they had reached the double doors, then he swung into the study. Father was seated in the brass-studded wing chair, his chin tucked into his chest so Gordy couldn't see his expression.

"Your wife—Mrs. Kincaid—Maggie—she hasn't come in and it's raining. . . ." Criminy, he was babbling like a baby.

Father looked up. A strange sort of smile softened his mouth. "You called her Maggie."

Had he? Gordy didn't know, and that wasn't important anyway. "Dr. Chatham," he said. "I think he was threatening her and I didn't know what to do—"

Father jerked up from the chair. A sharp sound came from his throat, and he reached out, grasping at air because there was nothing to grab. Gordy watched, frozen in horror, but Father caught himself with a jerk of his weight onto his good leg. Gordy closed his eyes. His breath was hitching and pitching, and words were trying to get out, but he could hardly even breathe around the knot in his throat.

"Gordy." Father's arms were suddenly around him, hauling him up tight against his chest. "Shh, it will be all right, son. Everything will be fine."

It felt so good to be held by Father, and he thought he must have been waiting for this his entire life. He wanted to stay there a long time, but he was nearly a man.

He made himself start to pull away. For an instant, Father's hold tightened and Gordy felt strong fingers curling into the muscles of his back. Then Father dropped his arms and stepped back. His face looked funny, softer somehow, but maybe that was the tears brimming in his own eyes.

Gordy saw Uncle Royce then, standing with his shoulder leaned against the study door, his expression so serious it was almost sad. Their gazes caught, held, then Uncle Royce winked.

"Where's Maggie?" asked Father.

Uncle Royce straightened. "I don't know."

Gordon stepped out the door and into a storm so violent it stole the breath from his throat. His thoughts were caught up in imaginings almost as wild.

When Gordy related the incident over the fox tail, Gordon had recognized immediately the veiled threat mixed in with the racist malediction. And while he laid down the edicts to his former lover concerning Clara's future, Maggie had been forced to face Chatham's threat alone.

She had needed him and he hadn't been there.

If that bastard had hurt her . . .

He topped a rise and saw her where he would never have thought to look, inside the wrought-iron fence, rocking and crying over Gussie's grave.

She looked small and forsaken, huddled on the ground against a backdrop of gravestones and roiling sky. Long lengths of black hair lashed like ropes around her head. Her clothes were soaked and clung to her body so closely she may as well have been naked.

He gave her no warning, coming to her from the side. He gripped her arms and hauled her against him. She looked up at him, her green eyes glittering like shattered stars.

"Did he hurt you?" he shouted. "Dammit, Maggie, did he hurt you?"

"Who? No." Her head moved, shaking a denial, and then her gaze became caught in his. She was lying. He knew her. In some ways, he knew her better than he knew himself.

He took her face between his hands. His kiss was hard and desperate. He was being too rough, but he wanted her, dear God, he wanted her. Her hands grasped his waist and she melted against him, meeting his tongue with her own, and for that heartbeat in time, she was his alone, and she filled his universe.

She pushed against his chest so hard he almost stumbled. "No. Not here."

"Here." He pulled her back against his hips. "She's dead, she can't be hurt. But you can, Maggie. Dammit, you are."

"Blessed Mother, what am I going to do?" she whispered.

His breath stopped, his whole body tensed. "What do you mean?"

Her eyes, haunted and dark, stared into his. "I will never fit into your world."

His hand clenched into a fist and he drew it up, hard, against his chest. "Here, Maggie. You fit here."

She blinked and turned her head away. He searched for the words to make her look at him so she would see on his face what was constricting his heart, but words always seemed to fail him with her.

He swung her into his arms. Her skirts whipped around them as he carried her into the meadow.

"Your leg," she murmured. "Put me down."

He ignored her. He was taking her home, to Old Riverbend. Where she belonged, whether she knew it or not.

Chapter 25

The morning sun poured through the window in the dining room, catching him full in the face. He spread some salve he'd mixed over her palm. His touch was gentle, a healer's touch.

"You're going to have to be careful until this mends." His voice sounded rough, like something was caught in his throat. "Infection sets in to these open sores and you'll lose a hand."

"Aye, I'll be careful." Maggie tried to force a smile, but her mouth refused to cooperate. At least the tears had dried sometime in the night while he held her in his arms.

She watched him as he wrapped a clean strip of linen around and around her hand, cradling her thumb in linen folds, up and around her wrist. His long, graceful fingers brushed her skin. His hands held so much power to seduce her: those gentle, healer's hands, the insistent lover's hands that wrenched such trembles and shudders from her body.

Maggie looked away from him, out the diamond-paned

window into a sky of brilliant blue. The storm had passed in the night and left winter in its place.

"Clare," she said hesitantly. "Her mother . . ."

"You are Clara's mother." He cut the end of the bandage with a pair of steel scissors. "Don't feel sorry for Aurora. She has two children who were suckled by black mammies, turned over as toddlers to the English nanny and shipped off to boarding school at the earliest possible moment. Clara got more attention inside that orphanage than she would ever have received from her birth mother."

"She was coming back for Clare. For you."

He paused tying off the bandage. "She spoke to you?"

"Aye."

"I'm sure she put on a prizewinning performance," he said through tight lips. He finished tying the bandage and set her hand in her lap. "As long as Aurora stays away from our daughter, my lawyers will send her an annual report accompanied by a sum of money. When Clara is eighteen, I will tell her about her birth mother, and it will be up to our daughter to make the decision as to whether or not she wants to contact the woman."

"If something should happen to me," he continued, his intense blue eyes fixed on her face, "my lawyers will either finish buying her off or continue the payments and reports. Aurora didn't want Clara so much as she wanted money. Leland died close to bankruptcy."

He lifted his hand, his curled fingers lightly tracing the line of her jaw. "And since we're finally talking about what happened yesterday, what did Chatham say to you?"

Her heart seized. That gun at his waistband, his coldly determined anger. What would Gordon Kincaid do if she told him the truth? She swallowed, not answering, trying to form an answer.

"Talk to me, angel," he said, so soft it might have been only a thought.

She drew in a deep breath and chose the lesser sin. "Only something about the sport of a fox hunt."

She saw it on his face, disbelief. She wanted to reach up and touch his mouth, smooth away the lines of worry. She wanted to tell him it would be all right. That they would work through all these problems, and make a family together.

She didn't, though, because she knew there were danger-ous men and terror-filled nights; and wanting to solve a prob-lem was not enough to see it solved.

He was pouring another cup of tea now, added milk, and set the cup in front of her at the table. They both looked over as Dulcie entered, her stiff petticoat announcing her presence even before she appeared in the doorway.

"Where you want your newspaper, Doctor?" she asked.

"I'll take it here."

Dulcie set the silver tray beside his coffee cup and gathered together the bandages and bowl containing the remnants of the salve. "Did you tell Mrs. Kincaid she's not to be working like one of the staff, least not until those poor hands heal up?"

Gordon peered over the rim of his coffee cup, amusement shining in his eyes. "I tried; might mean more to her coming from the head honcho."

"Humph." Dulcie shifted the clay bowl into the crook of her elbow and reached out with the other hand, smoothing a wrinkle in the yellow tablecloth. "I remember when you were just another little boy wearing knickers. Don't you go getting all smart-mouthed with old Dulcie."

Gordon leaned back in his chair, his hands pressed hard over his heart. "Dulcie, Dulcie. You wound me so."

"Humph," said Dulcie, but she was trying hard not to laugh.

Maggie ducked her head, hiding her own smile. Dulcie's petticoats crackled like dried leaves as she made her way to the door. She stopped and looked back.

"You heard him, Mrs. Kincaid. You won't be polishing any more chandeliers, least not when Dulcie's around."

"No, Dulcie," she managed with a straight face.

"Humph."

As Dulcie's rustling sounds faded down the hall, Maggie

met her husband's gaze. They shared a real smile. For an instant, she felt a little breathless, even shaky.

With her bandaged hands, it was awkward, but she stirred the milk in her tea and then lifted the cup to her lips. Gordon opened the newspaper. His eyes scanned the columns, then he let out a long slow breath and folded the paper back on itself.

His face was rigid and hard. She set her teacup down slowly, very carefully. "What is it?" she asked.

He looked at her as if he'd forgotten she was there, then shook his head a little and came around the table. "Read this," he said.

She looked to the black-bordered column where he pointed and read:

> *The Moon Rises*
> *The Bear tracks the Wolf*
> *As the Hound the Fox*
>
> *Our Shrouds are Bloody*
> *And the Midnight is Black*
>
> *Some Shall Weep and Some Shall Pray*
> *The Watch is Set*
> *The Hour Cometh*
>
> *Meet at the Den of the Cottonmouth*
> *The Guilty Shall be Punished*

Maggie reached for her teacup, needing something to wash away the fear that was raw in her throat, but her hands trembled and the china clattered against the saucer, so she carefully set it down.

"That's a calling of the Klan," he said. "I haven't seen one of those in the *Fredericksburg News-Leader* since Grant pulled the army out of Virginia in 1870."

"And you think it's . . ." She knew. Chatham had made the threat clear. *Leave or we'll make your husband sorry.*

"I think they don't have the guts to go after a Kincaid," he said. "But just in case, you and the children stay close to the house until Annie delivers her baby and I can take you all in to Richmond."

She smoothed the edge of the paper as she read the words one more time, trying to make sense of them.

Gordon took the paper away from her and folded it. "The ghouls will probably go after my sharecroppers, or Royce's tenants. Maybe both." He laughed, but the sound had no amusement in it. "They actually call the white trash that does the dirty work *ghouls*."

"What can we do?" she asked, feeling a suffocating weight settle around her like a shroud. And she knew what she must do, for she had brought this on her husband, his family, his workers. She nudged her chin up, and it trembled a little. "I'll go back to Balti—"

"Like hell you will."

But before she could insist it was the only safe answer, Dulcie returned. She stopped in the doorway, her wiry body held rigid, and then her shoulders seemed to slump.

"The general sent word," she said. "Miz Annabelle needs you."

Gordon's eyes winced shut. "Damn," he muttered.

"I'll go with you." Maggie pushed back her chair.

His throat moved as he swallowed. "All of you will come," he said. "Even you, Dulcie."

Gordon eased the sheet down over Annie's legs, restoring her dignity. "It's real labor, Annie-girl," he said.

He moved up and sat on the edge of the mattress beside her, shifting somewhere between his role as doctor and brother-in-law to this woman he'd known, and loved, all his life. She gave him a tired smile that became generous when Royce moved from the window to join them.

"That's not blood you're feeling, but amniotic fluid," he explained, hoping to ease some of her fear. "The sac is leaking, which means we've got to bring this baby into the world." She nodded and then grimaced, reaching beneath her body. "Your back hurting already?"

"Some."

"I can't give you anything for pain. The baby's going to be small; laudanum might kill it," he said as he eased her onto her side. His fingers kneaded the tight muscles at the small of her back. Back labor was hell on the mother; he hoped this didn't continue into the long hours ahead of her.

"I sent for Patsy when I sent for you," said Royce, taking his wife's hand in his own, rubbing over her knuckles with his thumb. "I guess we try to get Levin out here next."

Patsy was Clarence's wife and had attended Annabelle at all her confinements. Dr. Levin wasn't scheduled to come out from Richmond for another two days. Hopefully, they could reach him by telegraph. Gordon didn't want to be attending physician for a woman who was not only closely related, but also had a history of complicated labor. He hadn't delivered a baby in over five years. Worse, he doubted he had the courage to preside over the death of his brother's wife—he calculated her odds at fifty-fifty, the infant's much worse.

Just then, the door opened and Patsy entered. Without being instructed, she walked over to the porcelain bowl on the dry sink and began to scrub with the lye soap. He could leave Annie in Patsy's capable hands for a few minutes. He nodded to Royce.

Royce leaned over and kissed his wife's forehead. "I'll be back in a minute, dear heart," he said. "Let me get the children squared away and someone sent into town, then I promise I won't leave you again."

Gordon left them alone and waited for Royce in the hallway. He fingered the news clipping in his pocket.

How close or real the danger, he didn't know. The message was too cryptic to make any sense to the uninitiated. What he clearly understood was that Johnson and Chatham had made threats against Maggie yesterday, and it was his own doctoring among the county's black population that had brought those threats down upon his wife.

Royce stepped into the hallway and pulled the door closed. Gordon heard the children's voices from somewhere downstairs. He closed his eyes a moment, then opened them and turned to his brother. "Did you get a chance to read this morning's paper?" he asked.

Royce shook his head. Wordlessly, Gordon handed his brother the clipping, watching the stone face for any reaction.

"They're mustering the ghouls," Royce said. "Christ, why today?"

"We'll just have to muster our own troops. Clarence owes me a favor."

"Clarence will come through." Royce studied the clipping again. "The moon rises and the midnight is black," he murmured, then looked up. "I'd interpret that as they gather with the rising moon and attack at midnight. What I can't get from this is where they form up or where they plan to attack."

"Pretty much my own interpretation," said Gordon. He took the paper back and slipped it in his pocket. Right now Annie needed her husband more than she needed her doctor. "I want you to go back in with your wife and see that she's bathed and put in a clean nightgown on clean sheets. Have Patsy see to it that I've got at least a dozen boiled sheets and lots of towels."

"What are you going to do?"

"I'll take care of the telegraph to Levin."

One to Father Fitzhugh too, he decided. Richmond's new bishop would make an effort to search for the obstetrician if the doctor was out on calls.

"After that, I'll swing by to speak with Clarence, then stop by Chauncey's to see if he can round up some white skin that isn't Klan to post a guard between our two houses." A low, muffled moan issued from behind the closed bedroom door. Gordon thought he saw a tremor race through his brother's body. "I'll be gone an hour, no more," he said quietly. "I can't send Franklin or Gordy."

"No," said Royce, and their eyes met. "You can't."

The tall clock in the entrance foyer chimed nine o'clock.

* * *

Maggie had thought the day would drag by, filled with a sad kind of anxiety over Annabelle's labor and a dreadful worry over the Klan's threats. Instead, the hours flew, filled near to bursting with tasks for the laboring mother and her hoped-for infant, and meeting the needs of the children.

A little after ten o'clock, Maggie was in the kitchen with Dulcie, stirring sheets in a tin washtub. Gordon had come through then, returning from town, where he'd seen to summoning Dr. Levin. She kept looking at his mouth, his eyes, waiting for a smile to spark there, but it didn't. He touched her, though, as he passed by, briefly, just below her ear.

At noon, she saw him again. The children were seated around the plain pine table in the large kitchen, finishing their lunch of chicken and carrot soup, when Gordon came down to join them. He answered their questions in simple terms that told them nothing; then, while the children helped Dulcie clear the table, he took her hand for a walk outside. The sun spilled white light over the river, the leaves crinkled beneath their feet. And when he kissed her, she felt a roughness in it, a desperation that caused her to lean into him and kiss him desperately back.

She was folding the dry sheets when the clock chimed two. She carried the clean linens upstairs and handed them to Patsy, and afterward, she walked the river path to Old Riverbend, even though Gordon had told her not to. But Franklin was not in the stables, only his son Cyrus. So she gave Cyrus the warning and wondered how he knew when he tipped his hat and said, "Thank you, ma'am, but we've already got the word."

The general emerged from his laboring wife's room shortly after three in the afternoon. Maggie fixed him a sandwich in the kitchen. She poured him fresh coffee, and something she saw in his face caused her to touch him, laying her palm on his shoulder. He reached up and grabbed her hand, squeezing hard. She had to fight to hold back her tears.

Now it was going on five o'clock, someone was banging the brass knocker on the front door and there was no one else available to answer the knock. The sun had not yet set, and surely the Klan did not knock at the door, tip their black silk hats when the door opened and announce their intent to wreak mayhem in a syrupy Southern drawl.

The thought made her smile, and so she was smiling when she pulled the door open to see the biggest, darkest man she had ever stood face-to-face with. She looked up into brown eyes as deep as the oceans, set in a proud, almost haughty face.

She didn't think this was a man to ever drink from an old jelly jar, and it occurred to her that she had never checked her own kitchen cupboards. But then, she had never seen Dulcie drink from an old jelly jar either.

He pulled a felt bowler from his head and nodded. "I'm Clarence Hallston," he said, "and I'm supposing you're the new Mrs. Kincaid."

"Aye." She opened the door wider and gestured. Something like amusement flickered around his eyes.

"I've known the general my whole life, and he isn't one to send a black man to the back door," he said. "But just in case anyone's watching, why don't you go for one of the menfolk while I wait here with my hat in my hand like a good nigger."

Maggie craned to see around his shoulder, then stepped out on the front gallery, pulling the door closed behind her. "I'd need a crowbar to get the general out of his wife's room, and my husband . . . well, I don't think I ought to call him out unless it's truly urgent."

"Give your husband this, then," he said, holding out a yellow telegraph. "Tell him I'll meet the train and bring the doctor out."

Relief flooded through her with such intensity that she swayed on her feet. Dr. Levin was coming. And then she realized what danger this man was willingly placing himself in, and she almost swayed again. "Why are you doing this?"

His thick, dark brows drew together. "I don't rightly know how to answer that, Mrs. Kincaid."

"I read the Klan notice in this morning's paper," she said. "I understand the danger. So why are you doing this?"

"Because my wife and the other Mrs. Kincaid are friends and because the general and I grew up together, slave and master, and friends as well. But mostly because your husband did me a favor."

She watched a flock of Canada geese cut across the horizon, their honking cries echoing inside her head. After a moment, Clarence stepped to the edge of the gallery, his dark gaze skimming the yard, the stable yard, and beyond to where a grove of hemlocks cast dark shadows that could hide a man.

"You didn't know about the favor?" he asked in a low, rumbly voice.

"No," she said, holding back a sigh. More mysteries her husband had chosen not to share with her. But then, she wasn't being fair; just this morning she had deliberately chosen to lie to him.

Clarence turned to face her again, his eyes even darker than before. "Your husband has been doctoring my people— won't even let them pay him for his services. If someone gives him a bag of turnips or a skinny chicken, he drops it off at the next tar shanty he stops at. That's why I'm doing this, Mrs. Kincaid. So you tell him he's got willing men with fire buckets handy, if it comes to that. We're colored men, which means we can't stop them, but we can help limit the damage. And tell him too that Chauncey Pettigrew has the harder job, but he'll have some decent white men on the grounds here by eleven tonight."

She pushed a dead leaf around with the toe of her leather half boot. He let out a heavy sigh.

"Your husband was only doing what he thought best for you, ma'am, not saying anything. It isn't his fault you're being blamed for something you have no cause to be blamed for. But life's not fair. It's just plumb not fair."

"And don't we both know that for truth."

He smiled, and she smiled back, although she thought there was a sadness in it for both of them. "Aye, then, you'd best be getting back while it's still daylight."

"You stay close to the house tonight," he said, then settled his hat and turned away.

The wind swirled suddenly through the trees, pelting the gallery with a hail of oak leaves. She was inside with the door closed before she opened the telegraph.

ARRIVE 9:05 FREDERICKSBURG. ONE DOCTOR. ONE PRIEST.
FATHER FITZHUGH.

Darkness settled over Riverbend. The lamps inside the Big House were lit and the children fed. And still Annabelle continued in labor.

Maggie pushed open the door to the kitchen, thinking she'd make some hot chocolate for the children, and stopped when she saw Gordy there, alone. He was at the pine table with his head in his hands. And his shoulders were shaking with the strength of his sobs.

Her footsteps sounded on the brick floor, but he didn't hear her, so she touched him briefly on the shoulder, then proceeded on for the milk jug.

"In Ireland," she said, "we have a saying. Those things that cannot be explained are either miracles or mysteries, and must be taken on faith. And isn't birth a miracle, and death the greatest of life's mysteries?"

He slanted her a glance from red-rimmed eyes, but said nothing. She poured the milk into a copper pan, and set it on the stove to scald. She rummaged in a cupboard until she found the chocolate bar wrapped in white paper, then picked up a knife and cutting board and set them all in front of Gordy. He rubbed his nose with his shirt cuff.

"Cut it in shavings, like whittling a stick," she said, and went back to the cupboard for the sugar. She set the sugar cone on the table and watched Gordy, still silent, but he was cutting the chocolate. His hands trembled a little, but she didn't take the knife away.

She picked up a wooden spoon and turned back to the stove, slowly stirring the milk over the heat.

"When I was a wee lass in Killady," she said, "I lived with my mum and my father, Seamus Quinn, who wasn't really my father but loved me anyway, and a boy who fostered with us. The boy's name was Jamie O'Connor and my da took to him so, as the son he never had."

She watched her hand stir the milk, remembering. "Once, after Jamie had been with us a year or so, we were working together pitching hay in the stables and he was talking so grand, about how one day he would own a piece of land and fill it with fine horses. It was an impossible dream, so I told him one day I would grow up and marry a duke." She smiled briefly, picturing Jamie with his shock of red hair and the disgusted look on his face. " 'Are you daft, Mary Margaret?' he said to me. 'When you grow up, you will marry me.' "

She looked over her shoulder to see Gordy was looking at her, not with the deep blue frown that was so familiar, but with an uncertainty in his eyes that made her believe this was the right thing to do, to share with him words she had shared with none other.

"And perhaps if we had stayed in Ireland," she said, "I would have married Jamie O'Connor and your father would have married some other woman, maybe Mrs. Hammond. But it didn't happen that way, after all . . ."

. . . Hours.

Gordon allowed himself to lean against the newel post across from the tall mahogany clock, taking some weight off his aching leg. He pressed his fingers against his closed eyelids. When he looked again, the hands on the porcelain clock face still read a quarter to eight.

Somewhere in the darkness outside, men in white hooded

robes were beginning to gather. On the tracks of the RF & P, a train was bringing the right doctor closer to Riverbend.

If he could keep Annie alive long enough . . . a hundred minutes or thereabouts.

God, he'd almost lost her once this afternoon when she slipped into unconsciousness. He'd sent Royce from the room, ostensibly to eat, and Royce had gone, so he was confident his brother didn't know what a close thing it was. Annie, bless her, had rallied, but she knew. Oh, yes, brave lady, she knew death was a near thing, and she wanted to say her good-byes.

Gordon mustered himself and walked down the central hall to the second parlor. Dulcie was sitting on the sofa with Clara curled on one side of her, sleeping with her head in Dulcie's lap, and Hope Ann at her other side, Dulcie's arm curved around the child's shoulder. Hope Ann looked at him through eyes so like her mother's that he had to swallow before he could speak.

"Your mother wants to say good—night." He caught himself at the last moment, but Dulcie's eyes closed anyway.

He brushed his hand down Hope Ann's hair as she came by him. Her hair was her father's, but in every other way, she was the image of her mother. He wondered if his brother would find peace in that, or if the resemblance was going to shred Royce's heart when—if—the future unfolded in the manner he feared.

"Where's Gordy?" he asked.

"In the kitchen with the missus." Dulcie's dark hand stroked Clara's brow and the child snuggled closer. "Don't you be botherin' them just yet. The missus is talking and the boy is listenin'."

At any other time, he'd reflect on that; he'd even probably follow Dulcie's advice. But he was a doctor and his patient's needs had to come first, so he made his way to the back of the house where Royce had added a new kitchen addition just last year.

The door stood ajar, and his footsteps slowed when he heard his wife's voice. He quietly eased through the door and leaned his shoulder against the blue cornflower wallpaper, hidden in shadows.

"It was a good life we had, for Ireland," she was saying. "Our landlord was of old Anglo-Irish stock, his own roots deep in the land, so he helped when the potato crop failed again and stood down the constabulary more than once when they came to evict a poor Catholic family for not paying their tithes to the Church of Ireland.

"I had to leave Ireland before I ever began to understand how complicated it all was. Men such as my da would argue the point, but I think now it was the Anglo-Irish landlords who were caught in the tightest bind, those that gave up their faith in order to keep title to the land. Perhaps it will never be solved, the problem called Ireland, and the people there will go on killing each other forever."

She breathed, and the sound of it was like a sigh, only deeper. "If you ask me, 'tis a poor addled brain that claims to kill for love of God. The land, always the land, and those that die—it's for that precious thing called freedom. It's a courage I don't have, and I'll not fault those who do."

For the first time since he had spoken to her outside a Catholic orphanage, Gordon made the connection between his wife's background and his own. It was more than pride, more than defeat, more even than suffering the humiliation of an army of occupation governing your every move.

It was a love of the land that went so deep into your bones that you couldn't separate the land and its heritage from yourself. The need to defend that heritage, even when deep inside you knew the sins of the fathers were being dealt to the sons. All the unanswerable questions and bitter choices, and the sorrow that inevitably followed. And he thought, perhaps, his son needed to hear this almost as much as he did.

Gordy lifted his head. "My father, Uncle Royce . . ."

She looked over her shoulder at Gordy and the curve of her lips wasn't a smile because it cut too deeply. "Aye, they are men who understand that one man's freedom is another man's chains. They've looked for the right answers, Gordy, and perhaps they've even found them."

She took the cutting board and scraped the shavings into the scalding milk. For a minute, the only sounds were that of the wooden spoon scraping the bottom of the pan and Gordy's occasional sniffle.

"One day the soldiers came to Castle Lachlan," she said finally, and her voice was strange, with none of the emotion that filled it when she sang or told her stories. And as he listened from his place in the shadows, Gordon began to understand why.

"They were searching for smuggled guns," she said, "and they found them buried on the Lord Lachlan's estate, behind the stables where my da worked. I think Geoffrey Fitzhugh knew the guns were there; he was a peer, an earl, but an Irish one, and the Fitzhughs loved Ireland every bit as much as my da and Jamie loved her. They, the Crown, would take the earl's land, you see, strip it away from him and give it to a true Englishman, and m'lord knew what would happen then to the poorest of his tenants. They would die, Gordy. They would be evicted from their homes and starve in the ditches, those that didn't freeze to death first.

"So Geoffrey Fitzhugh said little to the soldiers, except to take the guns and that he would hold an inquiry. He spoke in his arrogant way and it might have worked, him being a peer and the soldiers in awe of his title. It might have worked, except for my da.

"My da admired Lord Lachlan for his love of horses and his secret support of the Brotherhood, and he hated him too because . . ." She paused and brushed her fingers over her temple. "Well, because my da wanted to be the man my mum loved and he thought the earl was that man.

"It was my da who grabbed the hay rake to attack the English lieutenant. He'd taken only a step when one of the soldiers shot him in the leg, not wanting to kill him so easy, now. Me mum was on her knees in the dirt, keening, and my body was shaking so I thought I'd fall into pieces, but there was naught anyone could do for poor Seamus Quinn now, not even the earl could be heard over the soldiers' shouting. And they had the guns."

She set the spoon down and curled her hands in the apron tied around her waist. Gordon waited for her to turn again, to look at Gordy, who was sitting at the table with his head bowed, but she didn't.

"They set a torch to our cottage, and made us watch while it burned." Her head tilted back for a moment. She swallowed audibly in the silence, then said, "They put a rope around my da's neck, him twisting and turning and fighting them as best he was able, and poor mum so weak with fear she couldn't even stand. And myself being held back by the earl, I was that mad with my own fear. The horses started screaming about then because the stables had caught fire, but nobody moved to save them. The soldiers were shouting to string him up, lads, string him up, sounding just like Mr. Johnson shouting at his hunting dogs yesterday. Kill, kill."

But she didn't shout when she said the words: Hers was a hoarse, rough sound, not quite a whisper. "And they did that. They threw one end of the rope over the branch of a yew tree, two men pulling my da up slow, so he'd not die easy.

"It took him a long time to die."

She picked up the spoon and then set it back down. Took a deep breath, and let it out slowly. "It was the earl who cut him down, and gave up the wood to build a coffin. We buried him the next day on a hill above the pasture. Such was the way Mum looked that morning, all staring eyes and white face, that I knew there would soon be another grave on that hill. And Jamie . . .

"Jamie went out in his father's fishing boat, after the burial, even though the skies had gone black with a storm. I waited for him on the beach, near blind with fear that I'd lost him too. But he came back, and I helped him pull the boat on the shore, and only when that was done did he look at me. I saw it in his eyes then: the empty, bitter look where once his laughter had been. To this day, it lives in him still. So in a way that is maybe hardest of all to understand, I did lose him after all.

"Lord Lachlan was on the beach that night too, standing all by himself at the edge of the river. He looked as alone as I felt, and I wanted to go to him and take his hand, and tell him it was only a nightmare and that tomorrow we'd all wake up and the sun would be shining so bright, and life would be the same as it had always been. But I didn't; he was the Lord Lachlan, and I was the child of his murdered horse trainer. So I went back with Jamie to his family's poor *shibeen*, where Mum lay on a straw pallet, silent except for her coughing.

"It was the earl who came to us the next day. He explained how he was chartering a boat to take all those who wanted to leave Ireland, to go to America, where there was so much land even a poor man could own his own piece of it. Afterwards, he took me outside and spoke to me alone. When I think back on it, it seems he talked for a long time, but I wasn't hearing much of it. Except the last words—those I can hear him saying still.

" 'Someone . . . special . . . will meet you there.' And someone special did meet me. The Lord Lachlan's brother, Father Hugh Fitzhugh."

She stared straight ahead at the flowered wallpaper, but Gordon thought she was seeing beyond it to a long-ago day when a frightened young girl stepped foot on this shore to be met by a priest, who was her father's twin brother.

"Mum never saw America. She died on the crossing. I was twelve years old, just like you now." She turned slightly and gestured. "Would you hand me the chocolate pot?"

When Gordy moved, his head turned to a profile and Gordon saw the tracks of tears on the boy's cheeks. Maggie set the ceramic pot on the stove's chrome fender and lifted the saucepan.

"When she died, Gordy, I felt like my world had ended—and sure in a manner of speaking it had, with me da dead as well and me never to see Ireland again."

The gas jets hissed. Maggie poured the chocolate from the saucepan into the pot. Gordy scraped his sleeve under his nose.

"But I found a new life in your country," she said. "A father of a sort in Father Fitzhugh and a mother of a sort in Mother Bernadette, and then the children in the orphanage who made me feel so needed. And I was happy there, Gordy. The hurting never goes away, but it becomes a sweet kind of hurting, and you open your arms to it when it comes because it's a part of you and means you're still a part of that person you loved and lost."

She set the saucepan down and half-turned so she was facing his son. She brushed her bandaged palm over his hair and Gordy didn't jerk away.

"You've loved your Aunt Annie as you would have loved your own mum. Whatever happens tonight," she said, "have faith in your father to do his best, and faith in—in what would call God's wisdom."

Gordon stared in wonder as his son put his arms around his stepmother's waist and buried his face against her shoulder. "I'm s-s-sorry, Maggie."

"And didn't I know that all along," she said softly. She ducked her head so her cheek rested against Gordy's shimmering gold hair, and when she did, Gordon knew she had seen him in the shadows.

Their eyes met and held forever, and night flowed into dawn and there was no clock ticking in the hallway, no death hovering on black wings just outside the door.

Then forever ended and became now, when she gently took his son's shoulders and set him back. She turned her face away, but not before he saw the raw anguish pulling at her mouth and darkening her eyes. "Your father's come for you, Gordy," she said.

"Use your handkerchief, son," he said as Gordy lifted his elbow again. Gordy dug in his hip pocket and pulled out a crumpled linen square. Gordon said, "Aunt Annie wants to say good night."

Gordy swallowed and nodded. He cut a swift glance at Maggie, and her mouth tilted in a sad smile. Gordy's footsteps echoed in the silence as he crossed the brick floor. Gordon reached out, laying his palm on his son's shoulder, and then Gordy left and he was alone with his wife.

His wife, who had never shared her tragic story with anyone. Until now, and she had chosen to give the gift to his son. His heart was in his throat, and he feared if he so much as breathed, this woman whose beauty shone from within would disappear from his life, and his world would come to an end.

She was folding a blue-and-white-striped towel, not looking at him. " 'Tis bad, then?"

"Breech." He took a step forward. "You can go up, say good—" He choked and had to swallow.

She set the towel on the table and came to him, and her arms went around his waist. She looked up and he saw himself reflected in her eyes.

"Annie was saying farewell to me yesterday. Let her have this time with her husband and children."

She tucked her face in his shirt, and he rested his chin on her head, hugging her closely. Her body pressed into his, and it seemed as if her blood flowed into him, her heart beat inside his chest, and it was a closer joining even than when he took her beneath him.

He rested his chin on her hair, and she smelled so incredibly sweet, of chocolate and spring flowers. "I never knew these things about your life, Maggie. Why did you tell Gordy now?"

She was silent for a long time.

"I thought it might help Gordy to hear it," she said finally, and he knew he had never loved her more than he did at that moment.

Somewhere beyond the double green doors, a barn owl hooted a mournful cry into the winter night. Maggie looked at the tall clock in front of her, praying it would read after nine o'clock, which would mean Dr. Levin was only minute away, but it was one of life's unanswered prayers. Both black hands were pointed at the Roman numeral IX.

She felt stifled suddenly, as if she would scream if she didn't get a breath of fresh air. Maggie stepped out on the gallery, drawing in great lungfuls of biting night air. The owl hooted another sad lament to the deepening night.

She thought at first it was a falling star she saw through the tree branches. But then she saw another against the black streaming river.

Only it wasn't stars. It was the Klan, carrying blazing torches.

Chapter 26

"Christ, Gordon, tell me what's happening."

"It's a footling breech." Gordon slanted a sideways glance at his brother, then looked away from the stark anguish on his brother's face.

Annie stared at him through pain-wracked eyes as he draped another clean sheet over her knees. He'd never felt so humbly mortal in his entire life, but he reached for an encouraging smile. "Hang in there, Annie-girl," he said. "Not much longer, but this is going to be tough for a few minutes."

She started to nod and then another contraction gripped her. A scream slipped past her lips. Beside him, Royce went rigid as his face paled. Gordon knew he couldn't handle two patients. He needed Royce right now as much as Annie needed him.

"Get behind her, Royce," he said calmly. "Hold her in your lap and keep her legs open." As Royce followed his instructions, he spoke to Annabelle. "This is going to hurt, Annie-girl. A lot. I'm going to try to bring the other foot down and you can't push. No matter how bad it gets—don't push."

Royce straddled her with her back pressed hard against his chest, his hands clasping her knees, holding them open. Gordon gave her calf a gentle squeeze. "Concentrate on breathing. This will all be over soon."

Her eyes winced shut as another contraction ripped through her body. Gordon said a silent prayer to Maggie's God as he waited for the contraction to pass. "All right. Now."

Annie screamed again as his hand invaded her body. He gently grasped the unborn infant's foot. He listened to Royce's low voice as Royce talked his wife through the pain. Gordon found the infant's thighs and guided the second foot down into the birth passage.

Annie made a mewling sound, then went still and silent. Gordon glanced up and realized she'd lost consciousness. "She breathing?"

Royce jerked a nod.

"Hold on to her, it's almost over." Gordon struggled to keep the infant's feet together and guide them out. He withdrew his hand as another contraction struck her. Almost immediately, tiny feet appeared. "We've got two feet showing," he said quietly, for the first time in hours beginning to hope for the best.

Royce looked over his wife's head. Tears were streaking down his cheeks. Annie stirred, pain fluttering across her features as she regained consciousness.

"You can push now, dear heart. It's coming," Gordon said in a hoarse voice. He grasped tiny feet slippery with blood, then felt something give as the thighs appeared. A moment later, a torso and two tightly crossed arms slid into his waiting hands.

"A son," he said.

A savage cry wrenched from Annie's chest as the baby's head spurted clear in a gush of blood and fluid. Gordon was holding his nephew: a perfectly formed boy-child, covered with patches of white vernix and splotches of blood—and very much alive.

He deftly wiped the infant's face with a clean cloth, then turned him over and patted his back. A glob of mucus came from the baby's mouth and then he was squalling. It was a beautiful sound, as beautiful as the nonsense words and quiet laughter he dimly heard being passed between Royce and Annabelle.

The clock downstairs pealed nine times as Gordon laid the infant on his mother's stomach. While Royce and Annabelle were engaged in falling in love with their new child, Gordon looped the umbilical cord, tied it off, then cut it.

Patsy scooped up the baby, wrapped him in a towel and carried him over to a washbasin for his first bath. Royce eased his wife down on the bed. He looked over to where Patsy was working, grinned broadly, then leaned over Annabelle and showered her wan face with tender kisses.

Gordon didn't think either was aware that the placenta was delivered. He gathered the placenta into a bowl to be buried later and went about cleaning Annie and stitching her torn tissue. No worrisome bleeding. He placed a cloth pad between her thighs and gently lowered her legs. Levin would be arriving any minute now to find the job completed. Relief flooded Gordon's veins, surging with an actual heat.

"Dry gown for our new mother," he said, handing Royce the garment. He turned his back as Royce changed his wife into the clean gown, and crossed over to check on the baby.

Perfect. Tiny, wizened face with all the working parts, ten fingers and toes, and a healthy set of lungs, if the lustful crying was any clue. Gordon wrapped his nephew in a swaddling blanket and exchanged a relieved, giddy grin with Patsy. He carried the baby over to Annie, who settled him in the crook of her arm. Immediately the tiny boy began to root, searching to suckle at his mother's breast.

"We have a son, dear heart," said Royce, awe and tears both evident in his voice. "A son."

Royce gently stroked his son's bald head. Annie was too

exhausted to do more than smile, but the smile was more than enough. Gordon looked into her large brown eyes, glazed with both pain and joy. He felt a pressure in his chest, a hot stinging in his eyes.

When winter passed and the trees were once again turning green, he'd be attending another birth; not as a doctor but as husband and father, sharing his wife's pain, her exhaustion, her joy. Tonight, he wanted to share hopes and dreams. And triumph.

Maggie's feet slid out from under her and she scrabbled for purchase on the freezing ground. She ignored the pain shooting through her hands and scrambled back to her feet, running toward the back of the Old House. Clouds raced across the face of the moon. In the dark, she nearly tripped over a body, trussed and lying in the cold mud.

"*Wirra*, Franklin," she said, kneeling beside him. She pulled the gag from his mouth and began to work at the knots with stiff fingers. "Are you hurt?"

He shook his head. "Reach in my pocket—there—that one—penknife."

She sawed through the rope binding Franklin's arms and then he grabbed the knife from her trembling hand and began to work at his ankles. "The boy," he said in a hoarse voice. "Out front—"

Maggie was already running. She raced through the back of the house to Gordon's study, where she stopped and stared at the rifles mounted on the gun rack. Her heart pounded against her rib cage. She reached out and touched the barrel of a shotgun. No, she knew nothing of rifles and wouldn't have the courage to aim the thing at a man even if she did.

A horse blew a snort. She heard a man's shout. The noises came from the front lawn. She brushed her sweaty palms on her skirt and ran to the foyer, where she came to an abrupt halt.

A dancing glitter of red and gold was reflected in the leaded glass framing the front door. Fear turned her blood to ice. For a moment, she heard the clipped accent of British soldiers, smelled the bitter odor of burning thatch. . . .

This wasn't Ireland and she was no longer a child. Maggie drew a deep breath. She yanked open the door and stepped onto the front gallery.

A flaming cross illuminated the grounds, the madly dancing firelight etching the forms of a dozen men mounted on horseback. The horses were restless, spooked by the hiss and crackle of the burning cross. Curled, feathery ashes drifted up like rising snow and disappeared into the night.

Gordy stood at the top step, a raised shotgun held firm in his hands. One flaxen-haired boy, his narrow, boy's body delineated by a hellish orange light, standing alone to face down a dozen grown men mounted on horseback. She couldn't have loved him more at that moment if he'd been the child from her own womb, nor could she have felt such mingled pride and fear for him.

Maggie moved beside him. "You'll be leaving now," she said in a steady voice that displayed none of the rage and fear that were battling for dominance inside her belly.

Someone laughed harshly. Another man rode up to the burning cross, carrying a torch in one hand. He reached out and flame leaped with a hiss from the cross to the pine torch. With a jerk of the reins, he turned the horse and spurred him toward the stables. Gordy's arm trembled as he released the safety on his shotgun.

She placed her hand on his arm. "You cannot stop them with two shells," she said in a low voice.

"I can stop two of them."

"Aye, maybe. And it would be just like my da, only they wouldn't hang you; they'd hang Franklin."

He jerked a nod but held the shotgun steady.

The yard erupted into frenzied activity—silver hooves pawing the sky and then thundering against the cold ground. Men shouted, waving brands of fire over their heads, and flaming torches rode the wind, hurled one by one into the stables where horses were screaming.

Then, so quickly it might have been a dream, the men seemed to disappear into the black night. One man remained behind. He set his horse to a slow walk and approached the gallery where she and Gordy stood.

The fires lit the sky with a flickering red glow. Dreadful noises filled the night: the crackle of flames and the screaming of trapped horses, Lucky's yelps and the pounding of her own heart.

The man brought his horse right up to the bottom step. He leaned over his shotgun, peering through the slit of his hood in a firelit stare. "Tell your father, boy, that the war isn't over. You tell him it's just begun and he better get himself back on the right side."

Maggie couldn't see the face behind the hood, but she had stared into those same eyes yesterday until his entire wine-red, whiskered face was burned into her vision.

Chatham laughed, turned the horse and rode into the night.

Black smoke billowed through the opened doors, flowing upward into oblivion. Beyond, Maggie could see bales of hay burning, flames licking along the floor and against the stalls. The sound of the fire came like an onrushing train, bellowing, whooshing, roaring like a dragon from the nether reaches. Over it all was the wild screeching of horses.

She grabbed Gordy by the shoulders. "No," she screamed. "You will not go in there."

He struggled in her grip. "Colonel, Firenza—"

Franklin appeared like an apparition through the smoke, leading a blindfolded black stallion. Firenza. Even blindfolded, the huge animal was frantic with fear, tossing his head, shying and pulling against the rope halter.

"You take them as they come out," she shouted at Gordy. "Into the far paddock."

It took him a moment to understand, and then he nodded and grabbed the halter from Franklin. He used all his strength but managed to control the big horse, calming him with some innate horse sense that seemed to be a Kincaid trait.

Maggie leaned over and ripped at her petticoat, tearing several strips. She dunked one in the horse trough, then tied it around her face, covering her nose and mouth.

"You're not going in there either, Mrs. Kincaid," said Franklin.

"Only the two of us. We'll save as many as we can." She didn't give Franklin an opportunity to argue, diving past him and into the holocaust.

Smoke and heat engulfed her. Hungry flames licked at wooden stalls and climbed the support posts, crept like undulating serpents along the rafters. Orange and yellow light skittered and leaped, reflected in the wild eyes of rearing horses.

She worked her way as far back into the structure as she dared, stopping at Shenandoah's stall. The mare's hooves struck hard at the wooden slats. Maggie touched the metal latch and cried out from the searing heat. Franklin appeared at her side.

"I'll bring them out of the stall," he said, and then leaned over, gagging and coughing. He raised up, peering at her through streaming eyes. "You take them out."

"Aye." Maggie backed up, watching as Franklin battled the mare, finally managing to tie a blindfold over Shenandoah's eyes. The horse calmed enough that he could slip the halter over her head. Maggie grasped the rope and led the animal through thickening clouds of smoke toward the cold darkness of the opened doors.

Gordy was waiting. She turned Shenandoah over to him, then leaned over, choking and gasping to draw clean air into her lungs. Smoke and tears blinded her, made everything into a smear of light and shadow. She wiped her streaming eyes with the back of her hand and plunged back into the barn.

Time was measured in the spread of the flames. They worked as a team, managing to save all the Thoroughbreds, turning next to the draft horses. Her throat was raw. Every breath was like swallowing flame. The heat burned her lungs and scorched her skin. But worst was the noise, the roaring of the fire, louder than any wind, mixed with the screams of the trapped horses.

Every muscle in her body ached from fighting large animals. She took one more lead rope and yanked, bullied and cajoled the horse down the center of the barn. The fire had become a living thing, consuming everything in its path and moving on voraciously, ever hotter and hungrier. A fiery beam fell from the roof, landing with a loud roar just behind the gelding. A shower of sparks rained down on the horse, in her hair and across her shoulders.

Terror squeezed out what little air she had left in her lungs. The horse reared, jerking rope across her injured palms. She bit back a cry of pain. Franklin was there, shoving her forward. Maggie staggered toward a doorway framed by curling yellow flames.

She made it out into blessed cold air and leaned over, sobbing and choking. Her knees were trembling, her head reeling, and she couldn't seem to draw enough air into her lungs.

"Away from here, Mrs. K." Franklin grabbed her around the waist. "Get away, the whole thing's gonna go."

A rider came thundering from the direction of the Big House. Terrified by the fire and screams, the galloping horse reared, his front legs pawing the air. Gordon leaped from the animal's bare back.

"Maggie," he roared like a man demented.

Franklin reached him in time to keep him from plunging into the burning stable. "She's safe. There—by the fence."

Gordon rushed to her. He clutched her shoulders hard, his fingers biting into her skin.

"Maggie." His eyes closed briefly. "Look at you. Dear God, look at you." He grabbed her head between his hands and kissed her roughly.

She was crying and gasping, half-crazy from fear and relief. Suddenly it seemed as if men were everywhere, running with buckets of sloshing water in an effort to limit the spread of the flames. She saw Clarence, red light reflecting off his dark skin, looking like some avenging angel as he issued orders to a throng of men.

And then she saw another man, a tall, black-haired man coming toward her in long, ground-eating strides. Father Fitzhugh was here. The entire evening came back to her in a rush.

"Annie?" she asked in a voice that croaked from swallowed smoke.

"She's fine," said Gordon, his face sparking in a smile in spite of the mayhem surrounding them. "A son, they have a son." He looked around, over each shoulder. "Speaking of which—where's Gordy?"

"The paddock." Maggie turned, searching the far paddock where horses milled restlessly. "No. . . ." She swung around as her stomach clenched tight. "Colonel," she murmured, and then cried out, "Franklin. We didn't get Colonel!" She jerked her head toward the flaming barn. "Dear Blessed Mother." And she started to run.

She could feel the fire's heat on her skin when Gordon grabbed her from behind and shoved her into Father Fitzhugh's chest. "Keep her safe," he yelled over the roar of the fire.

She reached for him, but he was already lunging into the inferno. "Gordon," she screamed as he was swallowed up in billowing, red-tinted clouds of smoke. Father Fitzhugh's arm wrapped around her waist and he pulled her back, away from the heat and flames. She turned in to him, sobbing into the rough weave of his coat.

"*Sha, sha, mó cailín,*" he murmured as he held her tight. "Have faith."

She could not look, could hardly breathe. Her stomach knotted up tight. She knew a fear such as she'd never experienced and then Father Fitz spoke.

"Look, my Maggie," he said softly. There was subdued encouragement in his voice.

Maggie turned, supported by Father Fitz's arm. Gordon was emerging from a cloud of smoke and flames. His beautiful face could have been carved from stone, it was so expressionless. He cradled a limp Gordy in his arms.

She wanted to scream. Scream against the raging fire that consumed wood and horses and little boys, and against the hatred that set that inferno.

She took two steps toward them, but a crushing pain hit hard in her belly and she doubled over. Maggie reached out, grabbing the fence rail, as another pain exploded deep inside her center, seeming to splinter her into fragments. A hot gush of liquid spread down her legs.

"Gordon," she cried, but if any sound came out of her throat, it was lost in a thunderous roar as the barn roof gave way and crashed into the voracious flames.

Another pain wrenched her body into a tortured knot. Someone's hands caught her and lowered her to the cold ground. She thought it was Father Fitz, but the world had gone dark and she couldn't be certain. She heard voices, sounding as if they came from a vast distance.

After an eternity of pain and cold, she recognized one voice reaching through the pain. A large man was kneeling beside her, touching her with gentle, healer's hands. He spoke her name again, and she knew it was her husband.

"Gordy?" she asked through lips that were growing numb.

"Father Fitzhugh has him. He's coming around." Gordon lifted her soaked skirts and placed some type of cloth between her thighs. "Levin," he said urgently to someone who hovered over her. "Get him down here now, she's hemorrhaging."

Gordon lifted her into his arms, causing a wrenching agony. "Draw your knees up as much as you can, angel."

Maggie tried, but the struggle was too much. She gave in and let the dark peace claim her.

Chapter 27

*H*e had no tricks in his black doctor's bag to save her.
Gordon reached out and brushed his wife's cheek.
Those decadent black lashes shed no shadows on her cheek-
bones now. They'd been singed in the fire.

She gave the appearance of a battle casualty, with bandages wrapping her burned hands and arms, that awful gray
pallor to her face. The worst wounding, the loss of their child
and a goodly portion of Maggie's lifeblood, didn't show. No
bandage could heal that wound.

"I did this to her," he said in a low voice.

"We men have a tendency to think we're much more important than we actually are." The eyes Father Fitzhugh
turned to him were deep and dark. "You're no more responsible for what happened than you're responsible for the next
sunrise. It's a battle as old as creation. Sadly, evil endures."

"It should be me," he said hoarsely. "I should be dying in
her place."

"No, son, it's not your choice to make." Father Fitzhugh

sighed. "There is no pain like losing a wife or child. No man should have to endure it, but they do."

"How would you know, Father?"

Father Fitzhugh stiffened and looked away. When he looked back, betraying tears filled his green eyes. Gordon glanced at the rosary Father Fitzhugh held in his hand, Maggie's rosary.

You gave that to her mother, he thought. Maggie is *your* daughter.

How different we all are, he thought, watching the priest who was a mortal father, thinking of Royce's vulnerability the other night, his own blinding terror now. And yet, so much the same in our men's arrogance and fear and pride.

Father Fitzhugh was wrapping the rosary around Maggie's still hands. Gordon looked away, and then the priest said, "Can she hear, do you think?"

His throat was so tight he could hardly speak. "Maybe."

"Her music? Would you mind if I played the harp for her?"

"Go ahead, Father."

Gordon stepped onto the balcony and after a moment the haunting sound of an old Irish air drifted out after him. He leaned his palms on the cold railing, remembering the night of the concert in Baltimore . . . Maggie with her children's choir, Maggie's voice lifted in song as she plucked the harp strings and enchanted a concert hall full of strangers. Enchanted a lost, lonely man named Gordon Kincaid.

He had no pride left. He wanted to drop to his knees and shed the tears that scalded his eyes. He wanted to rage and bellow and slam his fists against hard surfaces. The part of him that was dying with her wanted to throw the whole of him over the balcony onto the ground below.

He was a father now and his children needed him more than ever, so he did none of those things.

He stared at the river. The sun setting behind the clouds cast a pinkish glow over the horizon. Before Maggie, he would never have noticed that subtle light in the heavens.

She had given him so many priceless gifts: Clara, even Gordy. The simple pleasures of life he had almost forgotten. And he had taken them all, and taken her from her safe haven because he wanted what she could give him so very much.

A choking sensation closed his throat. He bowed his head. And Gordon Kincaid made a promise to his wife's forgiving God.

Let her live and I'll give her back to You.

The sounds of the harp ceased. After a while, the French doors opened and he heard Father Fitzhugh's urgent voice speak only his name. As a priest, Father Fitz would have attended many death vigils, would recognize the final approach of death as well as any doctor. Gordon stared at the ice-edged river, trying desperately to memorize this last moment he would spend as a complete man.

"I'm coming," he said, straightening his shoulders. Somehow, he'd find the strength to hold her hand as she took that final breath. He didn't know where he'd find the strength to face what came after.

Maggie, you never knew how much I loved you.

The music was insistent, the familiar Irish airs played on a harp, beguiling and treacherous sounds pulling her back to someplace she didn't want to go.

She was brittle and barren inside, her mind was wrapped in a thick mist and she couldn't seem to force her lids open. If she could just touch the harp, maybe she could find her center, make some sense of this bleak, fog-shrouded world.

Maggie tried. She focused her mind and issued orders to her hand, but the only thing she accomplished was stopping the music. She felt herself drifting back to that other place where silence and darkness reigned.

"Where's that Irish spirit? Come on, angel, you moved your fingers. Try again."

A brush of her face, a man's gentle touch. Her hand was lifted and cradled in something warm, a man's larger hand.

"Maggie, come back."

Come back. Something had happened. Something terrible. She didn't want to come back, didn't want to remember. Sleep was safe.

"Move your fingers, Maggie. Come on, angel, try again."

She knew that voice, that touch. Even through the thick mist in her brain, she knew him.

For you, *á mhúirnín.* Anything for you.

They rode into the outskirts of Fredericksburg, three men, one boy. The morning fog was thinning as they drew up on Princess Anne Street and dismounted.

Another figure approached from beneath the awning of the neighboring building. Gordon gave a slow look up the cassocked length of the priest, and then their eyes met and locked.

A damp wind ruffled Father Fitzhugh's hair. "Vengeance is mine, saith the Lord."

"Justice is mine." Gordon turned on his heel and shoved open the door.

Father Fitzhugh followed him through an anteroom and into Dr. Chatham's office. Chatham looked up, his jaw sagging open. His pupils went wide as his gaze shifted from one man to another.

"Now, now . . . Gordon." He smiled between his side-whiskers and held out a hand as if to fend them off.

Gordon kept going. He picked up a chair by the top rung, swung it around backward and straddled the cane seat. Without moving his gaze from Chatham's face, he reached down and pulled the Colt from his holster. He half-cocked the pistol and reached for a cartridge.

"Why are you here?" Chatham's gaze shifted to the priest.

Gordon cocked one brow as he emptied powder into the gun chamber. He tore the paper from the ball and rammed it into the cylinder. Chatham watched his fire-blistered hands as if mesmerized, then shook his head.

"Gordon, I swear by all that's holy . . ." His hand moved furtively toward the desk.

"I wouldn't do that," Gordon said, his voice cold. "I don't want to have to kill you, but I will if you touch that gun." He narrowed his eyes. "Remember the war, Chatham? I rode with Stuart. Where the hell were you then?"

"I was in Richmond. You know that. I did my share. In the Treasury Department."

"The war is over, settled on the battlefield between men of honor." Gordon grabbed Chatham by the collar and jerked him up, bringing their faces so close together Chatham's side-whiskers brushed his face and he could smell the man's breakfast.

"You yellow-bellied son-of-a-bitch," he growled. "You burned my barn and killed my horses. You damn near killed my son." His grip tightened on Chatham's throat until the man's eyes popped and he gasped vainly for another breath. "My wife . . . damn you, what you did to my wife, our un-born child."

Gordon let go. Chatham staggered and fell, sprawling into the desk chair. His chest heaved as he gasped to pull in air.

"It wasn't supposed to happen that way. By God, we didn't mean to hurt anyone."

"You'll talk, Chatham." Gordon dropped the gun muzzle, carried a cap to the exposed cone and pressed it on with his thumb. The cylinder clicked ominously as he turned it. "Remember Judge Pleasonton? Old friend of the Kincaids. He has the absurd notion I saved his son's life at Antietam."

Gordon leaned closer. There was no mercy in his voice. "When you're done talking, there'll be no Klan in this county, Chatham. No more lily-livered night riders." He let down the hammer of the safety notch. "I won't give up until you pay for what you've done."

Chatham's face went white. Footsteps sounded in the anteroom and then the door opened to the mayor and Judge Pleasonton. Behind them stood Royce and Clarence.

Gordon's foot lashed out, catching the base of the roll chair and sending man and chair crashing backward into the wall. His lips pulled back over his teeth. "Talk, damn you. Names, every name of every Klansman."

Chatham sneered at him. Gordon raised the pistol, taking dead aim at a point between Chatham's shifting eyes. His finger tightened on the trigger.

"No, son."

Gordon ignored the priest. Tears splattered down Chatham's cheeks and onto his whiskers. Gordon dropped the muzzle and fired a shot into the floor between Chatham's feet. The stink of sulfur filled the small room. A wet stain spread slowly down Chatham's pants legs.

"Talk, damn you!"

Chatham talked.

Gordon rode back into town the next morning, alone. He mailed a letter to Baltimore. The answer came a week later.

He spoke with his children. He spoke to the priest.

And then he saddled Firenza and rode for hours along the riverbank, planning what he must say to Maggie.

Chapter 28

Maggie knew she should have faith in God's mysterious ways, had always had such faith, but it didn't matter. The dark and dangerous men had stolen her life again, and this time, she felt more than broken inside. She felt empty.

"Maggie," Gordon said in an insistent voice. "We need to talk."

Maggie wanted to turn her head to the wall, wrap herself in the safe mist where there was no past and no future, but some spark of living caused her to look at him. He took her hand in his larger one, staring down at their hands clasped together.

For no reason at all, she began to cry. She cried until his taut face became a blurred wash of features. The mattress sagged with his weight as he sat on the bed beside her. He brushed her hair back from her forehead.

"I've made arrangements to send you back to Saint

Columba's," he said. A muscle clenched along his jaw. "Tomorrow morning. Father Fitzhugh will accompany you."

Maggie sucked in a breath as agony shot through her. He was sending her away. Some tiny shred of pride remained and she tried desperately to swallow her tears. "Might be 'tis for the best," she said dully.

"You'll recover faster there, under the care of the nuns." He tilted his head back and blew a harsh breath from between his teeth. "If you decide you don't want to come back, I won't put any obstacle in your way. An annulment . . . nullification, whatever it is your Church provides for divorce."

She said nothing, her mind reeling. He said, "I won't keep Clara from you. She can visit as often as . . ." He shrugged. "I don't know how it works—a convent—but I can stay at Drew's, and you can have your time with her."

He was staring at her hard. His eyes were so blue, so beautiful. She suddenly wanted to be back at St. Columba's where it was peaceful. Safe.

"I don't know what I want," she said finally.

"I think I do." He stood and moved to the foot of the bed, leaning one shoulder against the walnut poster.

She was horrified with herself. She should reach out to him, put an end to this strange distance between them. Instead, she lay frozen.

"How would you know what I want?"

He smiled faintly. "I know you, Irish."

She curled into a ball, clutching an arm around her empty abdomen. "I want you to leave me alone. Just leave me alone."

Gordon wandered into the back parlor, a bad choice under the circumstances. Maggie's presence was everywhere in this room, in the bright paint, the flower chintz of the reupholstered chairs, the touches of color, and laughter, she'd brought with her into this old house.

He lowered himself into one of the chairs and stared glumly out the window. He was sending her back to the safety of St. Columba's, firmly convinced he would lose her to her Church once she returned. Or maybe to James O'Connor.

He didn't tell her what it cost him to give her up. She lived, and that was all that mattered.

"For love is as strong as death; jealousy is cruel as the grave; the coals thereof are coals of fire which hath a most vehement flame."

Gordon looked toward the sound of Father Fitzhugh's voice. He couldn't tell if there was censure in the tone, wasn't quite certain of the point Father Fitz was trying to make.

"Song of Solomon," Gordon said, more as an effort to fill the heavy silence than for any other purpose.

"A rather unique book of the Old Testament, subject to widely varying interpretations." Father Fitzhugh came into the room and walked over to the brandy decanter. He lifted the crystal bottle and raised one brow. Gordon shook his head to decline. He waited for the older man to state his real purpose. Father Fitzhugh poured himself a finger of brandy and said nothing.

"You disapprove," said Gordon at last.

The priest smiled faintly and shook his head. "I don't understand why."

Gordon pushed up suddenly, wincing as pain shot through his leg. He walked to the window, staring at the charred remains of the stable. "She'll be safer there," he said.

"That's not the reason," said Father Fitz. "I was with you the other day, remember? The Klan will be quiet for a long while. Could be you've put a permanent end to that evil here."

So Gordon would have wished but found it hard to believe. "I coerced her into marrying me," he said. "Arrogant fool that I am, I paid no attention to any of her fears."

Gordon ceased the restless drumming of his fingers against the shutter and slanted a glance at the priest. "I was going to be her knight in shining armor—protect her with my name." He laughed harshly. "Some knight. I damn near killed her."

"There are innumerable ways to kill those we love. Death just might be the kindest of those."

"As well you know, Father?"

"As well I know." Father Fitz studied the amber liquid in his glass.

Gordon walked out of the room. He saw no need to explain himself to a flawed priest, even one who loved Maggie with something akin to the same blinding emotion he himself felt for his wife.

He continued out the door and on to the makeshift stables erected during the past days. He could drink himself into a stupor or he could ride. Since he suspected the stupor would be tomorrow night's solution, he bridled Firenza and swung onto the stallion's bare back.

The big black seemed to sense his owner's mood. With the barest touch against his flanks, Firenza took off across the fields, taking the first fence in a soaring leap as if all the hounds of hell were snapping at his heels.

Maggie forced herself onto her feet. Her legs were as weak as a newborn lamb's. Bright, floating pinpricks of light swirled in her vision. She wrapped her arm around the foot post and held tight until the dizziness cleared.

She'd floundered in this self-imposed prison long enough. She set a small goal: to walk across the room as far as the vanity. Just setting the goal seemed to give her strength. She walked the distance and sank down onto the velvet bench.

Beyond the curtains, night had fallen. A full moon was rising over the river. Maggie blinked back lingering tears, remembering another night with a full moon when she'd danced in a summerhouse and given her heart to a man.

She shuddered, breaking her reverie. She reached for her hairbrush, and the light from the gas lamps caught the diamonds in her wedding band and made them flash. She carefully replaced the brush on the runner of Irish lace, then rolled the beads of Mum's rosary between her fingers. Not praying, but thinking.

Finally, she lifted the lid to the heart-shaped trinket box painted with pink roses that Gordon had given her for no reason at all. Inside was one small object, and she picked it up, holding it between her thumb and forefinger so that the light caught the brass ring.

And she understood how, in so many ways, her husband had shown her the depth of his love. Even—especially—now, by sending her away.

A glimmer of gaslight shone from the family parlor. Maggie's legs trembled with weakness as she descended the stairs, gripping the railing with both hands. But she felt triumphant as well. She had survived, but she'd done something even better.

She'd found that grand, good place. And now she would make it theirs. Hers, her husband's, the children they both loved, and the children who would come in the future.

Someone stirred in the flower chintz armchair that sat before the fire. "Father Fitz," she said.

He stood up, and then she saw the children, sitting together on the floor in front of the fireplace. Their faces were drawn, worried.

Father Fitzhugh came to her, taking her arm and leading her to the chair. "You shouldn't be up, child. Sit."

She eased into the chair and smoothed her dressing gown over her knees with hands that shook. But she felt good inside. "You would help my husband send me away?"

Father Fitzhugh stared at her through green eyes so like the earl's. So like her own. "I don't know what I'm going to do," he said. "Why don't you tell me what you want me to do."

She held out her hands to the children, and they came. Both of them, Clare beginning to smile, Gordy looking so sad, so worried.

Gordy took her outstretched hand. "What can we do?" he asked in a broken voice. "Father won't listen."

She'd lost her way for a while, but she had found it again, and she could feel the ripening of joy deep inside her heart.

She wasn't sure how she had come to this place. It had be
gun on a cloud-shrouded morning when Gordon Kincaid ar
rived at the orphanage where his daughter lived, and it wa
ending here, with the hands of both his children claspe
within her own.

"I need your help, Gordy."

"Anything, Mother."

She was giddy with joy, and she laughed. "Help me wav
a rowan wand and weave a spell of enchantment."

The wind was still, and the silence deep. Tree branches she
dark shadows on the footpath. There was mystery in the air
but somehow, she knew all the broken pieces of her life wer
coming together.

She smelled the water before she came in sight of it, hear
its soft murmuring against the shoreline. The moon wa
risen, full and white. In the distance, where the bluff loome
over the river, she saw the small orange light flare as Gord
lit the bonfire.

Father Fitzhugh's arm tightened around her waist as sh
lost her footing, and she leaned into him. "Mum's last word
to me were to be proud," she said softly. "That my father wa
a good man."

"Your mother always had more faith in him than he de
served."

She leaned her head against his shoulder. The scents of th
Church were in his cassock and she breathed them in. "
think she knew he loved her, but she gave him up to a Greate
Love."

They walked through damp leaves. The bonfire caugh
and blazed up ahead. Father Fitzhugh let out a long, slow
breath.

"How long have you known, *mó cailín*?

"I was never certain." She smiled into the moonlight. "Un
til now."

"My greatest unanswered prayer was that Deirdre shoul
live long enough to reach this country. I wanted to thank he

for . . . well, for many things, but mostly for the gift of a daughter."

"And don't you think she hears you now?"

He tipped his head back and silvered light bathed his face. His eyes were wet and his voice hoarse. "And surely she does, my child. She does."

Chapter 29

*A*n owl cried into the night and Firenza shied nervously. Gordon calmed the horse with subtle pressure on the reins. He peered through the inky hulks of tree trunks. On the river bluff, a bonfire danced against the night sky.

Pure, unadulterated rage consumed him. He put his heels to the big Thoroughbred and drove forward. Firenza made three galloping strides and launched into the air over the creek; a moment of suspension, and then they were down with a splash of hooves in a puddle near the creek bed. Another two bounds and they were into the forest. Gordon reined back. He ducked his head to avoid low-hanging branches as they plunged down a path through the underbrush.

He pulled up at the edge of the woods, still hidden in the darkness. Firenza blew restively. He listened, straining to control his breathing and the horse's movements so he could hear. The light wind brought the wispy sound of a harp.

He held his breath, convinced he'd finally gone mad,

tipped over the edge into lunacy, and heard the unmistakable sound of Maggie's singing.

He nudged Firenza forward, climbing the last rise, stopping when she came into view. He dismounted and led the horse forward. She must have heard him, but she continued playing, ethereal music drifting like the fog.

A paralysis seized his body. He could not move or speak, could only watch her. She lifted her head and looked at him. In the glow of the bonfire, the white lace of her collar seemed to catch the light and make her skin glow.

"The night is cold." He looked at her with a grim curve of his mouth that was not amusement. "You catch a fever, and I swear I'll kill you."

She tilted her head, plucked a harp string. "You could keep me warm."

He backed up until he stood against Firenza's shoulder. She was here on the river bluff. How she got here in her weakened state—with a harp, no less—he couldn't begin to guess. Why?

A terrible uncertainty washed over him. He let go of the reins and walked to the edge of the bluff. He didn't want to know, didn't want to believe she was here, waiting for him.

"You would send me away?" she asked.

"No, not send you away. Give you up." The river lapped against the shoreline, the sound queerly muted by the mist. "Dammit, Maggie, I know it's the right thing to do. I just didn't know it was going to be this hard."

"Aye, 'tis hard. But you've done the same before, with Gordy."

"It was the right thing to do then. The right thing to do now." He turned. She was looking at him now, and he thought he must say more, for once in his misbegotten life find the right words, to explain to her why he had to let her go.

"You gave Clare to me, brought Gordy back. And what did I do? I nearly got you killed. Our child . . ." A tightness gripped his throat, his chest. The sharp needles on the pines seemed to blur and run together. He wiped the heels of his palm against his eyes, and they came away wet. He half-turned away from her so his face would be shielded from the firelight.

"Gordon."

"I don't know how to rectify any of that. The only thing I can do is give you back your life."

He didn't realize she had moved until her hand touched his arm. He shook his head to clear his vision, and then saw she was still so weak she was swaying on her feet. "Dammit, Maggie, sit down."

Light from the bonfire spilled across her face, highlighting the high angles of her cheekbones. He studied the arch of dark brows, the full, moist curves of her mouth, the green eyes staring back at him, storing the memory so he could pull it out later in the bleak days ahead of him. The lifetime of days he would have to go on without her.

He eased her down on the stool, then removed his jacket and draped it over her shoulders. He stepped back one step, then another. She looked down at her hands, folded together in her lap.

"Our child," she said, her voice breaking, and the sound was like a rip in the fabric of his soul. "It near broke my heart to lose the babe." She looked up then. "But how can you believe I would blame you? What you did was brave; more, it was right."

"I knew it was a risk with the Klan back in action, but courage never entered into it." He kneaded the ache in his thigh with his hand. Tipped his head back and watched a wisp of cloud race across the round white moon. He let out a breath and brought his gaze back to her.

"I did it for me. You gave me reason to live again and I wanted it all, you see. You, the children, my sense of pride in being a man. I never said anything because I thought it would only frighten you needlessly—too arrogant or stupid to believe they'd actually attack a Kincaid."

A grave smile softened the curve of her mouth. "And so

now, because of what happened, you would give me back my life. When it is not yours to give."

He took a step forward and touched her face because he needed to touch her one last time. He thought of another night when the sky was filled with a lover's moon and he had walked along the river path with this woman. Something swelled in his chest, a sensation of loss so fierce and terrible it made him ache.

He dropped his hand and tried to smile, but his face felt too tight. "It's not mine to take either."

"Here is my life." She fisted her hands between her breasts. "You are as much a part of me as my heart."

The world spun all around him, and his lungs seemed to collapse so it was an effort to draw in a breath.

"What are you saying, Maggie?"

"I am saying that I love you. That we both love the two children waiting back at the house, and that someday, God willing, more children will follow. I am saying you are my life, my dreams, my hope, and that I will not leave you."

"You love me?"

"With all my soul."

The breeze ruffled wisps of hair at her temple. He knelt down in front of her so he could see into her eyes, daring to hope again. What he saw there was not pain, but strength. And love.

"I never thought I'd hear you say those words."

His heart was beating so hard, so full up with loving her. He took her hands in his own and ran his thumb along the edge of the bandage wrapping her wrist. "I wanted to give you the best of everything, the best of myself. I've given you only pain."

"You do not know the best of yourself." She reached up to play with a lock of hair at his temple. "You are not so much a gentleman as you are a gentle man, and courageous, and sometimes I fear you so, or fear myself, that I cannot be the woman you need."

"You are everything I need." He swallowed and cleared

his throat. "I'm a selfish man, Maggie. This is your last chance—if you're not on that train when it pulls away from the station tomorrow morning, then I'll never let you go."

"You see, then," she said. "We are equal in our sins."

"Hardly." He laughed wryly. "Not even close." He brushed his fingers along the angle of her jaw. "How did you get here, with a harp, no less?"

"Gordy carried it down." Tears welled in her eyes. "He called me Mother."

"I know, ever since that—that night." A tremor raced through her body and he didn't know if it came from the memory or from the cold wind off the water. He drew the edges of his coat tight around her neck. "You shouldn't be out in this night air. I should whip the boy, but I think I'll thank him instead."

He looked at her flushed cheeks, her lower lip trembling slightly, and saw that she was trying hard not to cry. He leaned forward, his mouth close to hers.

"Maggie," he whispered. He brushed the corner of her mouth.

She turned her head and met his kiss with a sudden desperate urgency that equaled his own. He drew her hard against him, his eyes closed, holding her tightly. His life. His Maggie.

So many gifts she had given him. And he thought of one he could give to her. After a long time, he managed to pull himself back. He looked into her eyes, those beautiful green eyes that were the window to her soul.

"Would you marry me, Maggie?"

Her fingers found his and slid between them. "I thought I already did."

"Again. In your Church. I'll convert, if Father Fitzhugh will allow—"

She was smiling while a wash of sudden tears ran down her cheeks. "You don't have to do that for me."

"For us, then. For our children."

The river gurgled over stones, and somewhere in the forest a nightingale began to sing. He stared past her, beyond the rim of firelight and into the silvery glow through the tree branches. He thought how odd it was to hear a warbler this late in the year, and yet, something deep inside told him it wasn't odd at all.

He took her bandaged hand gently within his own and lifted it, kissing each one of her fingertips. Loving her. "Let me take you home, Maggie."

He stood and kicked dirt over the dwindling bonfire. When he was done, he lifted her onto Firenza and swung up behind her. He brought both arms around her, enveloping her in his body's heat.

They rode in silence up the dirt trail and then broke out of the tree line. Old Riverbend rose before them, soft light beaming from the first-floor windows to welcome them.

Home, and he saw a sudden vision of the future when the house would be filled with children: his, theirs, orphans from St. Columba's for long summer holidays. There would be troubles ahead because life was imperfect, but they would meet those problems as a family. And there would be happiness too, found in the hours and days, stretching into the weeks and years they would spend together.

She shifted against him and he felt her release a long, slow breath. "The ladies will never want me on their committees."

"Ah, you're wrong there. Mrs. Neal came by to leave a calling card. She asked me if you were the type of woman who could forgive and forget."

"What did you tell her?"

"I told her you were an angel and their damn committee didn't deserve you."

A quiet laugh escaped her. "Gordon, you turn the world upside down."

"Inside out." He splayed his fingers wide on her waist, touching her. "Topsy-turvy," he said, leaning his head to nuzzle that sensitive spot below her ear. "Better, Maggie. You make my world better."

She tilted her head back against him. "Every day for the rest of my life, I will tell you how much I love you."

Awe filled his chest, that she was his, and a sweet kind of aching too, that she should love him back. And he understood that this . . . this was joy.

Gordon's arm tightened around his wife. Arrogant bastard he might be, but he could recognize a miracle when he saw one. Lucky fool—God had seen fit to give him two.